Beneath Bone Lake

"Let them go. I'll do anything. Please."

"You *will* give me everything. No arguments, no tricks, and don't even think of telling the authorities or anyone from the media about this call. Defy me, and I promise you I'll be the first to know," he hissed. "And the next body you find is going to be your daughter's."

"Let me talk to her," Ruby blurted, thinking that something in his voice, something buried in his malice, was familiar. "Please, she must be so scared, and I—I need to hear her voice. I have to, you know to—uh, to assure myself that they're both really okay. That you have them and they're still safe."

"But they *aren't* safe. And they won't ever be safe unless you follow my instructions to the letter. Can you do that, Ruby? Can you follow them exactly?"

"I swear I will. Just don't hurt—"

"Then wait for my next call. And remember, whatever you say to the authorities, any authorities, will come back to my ears, so have a care…You don't want to go and lose your head. *Or theirs.*"

Other books by Colleen Thompson:

TRIPLE EXPOSURE
THE SALT MAIDEN
HEAD ON
HEAT LIGHTNING
THE DEADLIEST DENIAL
FADE THE HEAT
FATAL ERROR

RAVE REVIEWS FOR COLLEEN THOMPSON'S ROMANTIC SUSPENSE!

TRIPLE EXPOSURE

"Thompson packs this well-paced thriller full of twists and the local color of a small Texas town...The climax will surprise even the most jaded of suspense readers."

—*Publishers Weekly*

"Thompson leads readers on a twisted course...only to stand the plot on its head again in the finale. The only constant is the steady revelation of the characters, who are shown in... more depth with each exposure."

—*Romantic Times BOOKreviews*

THE SALT MAIDEN

"Poetic use of language, intricate plotting and a wealth of fascinating details make Thompson's latest novel a masterful work of suspense. Readers will come for the action and stay for the three-dimensional characters and well-crafted narrative. This is a fabulous read!"

—*Romantic Times BOOKreviews* (Top Pick)

"I could not bring myself to set the book down. I simply HAD to know what would happen next...Non-stop action, drama, and mystery. Fans of Tess Gerritsen, Tami Hoag, and Sandra Brown will adore this tale. Phenomenal!"

—Huntress Reviews

HEAD ON

"Well written with realistic and appealing characters, *Head On* is a mesmerizing story that keeps readers guessing as the murderer draws closer and secrets are revealed. A compelling tale of romantic suspense, it is a strong, satisfying read."

—Romance Reviews Today

"Filled with realistic dialogue, compelling narrative and believable conflict. The multiple viewpoints add dimension...and the characterizations are very well done."

—*Romantic Times BOOKreviews*

MORE PRAISE FOR COLLEEN THOMPSON!

HEAT LIGHTNING

"Thompson has crafted a top-notch, thrilling romantic suspense."
—*New York Times* bestselling author Allison Brennan

"This nicely complicated tale has plenty of edge-of-your-seat suspense."
—*Romantic Times BOOKreviews*

THE DEADLIEST DENIAL

"Captivating...Thompson, a RITA finalist, is skilled at building suspense."
—*Publishers Weekly*

"Thompson's style is gritty, and that works well with her flawed and driven characters."
—*Romantic Times BOOKreviews*

"*The Deadliest Denial* is a spellbinding read with a gripping, intrigue-filled plot. There are twists and turns around every corner...This is a great read. Ms. Thompson has gifted us with another all-nighter."
—*Fresh Fiction*

FADE THE HEAT

"RITA finalist Thompson takes the reader on a roller-coaster ride full of surprising twists and turns in this exceptional novel of romantic suspense."
—*Publishers Weekly* (Starred Review)

"The precise details of Thompson's novel give it a rich, edgy texture that's enthralling...For keen characters, emotional richness and a satisfying story that doesn't fade away, read Thompson's latest."
—*Romantic Times BOOKreviews*

FATAL ERROR

"Fast-paced, chilling, and sexy...chemistry that shimmers."
—*Library Journal*

"Thompson has written a first-class work of romantic suspense."
—*Booklist*

Beneath Bone Lake

COLLEEN
THOMPSON

LOVE SPELL NEW YORK CITY

*With love and appreciation to all those who journey
far from home to serve our country and to the
families, friends, and lovers who await them.*

LOVE SPELL®

June 2009

Published by

Dorchester Publishing Co., Inc.
200 Madison Avenue
New York, NY 10016

Copyright © 2009 by Colleen Thompson

All rights reserved. No part of this book may be reproduced
or transmitted in any form or by any electronic or mechanical
means, including photocopying, recording or by any information
storage and retrieval system, without the written permission of the
publisher, except where permitted by law.

ISBN 10: 0-8439-6243-7
ISBN 13: 978-0-8439-6243-7
E-ISBN: 978-1-4285-0687-9

The name "Love Spell" and its logo are trademarks of Dorchester
Publishing Co., Inc.

Printed in the United States of America.

10 9 8 7 6 5 4 3 2 1

If you purchased this book without a cover you should be aware
that this book is stolen property. It was reported as "unsold and
destroyed" to the publisher and neither the author nor the publisher
has received any payment for this "stripped book."

Visit us on the web at www.dorchesterpub.com.

ACKNOWLEDGMENTS

I'd like to express my appreciation to many people who helped bring *Beneath Bone Lake* to fruition. First and foremost, thanks to my husband Mike, who's always up for a research trip or a plotting session and who scarcely bats an eye when I point to random items in the local home improvement center and blurt, "Wouldn't that make an *excellent* murder weapon?"

Thanks to Dottie Carter of the Spatterdock Cabins in Uncertain, Texas, for the hospitality and to local guide David Applebaum for showing me around beautiful Caddo Lake, the inspiration for the Bone Lake of this story. Your stories of life on the lake were as fascinating as the place itself.

I'm extremely grateful to first readers Barbara Sissel, Joni Rodgers, and Jo Anne Banker for their helpful feedback on the manuscript, along with Wanda Dionne and T. J. Bennett, two of the sharpest critique partners out there. I count your friendship, intelligence, and assistance among my greatest assets.

Finally, thanks to my agent, Karen Solem for the insightful suggestions and amazing support, to Jennifer Schober, also of Spencerhill Associates, for her assistance, and to editor Alicia Condon and all the wonderful people at Dorchester Publishing who work so hard to get my stories in the hands of readers.

Beneath
Bone Lake

CHAPTER ONE

"The very emphasis of the commandment: Thou shalt not kill, makes it certain that we are descended from an endlessly long chain of generations of murderers, whose love of murder was in their blood as it is perhaps also in ours."

—Sigmund Freud

The boatman's paddle dug deep beneath the moss green surface, biting and twisting like a switchblade's killing thrust. Pulse thrummed and muscles burned as he dragged the canoe forward, threading through a swamp-dank maze of pale trees, the ghost sentries of a forest flooded years before. Above, the skeletal branches reached skyward into silver, their bony fingers veiled in Spanish moss and predawn mist.

A harsh cry heralded a white egret's low flap over the water, and a higher-pitched, more melodic twitter warned that the sun was close to rising. With a glance down at his watch, he swore, then flipped away the cigarette he'd been smoking. He had to get moving, get the hell out of here, because cold or not, the damned bass fishermen would be out at first light. He couldn't take the chance that the silent incursion of an electric trolling motor would bring one close enough to notice that he carried no tackle—close enough to hear the splash as his loathsome cargo slipped over the canoe's side.

Easier said than done, he soon learned. Sweat erupted and his back screamed as he hauled and cursed, dragged and swore. He might have given up then, put ashore somewhere, and abandoned the old boat with its grisly cargo. But he had given his word to do this right, and that alone meant something to him. Separated him from the animals whose instincts ruled them, from those hollow beings who called themselves men and women but were, he knew, nothing more than shadow. Including that shadow to which he'd bound himself for the duration of this contract.

Finally, he thought to make a lever of his paddle. Using a crossbar for a fulcrum, he wedged the blade beneath the plastic-shrouded lower torso, then grunted with effort as he pushed down on the handle. At long last, his burden shifted to flop heavily, its shoeless feet disappearing among dark-olive wavelets. Where the bound and weighted legs went, the body clumsily followed, the head banging a final, sickening *thwoppp* against the aluminum hull before it splashed down.

The canoe rocked dangerously, threatening to flip until he shifted from his knees to sit flat on the boat's bottom. Wincing as his pants wicked up moisture from an inch or so of cold, mud-and-blood seepage, he peered at the bubbles fizzing to the water's surface and stared deeper to detect—or imagine he detected—pale fingers fluttering. A farewell wave that swiftly vanished into the murk beneath Bone Lake.

He heaved a tired sigh, then turned the canoe back toward the spot where he would pierce the hull and send it to the bottom. Amid the nearby lily pads, a pair of eyes sank and a tail flipped—a huge gator's.

The boatman started at the sight, then offered a wry smile . . . and a little wishful thinking, colored with an accent he turned on and off at will. "Today's breakfast's on me, big boy. You be sure'n eat hearty now, you hear?"

Then he gave a tight nod, acknowledging the only

kind of partner a man could trust to keep his secrets, the only kind he knew for sure he'd never have to kill.

April 4

As the plane touched down in Dallas, a wave of pure elation buoyed Ruby Monroe's spirits. Elation fused with indescribable relief.

Despite her nervous stomach, she'd sailed right through customs in Atlanta. Breezed through with her possessions and boarded the connection that would take her home. After a year spent working as a contract bus driver shuttling personnel around Iraq, she would finally be free to trade that sandbox for Zoe's, to hug and kiss the four-year-old daughter she had missed so desperately.

While the plane taxied toward the terminal, Ruby ignored the canned warning to keep her seat belt fastened. Instead, she jerked her backpack from the space beneath the seat in front of her and slid forward, her muscles drawn like bowstrings, tensed for the moment they could carry her into the heaven of SpaghettiOs and storybooks and Zoe's endless schemes to drag out tuck-ins.

Her daughter's phone conversations might have teemed with "Aunt Misty took me for a pony ride" and "Aunt Misty braided my hair," but Ruby was certain Zoe had missed the only parent she'd ever known. Ruby vowed to make the separation up to her—to put this past year in the rearview of their lives and do her best to forget it.

And she would forget, the moment she made public the information she had. She wished she could do more. Wished she could risk going forward with her suspicions regarding her employer, DeserTek. But her family's future had to come first, so she planned to drop the item she'd brought into a mailbox and move on.

The instant the plane stopped rolling, other passengers—nearly all of them in front of her—popped out of their seats and went for the overhead bins to wrestle winter coats and carry-ons and ostriches and elephants down into her path. Ruby, all of five-three on her tiptoes and a light-weight besides, had no luck pushing her way forward, and by the time she thought to play the just-back-from-Iraq card, it was entirely too late. Though a few sympathetic souls allowed her to squeeze past them, there was no breaking up the bottleneck. Shifting anxiously, she fought for patience, prayed for release, and did her best to keep from swearing.

After two centuries and an epoch, she squeezed out the exit and bolted down the Jetway—until a large woman huffing hard behind a walker blocked her path. Skidding to a stop, Ruby whimpered, but since she'd been raised far too southern to say anything, she forced herself to wait. When at last she made it to the terminal, she sprinted along the moving sidewalk, her backpack punching at her shoulder blades with each step.

"Excuse me. Sorry," she said as she trotted toward a revolving door leading into the baggage claim area. Once inside, she scanned the crowd for the top of Misty's golden head. No sign of her in the crowd, or Zoe, either, so Ruby jogged, heart pounding, to see which carousel would have her luggage.

After reading the information from a screen, she raced to the correct location. Grinning as she peered right and left, she wormed and jostled and apologized her way through knots of people. The conveyor buzzed and lurched to life, but by the time the first few suitcases began their orbit, Ruby understood that her family wasn't there.

Her smile withered like a cut flower.

"Probably out parking," she guessed. Or maybe her sister, who tended to zone out to music during long drives, had missed the airport exit. Or there could be traffic, even at one thirty, since Dallas was about a million times more crowded than the East Texas hometown where they'd lived since their teens.

Doubt flickered, and Ruby felt the slow burn of annoyance. Could her sister, who was *never* late, have somehow lost track of the time? She *knew* what this day meant to Ruby. Knew this was the most important homecoming of her life.

"Damn it, Misty." Ruby knew she had no business begrudging her sister a few minutes. For a whole year, Misty had juggled her own classes and part-time job while seeing Zoe through skinned knees and stomach bugs, through moods that ranged from bubbly to demonic. All so Ruby could save enough to finish her nursing degree and secure her daughter's future.

She swung her backpack off her shoulder and pulled her mobile from one pocket, then pressed the number 1 on her speed dial. A digitized voice announced that Misty's cell phone was no longer in service.

"Well, shit," Ruby said, forgetting her resolution to clean up her language before coming home to Zoe.

Had to have been a mistake, Ruby decided, since she had spoken to her sister earlier that week. As she hit REDIAL, a fortyish man in a loosened tie and rolled-up shirtsleeves jostled past her, bumping the corner of her backpack and knocking its strap off her shoulder. Her arm jerked downward, the pack's weight pulling the phone away from her ear.

Waving off the man's apology, Ruby set the pack at her feet and brought her cell phone back to her ear. In time to hear the canned message repeating, maddeningly insistent.

"Come on, Misty. You couldn't get the stupid bill paid?" Indebted to her or not, Ruby felt like throttling her younger sister for the lapse. It wasn't as if Misty didn't have the money; Ruby had given her access to her bank account so she could replace the leaking roof and keep up with Zoe's day care. With Ruby covering the utilities as well, the least Misty could have done was send the payments on time. And without a landline at the lake house, Ruby had no other way to reach her sister.

The bright notes of a child's voice caught Ruby's attention. Relief bubbling through her, she looked around eagerly. Her breath hitched at the sight of the man who'd bumped her scooping up a giggling, red-haired toddler who threw her chubby arms around his neck.

With a sigh, Ruby turned away and reached down to snag her backpack's strap, then froze. *Shit!* She'd taken her eyes off it only for a moment. Heart thumping, she looked around frantically, glancing from an older woman to two teenagers to several people she'd seen aboard the plane.

"Did anyone pick up my backpack?" she asked loudly. "Did someone accidentally grab the wrong—?"

She saw several nervous glances. A few people looked around, too, half pretending they'd know her pack from anybody else's. But no one made eye contact, with the exception of a rumpled-looking man who nodded toward an airport security officer and said, "Better go report it."

She cursed again, unable to believe that she'd survived a war zone, only to fall victim to a random crime as soon as she set foot in Texas.

What if it isn't *random? What if management's figured out I was the last to speak to Carrie Ann, the only person she had the chance to give . . .* Dread pierced Ruby like a needle. She *knew* she shouldn't have allowed herself to get involved.

Trembling, she hurried over to the airport security officer, a squatly muscular young black man who asked her to describe her backpack, then radioed for help. After a maddeningly long interval, during which she filled out a loss report and kept a lookout for her family, the officer returned, shaking his head.

"Wish I could tell you we'd recover it, but that's not likely. Security cameras show a skinny dude, dark hair—Caucasian or Hispanic. Jogged out with a pack that could've been yours, hopped into his buddies' light-colored Chrysler—we couldn't get the plates—and lit out. Your wallet in that backpack?"

Nodding, she handed him the form, where she'd listed all except one of the contents. Other than the driver's license she'd tucked inside her pocket to go through security and the credit card she'd last used to buy a magazine and a drink back in Atlanta, she'd left all her cash and cards inside—even her passport—along with a stuffed animal she'd picked up for Zoe while awaiting her connection and several family photos. But those losses meant nothing, nothing whatsoever against the theft of the flash drive Ruby had sewn into the pack's lining. Her knees weakened at the thought.

If DeserTek knows somehow . . . She thought of the surreal offer management had made on her final day in-country. Remembered the upwelling of revulsion that had prompted her to turn down many times the salary she could expect as an RN.

The officer told Ruby, "Those dudes are nothing if not efficient, so you can figure on them running up charges all over God's creation inside the next hour."

"This goes on a lot, then?" Anger surged past her worry. "Why isn't something done to stop it?"

The security officer shrugged shoulders that looked as if they could bench-press a Humvee. "Sorry, miss, but for every two of those damn cockroaches we smash flat, ten more crawl in off the streets. They're organized, for sure,

probably gangbangers. Best thing's just to call this number." He handed her a printed sheet. "They'll help you
contact your credit card providers and your bank. And if
that's your luggage, you'd better collect it before somebody else gets the same idea."

Ruby *had* been watching the other baggage being
claimed as her two lonely suitcases rode an endless loop
to nowhere. She'd been waiting, fear in full bloom, to
see if anyone approached them. In which case she'd
planned to raise such hell that the thief would be caught
for sure.

"You going to be all right, miss?" the young officer
asked as they walked to the carousel. "Is someone coming for you?"

"Thanks," she said. "I'll be fine. My family's on the
way. Just running a little late."

The officer's radio squawked. He frowned and quickly
excused himself, hustling in the direction of the shuttle
pickup exit.

Ruby wheeled her suitcases toward a bench where she
could sit. While waiting, she used her phone to cancel
the credit cards she'd left in her wallet. By the time she'd
finished, Misty and Zoe still hadn't turned up. A glance
down at her watch made Ruby's stomach cartwheel.

Where on earth could they be? Had they had car
trouble, a flat tire? An accident on the way?

Ruby bit down on the thought. Because thinking of
accidents jerked her back to the beeping monitors and
the hissing respirator and the sad-eyed doctor glancing at
her pregnant belly while suggesting that organ donation
was a way to wrest some good from her family's tragedy.
Thinking of her husband, Aaron, reminded her that war
zones weren't the only places people died, that even
those she loved were never truly safe. She imagined the

little Honda she'd passed on to Misty as smashed as Aaron's motorcycle had been . . . her daughter's tiny, broken body pulled from twisted wreckage.

Not going there, Ruby told herself. *Not* going. Think instead of hugging Zoe, of smelling her strawberry-sweet hair and lifting her into her arms. Think of seeing the real girl, not just pictures, and of hearing her laughter in person instead of settling for a phone call that was no doubt being monitored, recorded . . . analyzed.

But a quick call to Mrs. Lambert, who ran the home day care her daughter attended, made Ruby feel no better.

"Praise the Lord that you're home safely," the older woman told her. "But Zoe hasn't been here for the past week. Has a fearsome cold, I understand. Stuffy nose and cough and fever. Misty wanted to keep her away from the other children until she's certain—"

"Zoe's been sick?" That didn't make sense. Misty hadn't said a word about it Monday.

"I've put that precious child on my prayer list," Mrs. Lambert assured her. "But what about you? Do you need someone to pick you up there? You're in the city, you said?"

"DFW," Ruby answered, naming the larger airport that served the Dallas/Ft. Worth metroplex. "But I'll be fine, thanks. I'll rent a car if they don't show up."

Ruby had no intention of waiting around for three hours for one of Myrtle's church friends, who would doubtless preach to her every mile of the journey back home. More than likely about the Lord's preference for the kind of mothers who remained in the same country as their offspring. "Probably Misty's just taken Zoe to the doctor. Or maybe they both fell asleep and—anyway, it'll be better if I drive out."

As soon as Ruby disconnected, she tried Misty's best

friend, Crystal, but her phone went straight to voice
mail. At Hammett's on the Lake, where both Misty and
Crystal waited tables, Ruby connected with yet another
recorded message, this one telling her that the restaurant was closed but would reopen "for all your bar,
grill, and recreational needs" in time for happy hour at
five p.m.

Frowning, Ruby racked her brain for anyone else who
might have some idea of Misty's whereabouts. Finally, an
idea struck: *Call Sam McCoy,* though turning to a near
stranger—particularly *this* stranger—didn't set well with
her. Sure, Aaron had always stuck up for his foster
brother, ignoring any whispers about "bad blood." But
that had been when McCoy was a big-shot computer
security wizard and partner in his firm in Austin, not
some disgraced felon who'd moved back to the area—
after purchasing the house next door—to lick his wounds.
She saw him in her mind's eye: the dark hair so close-
cropped it brought out sharp-looking honey brown eyes,
and a fine set of muscles straining as he'd helped the movers manhandle a king-sized mattress off the truck only a
couple of months before Ruby had left the country.

"I could stand to help him christen that," Misty had
commented with a grin.

"Don't even think about bringing that criminal around
my daughter," Ruby had warned her. He'd been polite
enough when they'd met briefly at the mailbox, but
she'd heard of his conviction, even if he hadn't actually
served time. She knew, too, that the Monroes, whose
patience had run as deep as their faith, had given Sam the
boot a few months shy of his eighteenth birthday, though
she'd never heard why he was kicked out.

Before she could lose her nerve, Ruby tried information: "Unincorporated Preston County, please, Dog-

wood area. I'm looking for a listing for a Sam or Samuel McCoy on South Cypress Bend."

"I have a business listing," the operator told her. "At Forty-one South Cypress Bend. Could that be it?"

"Has to be." Since there was nothing else but state preserve within a half mile of her own place, Ruby scribbled the number on the back of her drink-and-magazine receipt and punched it into her phone.

The machine picked up on the fourth ring before regurgitating a recorded message that took her by surprise. "You've reached the Reel McCoy, Bone Lake's premier fishing guide. I'm most likely on the water at the moment, but if you'll leave your name and number . . ."

Fishing guide? Ruby frowned, wondering if she'd dialed the right number. But that address had to be his. She disconnected, feeling more anxious than ever about Zoe's and Misty's whereabouts.

Frustrated, Ruby watched a fresh crop of passengers begin picking up their luggage. Any second now, she told herself, her sister would show up apologizing, with Zoe bouncing along at her side and shrieking with excitement.

Imagining that moment, Ruby took a deep breath and filled her lungs with painfully sweet anticipation. Anticipation that ticked inexorably toward panic as she watched the steady stream of travelers welcomed home by loved ones, as she felt the minutes and the hours hurtling toward eternity.

CHAPTER TWO

Things fall apart; the center cannot hold;
Mere anarchy is loosed upon the world . . .
                              —William Butler Yeats,
                              from "The Second Coming"

When blaring music pressed past the sound of his boat motor, Sam McCoy told himself it was none of his damned business. Better he should think about beating the encroaching darkness, getting off the water, and cleaning his catch. Keep his thoughts tuned to an evening filled with fried bass, cold beer, ESPN, and a warm shower, not necessarily in that order.

So what if his only close neighbor, Misty Bailey, and her new "friends" wanted to spend another evening blowing out their eardrums with that noise? It wasn't as if anyone had asked for—or would welcome—his opinion. Let Mama Bear deal with the current problem when she came back. Should be any day now, the way he'd heard it. Bass notes thumped, and Java, who stood on the johnboat's flat bow, turned to whine at him.

"What are you lookin' at?" he asked the chocolate Lab, but the soulful brown eyes kept staring, begging for permission to jump ship.

A few months back, Java had discovered the little girl next door, and it was love at first sight. Since that happy wag-and-squeal-fest, Sam had had a hell of a time keeping the young dog from wandering—make that *galumphing*—over to the neighboring cabin. Though Misty had carefully kept him at arm's length, she had put up with the impromptu visits for her niece's sake.

For the sake of Aaron's daughter . . . Sam's stomach knotted at the thought, for he'd seen Aaron Monroe in Zoe's face, in the child's flyaway blonde hair, in her showstopper of a smile. Strange that the resemblance affected him, considering how pissed he'd been the last time he saw Aaron. Stranger still, since he'd never before warmed to kids, the sight of Zoe romping so happily with Java had reminded him of one bright spot in a past he'd worked damned hard to put behind him.

As Sam stared in the direction of the Monroe house, he couldn't help wondering. How was Zoe faring, now that her caretaker had apparently gone off the deep end? How could a little kid like that cope with all the noise? And not just noise, Sam imagined, for even by Bone Lake standards, the one woman and two men he'd glimpsed over there looked pretty rough. What if they were drinking, drugging, doing God knew what else around the little girl?

What the hell could Misty Bailey—who was a knockout as well as whip-smart—possibly see in such lowlifes? Over at Hammett's, where she waited tables part-time, she fielded better offers almost daily from good men with decent jobs, handling the kiss-offs with an easy grace that he admired.

Even when he'd been the one summarily dismissed.

So stay out of this, his better judgment warned him. *Hasn't sticking your neck out over other people's business caused you enough trouble for one lifetime?*

The music shut off, and the sound of shouting drifted down from the Monroe place. This time, Java didn't wait politely for Sam's say-so. Instead, the Lab jumped into Bone Lake and paddled for the shore.

"Damn it, dog, get back here," Sam called after her, but it was hopeless. The Lab was swimming for all she was worth, making for the wooded shoreline nearest the Monroe property.

Cursing, Sam maneuvered the small boat's outboard to avoid the jutting cypress knees and follow the bobbing brown head toward the shore. The dog scrambled up the roots of a huge tree and shook, tail wagging, before racing in the direction of what had sounded like a man's voice. As Sam tied up to the Monroes' dock, he hesitated, then shook his head and followed, eager to grab his wandering dog and get back home.

"Java, come," he called, more to alert the human inhabitants to his presence than out of hope his exuberant young Lab would deign to listen. Moving from the dock onto the sparse lawn, he whistled and made his way uphill toward the house. His gaze swept the unscreened porch and the back of the faded cedar two-story, which was in dire need of a new roof. From inside the house, he heard what sounded like a couple of big brutes barking—though he'd never seen dogs here in the past. He noticed an odor, too, a strange, cat-piss stink that made him wonder if some animal had been spraying musk.

Along the left side of the house, a shirtless man, all corded muscle and tattoo ink, stood near the driveway's edge. His back was turned, probably because he hadn't heard Sam over the barking from the house.

"I told you to get lost, bitch," the man yelled at someone inside a small, new-looking Chevy parked next to a mud-spattered black sedan. "Turn around and get the fuck out before I set my dogs on your ass."

Startled by his harsh tone, Java froze in her tracks only a few yards short of the man she'd meant to greet. Crouching low, the Lab whined, drawing his attention. When he turned toward her, Sam spotted the man's handgun—saw him aiming toward the dog.

"Whoa, whoa—hey, I've got her." Sam edged forward,

keeping his movements and voice deliberately slow and calm: the harmless neighbor. As concerned as he now felt for both Zoe and her aunt's safety, he wouldn't do anybody any good if he got himself killed.

"What the—" The gunman jerked in surprise, eyes wild, before swinging the weapon to point straight at Sam.

Sam raised his palms, as if they could stop bullets. "Sorry for the bother. Just let me get my pup, and we'll be out of your hair." He could call the sheriff's office from his own house, then wash his hands of the situation.

With his arms shaking, the greasy-haired man blinked at him, displaying a crudely inked 666 in the hollow of his cheek. To Sam, he looked confused, seriously strung out on something. His bad teeth and dark-circled eyes told Sam this was no three-day drunk but a serious, long-term addiction.

"I'm a friend of Misty's." Sam hoped the half-truth would tip the balance in the tattooed man's addled brain. "Are she and Zoe around?"

"Who the fuck's Misty?" the man slurred.

A woman shouted from inside the car parked in the driveway, "Deputies are coming. They'll be here any minute."

Though he couldn't see the face inside the little blue car, Sam thought it might be Ruby Monroe. Before he could react, her unwelcome houseguest wheeled around and hurled curses at her.

Ruby executed a three-point turn that sent gravel flying, then peeled out of the driveway—an exit punctuated by three shots.

"Java, come," Sam urged, racing for the cover of the trees that separated his place from the Monroes'. The massive cypress trunks should offer him some shelter in case the gunman sent a hail of bullets his way.

As Sam ran, he heard another shot—followed by a canine yelp.

"Son of a bitch," he snarled, turning reflexively with fists clenched. Java scrambled past him, bolting for home. Injured or not—Sam couldn't tell in the dim light—the dog disappeared in no time, vanishing into the hundred-yard-wide buffer of trees between the houses.

Sam ran after her, tripping over fallen branches in his hurry. By the time he emerged panting near his own boathouse, he was brushing stinging fire ants from his forearms as he looked around for Java.

The blue car, which bore a rental sticker, idled in the street nearby. His heart lurched at the sight of the bullet hole piercing the rear window.

He raced over to the passenger-side door, only to find Ruby staring at him through the lowering window. "What the hell—are you all right?" he asked her.

"Where's my daughter?" Her blue eyes were wide, her face pale. "Where's Misty? And who *is* that crazy person?"

Sam glanced back toward her place, opened the car door, and swung inside. "Drive down a ways and turn around. If trouble's coming, I don't want it sneaking up behind us."

"Okay, but what's going—"

"You sure you aren't hit?"

As she shook her head, her chin-length, light brown hair swung around a worried face. "Not hurt. What about you?"

"I'm okay—and those deputies are coming, aren't they?" Only two regularly patrolled this end of the lake, but he'd be glad to see them. "You weren't bluffing about that?"

"No, I called. Of course I called." Her glance snapped from his face to her house to the road and back again. "*Where's my family?* Misty was supposed to pick me up at the airport."

"I haven't seen them in a few days." But he was wondering, could it have been longer? He'd been busy guiding fishermen eager to take advantage of the spawning run. It might have been a week, Sam realized, since the last time he'd spotted Zoe or her aunt, and Misty hadn't been at Hammet's since she'd . . . A chill slashed up his backbone at the thought of what an armed drug addict could have done to them in that time.

"I—I called Misty's cell, but her number's out of service. I tried your place, too, but you weren't in."

"Out fishing." Even when he wasn't guiding, a rod and reel kept his hands busy. Kept his mind off the terms of his probation . . . mostly.

"That man—that horrible man—who is he?" Ruby asked.

"Sorry, no idea. I only went to get my dog."

"If he's done anything to Zoe, if he's touched a single hair on her head, I swear"—Ruby's blue eyes burned with conviction, and her voice went strangely flat "—I'm going to kill him."

Sam more than half believed her, a gut instinct that had the fine hairs rising behind his neck. He supposed she'd seen some ugly shit this past year, overseas. Supposed it might have left her capable of killing a man. "I didn't see your sister's car there. I'll bet she took Zoe somewhere," he said, needing to ease Ruby's desperation. For Aaron's—or his parents'—sake at least. "Somewhere safe, away from those people."

"What people? There's more than one of them? In my house?"

He nodded. "A few days back, a week maybe, I saw

three over there, kind of a rough-looking bunch. But your sister was with them. They were having a few laughs and beers on the back porch. Zoe was running around playing, didn't look a bit bothered."

"God, where are those deputies?" Ruby gritted her teeth and turned again to look back up and down the road. "They should be here by now."

"I was thinking the same thing. Give them a few minutes, and try calling again."

There was an uncomfortable lull as both watched, until Ruby gasped at some movement in the roadside brush opposite the houses. Before Sam could shout at her to drive, a small doe broke from the trees. More deer followed her across the street and into Sam's yard, two with fawns at their side.

"Sorry," she said. "For a moment, I thought . . ."

The deer settled in to graze on the sparse spring grasses in front of his house, as they often did around dusk.

"These people you saw at the house—" Her fingers jittered over the steering wheel as she spoke. "You didn't recognize them?"

He shook his head. "No, and I thought I'd met most of the folks living on this end of the lake. Maybe they're from Dogwood," he said, referring to the town proper, a twenty-minute drive north. "Or maybe they were passing through, just some people she met at Hammett's while she was waiting tables. Except that Misty—"

"She might tend to see the best in everyone, but I can't picture my sister inviting strangers home," Ruby interrupted, "especially not with Zoe around. I specifically asked her not to—"

"People screw up," he said. "They make mistakes and they learn from them."

If they get the chance. . . . Sam's attorney had drummed

that message into him. That this was the only chance he was getting. That he'd lose everything if he was too stupid—or too much of a McCoy—to take it.

As Ruby studied him, her gleaming eyes reflected red and white. "*Finally,*" she said. "I thought they'd never get here."

Following her gaze, Sam blew out a relieved breath at the sight of two patrol vehicles, their lights flashing and sirens muted.

"Better go fill them in," Sam said. "They'll need to know about the gun and dogs—you hear all that barking?"

"I did. Right before that man ran out waving his gun around. Took ten years off my life."

"Damned lucky he didn't take the rest of them while he was at it." Sam fingered a hole in the dashboard between them. "You should've driven off and waited for help."

She shook her head and grimaced. "I know, but I thought—all I could think about was Zoe."

"Must've been a hell of a shock." As the two SUVs approached, Sam opened his door. "I'll tell the deputies what I know. Then I'll have to see about my dog."

See to his dog and let the law handle whatever was going on inside the Monroe house. Try not to feel responsible, because this wasn't any of his business. Try not to let the past tangle with the present, though hadn't he risked that by moving back here in the first place? By moving right next door to Aaron Monroe's widow? Abruptly, he wished he could go back a year and change that decision, tell the real estate agent to forget the great deal she'd found and look for something elsewhere. Wished he hadn't, like a damned fool, been sucked in by sentiment.

Java slunk toward Sam, her tail tucked and her brown eyes worried. He squatted down to greet her. "There you are. C'mere, Gator Bait. It's okay. You're going to be fine."

He ran his hands along her flanks, her legs and belly, but to his relief, they didn't come up bloody. Probably, the dog had yelped in fear instead of pain.

The moment the first deputy left his Suburban, Ruby was on him, pointing to her house and saying, "There's a man inside. He has a gun, and he could have my little girl there. My sister, too."

"He shot at both of us. Put a bullet through the rear window," Sam told Deputy Calvin Whitaker, an over-grown, eager type in his midtwenties who had mooched a few fishing expeditions off him these past few months. "And there're dogs inside the house. Big and vicious, from the sound of them."

"We're here now." With his attention trained on Ruby, Calvin looked as upright and earnest as an Eagle Scout. "So don't you worry, Ms. Monroe. We'll get this taken care of."

Deputy Oscar Balderach, a soft-bellied man in his late fifties, stepped down from his Suburban and took the lead questioning Sam and Ruby about the situation. Clearly concerned about the possibility of a young child in the house, Balderach was on his game as Sam had never seen him. Maybe he'd been saving himself for a true emergency.

"I need to call this in, get us some backup," Deputy Balderach said, his voice deep and assured. "Nine chances out of ten, this ol' boy'll give up peaceable and let us run him in to sleep it off. Or if he's got outstanding warrants, he might try and scurry off for cover. But we can't get caught off guard if it occurs to him to go the hostage route."

"Hostage?" A tremor passed visibly through Ruby's

body. "You can't mean he'd take Zoe. Can't you get some snipers, someone who can take him down before he—"

"I understand you've just come back from the war," Balderach said, "but in this part of the world, they don't let us do preemptive killings."

His tone implied he would enjoy his workdays a hell of a lot better if "they" would. "We'll need you to stay back, Ms. Monroe," he went on, "so we can prepare for every contingency and focus on getting your family out safely, if it turns out they're inside."

Balderach's western boots crunched gravel as he strode back toward his SUV to make his call.

Calvin Whitaker speared Sam with an earnest look. "Be best to take her to your place. Keep her inside and stay away from the windows until somebody comes for you."

Tell him you can't get involved. Sam could hear his lawyer—a fighting gamecock of a man who'd grown up in a border barrio—as plainly as if Pacheco stood right here beside him. *Tell him you won't do it, 'padre. Set your boundaries straight off, because I guarantee you, they'll be watching. Watching and waiting for a chance to put your cojones in a wringer the second you step outta line.*

Before Sam could think of how to say no to a terrified young mother, Ruby stared Calvin down.

"Don't talk about me like I'm not here, Deputy," she told him, arms folded across her chest. "This is my family, and my home. Zoe's only four years old. She's going to want her mother the second she comes out. And I'm going to be here for her. Right here."

"I've seen the way Misty watches out for your girl— never takes her eyes off her a minute." Sam figured not even Paranoid Pacheco could fault him for giving Ruby a little reassurance. As long as that was the sum total of his contribution. "I can't imagine her taking her car and leaving Zoe with the likes of that freak."

Sam tried not to picture the little blonde girl hiding beneath her bed or in a closet. *Aaron Monroe's little girl,* which made her the closest thing to a niece that Sam would ever have. The thought struck like a gut punch, though he knew it was bullshit. Even if Aaron were alive, Sam couldn't imagine being invited to a kiddy birthday party or a backyard barbecue. Or accepting if, by some miracle, he were.

Ruby grimaced. "Misty and Zoe could still be inside, held against their will. And scared out of their minds, with all the barking and the shooting."

"Did you hear that guy?" Sam asked. "He didn't react to Misty's name when I asked." Maybe he'd just been too stoned to respond, but was it possible the man didn't even know her? As Sam thought about it, he realized the tattooed invader might not have been one of the people he'd seen on the Monroes' porch last week. After all, Sam had been on the water at the time, playing the amiable host to a particularly difficult angler, so he hadn't homed in on specific details.

"At worst, you could get hurt out here," Calvin told Ruby. "At best, you'll be a distraction."

"Look, I'll keep my distance. I won't go any farther than"—she looked around, then pointed out a huge, moss-draped cypress tree slightly closer to Sam's house than her own—"than that spot. But I will not be shuffled off, you hear me?"

"I have a phone book inside," Sam said, offering no more than any decent person would. "We can call some of Misty's friends, see if your sister's been in touch."

She shook her head. "Just bring me the book. We can call from out here."

"I can do that," Sam said, half relieved she wasn't budging.

Apparently, Calvin had come to the same conclusion. "Just stay here, then. Promise me that."

When the deputy turned away, her hand shot out to snag his arm. "I will, if you promise me you won't do anything—anything at all—to risk my daughter's safety," she said. "I've seen what happens when operations go wrong, somebody gets excited. And today's supposed to—I haven't seen her for a whole year."

Her lips went white as she pressed them together, trying to keep from crying. Sam gave her credit for that, for not compounding a terrible situation with hysteria. She might lack her sister's flashier blonde beauty, but to his mind, Ruby's brand of grit went a long way toward explaining what Aaron had seen in her.

Flushing, Calvin stared down at her hand, then cleared his throat. "We'll do our best," he said before striding—or escaping—toward Balderach's Suburban.

Sam told Ruby, "I'll be right back with that phone book and my cell. Somebody around here's bound to know something."

He could at least help her make a few calls, he thought, even as his mind whirled through those possibilities he couldn't offer: cellular phone hacks, triangulation, credit card traces.

Possibilities that made his long-idle fingers cramp in protest; memories that lodged inside his throat like splintered glass.

CHAPTER THREE

Other sins only speak; murder shrieks out:
The element of water moistens the earth,
But blood flies upwards, and bedews the heavens.
                                        —John Webster,
                              The Duchess of Malfi, act IV

A loon's cry drifted off the water, echoing through the deep green cypress shadows like a lost soul's lamentation. Ruby shivered and hugged herself against a damply cool breeze, a harbinger of evening. She couldn't see the deputies and couldn't stand to think about what they might be doing, what might be happening inside.

But she could make out one weathered corner of the weekend lake house Aaron had inherited only months before his accident. One algae-stained corner and a section of a roof that clearly hadn't been replaced last month, as Misty had reported.

What the hell was going on here? Had her sister, the person Ruby trusted most in all the world, gone crazy? Or had something—or someone—compelled Misty to lie?

Ruby's chest constricted as she recalled the excuse her sister had given Myrtle Lambert for keeping Zoe out of day care. What if Misty had lied about that, too?

What if DeserTek was involved in all of it, from the backpack's theft to her missing family? If her failure to jump at the offer of a highly paid consulting job—a ridiculous offer for a woman who'd been driving buses—had been construed as a sign that she had damning information and meant to use it? Ruby pressed a hand to her mouth, nausea vying with a wave of dizziness. What if all of her suspicions about Carrie Ann's death were true?

Ruby sucked in a deep breath and forced herself to turn away, toward the recently remodeled house where Sam lived. With no sign of his return, she decided to try calling Hammett's once more, to keep herself from going crazy.

Paulie Hammett's wife, Anna, answered, amid a clatter of utensils.

"Anna, this is Ruby Monroe." Ruby whipped past the obligatories, far too freaked for chitchat. "I'm looking for my sister. I need to get hold of her right away."

"Misty didn't tell you she'd quit? A week ago last Friday."

"She *quit?* How could she have quit?" Misty had worked at the restaurant for close to ten years, since her junior year of high school. Unlike most of Hammett's "girls," she'd kept at it, too busy helping Ruby with their dying mother to attend college immediately after high school. And too practical to give up the stellar tips her long legs and sunny smiles attracted, tips she now needed to put herself through school.

"Got crosswise with the old man about something," Anna answered. "You know how Paulie can get sometimes. I asked him about it, but he just grouched at me to leave her be. Said she'd either come to her senses or she wouldn't. He's not crawlin', not after the way she stormed out in front of customers."

"Misty?" Though Paulie had scared away plenty of waitresses in his time, Ruby had only known her sister to laugh off her boss's moods.

Anna lowered her voice. "You ask me, wouldn't hurt that man to do a little crawlin'. Misty's been here, what?

Ten years? She's practically family and always such a great friend to our Dylan. I give her a lot of the credit for gettin' him on track again, back in that stretch where he was havin' his troubles."

Before Ruby had left the country, she and Misty had received an invitation to his wedding. Ruby considered this, along with his solid reputation as a contractor, proof positive that the Hammett family's Peter Pan had finally grown up.

"You know if Misty's working someplace else now?" Ruby asked. "Have you heard anything at all?" The de facto nerve center for area politics and gossip, Hammett's was a far better source of lakeside news than the paper. Since her sister was a fixture there—and a much-loved one at that—any post-meltdown sightings would be reported and analyzed more avidly than the last Super Bowl.

"Not a word, but I'm surprised you haven't got an earful by now. You're back home, aren't you?"

"Sort of," Ruby said, unwilling to go into the details, "but she didn't meet me at the airport. So do me a favor, will you? Call me back if you hear anything. Anything at all. Please, Anna."

After eliciting a promise, Ruby ended the call as Sam jogged toward her, the area's thin telephone directory in one hand, two water bottles in the other.

He passed one of them to her and asked, "Who should we try first?"

"Thanks." She cracked open the plastic top but didn't spare a moment for a sip. "I just got off the phone with Anna Hammett. She told me—"

"Misty quit. I started to bring that up before. I—uh—I'm over there a lot. I have this deal worked out with Paulie. I pick up the tourists from their rental cabins, give 'em the eco-tour or take 'em fishing, birding, whatever they want."

This made sense to Ruby. Hammett's used to rent boats to anyone who wanted to explore the labyrinth of cuts and bayous bordering the south end of the lake. But lost tourists were bad for business, drowned ones far worse—especially when their half-eaten bodies were recovered.

"I can't understand it. Why would Misty quit? Did this happen around the same time you started noticing these strangers hanging round the house?"

A loud pop—then two more in quick succession—had her ducking behind a thick trunk, a reflex quicker than the conscious realization: *gunfire.* Sam crouched almost as quickly, peering in the direction of the sound.

Ruby dug her nails into her palms, survival instinct warring with the marrow-deep conviction that Zoe was terrified or hurt and wailing for her mother. Sam latched on to Ruby's shoulder, as if to hold her back. Before she could decide whether to be furious or grateful, a deep *whumpff* reverberated through her bones, a boom that sent a squawking flock of blackbirds rising from the trees.

"Oh my God." Ruby jerked away and started running.

"Damn it, Ruby, hold on." Sam caught her elbow and forced her to stop. "There could be more shooting."

She tried in vain to free herself. "That was an explosion."

She knew that sound. She *knew* it. Though the bus she'd driven was never hit, she had heard the improvised bombs and large artillery, had watched blasts rip open vehicles and collapse buildings. She'd seen the dead, too: women, children, sometimes whole families, along with the combatants. For one dizzying moment she was certain she'd drawn the war-zone violence home in her wake. She smelled the smoke of it and saw the glow of—

Staring, Sam released her. "It's your house."

Ruby followed him as he ran toward the department vehicles parked in front of the trees dividing their two properties. Both SUVs sat empty and untended, their lights flashing. Beyond them, the two-story lake house blazed, flames rolling and thick, black ash billowing from the blown-out ground-floor windows and the outward-flung front door. If anyone was inside—

"*Calvin.*" Sam pointed out a crumpled form on the front lawn before running toward the younger deputy. Ruby was right behind him, keeping low to duck the worst of the smoke. Still, the heat pushed at her, its malice palpable in the prickling of her skin and the tightening of her lungs. Squinting, she scanned around for the other deputy, but seeing no one, she focused on the downed man.

"We have to get him away from this," Sam said, grabbing the broad shoulders and gesturing for Ruby to take Calvin's feet.

"Wait a second," she said, seeing the weapon hanging loose in the deputy's hand. Unwilling to risk leaving it, she picked it up and shoved it under her belt. "Okay, now."

They both lifted, carrying the limp form to the street side of Whitaker's SUV, where its bulk offered some protection. While Sam called for more help on the radio, Ruby drew upon the primary assessment training she'd had in nursing school. First, she shook the injured man, calling, "Deputy Whitaker, say something. Calvin?" When he didn't respond, she went straight to *A for Airway*—neck straight, head tipped back, mouth clear and unobstructed. *B for Breathing*—bending lower, she could hear him, rasping a little, but clearly moving air. *C for circulation*—no blood . . .

The deputy groaned and coughed spasmodically, but before Ruby could go further, Sam yelled from the open door of the Suburban, *"Shoot it."*

Only then did Ruby register the savage barking. Turning her head, she saw a blur—a snarling gray shape streaking toward her. Without Sam's warning, she never would have reached the gun in time. As it was, the huge beast was leaping, close enough to see the white teeth flashing only a few feet from her face as she fired twice.

The mastiff, singed hair stinking, struck her, the momentum of its attack knocking her onto her rear end and causing her to drop the weapon. She stared as the animal's jaws worked and its massive paws twitched before it went still, its long tongue lolling from a bloody mouth.

Shuddering, Ruby scooted clear of it and peered around the front of the Suburban. A breeze rolled off the water, lifting a host of sparks like fireflies. She heard the crackling, roaring voice of flame, saw it reignite an eerie, second twilight. Thick smoke drifted their way, bitter-hot with wood ash. Eyes streaming, Ruby realized no one could get inside now.

And no one could possibly get out.

Zoe and Misty aren't in there, aren't inside: burning, screaming, dying. Instead, Ruby forced herself to picture the two of them on their way home, having somehow missed her at the airport. A tire maybe—only a flat tire had made them late—and Misty's spare had been bad. She'd had trouble with the lug nuts, lost her directions . . .

But what if she was wrong? Sick with fear, Ruby stood abruptly. "Maybe it's not so bad in back. I need to check and—"

"I'll run back and do it. Stay here and do what you can for Calvin."

Afraid of what she might see behind the cabin, Ruby swallowed hard and nodded. As he jogged off toward the house's lake side, she turned her attention back to Calvin, who was on his side and groaning, struggling to sit up.

"Don't try to move," she said. "Help's coming."

And with one last, heartbreaking glance in the direction of her burning house, she turned back to what needed to be done.

As Sam rounded the corner of the blazing building, he prayed there wasn't another of those gigantic dogs waiting.

Instead, he found the deputy's boots. A few feet from the flaming hole of the back door, Sam made out the smoldering, black soles and scorched, tooled leather. Bending low and choking on the acrid smoke, Sam grabbed Balderach by the ankles and pulled the man away.

Too late, Sam realized the moment he blinked clear his vision. Balderach's arms trailed limp behind him, his uniform shirt smoking. The thick mustache had burned off; the face was bubbling, peeling—Sam looked away from it, horrified but certain the deputy was past help.

Hacking in the thick air, Sam moved back from the body, stepped away, and peered up at the second-story windows above the porch roof. As he struggled to catch his breath, he looked around for some safe way to climb up, at least to peer in, but the siding was ablaze now and every window glowing. Including the single upstairs bedroom, where Sam was nearly certain he saw movement. . . .

A feminine silhouette lurching forward and then dropping out of sight.

"Misty?" he shouted as he stepped up on a flower box and onto the porch railing. The porch roof proved more challenging. Though it hadn't yet caught fire, a piece of trim broke off in his hands and he nearly fell.

On his third attempt, he swung a leg up, then pulled his body onto the sloped surface. By this time, those shingles nearest to the house's outer wall were smoking, triggering more coughing as he edged toward the window.

He stared in the direction of the soot-stained glass, but the only movement he saw from inside was the throbbing pulse of flame, its color muted by the swirling black clouds. If he kicked through the window, would the rush of oxygen cause the fire to leap out and ignite him, burn him to death like Balderach? The thought tightened Sam's gut, but only steps short of the window, he was too damned close to back off—too much committed to give up the chance to help whomever he had glimpsed.

As his foot sank into a soft spot, Sam fell hard, slid, and barely managed to stop himself from rolling off the roof. Cautiously, he stood again, then moved forward once more, feeling for depressions where the wood beneath the shingles might have rotted.

Which put him about six feet away when a second blast blew a thousand shards in his direction and sent him flying backward.

Flying, falling, and all too quickly landing a few feet from the deputy's still-smoldering remains.

CHAPTER FOUR

We are the hollow men
We are the stuffed men
Leaning together
Headpiece filled with straw. Alas!
Our dried voices, when
We whisper together
Are quiet and meaningless
As wind in dry grass
Or rats' feet over broken glass
In our dry cellar.

—T. S. Eliot,
from "The Hollow Men"

April 5

After three months in office, Justine Wofford still hated these meetings with her deputies, hated the awkward silences that followed her orders, the resentful looks, and the less-than-subtle attempts to call her experience and judgment into question. Exhausted from a night spent working and emotionally wrung out from their department's loss, Wofford was in absolutely no mood for a challenge.

Perhaps, she hoped, this could be the day they put aside past politics and came together as one. For Oscar Balderach's sake, as well as that of their injured rookie, Calvin Whitaker. But she'd barely started divvying up assignments when Deputy Roger Savoy interrupted.

"You ask me, we oughta haul the neighbor out of his

hospital bed and let some of the more experienced inter-
viewers sweat him till he coughs up something. I'll lay
you odds, Mrs. Wofford, if McCoy's not involved, he's at
least seen something," Savoy said, looking for all the
world as if he meant to be helpful.

He had a way of doing that, of casting himself as the
seasoned professional who knew this jurisdiction inside
and out—in contrast to her, of course. He'd emphasized
this difference when he'd run against Justine, presented
himself as her late husband's heir apparent, a deputy
who'd spent close to thirty years as Lou's right-hand man.
A man comfortable in what most saw as a man's role.

Too bad for him he didn't bear the last name Wofford.
Or understand he'd provoked some powerful grudges
with his stiff-necked ways. Or that he didn't appreciate
how well the ten years she'd worked as a Morton County
deputy and the two years she'd been married to Lou
Wofford had prepared her to play hardball.

"It's *Sheriff* Wofford . . ." Justine corrected, giving him
a half smile he would doubtless describe later as ball-
busting. If one listened to Savoy, she was Wonder Bitch,
capable of emasculating legions of East Texas law enforcers with a single glance. Which was a pretty neat trick,
considering how ignorant and ineffectual he also made
her out to be. "And I'm certain you didn't mean to imply
that my interview skills are in any way lacking. I said I'd
handle it."

She saw surprise register in the split second before he
slapped on a fresh coat of professionalism, saw the discomfort flash over another half dozen faces, too. Normally, she pulled men aside to redirect objectionable
behavior, with the idea that embarrassing them before
their peers was no way to win allies. But increasingly,
she'd come to realize that this tactic made her look weak

to them, so she'd decided on a new strategy. Fuck with her in front of others, and they could expect to be treated in kind.

"Or course I didn't mean that, *Sheriff*. But it occurred to me you weren't around back when we had regular dealings with the McCoys. White trash, the whole lot of them—steal anything that wasn't nailed down."

"Yes. Well, thank you for the history lesson. I'll be stopping by a little later, to thank Mr. McCoy for his assistance last night."

"*Thank* him?" another of the veterans muttered, but Justine's hard look shut the commentary down, a truce she knew would last only until she made it out of earshot.

Which didn't take as long as she expected, thanks to Larry Crane—cruelly nicknamed Ichabod in the department, in honor of his Adam's apple and gangly gooberdom. As far as she'd seen, Crane was the butt of every joke, the deputy no one respected, which had made him the perfect person to recruit as her first ally. Left to man the phones, he interrupted to tell her, "Made that call to the bank, Sheriff. And I know you're going to want to hear about this right away."

At the sound of approaching footsteps outside his hospital room door, Sam braced himself for another visit from the duty nurse, Elysse Steele, a tall blonde he had dated briefly. And apparently none too successfully, judging from the muted glee he'd seen on her face when she had come to jab his ass with a needle the size of a turkey baster.

He forced his eyelids open, intent on banishing the enemy before she marched in a troop of student nurses working on their urinary catheterization merit badges.

As he blinked away the medication haze, he made out sunlight filtering through the window shade. The breakfast tray came into focus next, its presence assuring him the night shift should by this time be off duty. He sighed and felt it in his ribs first: a knifing pain that awakened a constellation of aches and twinges.

The door opened, and Ruby poked her head inside. "You awake?" she whispered.

"Come on in." His voice came out gravelly and slurred.

She slipped inside but remained close to the door. "I— ah—I'm meeting a friend of mine here as soon as she gets finished with a few charts. She's letting me stay at her place for a while. Anyway, I thought—I thought I ought to check to see how you are. My friend couldn't tell me anything, except that you might be the luckiest SOB in Texas."

"Your friend's *Elysse*?" He winced, a movement that telegraphed a neon-bright sting from those stitches closest to his mouth. "Listen, whatever she has to say about me . . ."

He stopped there, reminding himself that anything he said could and would be used against him in a court of feminine opinion. And unlike his last trial, no defense would be allowed. Instead, he changed the subject. "I'll be okay. What about you? Did you get hurt?"

As his vision cleared, he'd noticed the blood spotting the same jeans and turquoise top she'd been wearing yesterday. She clearly hadn't taken time to sleep, either, judging from the dark circles beneath her eyes.

"It's *your* blood." She moved nearer to his bedside, took a closer look at the bandaged spots: the bridge of his nose, his forehead, and his jaw. Wincing sympathetically, she asked, "How's that feel?"

"Like sixteen stitches," he said. "The doctor fished out a few shards from the window, but Elysse's right. I'm damned lucky I didn't break my neck flying off that porch roof. Or burn up in the fire. Thanks to you."

"I spotted the deputy first, and—and I thought you were dead, too." Her blue eyes looked haunted. "There was so much blood. But corpses don't gush like that. I—ah—I've seen my share this past year. And then you blinked up at me."

"I was pretty damned surprised to be alive. Listen, I want to—I want to thank you. For getting Calvin on his feet and for—for the two of you—" It sucked the air from his lungs, the thought of how they had risked their skins to drag him toward the water. "I would've cooked right there. Burned up like poor Balderach."

Lying on his back, stunned, as the flames had crackled their way closer, he had realized that if he died, no one would be much inconvenienced. Oh, maybe his former partner or Paulie and Anna Hammett and a few running buddies would raise their beers in tribute, or Pacheco would curse him for a stupid bastard, but sand would swiftly cover the faint footprint he'd left on this earth.

But wasn't that what he'd been going for these past years? Hadn't a lack of complications, of connections been his goal?

Unsettled by the thought, he asked, "How's Calvin?"

"I ran into his mother out there." Ruby nodded toward the door. "She says he's got a mild concussion, but she's taking him home as soon as they get his discharge papers finished."

Sam nodded. "I imagine he's pretty busted up about Oscar."

"They all seem to be, the whole department. And that poor family . . ." Ruby shook her head. "I don't understand it. Why would the house—how could it just explode like that? It makes no sense—the place burned so fast. Too fast. It really makes me wonder . . ."

She turned her face from him, but not before he took note of its pallor.

"Ruby? Are you—have you had any word yet? About your family?" When no answer came, he added, "Maybe you'd better sit down."

She wobbled toward the chair beside him and sank down, hugging herself tightly.

Sam used the controls to raise himself, fighting off a groan with the shift in his position. "Tell me," he said.

"I spent most of the night answering questions, or waiting around the sheriff's office. While I was there, I called everybody we could think of." Ruby rubbed at damp eyes. "I must've woken up half of Dogwood, but I couldn't find a single soul who's seen either of them. Misty hasn't called her old boss. She hasn't called her friends or shown up for her classes. And Zoe—I managed to reach the pediatrician, too. The doctor hasn't see her in months, hasn't heard a word about her being sick. I talked to Misty on Monday but no one else has heard from them in the past week, unless you—"

"It might've been that long ago for me, too. Sorry I can't be sure." Sam pulled the bedside table close enough to pour a cup of water from the pitcher. "Does Misty have friends out of town? Someone she might visit? A boyfriend, maybe, where she might lose track of the time?"

He held out the water to her, but Ruby shook her head.

"No one I know of," she answered. "But I should try her friend Crystal again. You know Crystal Kowalski, don't you? From Hammett's?"

"Sure." Also a waitress, Crystal was as much a fixture at the restaurant as her best friend, though Sam found her constant, self-absorbed chatter annoying enough that he avoided sitting in her section. "She and Misty have been practically joined at the hip, always talking about that court reporter program they're in."

"I haven't been able to reach her, either."

It was on the tip of his tongue to ask Ruby what he could do to help her. To let her know that despite his aches and pains, he'd be going home today. But instead, he said, "Well, the new sheriff's taking care of things, I'm sure. She'll be hell-bent on getting to the bottom of this, especially since she's lost a man."

And because she had something to prove. There had been a huge hullabaloo when Justine Wofford, a fairly recent transplant from a distant county's sheriff department, won the recent special election, claiming the right to complete her husband's term. But there were plenty who argued that she wasn't qualified, plenty waiting for the chance to run the woman they considered an upstart out of office at the first sign of trouble.

When Ruby stared at Sam, her blue eyes welling, he had to look away to continue. "She's probably already working with the volunteer networks and putting out an AMBER Alert. And other law enforcement agencies will come in, too."

The state fire marshal, he thought, and maybe ATF, if there had been some sort of explosives in the house. The more investigators that showed up, the more closely they would look at any handy suspects.

And who could possibly be handier than the felon living next door?

"The firefighters . . ." Ruby started. "Sheriff Wofford told me . . ."

He swallowed hard, dread pooling in his gut like liquid flame. Though he didn't want to know, he couldn't stop himself from asking, "What did the sheriff tell you?"

"She said the firefighters pulled two bodies from the rubble. Just a few hours back. There were two adults and another of those big dogs. They don't know a lot more yet, but they think maybe one of the—the victims was a woman."

A nightmare memory constricted Sam's chest. A memory of the falling figure he'd seen through the window. The woman he had tried and failed to reach.

"They asked me for the name of Misty's dentist," Ruby went on. "They need—they'll need the records for the medical examiner."

"It can't be Misty." Sam shook his head, his mouth two steps ahead of his better judgment. "Can't be. Because she's with your daughter, keeping her safe. She is because she has to be, because they're damned well going to find them both alive."

Nodding, she whispered, "Thank you. Thank you so much for that. And last night."

She slipped out of the room, leaving him feeling for the first time like the criminal the federal court had named him. Feeling like a coward and a monster for placating his foster brother's widow with false hope.

CHAPTER FIVE

The sun, the moon and the stars would have disappeared long ago, had they happened to be within reach of predatory human hands.

—Havelock Ellis,
The Dance of Life

Above the algae-filmed green waters of an isolated slough, dragonflies glided, darted, or hung suspended in the sunlight: dashers and skimmers, eastern amber-wings and clubtails. To the uninitiated, they looked harmless, living jewels that studded the swampy bottomland. But the man watching knew that his old friends were killers, winged assassins waiting for the slightest flicker of prey movement to send them into action.

As he stood smoking on a wooden walkway, he imagined himself much the same way. Not stagnating near some backwater bayou beside a cheap vacation rental, but hovering in place and waiting for his true target to panic and break cover. Waiting for the perfect moment to fulfill his promise and do what he'd been born to do, as efficiently and guiltlessly as the tiny hunters of his temporary kingdom.

Amid the calls of birds and the rustling of breezes through the bright, spring leaves, a discordant sound—unnatural and unwelcome—had him turning toward the shabby little cabin he was using as a base. Turning toward a high-pitched cry from inside. A human cry that fractured his peace, in spite of his precautions.

He could not have this, would not allow the interruption.

So he pushed past overgrown brush and stalked toward the steps, the world darkening as thunderheads obscured his inner vision. He would have the quiet he craved, to plan, to calculate, to think out every angle.

And if that meant having to treat his reptilian allies to another carcass, so be it.

Elysse drove, since a helpful deputy had arranged for the rental company to pick up Ruby's damaged car.

"I hate not having my own wheels," she complained. She'd intended to buy another used vehicle upon returning, but car shopping was the least of her concerns now.

"You can borrow mine whenever you need it," Elysse said, "as long as you run me back and forth to the hospital for my shifts."

"Thanks. I promise it won't be for long, and I'll be careful with it." The small car was just over a year old, with nary a ding marring its gleaming white exterior.

"Just try not to get it shot, okay?"

Ruby gaped, then faltered through a weak laugh at the rise and fall of her friend's eyebrows. But Ruby didn't have the heart to joke, so she was grateful when Elysse pulled into a yard dominated by an old magnolia tree festooned with Spanish moss. Rather than parking beside the house, she pulled beneath it, for the one-story cedar structure had been built on pilings to raise it above the occasional floods that washed through the canal neighborhood. Located on a narrow spit of solid land, the house was flanked by shuttered and elevated vacation cabins overlooking the man-made channel. Behind the houses and across the single-lane street, a domelike beaver lodge presided over a swampy wetland of the rodents' making.

After pulling her suitcases from the back of the Corolla, she followed her much-taller friend to a flight of wooden stairs beneath a screened porch that faced a green-brown strip of water lined with docks and houses on both sides. Elysse's own dock—currently boatless— slumped in defeat beneath the waterline, but the small house itself appeared to be in good repair.

"This is it." Elysse introduced her recently purchased home—the first she'd ever owned—with a halfhearted flourish. Though she still wore her violet scrubs from work, she'd unclipped her ash-blonde hair, so the loose waves framed a face lined with the fatigue of a long night shift.

"It's really nice, Leese. Thanks for having me," Ruby managed, her mother's gentle insistence upon manners bubbling through the layers of despair, and terror. She wished her mother were alive and healthy now to take charge and see her through this nightmare, though in her heart Ruby knew Althea Bailey had been a gossamer magnolia, the kind who locked herself in dark rooms with a cold compress and a fifth of Southern Comfort. At least she had until her liver had cried uncle.

"Place sat empty for years. It was a fine mess, first time I saw it," Elysse told her. "Sam was the one kept saying what great potential it had. Helped me negotiate a bargain price and clean it out and fix it up, too. And silly me, I supposed that must mean something. Really, what man puts that sort of effort into a house he doesn't mean to live in?"

Disappointment appeared in Elysse's hazel eyes, and bitterness shot through her honeyed voice. Grimacing, she flushed, something she'd been prone to since the two of them had met in high school. "Sorry, Ruby. I'm sure the last thing you're in the mood for's another laugh-a-minute episode from the archives of the Elysse Steele Love Files. Served me right anyway for getting myself hooked up with a guy like that. McCoys steal—everybody knows that. Expect anything different, and you've got nobody but yourself to blame."

The comment reminded Ruby of rumors about the father, who had driven his wife to abandon both him and their two sons, of the stories she'd heard about Sam's brother, J.B., and his dangerous behavior. The family reputation was at odds with what she'd seen of Sam so far. Yet she wanted to tell Elysse it was all right. Because Ruby would give anything to put things back the way they'd been the last time the two of them had spoken, with Elysse encouraging Ruby to take the job she'd badgered her insufferable stepbrother to set up and Ruby—considered the expert for having been married—talking her friend through her latest relationship implosion. But all Ruby could think of was Zoe.

"I can't just wait around here," Ruby burst out, the truth of it slamming her like a two-by-four against the skull. Pain and panic pounded at her temples. "I should be out looking for them. I should be working with the volunteers to organize search parties—"

Elysse touched her arm. "There's an AMBER Alert, Ruby. Which means that you've got every officer in the state—probably a few states—looking. And it'll go out on TV and the radio, too, right?"

Ruby nodded mutely, and in her mind, she saw the information scrolling across the bottom of a screen or splashed across the e-mails that went out to thousands. Zoe's description and the plate number of Misty's Honda Civic. The photos deputies had collected when they'd awakened Myrtle Lambert and Anna Hammett. Because Ruby herself no longer had a single picture. The little album in her backpack had been stolen, and all the rest had burned up with her house.

I'll never get them back again. Not the baby photos nor the wedding pictures nor the last shots she'd taken of her husband. *And what if I never get another chance to take more of my daughter, either?*

The premonition hit her so hard, the earth fell away beneath her feet. She couldn't swim; she couldn't fly, yet somehow, she kept standing, like a dead tree in a flooded hollow.

"The police will find them for you, Ruby." Elysse braced her, with arms wrapped around her shoulders and words insistent in her ears. "They'll search every place you'd think of and lots of places you won't. They'll find them and they'll bring them right here, so you'll want to get some rest now. That way you'll be fit to take care of Zoe and Misty. You'll be strong and ready."

Ruby wanted to thank Elysse, but she couldn't speak for fear of completely losing the calm that had been drilled into her, the clear-eyed inner stillness needed to survive a world where at any moment, a complete stranger might make it his business to kill her. It seemed surreal to feel in greater danger on her home turf than she had ever felt in Iraq.

"Let me get this for you." Elysse snatched up Ruby's larger suitcase and preceded her upstairs. At the top, she unlocked the screened porch, where she kept a ceiling fan, a couple of deck chairs, and an old, chain-hung porch swing. Elysse's flat-faced black Persian cat stared out at them through a sliding glass door, its demonic stare as unnerving as ever.

"This part's Margarita Central." Elysse ignored the cat to glance around her porch. "We'll have the party here to celebrate when Misty and Zoe come back safe and sound."

She pulled open the sliding door and said, "Hey, Bubba-Boo, we're home."

The cat's orange eyes stared evilly before it turned its tail to them. Probably at the indignity of being referred to by such a cornpone name instead of one following a noble title. *Baron Beelzebub,* thought Ruby, who liked normal cats just fine, had even promised one to Zoe. *Lord Lucifer,* maybe.

"He's really missed you," Elysse assured her. "He's just too proud to show it. Let me stow your suitcase in the guestroom. Then we'll have a little breakfast before you get showered and into bed."

Ruby's stomach shocked her with a pang of hunger, reminding her she hadn't eaten since yesterday's mid-morning snack at the Atlanta airport. Her brain buzzed with exhaustion, too, though sleep seemed even more unthinkable than food.

Yet Elysse was right, Ruby realized. Unless she forced herself to regroup, she'd be worse than useless. Unless she found the strength to plan and act, she'd spend eternity in a hell far more insufferable than the one she'd left behind in Iraq.

Smooth and untroubled, the water's surface reflected a lurid bouquet of dawn color. Gliding upon white wings, Ruby looked down at the lily pads and shore weeds, at the cypress trees and finally the bleached trunks that had given rise to the lake's unofficial name.

Circling, she peered down, heart thumping with the urgent need to see beneath the surface, to find the truths the water hid. But no matter how hard she tried, how desperately she struggled as her wings tired, she saw no farther than the mirror image of the sunrise, a bloody spill highlighted by a gleaming, golden orb.

The blinds were closed, so Ruby had no idea how long she'd slept by the time Elysse shook her awake. Heart spasming, Ruby jerked upright, jagged bits of her dream giving way to an equally unsettling reality. "Have they been found? Zoe? Misty?"

Elysse shook her head, her mussed hair and oversized T-shirt hinting that she, too, had just awakened. "Sheriff Wofford's here to see you. She's waiting for you in the living room."

Ruby could scarcely breathe, her heart was pounding so hard. "Where are they? Where's my daughter?"

"She didn't tell me, Ruby." Elysse hugged herself, the nail beds going white as her fingers dug into her arms. "She won't say why she's here."

"Oh, shit." Ruby sprang from the bed and bolted past Elysse. "Oh, *no-no-no*."

Justine Wofford stood waiting with her hands clasped before her. An attractive woman in her late thirties, she wore an expression as funereal as her sleekly pulled back, coffee-colored hair and a black suit cut to downplay generous curves—and most probably a holster. Or maybe what looked like grimness was fatigue, for Ruby knew the woman had worked straight through the night.

At the sight of Ruby rushing toward her, the sheriff raised her palms, her dark eyes softening. "No, Mrs. Monroe. It's not that. I still don't have any word about the identification of the burned bodies."

Ruby stopped, her limbs quivering from the surge of raw adrenaline. Abruptly, ridiculously, anger surged through her, resentment toward this woman whose concern was tempered by official distance. Ruby's own emotions were so raw, she wanted to howl with pain, wanted the whole world to scream with her. Yet somehow, she forced herself to gear down, to listen as the sheriff spoke.

"I've asked the medical examiner to make this case a priority. I hope to have an answer for you soon. Meanwhile—"

"What about the AMBER Alert? Has anyone reported seeing my family, or the car at least?"

"I want you to understand that when it comes to cases involving missing children, there are always going to be reports. People who think they might remember seeing something. People who want to help so badly, they try to fit round memories into the square holes of the scenario. We get other calls as well, unrelated reports, false confessions from disturbed citizens, intentional efforts to mislead."

Ruby swept her sleep-tossed hair from her eyes, tugging it hard enough to feel the pricks of pain at her scalp. "So you've gotten some of these already? But how do you know which ones—which calls are the real ones?"

Wofford shook her head. "I could tell you there's some litmus test or that we have some sixth sense that helps us tell the accurate tips from all the false leads. But that would be a lie, and I promised you last night I wouldn't do that."

Ruby knew lies could be shortcuts, that they made the authorities' jobs easier. But she was beginning to appreciate that Sheriff Wofford wasn't the type to cut herself much slack, or maybe she couldn't afford to as a woman in what had always been a man's role in this county.

"No lies, no omissions," Ruby said, echoing—and holding on to—Justine Wofford's words.

The sheriff nodded an acknowledgment. "The truth is, we have to check them all out, and I won't be bothering you with any that I'm not reasonably sure of. Otherwise, I'll be running your emotions up and down the flagpole for no reason. And I won't do that, either."

"But you didn't drive out here to tell me that."

"You're right. I do have news. I couldn't reach you on your cell phone, so I'm glad you let me know where you'd be—"

"Oh no," Ruby cried, remembering. "I meant to plug it in here, but I . . ."

What if Misty had tried to reach her? What if she had missed the call?

"I thought you'd want to hear," said Wofford. "We've checked with your sister's cell phone provider. Her service was suspended just days ago for nonpayment. I don't have the records yet—that takes a warrant—but I convinced a sympathetic employee to tell me the last recorded call came from overseas on March thirtieth."

"I called her, it would have been on that morning, your time," said Ruby, chills racing up her arms. Had anyone spoken to Misty or her daughter since?

"We should have the phone records in a few hours, and we've asked the carrier to restore service for now, to see if we can use it to reach Ms. Bailey, or if need be, use the GPS locater."

Ruby shook her head. "I don't think Misty's phone has GPS." Although her sister could have used it, it only came with more expensive models.

"Since our 9-1-1 system's been enhanced, we can locate any cell phone, as long as it's powered up. And assuming, of course, that your sister's phone didn't burn with the house."

"It didn't," Ruby said, hoping more than guessing. "Because Misty has it with her, and Misty's with my daughter." *Somewhere.*

"We've also contacted the credit card companies you mentioned last night and talked to someone from the bank. No activity on any of the cards in more than a week."

"And the bank?"

"Actually, that's why I came. I—"

Wofford cleared her throat, regret filling her dark eyes. "Two days ago, your sister's bank accounts were closed out, emptied. Do you know anything about—?"

"I—I don't understand that. Why would . . ." A rushing sound filled Ruby's ears, and her gaze drifted to the Persian, where it sat watching from atop the coffee table.

The cat's orange eyes stared back at her. Cold, aloof—then surprised as Elysse snatched it up in her arms and stroked the silky black fur, as if to comfort herself.

"I'm afraid there's more," Sheriff Wofford went on. "I'm sorry to have to tell you like this, but according to the bank, your personal accounts are gone, too."

"Gone? What do you mean? How could—?"

"Your money's been withdrawn," she said. "Right down to the last penny."

CHAPTER SIX

We know more about war than we know about peace,
more about killing than we know about living.
— General Omar N. Bradley

His discharge forms completed, Sam was half dozing in front of a TV fishing show when Paulie Hammett barged into the hospital room and said, "Holy shit, kid. You look like a sack fulla fish guts."

Sam jerked fully awake. "Thanks," he managed. "And same to you, pal. Only I have a prayer of getting better."

Paulie thumped down a twelve-pack of longnecks—wrapped in a blue ribbon—on the bedside table, a broad grin splitting the stubble of his grizzled beard. When Sam stared at the strange offering, he said, "What? You were expecting flowers?" Beneath the brim of Hammett's gimmee cap, he raised unruly gray eyebrows as he studied Sam's face.

Sam fought off a laugh, mostly because he knew it would hurt like hell. "Thanks—and I'm glad you could make it."

Paulie beamed at him, his faded Hammett's-on-the-Lake T-shirt straining across his paunch—and offering evidence that if a person wielded enough influence, he could make up his own damned dress code, thank you. A big man in height as well as girth, he tossed Sam a plastic grocery bag stuffed with jeans and what appeared to be—surprise, surprise—a new navy shirt bearing the grinning alligator logo. "Anna had me pick you up some clothes while I was taking care of that mutt of yours. Thought you might like something without blood all over it to wear home."

"Your wife's a goddess among women," Sam said.

"Tell me something she doesn't know already."

"She married way beneath herself."

Paulie rolled his eyes and snorted, as close to laughter as he ever came. "Tell me something *everybody* doesn't know already. Now put those on so I can run you home. We're shorthanded at the restaurant, so I need to get back before five."

"Sorry to take so much time out of your day."

"Not like you planned this, did you? Besides, I wanted to see you for myself, make sure they sewed you up straight." Paulie squinted, making a study of Sam's face, then abruptly sobered. "Seriously, McCoy, how're you feelin'?"

The concern in his expression was so unlike the King of Bullshit, Sam braved a response that few would dare. "You can tell your *wife* I'll be back in top form in a few days."

Instead of easing, Paulie's frown lines deepened. "All kidding aside, Sam. Anna—both of us—are plenty worried about Misty and that baby girl. If you know anything . . ."

Paulie looked away and rubbed the rolls behind his thick neck, but not before Sam caught the slippery shift of his expression. Was that suspicion he saw, or regret that Hammett had allowed Misty, an employee he considered family, to storm out of his restaurant over some meaningless squabble about a botched lunch order? Or was he simply pissed—which tended to be Paulie's default setting—about any sleep this disappearance had cost him and his wife?

"I'm worried, too," Sam said. He wondered if Paulie had heard yet about the bodies pulled from the burned house. But Ruby's face flashed through his mind, her desperate need to believe her family still lived, and he couldn't force himself to bring it up.

After an awkward silence, Paulie reverted to form. "You need me to call back that nurse to help you get your clothes on? Or you want maybe I should hunt up one of the younger ones? 'Cause I'm not helping you step into your boxers, no matter how pretty you beg."

"Well, in that case, wait outside," Sam grumbled.

Paulie grabbed the twelve-pack and headed for the door.

In spite of his discomfort, Sam tried to dress quickly, but a wave of dizziness—probably from the pain meds— left him clammy and exhausted. Stumbling into the bathroom, he bent to splash a little water on his face, then froze, catching sight of the bandages and bruises.

At least the shock cleared his head, allowing him to finish before his ride home lost patience. But when Sam opened the door to the hall, he found Paulie deep in what looked like a serious conversation with Justine Wofford.

Like most folks, the new county sheriff was dwarfed by Paulie's bulk, though her heels brought her within an inch or so of Sam's six feet one. He guessed she was going for an authoritarian look with her tightly upswept, dark hair and darker suit, but in spite of the effort, she looked all wrong for the role she'd claimed. Far younger than her late husband—Sam would guess late thirties— she had the kind of figure not even the most asexual suit could hide. Lucky thing for her, Sam thought, that Preston County's citizens, who weren't known for their open-mindedness, *were* well conditioned to vote "Wofford" when they saw the name on a ballot.

Or maybe, her opponent, the heavy-handed Roger Savoy, had made more enemies than just the Hammetts during his years as deputy.

The new sheriff offered her right hand, and Sam accepted, struck by the contrast of the firm grip with the woman's neatly polished red nails and diamond-studded wedding band.

"Mr. McCoy, sir." Wofford's gaze was direct and somehow unnerving; her eyes were so dark they were nearly black. "I came over here specifically to shake your hand. From what I understand, you put yourself at grave risk to save the life of Deputy Whitaker. Thank you, on behalf of Calvin's family and the citizens of Preston County, and I hope you'll soon be feeling better."

Sam, who had a McCoy's instinctive distrust of law enforcement coupled with a convict's desire to fly beneath the radar, wasn't certain how to handle gratitude from the enemy. Worse yet, she spoke like a damned politician, an association that made him want to rush off to wash his hand.

"I'm fine," he said, and attempted to deflect her attention by adding, "And Ruby Monroe's the one you should be thanking. You see the size of that dog she took out?

Would've ripped both of them to shreds if she hadn't thought to pick up Calvin's weapon."

Last night in the emergency room, he'd told another deputy all he could remember. Sam had hoped to quickly dispose of the questions so the department could get down to the business of closing this case without involving him further. But with Wofford here, that hope was gone.

Her smile didn't register in her eyes. "I read Deputy Savoy's notes, and it would seem that both of you behaved admirably."

She drew out the statement, leaving Sam to wonder if she'd meant to emphasize the words "would seem." He glanced at Hammett, only to see him nodding in agreement.

Paulie suggested, "Once everything gets settled and Misty and her niece are back home, I promise, we'll make one hell of a party of it. Boiled crawfish, cold beer, cake and punch for all the kiddies."

The new sheriff's demeanor changed at the mention of the missing persons, the fluidity of her expressions stiffening into what Sam recognized as the Official Law Enforcement Mask.

"I think it's premature, Mr. Hammett, to be planning celebrations." The stiffness of her tone contrasted with the merry wink of what appeared to be more diamonds at her earlobes. "For one thing, there's still a deputy to bury. A deputy who was a close friend of my husband's."

"Hell, Justine, they were both good friends of mine. You know that." Face reddening, Paulie rubbed the back of his neck. "I didn't mean to imply—I just wanted to—"

"I'm sorry I didn't get to Deputy Balderach in time to help him," Sam interrupted before Hammett could offer beer and "mud bugs" for the after-funeral gathering.

Wofford shook her head, the darkness of her expression reminding Sam she was a recent widow. Eyes trained on him, she said, "We'll talk more about what you did during the drive home."

Sam let that sink in before he answered, choosing his words carefully. "I'd be glad to do that. But Paulie here came all the way into town to pick me up."

It was a strain keeping his gaze neutral, an effort keeping his mouth shut; all he could think of were the reactions of those who might see him riding with the county sheriff. Surely, they would put it together with his neighbors' disappearance and the deputy who'd been killed. Most people in the area were willing to forgive a local boy, even a McCoy, of some crime they didn't understand that had only harmed some distant—and faceless—corporation. But what had happened last night related to a beautiful and well-liked young woman and a cute kid, a local lawman who'd been burned to death, and another who'd been injured. If people started associating him with that mess, he could kiss his new guide business good-bye. Though money wasn't Sam's problem—even after paying a huge fine, he continued to earn hefty royalties from some commercial security software he'd developed—what the hell would he do with himself for the next three years if he couldn't work his stopgap trade?

Instead of helping Sam out, attesting that they'd been close since Paulie and Anna had hired him as a scrawny, mouthy fourteen-year-old to clean fish for returning boaters, Hammett exchanged a long look with the sheriff before saying, "That's no trouble at all, Justine. I'll just ice this beer down back at the restaurant. Or maybe I'll drop by with 'em later, Sam. You and I can catch up then."

Sam felt like shooting him the bird.

As he and Wofford left the hospital, Sam did his damnedest to look innocent, unworried. He waved good-bye to the duty nurse as if the sheriff always escorted him back home. Once he and Wofford reached the sheriff's SUV, he quickly climbed inside the worn and grimy vehicle before anyone driving past could spot him.

The driver's side door creaked loudly as Wofford took her seat. When she turned the key, the Expedition's engine coughed and sputtered repeatedly before chugging to life. "Darned thing's beat to death." A light flush rose from her neckline, as if the vehicle's state embarrassed her. "Should get the new one in soon."

Ignoring the comment, Sam said, "Ruby stopped by the hospital this morning. She told me about those bodies in the house. Said you didn't know yet who you'd found."

Wofford pulled out of the hospital parking lot and said, "We think we have one male, one female, but the remains were burned so badly, we're not even one hundred percent sure of that much."

"Both adults, right?" he asked, the question tumbling loose as Zoe's bright smile flashed through his memory. "You—you didn't find a little kid in there?"

Wofford shook her head. "The firefighters looked hard, and the state fire marshal brought in a dog and handler earlier. But there's no sign of a child in that disaster. Thank God."

Sam released a breath he hadn't realized he'd been holding and willed his pulse to return to normal. This woman might sound compassionate, but something else beat beneath the surface. Something that warned him she was assessing his every syllable and each inflection.

"I understand you believe you saw a woman upstairs," she went on. "Did you recognize this person? Could it have been Misty Bailey?"

As the old Ford picked up speed, Sam felt every bounce and rattle transferred through the stiff suspension. With the street's neatly painted older wooden houses whirling past his window, he tried to focus on the shape he'd glimpsed so briefly last night: slender enough that a knee-jerk impression shouted *female*. At the thought of how close he had come to reaching her, he swallowed hard to clear the taste of bile. "It happened so fast, I can't be sure what I saw. But I hope to God it wasn't Misty, that she's somewhere safe with her niece."

The sheriff turned down a smaller residential street to bypass Dogwood's historic downtown, which would most likely be clogged with antiques-and-crafts-loving visitors on a beautiful Saturday in April. The town's namesake trees were blooming in showy white or pink displays. "Any ideas on where she'd go? She ever mention any boyfriend?"

Sam shrugged. "She never talked about anything too personal. We're just neighbors, that's all."

He cast the statement as carefully as a lure upon the water. Was Wofford simply fishing for additional information, as she would with any witness, or was she looking at him as a potential suspect?

Sure enough, the sheriff rose to snatch the bait, saying, "But you two worked together, right? At Hammett's, up until Ms. Bailey quit last week?"

"I wouldn't say we worked together. I'm an independent guide, but I do pick up some clients at the restaurant. Generally, I'm in there a few times a week, so yeah, Misty and I got to know each other. Casually."

"Casually . . ." Wofford braked as two mop-headed preteens crossed the street, both of them crowded onto a single bike. Lowering the driver's side window, she shouted, "Y'all run on home and get yourself some helmets."

The boys kept going, either not hearing or pretending they didn't. Shaking her head, Wofford said, "I'd like to sit those two down and show them what happened to the Bradley girl, poor darlin'. She was hit last year just a few blocks from here. On my husband's watch. Always bothered him that he never caught the coward who ran her down and took off."

He watched the corner of her mouth tic downward, saw regret flash over her expression—and almost liked the woman for it, though it was against his better judgment. "Was the girl killed?"

Wofford shook her head. "Not killed but maybe should've been. She'll never have anything close to a normal life, and neither will the family."

After a solemn silence, the sheriff made her way back to the topic at hand. "Getting back to Misty Bailey, I wanted to ask what you meant about knowing her casually."

"Casually as opposed to *biblically*." Unsure whether Wofford caught the reference, Sam put it more boldly. "I never slept with her, I mean. Passed the time with some flirting, but she didn't seem interested in more. Besides, I got to thinking she was living way too close for comfort anyway."

The dark eyes flicked an interested glance in his direction. "What do you mean?"

Sam shrugged. "I'm not looking for long-term now. Some women handle that better than others."

He could have elaborated that it would be damned awkward to end up stuck next door to an ex-lover, but instinct, along with the memory of Pacheco, screamed at him to watch his step.

To her credit, Wofford smiled, saying, "Don't shit where you eat, right? Isn't that what passes for male wisdom about dating too close to home? So you weren't involved in any kind of relationship with her?"

"That's right." Attempting to change the subject, he asked, "Do you have any idea what happened to the house? Was it a gas leak? Or did that guy with the tattoos set the explosion off intentionally?"

Wofford shot him another look, this one coolly appraising. After turning onto the oak-and-pine-bordered county road that would lead them toward the lake's south end, she said, "Second explosion could've been gas. Flames might've ignited what collected near the roofline after the initial blast."

"Which was caused by . . . ?" Sam ventured.

"Fire marshal thinks they were cooking in there," Wofford explained. "And I'm not talking about food."

"What do you mean?" Sam recalled a strong, ammonialike odor as Sam had walked from the Monroe boat dock toward the house. "Wait—yesterday, I smelled it. I thought it was an animal, but—it was drugs, right? They were cooking up drugs in the house."

Wofford nodded. "Methamphetamines, most likely. Explosive as all get out. Whoever was inside might've been trying to dismantle things in a hurry after Ms. Monroe showed up. Too much of a hurry for dealing with those chemicals."

"I've read in the paper about a few labs found in the county lately."

"They're popping up all over." She made a face at the mention. "Most of the time we only find them when the rocket scientists accidentally blow themselves to kingdom come."

"I can only imagine how it breaks your heart when that happens."

The smile flashed past so quickly it might never have been. "Only when innocent people end up hurt, too," she admitted. "But mostly, the meth-heads set up shop in isolated houses. Trailers rusting in the woods, old, tumbledown lake places. Anywhere the neighbors won't notice the stink of the chemicals or pay much attention to the traffic."

Sam shook his head. "I didn't notice anyone strange over at the Monroe house until last week. And even then, I didn't think much of it. Zoe didn't look upset, and hell, nobody put me in charge of what kind of company Misty Bailey keeps."

Wofford cut him a hard look, her black gaze boring through him. "No one's saying that, Mr. McCoy."

"Sorry." Sam grimaced. "Once a man's found himself on the wrong side of suspicion, he tends to get a little paranoid."

"But that last time," she said lightly, "there was something to the FBI's suspicion, right? Had your hand caught in the electronic cookie jar, didn't you?"

Sam snorted, knowing very well that Wofford had reviewed the details of his case, along with the terms of his probation. He could have explained about the elderly neighbors who had come, proud but penniless, to let him know what kind of corporation he'd been hired to protect. But he imagined she'd heard scores of excuses during her career in law enforcement. So what if this one came from a guy who'd once raked in big bucks defending rich companies from hackers?

So instead, he brushstroked the known facts, saying, "Yeah, I damned sure did, and it's cost me big time. Cost me a hell of a lot more if I screw up again."

"Then let's hope, Mr. McCoy," she said, currents of meaning flowing beneath the surface of her words, "that you're a faster learner than your big brother."

Sam flinched, blindsided, then wondered why he hadn't seen this coming. Of course, Wofford would bring up J.B. Considering the drug connection, it was only natural.

"It's been eight—no, more than ten years—since I've seen him. Bastard showed up uninvited at my place in Austin. Tried to shake me down for money."

Sam had been shocked that J.B., who had scared the hell out of him by breaking into his condo "to surprise him," looked so little like the smart-mouthed, devious brother he remembered. With the bloated face and red nose of a drinker, J.B.—only three years older—had aged fast and hard. But both substance abuse and prison could do that to a person, just as they had killed the brothers' father by the age of forty-eight. And like their father, J.B. had developed the same hair-trigger temper, the same intolerance for life's frustrations. When Sam had refused his demands for a "loan," the asshole had pulled one of Sam's own golf clubs out of his bag and smashed a glass-topped coffee table, a good laptop computer, and his brother's wrist, in quick succession.

Remembering, Sam flexed the fingers of his right hand. "I don't even know where he is now. Prison, I imagine, or dead, maybe. J.B. and I—we might've shared a set of parents, but we've never been what you'd call close. Best thing that ever happened to me was when our caseworker split us up for foster care."

If she hadn't, Sam suspected he might not have survived his childhood. Or even worse, he would have turned as violent as his brother as a means of self-defense.

"Feds are looking for him," Justine Wofford said, "in connection with a truckload found by a U.S. border patrol. Two tons of marijuana."

Sam gave a low whistle. "I always figured him for low-level stuff. An assault here, a B and E there, a few drunk and disorderlies thrown in for good measure. Maybe even murder, if he threw an unlucky punch. But big-time smuggling? The J.B. I knew couldn't coordinate a backyard barbecue, much less a drug-running operation. Not exactly what you'd call a people person."

Irritation spasmed at the corner of the sheriff's mouth. "Didn't say he did it *well*. This is his third offense. They get hold of him this time, they'll throw away the key."

Sam shook his head in disgust, thinking of the wasted potential. "What a dumb ass."

J.B., who'd started out life so damned smart, with such potential, had had the same chance to change his course as Sam had. But J.B. hadn't ended up with the Monroes. Would Sam, who bore the same genes, have fared any better without their influence? Even with it, he'd still screwed up plenty. But never once with his fists, never with a weapon.

Slowing for a curve, Wofford shot another glance in his direction. "Sure you haven't seen your brother lately? Or heard from him at all?"

Sam shook his head in answer. "Can't imagine he'd ever come to me for help again. Last *reunion* we had, I ended up pressing charges, put his ass in jail for six months. But you already know all that, don't you?"

"I know that part of it, yes," she admitted.

"Then you have as much information as I do—or more, it sounds like—on the subject of my brother. And if you knew as much as you think you know about me, you'd realize the last damned thing I'd mess around with is a bunch of hopped-up amateur chemists. I've got too much to lose, for one thing. I want my life back, once this supervised probation's over in a few years. Until then, I'm just killing time until the day I'm allowed to get my hands on a computer."

"You sound like you miss it."

"More than I can ever tell you," he said. "Which is why I'm staying as far as I can from any risks."

Most of them, anyway.

The SUV turned onto South Cypress Bend, the dusty, dirt road that would lead them past the state preserve and out to the lonely point of shoreline where only Sam's house stood at present. One tire hit a rut, and Sam felt sick, his headache vying with sweaty nausea for attention.

The sly look Wofford cut him made Sam feel even worse. "But this latest deal with the feds wasn't your first arrest, was it?" she asked. "There was that juvie theft charge when you were seventeen. A theft from your own foster parents."

"You can't be serious," Sam said, wondering where she'd gotten the supposedly sealed file. "First of all, it was nothing—just a big misunderstanding."

"Apparently, they didn't think so, since the Monroes had you removed to a group home."

Pain throbbed at Sam's temples, and he tasted bile. For three hundred fifty dollars, he had lost the only stable family he'd ever known. For three hundred fifty dollars that he hadn't even taken.

But he knew better than to argue. Had long ago learned exactly how far that would get him. Instead he told the sheriff, "Bullshit or not, it scared me into flying right for my last year in the system, so my sentence ended up adjudicated."

He could hardly blame the Monroes for giving up on him at that juncture. For years, he'd done everything he could to test their commitment, but their love and faith had held fast . . . until the night that blew up like a fire-cracker in his and Aaron's faces. . . .

"I'm not my brother," Sam insisted. *Neither one of them*.

"If I thought for one second you were," Wofford said, "we'd be having this conversation more officially."

Sam looked at her directly, not for a moment missing the implied threat. "And we'd be having it with my lawyer present."

They drove in silence for a while, until the trees opened up to reveal the charred ruins of the Monroe house, where scarcely a beam remained upright. Several SUVs were parked in the street, one bearing some kind of official emblem, the others unmarked. He counted four, no, five men milling about the property, including two wearing vests marked DEA.

Rubbernecking as she drove past, the new sheriff swore under her breath. "So much for keeping local control of this. . . ."

And so much, Sam understood, for limiting his role in this investigation to a "friendly" ride home from the hospital and a brief, informal chat.

CHAPTER SEVEN

Evil is unspectacular and always human,
And shares our bed and eats at our own table.

—W. H. Auden,
from "Herman Melville"

Though Elysse's cat stared at her accusingly from behind the sliding glass door, Ruby wasn't staying. For one thing, she didn't have it in her to wait around passively for those in charge to tell her that her sister had definitely betrayed her, or even worse, to say Misty was dead and they had found a child's body among the collapsed walls of the house. Panic bubbled at the thought. Whispering prayers, Ruby eased the screened porch door shut, her hand clutching the keys to her friend's white Corolla in a death grip.

If I keep moving, they'll still be alive.

If I keep acting, I will *find them.*

And if she didn't, Ruby understood that she would fall apart. That everything would blow to pieces like the supply truck she'd once seen struck by a rocket-propelled grenade.

Halfway to Hammett's on the Lake, her newly recharged phone rang. Glancing at the caller ID, Ruby winced but answered.

"What do you think you're doing?" Elysse demanded. "I turn my back on you one minute and you're off somewhere with my—"

"You'd been asleep at least an hour, Leese, and I left a note there on the counter." In it, Ruby had explained that she was meeting Crystal Kowalski, who had finally returned her call, at Hammett's before the dinner rush began. "Didn't you see it?"

"I read the note, but Lord, Ruby. You shouldn't be driving around by yourself. Not at a time like this."

"Listen, if you're worried about your car—"

"You're really stressed now, so I'm going to pretend you didn't say that," Elysse said sharply. "I'm worried about *you,* of course. After the sheriff left—"

"I know, I know." Ruby didn't need or want to be reminded of her tears. "But I'm fine now. Really."

Somehow, seeing her own heartache reflected in her friend's face had made Ruby's meltdown worse. She'd been relieved when Elysse had finally conked out and given her the time and space she needed to regroup.

"Besides," Ruby reminded her, "you have another twelve-hour shift tonight, so you really need to get some sleep."

"You can't seriously imagine I'd just go to work and leave you. I'm calling in sick tonight. Of *course* I'm stay-

ing with you—and don't even think of arguing with me
about it."

In spite of her anxiety, Ruby smiled at the fierceness in
Elysse's voice. With the rest of her life in turmoil, their
friendship was the one lifeline keeping her afloat.

"Thanks, Leese. Thank you so much. I'll be back
there in a little while. Then we can start making calls
and getting people organized. We'll figure out a way to
find them."

"We'll figure out a way to bring them home," Elysse
echoed fervently, and in her voice, Ruby heard the
promise that she and her daughter would be welcome to
share the house on stilts for as long as necessary. But perhaps not Misty, for Elysse hadn't been nearly as confident
as Ruby that her sister was innocent. And once provoked, Elysse held on to grudges with a vengeance.

After thanking her, Ruby ended the call, thinking
about her sister. After all, Misty was the only person
with access to the bank accounts, and Elysse's doubts
about her—but no. Ruby had spoken to Misty weekly
over the past year, had always either lived with her or
seen her almost daily, with the exception of this past
year. Misty had never given any indication she was having urgent money problems or involved with anyone.
With work and classes and Zoe's care all weighing on
her, she'd had no time at all for men, she'd claimed, yet
she'd seemed in good spirits.

With dusk still hours in the future, the huge, electric
alligator sign at Hammett's wasn't lit yet. But after a year
away Ruby was glad to see the familiar monstrosity,
which lorded it over what had started as a bar/bait house
and a clutch of fishing cabins on the shores of South Bone
Lake. The cabins remained rustic—an unchangeable
"tradition"—but the rest had been rebuilt: from a large

two-story cypress lodge-style bar and grill with covered lakeside decks to a modern marina. For all his supposed net worth and the small castle of a home he'd built nearby a couple of years earlier, Paulie Hammett still drove the same rust bucket of a pickup he'd had for as long as she could remember.

Though it was only four, about a dozen cars were in the lot, including Crystal's red Jeep Liberty with the booster seat in back. After parking beside it, Ruby started inside but hesitated, stomach tightening, at the glass door. Dread formed icy shards inside her stomach as she thought of Crystal, Anna, Paulie, or any of Misty's long-time coworkers swamping her with hugs and tears. Or worse yet, pelting her with questions to which she had no answers.

With her limbs tingling a pin-and-needles warning, she cursed but couldn't make herself move forward. Even when she heard a car door close behind her and an anxious female voice say, " 'Scuse me, please. My shift's about to start," Ruby couldn't manage to step out of the way.

An African-American teenager in a short skirt and Hammett's T-shirt edged past, then turned to look at Ruby with obvious concern. "You all right?"

"Could—could you send Crystal out here?" Ruby asked her.

The girl nodded, her brown eyes curious. "Sure thing, ma'am. I'll send her to you right quick."

As the waitress disappeared through the glass door, Ruby, who had turned thirty only the week before, realized with a start that the "ma'am" had been meant for her. But the prick to her ego was the least of her concerns.

Crystal soon appeared, wiping her hands on her apron. As feared, she immediately stood on tiptoe—she barely cleared five feet in heels—and flung herself into a tight embrace, treating Ruby to a mouthful of her curly auburn hair. Breath hitching, Crystal sputtered a greeting before bursting into sobs.

When she could finally speak, she wailed, "Oh, Ruby. I can't *stand* this. I just can't stand not knowing. If anything's happened to them, I don't know what I'll—what'll I *do*, Ruby? Misty's been my friend *forever*."

After a year in the war zone, where subdued reactions were a matter of survival, Ruby was taken aback by the onslaught of Crystal's emotions. But instead of toppling Ruby's control, as she'd feared, Crystal's drama felt like a hard slap. Was she expecting Ruby, of all people, to comfort *her* now?

"Let's take a little walk." Ruby extricated herself as she made the suggestion. "I need to talk to you about a few things."

Crystal glanced back into the restaurant, then furiously shook her curls. "Oh, to heck with that. They can do without me for ten minutes. I can't believe Paulie's making me work on a day like this anyway. I—"

Sobbing, Crystal again threw herself into Ruby's arms and squeezed her hard enough to hurt. "I should've known she wouldn't just stop returning my calls for no reason." High and squeaky, her voice sounded as girlish as ever, but there was nothing childish about the anguish in her tone.

Misty had often joked about Crystal's tendency toward drama, used to say she would probably spontaneously combust if ever confronted by a *real* emergency. Ruby pried herself free, wary of the flames. "Settle down, Crystal. Right now. I don't have the energy for this, and Misty and my daughter may not have the time."

Crystal nodded and fell quiet. "I—I'm sorry, Ruby.

I'm just—I wish I'd gotten your call yesterday, but I took Braden up to Mama's, and the cell reception's terrible out there."

Not wanting to rehash their earlier phone conversation, Ruby walked toward the docks, slowing her pace enough for Crystal to keep up on her killer heels. "What's been going on with Misty lately?"

"I should have known something was wrong," Crystal said. "It was bad enough she stopped showing up for classes, but when she said she needed some space from me, too—I was mad, hurt, really. What I should've been was worried. I mean, when has Misty ever 'needed space' from me before?"

Crystal had a point, though Ruby had always felt she wanted space when it came to Misty's best friend. Crystal meant well for the most part, but Ruby found her one of those people best taken in small doses.

"And right after that, she had some silly argument with Paulie about an order." Crystal shook her head and added, "I've never seen her blow up like that, and then, the way she stormed out . . ."

Ruby could scarcely believe it herself since the normally laid-back Misty hadn't said a word about the argument. "Before this all happened, do you remember her mentioning anything unusual? Hanging out with different people or behaving strangely?"

Crystal sucked her lip beneath her top teeth, her gaze drifting as she considered. "I remember a couple of days before she quit, we took the kids to the park—I guess it was about a week and a half ago. While we watched them playing, I tried to talk to her about coming back to classes, but she got real quiet. I asked if she was okay, and she said something about being tired. But then, I couldn't help wondering . . ."

"About what?" Ruby asked, trying not to feel distracted by the image of her daughter running, swinging, laughing . . . to feel heartsick, even jealous, that she hadn't been there. How could she have imagined that leaving her child, missing out on one-quarter of her young life, would ever be worth it? How could she have traded what she'd had in her hands for something as nebulous as a better future for them both?

"I got to wondering then." Crystal tucked a reddish spiral behind one ear while the breeze teased loose another. This close to the docks, the air smelled of gasoline from the boat engines mingled with the complex freshwater-and-vegetation odors of the lake. "I'd heard something at the restaurant, one of the cooks guessing, really, about Misty acting as moody as her daughter had when she was pregnant."

"Pregnant? But Misty wasn't even dating . . . was she?"

Crystal started to shake her head, then shrugged. "She never said she was, but you know Misty. Wherever she went, the men turned up. Take that neighbor of yours, the fishing guide, for instance. I saw them laughing near the bar a few times."

"Sam?" Ruby felt a jolt, recalling Sam's battered but still handsome face. Could it have been too handsome for her sister to resist? She thought of Elysse, who had been so hurt when she had fallen for a man unable or unwilling to return her love.

"He stops in a lot, and he's her type—pretty clean cut, especially for a fishing guide. But Misty's friendly with everybody who comes in. Laughs and chats and pulls in twice the tips that I do, but never lets anybody crowd her. Wish I knew her secret. Every time I try the flirting routine, I end up getting groped and having to call Paulie."

Ruby suspected Crystal had a tough time making

anyone take her seriously with her squeaky little voice and Tinkerbell-like stature. According to Misty, her friend never even tried to work "The Play Room," a dark-curtained video arcade parlor located upstairs, but not the kind where anyone underage was welcome. Misty had told Ruby it mostly served as an Internet café that allowed customers—nearly all male—to kick back with expensive drinks and offshore Internet gambling. In other words, it was only legal by a whisker but kept Hammett's in the black during the slow season.

But Ruby wasn't interested in Crystal's troubles at this juncture. "Did you ask Misty if she could possibly be"— the word caught in her throat, but she forced herself to ask the question—"if she might be pregnant?"

An old man in a fishing boat pull-started a noisy outboard motor and they waited for him to untie from the dock and rumble off toward the main channel.

"I didn't come right out and ask her, no," admitted Crystal, "but I mentioned, sort of casually, that with her acting so tired and out of sorts, there was this rumor at the restaurant. When she heard that, she stood up and told me I could tell anybody who said anything like that to go straight to hell."

"She was that angry?"

"Furious. Her face got all red, and she called Zoe. Made her cry, too, 'cause she was having so much fun with Braden she didn't want to go home."

Ruby squeezed her eyes shut. "How—how was she, Crystal? Zoe, I mean."

"She's doing great, Ruby. Growing like a weed and chattering like crazy. You'll hardly know her when you see her."

Ruby took a deep breath to steady herself, though *you'll hardly know her* had struck her heart like a guided missile. Unclenching her jaw, she asked, "I know Misty was mad, but did she ever *answer* the question? About being pregnant, I mean."

Crystal's forehead crinkled, and fresh tears glazed her eyes. "She said she couldn't believe I'd think she was that *stupid.* Which really hurt my feelings, as you might imagine." Crystal's son, Braden, only six months older than Zoe, had been born out of wedlock. Though Crystal never talked about it, Misty had confided that her old friend Dylan Hammett—long before he'd straightened up and met the woman who would become his wife—was the father, that Paulie and Anna paid the monthly support but didn't acknowledge their grandchild.

Seeing the pain in Crystal's eyes, Ruby touched her forearm and echoed something Sam had told her. "Everybody makes mistakes. My sister included, if she said something so thoughtless."

Crystal nodded. "Believe me, I've said my share of stupid things to her over the years. More of them than I can count. She's always forgiven me, and I'd forgive her, too, if she would only talk to me. But she hasn't since, and now—"

"She's either lit out for parts unknown or been taken somewhere with my daughter." *If she's still alive.* "With my money, too, according to the sheriff."

Could Misty have simply run off with her lover and Zoe, feeling she couldn't bear to relinquish the child? Was she starting a new life under an assumed name with the money?

Crystal gasped before insisting, "Oh no. That can't be right. Misty wouldn't steal, especially not from *you.* When I asked her if she minded your leaving her with Zoe so long, she told me you're the most determined, bravest person she's ever known in her life, and she'd give anything if someday she could be as good a mom and as good a person as you are."

Ruby felt her eyelids burning. "Thanks for sharing that. I, uh, I haven't been feeling like either one—a good mother *or* a brave and decent person lately." She felt doubly guilty because of the doubts she'd allowed to creep in about Misty, doubts she cast out of her mind and determined not to think about again. Her younger sister might be in trouble—might have taken Zoe and gone into hiding to avoid it—but she couldn't be a thief. Let alone a kidnapper.

"Did you ever see her with some skinny guy, tattoos all over?" Ruby shuddered at the thought of the man who'd burst out of her house waving a handgun. "Kind of a wild look in his eyes, like he might've been on something."

"Doesn't ring a bell," said Crystal, "and that *really* doesn't sound like anybody Misty would take up with."

Ruby nodded, then jerked her head toward the sound of car doors closing and people laughing in the parking lot.

Crystal, too, looked in that direction and saw the place was beginning to fill up. "I'm really sorry, Ruby, but I need to get back to work. We'll be swamped, and since Misty quit, we've been shorthanded."

"If you think of anything, call me right away. I don't care what time of day or night . . . just call me."

Crystal teared up, lip quivering. "I should tell Paulie I can't work. I should leave and help you find her. She was my best friend, Ruby. My very best friend in the whole world."

"Let's not talk about her in the past tense, Crystal," Ruby pleaded. "And while you're working, think as hard as you can about any men she might have mentioned, any financial worries or other problems she brought up. You saw more of her than anybody. You *have* to have heard or seen something."

"I promise you, I'll get in touch if I come up with anything."

As they started back, Crystal said, "I took some pictures of the kids playing in the park that day. I can make you copies—there's an especially nice one of Zoe on the slide."

"Thank you." Ruby tried to come up with words that would express how much the offer meant to her, but the lump rising in her throat defeated the effort.

Crystal smiled, sadness touching her eyes, then said good-bye and hurried off.

Ruby was unlocking Elysse's car when her cell rang. Pulling it from the borrowed purse, she saw *Prest Co Sheriff* in the ID window.

Her heart lurched and her knees weakened. For an instant, she didn't want to answer, couldn't stand any more bad news. But she couldn't just let it ring either. "Hello?"

"Ms. Monroe, this is Deputy Savoy."

Though much of last night was a blur, Ruby recalled a man in his early to mid fifties, graying at the temples, with the slight paunch of a lapsed runner and the smooth delivery of a TV preacher. But he'd been solicitous, she remembered, bringing her coffee, asking her how she was, promising he'd do anything he could to help bring her family home.

"Sheriff asked me to give you a call," he said, "see if you might be able to stop over to the office. If you'd like, I'll be happy to pick you up."

Ruby swung into the front seat before she crumbled into sand. "Have you found them? Do you know where they are?"

"No, ma'am, but we do have information."

"What? What is it?" she demanded.

"I'm sorry, but Sheriff Wofford asked that you come in

to discuss it." He sounded genuinely regretful, maybe even disapproving. "This wasn't my decision, mind you. Now, where can I pick you up?"

"That's all right, thanks. I'm already in the car. I'll be there as quick as I can."

"Drive carefully, Ms. Monroe. Be sure and buckle up."

Because of her shaking, it took Ruby three tries to jam her key into the ignition. What news was waiting for her at the sheriff's office?

All she could do was go find out, so she drove with terror riding in the seat beside her like the rotting corpse of an old dream.

Pacheco's disgust came through so clearly that Sam had to hold the phone several inches from his ear.

"Are you freaking kiddin' me?" his attorney demanded, his barrio accent stronger than ever in his anger. "If you're not involved, of *course* you want to cooperate with their investigation. You want to be the *most* cooperative citizen these hombres've ever seen, or somebody's bound to talk to Judge Phillips about rethinking the terms of your probation. You gotta be a Boy Scout, *ese*. Don't you ever listen to nothing I tell you?"

Sam wondered if Pacheco's advice would be any different if he weren't about to jump onto a plane to Cabo for a vacation. One undoubtedly financed, at least in part, by the exorbitant legal fees Sam had paid the sawed-off little jerk. "I don't want to end up as the handy suspect," he persisted, "and if that means delaying your trip—"

"Forget about it, *'mano*." Pacheco downshifted smoothly, speaking as if Sam were a true brother . . . or a client who required "handling." "You need anything, my associate, Alberto, will take care of you. You still got his number?"

"I don't want your cousin, I want you," Sam insisted.

In the background, he heard the buzzy, overamplified sound of a boarding announcement, followed by Pacheco's rushed "Sorry, didn't hear you. Gotta run now, amigo. This is the last call for my flight."

He terminated the contact, leaving Sam to curse his choice of attorneys. Why had he ever let Luke, his former partner, convince him that a streetwise little fighter like Pacheco was the way to go? Sure, he'd pulled off the feat of keeping Sam out of federal prison, but this bullshit—

At the sound of a knock, Java jumped up from her place at his feet to race barking for the front door. Sam was sore enough that it took him more time to get up from the sofa and follow.

"Sit, girl," he ordered, but Java continued her leaping, wagging, and whining, all hallmarks of her hope that whoever had come might prove to be a decent play-mate.

Sam peered through the peephole, fantasizing that Misty would be there smiling and apologizing for all the worry she'd caused. That standing next to her, Ruby would be holding her grinning daughter in her arms.

Instead, he saw a badge, held up to obscure his vision.

"Damn it. Just what I need," he grumbled, grabbing the dog's collar and unlatching the front door.

Two men, one white and one who might have been either African-American or Hispanic, stood on his door-step. Both looked fit, in their midthirties, and prepared for anything, with their right hands lightly touching their weapons and their booted feet in a wide stance.

"I'm Special Agent Acosta," said the darker of the two, still holding out a badge. A faint trace of a Latin American accent, smoother and more cultured than Pacheco's, colored his words.

Sam looked at the badge carefully, saw it identified Acosta as a Drug Enforcement Agent.

His partner, wearing wraparound sunglasses and a red-blond buzz cut that bore an unfortunate resemblance to peach fuzz, flashed his badge more quickly and mumbled, "Special Agent Felker. Mind if we have a few words with you about things you may've noticed next door?"

"I've already spoken with Deputy Savoy and Sheriff Wofford," Sam said, as if that might forestall them.

"The federal government's involved now," Felker went on, "and we'd appreciate your cooperation. *Sir.*"

Sam heard antagonism in the man's words, a willingness to push aggressively if necessary. Sam hesitated, weighing his impulse to push back against Pacheco's warnings about escalating an uncomfortable situation into something that might net him time in prison.

Acosta put in, "We think you might have seen or heard something that could help us in our investigation of the drug activity next door. You never know, something you tell us could help nab some bad guys—or even bring a little girl back to her mother. You do want Zoe Monroe to come home, don't you?"

"Of course I do. I want them both home," Sam said, knowing that Acosta had just backed him into a corner. That neither man would hesitate to lie or manipulate to try to trip him up.

He felt rather than saw the peach fuzz agent staring through the black lenses of his shades, felt the man's suspicion radiating like frigid waves off a block of ice.

"Or maybe you want a little family reunion with your brother in the federal pen. Our people in New Mexico are closing in on him, man." Felker glanced down at his watch. "Should be busting him as we speak, and we'd be just as happy to put two McCoys away for life as one."

"I don't give a rat's ass what you do with J.B.," Sam assured them. "Right now, I'm a whole lot more concerned about my neighbors."

"Then you'd better let us in, tell us your side of this story." Acosta shot him a dark look. "Before we can come up with any other versions of our own. Or get to wondering who was the brains behind your brother's operation."

With no better choice, Sam let them inside . . . and wondered if he would be arguing against assumptions already made. Suspicions born not of his own crimes, but his brother's.

Suspicions Sam could think of no way to combat without doing those things he did best—even if that meant taking the biggest gamble of his life.

THE BLOOD-DIMMED TIDE

Drugs hazing her awareness, Misty barely heard the voice from behind the locked door. She had a hard time differentiating it from the background murmur of a radio until the voice grew so insistent it triggered a painful thumping in her brain.

Except the noise wasn't *in* her; it was pounding from the outside. The beating of small fists against the heavy wood.

Zoe, Misty remembered, something akin to panic slicing through her muddled thoughts. Zoe was here with her, crying so hard Misty couldn't pluck a single word from the stream. Couldn't comprehend a damned thing except the noise chewing through her head like a chain saw.

"Zoe, *please* be quiet." Misty instantly regretted her outburst—the explosion of sound inside her skull. Had *he* heard it, too? Would he come back with another needle, maybe one for Zoe this time?

Anything to keep her quiet, out of his way while he—

No matter what, Misty couldn't let that happen.

"Go back and watch your movie." She fought to keep the fear from her voice. "Watch it like a good girl, and I'll talk to your mom about getting you a kitten. Two kittens maybe, to keep each other company."

To her surprise, the bribe worked, or at least the sounds of crying faded.

As Misty drifted off on the dark waters, she wondered how long something as flimsy as a promise could protect someone so small.

CHAPTER EIGHT

The blood-dimmed tide is loosed, and everywhere
The ceremony of innocence is drowned . . .
                            —William Butler Yeats,
                            from "The Second Coming"

Using a motorized craft this time, the boatman glided past the houses along the canal once, then twice before anchoring to "fish." Again and again, he expertly cast and retrieved a wicked, silver hook—left intentionally bare—until the mild spring afternoon sighed its last and faded into twilight. Courting frogs provided the bass notes to evening birdsong, while a great blue heron skimmed the water in search of a late meal.

Yet the house he watched remained dark, as did both its neighbors. Reasonably assured that no one was around, he tied up to the dock that ran alongside the boathouse next door. The single pontoon boat within was covered, supported by slings above the water, with thick webs suggesting it had not been moved in months.

Like all the others in the neighborhood, the boathouse owner's home had been built on stilts, but the place appeared long unused, with its windows shuttered and weeds shrouding a set of steps to the raised, canal-side deck.

As he walked next door, he assured himself that the target house and the one beside it also appeared vacant, with no vehicles or people in sight. No dogs, either, to raise the alarm as he mounted the stairs of the house belonging to Ruby Monroe's blonde friend. Earlier today, he had followed at a distance, watching through binoculars as she and Ruby had carried suitcases upstairs. With the white car gone now and no sign of life from inside, he presumed the two of them had left. . . .

Which would work out quite well if he'd guessed correctly, he thought, pulling on a pair of latex gloves and removing first a box cutter and then a cordless drill from the carpenter's apron he wore at his waist. If, on the other hand, he'd been wrong in his assumption, things could go quite badly for anyone inside . . . as well as for those "guests" he had left back at the cabin.

But come to think of it, no matter what he found—or didn't—this wouldn't end well for them. It couldn't, since they'd seen him . . . and since the one who'd bought his services had insisted they must die.

A slow-talking deputy with a world-class comb-over and an Adam's apple the size of a grown hamster ushered

Ruby into Sheriff Wofford's surprisingly well-appointed office. "Make yourself comfortable," he invited, "and I'll let her know you're here."

Inviting as the leather chairs looked, Ruby couldn't think of sitting. Instead, she paced the room, bypassing a large, potted tree beside the window blinds and angling around a desk topped with a neat stack of files, a phone and intercom, and a closed laptop computer. After glancing at the translucent glass door to assure herself no one was outside, Ruby walked around the desk to peer at a framed photo. In it, Justine Wofford stood behind an older, gray-haired man—the former sheriff—with her long hair down and her lean arms draped around his beefy shoulders. The photo had been taken locally, judging from the wisps of Spanish moss decorating tree limbs and the slice of sunlit water in the background. Handsome and relaxed, the couple laughed at something out of camera range, a clearly candid moment that reminded Ruby sharply of her own late husband, of the fact that Wofford's loss had been quite recent.

Would it prevent her from doing her job? Ruby thought about how muddled her own thoughts had been in the months following Aaron's funeral. She'd nearly miscarried soon after the services and had ended up on bed rest, but if she'd been able to return to work—she'd helped with billing at a local doctor's office at the time— Ruby couldn't imagine how she would have functioned. What if the new sheriff was so distracted, she missed something important? Something that could make the difference for Ruby's family?

After rapping lightly at the door, Deputy Savoy poked his head inside. "Ah, Deputy Crane told me you were in here. Sheriff had to run home to change her outfit or fix her makeup or some such." He glanced down at his watch, a frown creasing the corners of his mouth. "Said she wouldn't be ten minutes, but you know how you women can—"

"She left? For clothes and makeup," Ruby interrupted, disbelief quickly giving way to anger. "Why on earth would she call me over here if she meant to take off? Does she have any concept of what I'm going through, what it's like not knowing if my family—if they're . . ."

"I'm so sorry," Deputy Savoy said, his head bowed as if in prayer, his hair thick and dark save for the silver patches at his temples. "I'm sure Mrs. Wofford—I mean the sheriff—had no intention of upsetting you, but, well, the little lady had a mishap over by the coffeepot."

His silvery blue eyes flicked upward, and in that instant, Ruby saw his contempt for his superior. A year ago, she would have thought little of it, but overseas, she'd seen that look herself, had been on the wrong side of it a few times. She could be wrong, she knew, but intuition hinted that the coffee spill he'd mentioned hadn't been the sheriff's doing, that going home "to fix her makeup" had not been Justine Wofford's choice.

"While you're waiting, could I get you anything?" he offered. "How about some coffee? Water? Or a soda?"

Ruby shook her head, not wanting anything from the man except answers. "So, what about my family, Deputy? What did Wofford want?"

"She wanted to chat with you yourself—" he said.

"No. I came. I came right over here like she said, so—"

"—but it seems downright wrong," he went on, "to leave a worried little mama cooling her heels in this office."

He slipped around the desk and, after cutting a look toward the door, dropped into the sheriff's chair with a self-satisfied look that set Ruby's teeth on edge even more than the "little mama." But he could be as obnoxious as he wanted, as long as he ended the torment of waiting.

"Neither of the bodies found in your house was your sister's."

Tears sprang to Ruby's eyes. "I knew it. I knew she couldn't be . . . But who, then? I mean, I know about the guy with the tattoos, but who else was in my house?"

Justine Wofford stepped in, dropping her keys into her handbag. In spite of the expensive-looking tan suit and crisp white blouse she wore, she looked harried, with splashes of color at her cheeks and dark strands working their way loose from her chignon. But the look she shot Savoy had him leaping up from her chair with an alacrity that Ruby couldn't help enjoying.

"Sorry, Mrs.—I mean Sheriff," he said. "I was just telling Ms. Monroe here the ME says the body's not her sister's. I didn't think you'd want her to be kept waiting."

"Of course I wouldn't." Though Wofford's white teeth flashed against the smudged background of her lipstick as she spoke, no one would mistake her expression for a smile. "But I'll take it from here, Deputy."

"Yes, ma'am." Savoy slunk toward the door but rescued enough dignity to turn and nod toward Ruby with a promise. "We're going to bring them home, Ms. Monroe. You've got my personal guarantee on that one."

As he left, one corner of Wofford's mouth ticked downward.

"Trouble?" Ruby asked.

The sheriff dropped her purse inside a desk drawer. With a shake of her head, she said, "Nothing that should concern you. He's a fine lawman, smart, experienced. Just has a little trouble now and then remembering which of us won that runoff."

So it was more than sexism. "I have to admit, I haven't kept up with local politics, especially this past year."

"No reason you should have," Wofford told her, then unexpectedly came around the desk and offered Ruby her hand. "Now let's start this conversation over on the right foot. First of all, I apologize for your wait. Couldn't be helped."

Ruby nodded. "I have some questions. About those bodies found in my house."

"This case has been given the highest priority." The sheriff went around and reclaimed her own chair. "But we haven't yet identified them. I can say, however, that we have reason to believe at least one person escaped—or was helped to escape—the house around the time it started burning."

Ruby stared at her. "I saw that house just after the first explosion. How could you think anybody made it out of there alive?"

"One of those two dogs did, didn't it? The one you had to kill."

Ruby shivered, remembering the moment she had pulled the trigger. "Well, yes."

"And my deputy, Oscar Balderach . . ." Emotion shimmered through the sheriff's voice before she brought it under control. "It turns out he was shot before the body burned. The other two victims—we believe they were upstairs, in the front bedroom, when they . . . succumbed. So a third person must have been the gunman."

Ruby felt the cold cramping of fear in her stomach. It had been bad enough thinking the deputy was accidentally killed in the explosion, but knowing that someone in the house had deliberately shot down a law officer was even worse. Anyone capable of such a thing, she thought, wouldn't hesitate to murder an unarmed woman and a young child.

The sound of gunshots reverberated through her mind. "I—I think I heard it last night," she said, blinking back the burn of moisture. "I heard shooting, right before the first blast."

Wofford nodded. "Yes, that's in your statement."

Ruby barely recalled what she'd said, sitting in that starkly antiseptic interview room through the longest night of her life. "So you think—you're guessing someone came out through the back and shot the deputy, then escaped? But how? There wasn't enough time, and besides, I would've seen him."

"Not if he took the boat."

"The boat?" She was thinking of the beat-up old canoe she'd kept tied to a tree down near the water. She couldn't recall seeing it last night, but then, she'd been so distracted, she might not have noticed a flashing neon alligator, either.

"Sam McCoy's johnboat"—the sheriff's expression hardened—"wasn't tied at your dock as he reported. When we checked, it hadn't been moved to his dock or boathouse, either."

Ruby weighed the possibility that someone could have stolen it while she and Sam were helping Deputy Whitaker. It would have been doable, she thought, before Sam had gone around to check the lake side of the house. "You mentioned this shooter might've had some help escaping. Who would have done that? There was no one else around last night, no one I saw anyway."

"According to your statement, McCoy was out of your sight for a time, wasn't he? While you were busy helping Deputy Whitaker."

"Sure, Sam went around back to see if he could find . . ." It dawned on Ruby what Wofford was suggesting, and in some ways the theory made sense, in light of Sam's background and the fact that his johnboat was missing. But Ruby didn't buy it, not considering what she'd witnessed.

"He dragged Deputy Balderach back from the house," Ruby burst out, surprised by the heat in her own words. "He climbed up on the porch roof trying to save Misty and Zoe."

"That *is* what he said," Justine Wofford acknowledged, with one sleek brow rising. "But did you actually *witness* him doing either of those things?"

"You didn't see. You can't know—that man was upset. He was worried, almost frantic, about my family and *your* deputies. And he was definitely injured. You can't imagine he cut himself like that on purpose. My God, I found him lying near the body. It was awful."

Raising her palms from the desk, the sheriff shook her head. "I was only speaking as an investigator, looking at all the possibilities. And I wasn't aware you had any particular attachment to your neighbor."

Ruby stared at her, thrown off by the suggestion. When she recovered the power of speech, her temper took over. "You really don't have any idea about who took my family, do you? Otherwise, I can't imagine why you'd waste time on petty, ridiculous insinuations. I'm grateful to Sam for last night, yes, but when was I supposed to have formed this 'particular attachment'? While I was driving buses in Iraq this past year? *Please . . .* "

"I know you're upset. I know you're suffering a great deal. But I can tell you, I see nothing, not a damned thing *petty*"—the sheriff leaned forward in her chair, her dark eyes flat, relentless—"or *ridiculous* in any line of questioning related to the murder of a man—a family man—who devoted twenty-eight years of his life to this department. And what's more, Oscar Balderach was a friend of my husband's, a good friend for a lot of years."

Ruby rocked back, stung by the sharpness of the woman's voice. But she wasn't about to meekly tuck her tail and quiver. "I get that, and I'm sorry. Sorrier than I can ever tell you about his friends and family having to deal with this. But I won't apologize for keeping my focus on *my* family, because they're all I have now. And because I believe with all my heart that they have to be alive."

She held the sheriff's gaze, defying Wofford to contradict her.

Instead, the sheriff blew out a loud sigh. "I won't argue that point, Mrs. Monroe, because I think there's a good chance you're absolutely right. We know Ms. Bailey took the money last week—"

"I've already told you that's a lie, or a mistake at least. Misty's friend, Crystal, said the same thing. We both know—"

"You want to see the video?" Wofford challenged. "I've got it, from the bank. She came in alone, said she was unhappy with the customer service, so she was moving the accounts."

Maybe it *was* on video, but the sheriff—everybody— had misinterpreted what they'd seen. "Then that must be what she did."

"The branch manager tried to talk her out of it. I don't have audio on the recording, but the woman said your sister acted nervous, upset. When I asked if Ms. Bailey might've been on something—"

"Do you honestly think I'd have left my daughter with my sister if she used drugs?"

"I'm sure she didn't," Wofford countered, "not before you left, at least. But from everything I'm learning about Ms. Bailey, there have been signs, major changes in behavior. The branch manager was concerned, especially considering your sister's insistence on cash instead of some safer option. And my deputies have checked with every other bank in town. Ms. Bailey didn't open an account in any of them."

Ruby huffed out a frustrated sigh, her denial smacking up against the brick wall of the sheriff's facts. "When she took out the money, my daughter wasn't with her?"

"No, she wasn't."

"But she wasn't at day care, either. And I know Crystal Kowalski wasn't watching her." Ruby shook her head, eyes welling. "So where *was* Zoe?"

"That's an excellent question, Mrs. Monroe," said the sheriff. "I'm hoping your sister's phone records will help us find the answer."

"Do you have them yet?"

When Wofford nodded, the light flashed off her diamond earrings. "We received them this afternoon. We're in the process of cross-checking numbers against their registered users now. But there's one thing I *can* tell you. Your neighbor, the one you're so certain of—your sister called his house on the morning of March thirtieth."

Ruby slid to the edge of her seat. "Before I spoke with her?"

"Hours before your call. At five forty-two a.m., to be precise. You'd think a person would remember such an early call, especially from someone who's gone missing." Wofford leaned forward onto her elbows. "And yet Mr. McCoy never mentioned it to my deputy, or to me when we were talking. Did he say anything to you about it?"

With a lump rising in her throat, Ruby shook her head to indicate he hadn't. Could a handsome face and a fine body have swayed her judgment? Was Sam McCoy that good an actor?

The sheriff opened her mouth to speak again, but a tap

at the door interrupted. Her lips twitching downward, she said, "I'd better check on this. Please excuse me for a moment."

The interruption turned out to be considerably longer, time Ruby used to doubt each move she'd made, each word she'd spoken, since leaving the plane yesterday so eagerly. It seemed years ago that she'd looked down to find her backpack missing, since she'd thought of Carrie Ann's death or the possibility that all of this might somehow be connected. Convinced by the security guard that a criminal gang had been behind the theft, Ruby had barely mentioned it to the sheriff last night. And she'd said nothing whatsoever about her last nightmarish weeks in Iraq, partly because she couldn't imagine Wofford seriously considering that overseas deaths—a pair of abductions and beheadings quickly blamed on insurgents—could possibly have any bearing on a local case. Ruby could scarcely imagine such a thing herself, though memories of her surprising job offer and the upcoming hearings made her increasingly uneasy.

She decided she would bring it up now, push the idea so hard the sheriff would have to give it serious consideration. Maybe then, Wofford could latch on to some scenario that didn't cast her sister as a druggie and a thief.

Tired of waiting for the sheriff's return, Ruby moved toward the door to see if she could find out how long the delay might be. By the time she reached it, she could hear the low rumble of a man's voice on the other side. Leaning in to put her ear beside the crack, she recognized Deputy Savoy's voice.

"Eight calls to this number. The phone's registered to a fifty-seven-year-old woman, a file clerk for the city. No criminal record. But I found out she's got a grown son."

"You know him." Justine Wofford stated it as a fact, not a question.

"Unfortunately," Savoy said. "Leroy Coffer's a dealer out of Houston, goes by the street name 'Coffin.' We arrested him eighteen months ago, before you came on board here. Methamphetamine charges—possession with intent, but some greenhorn prosecutor made a procedural screwup, and the conviction got tossed on appeal."

Ruby turned the names Coffin and Coffer over in her mind, but neither meant a thing to her.

"Sounds like the type who'd set up a lab out near the lake," Savoy continued. "He and his associates—a real bunch of scum-suckers—are probably tied with some of those other cases, too, probably funneling the stuff back to his old connection in the city. I only hope the son of a bitch blew himself to hell with the Monroe place. Because if he was the one who got out, we'll have a hell of a time catching . . ."

A rushing noise filled her head, and Ruby's heart bounded against her ribs. There had been a *drug lab* inside her house? Her sister might be accepting of her friends' quirks, but she'd never stand for anything illegal— especially not with Zoe present. Misty would have fought like hell to prevent such an invasion.

Which meant, Ruby knew with a sickening jolt of clarity, that her sister had either been scared off or silenced somehow. *And what about my daughter? What about my little girl?*

"You remember if Coffer has a lot of body art?" asked Wofford. "Including a triple six on his face, right about here?"

"He's done a couple of short stints in prison, had the ink to prove it," Savoy responded. "I don't recall any facial tatts except a teardrop, but he could've added more since I last saw him."

"You think Misty Bailey could've been involved with somebody like that?" the sheriff asked. "Here's an attractive, supposedly responsible young woman, working on her education, looking after her sister's little one. Seems kind of a stretch."

Ruby felt a surge of gratitude that Wofford had done more than pretend to listen to her. Maybe she would listen to the part about DeserTek as well.

"Who knows what women see in these thugs?" Disgust weighed down the deputy's words. "But I've seen plenty of nice girls, pretty girls, throw their lives away on garbage. Hell, there's some that write love letters to complete strangers doing hard time."

"I've seen it, too," said Wofford. "I started out working in the jail in Morton County."

"Not so very long ago," Savoy said with clear disdain.

"Deputy, I asked for your opinion on Misty Bailey and this Coffer—" A warning hammered Wofford's voice flat. "Not my level of experience. Now, do you think the two of them might've been involved?"

"Could've been." His low tones sounded more resentful than contrite. "Man always had an eye for hot blondes, not that they keep their looks long once they start partying with Leroy. Aside from the drug use, he's pretty quick to lay down the law with his fists. He's had a couple of domestic battery reports on the books—one against his mama, and another on a girlfriend. I responded to one of those calls, and that girl was scared half out of her mind, refused to cooperate no matter what assurances I gave her. So Coffer walked, of course, and the girl with the cigarette burns and the black eye vanished."

"You look into it?" asked Wofford.

"Put in man-hours like you wouldn't believe, Sheriff, but we never could get the evidence to convince the DA to file charges. For one thing, her family thought our 'victim' might've took off with another friend of Coffer's, another bad seed. She had a history of poor choices when it came to men."

"You believe it? About her running off, that is?"

Deputy Savoy's voice dropped to a murmur, as if he'd turned his head away while speaking. Ruby couldn't make out his response, but Justine Wofford's next words sliced straight to her center like a white-hot blade.

"Men like Coffer," the sheriff said grimly, "aren't inclined to put up with any extra baggage. Especially in the form of kids they didn't father. Which means . . . goddammit, I hate this, Deputy, but we're gonna need to go beyond the volunteers' efforts to comb the woods around the Monroe place. We'll need to call in divers and dredge the south end of the lake for bodies. And tell them—tell them in particular, we're looking for a little girl's."

CHAPTER NINE

"Wild animals never kill for sport. Man is the only one to whom the torture and death of his fellow creatures is amusing in itself."

—James Anthony Froude,
Oceana, Or, England and Her Colonies

They'd be searching the house soon, Sam figured, either the DEA or the sheriff or God only knew what entity. In spite of his cooperation, there was no way they'd leave anyone with his background and proximity in peace.

Already, they'd impounded the johnboat. He'd discovered it missing when he'd gone out to take care of it. He couldn't imagine what evidence they'd whip up to establish probable cause to come inside, yet he felt certain they would get the warrant within a few hours and tear his place apart looking for any sign that Zoe or Misty had been here.

Sam could live with that, since he'd never so much as invited the two of them inside, and he wasn't worried the authorities would find anything to link him to illegal drugs. But before they came, he had to do something with the cell phone hidden in the insulation near the water heater in his attic. His possession of it was in direct violation of the terms of his probation.

He hadn't even used the damned thing, though he'd been sorely tempted, and he'd certainly gone to a lot of trouble to acquire it in the first place. He'd ended up buying several disposable telephones, removing the SIM card from each and trying the various cards inside several more expensive phones he'd purchased used and with cash. Finally, he found a combination that allowed him to activate what had turned into a completely anonymous cell phone capable of browsing the Internet.

An insurance policy, he'd told himself, in case of an emergency. He realized now it had been stupid, like a recovering alcoholic hiding a full bottle "just in case." The temptation had eaten away at him daily, forcing him out onto the water at all hours. Despite the risk involved, he meant to break it out now, to make a single phone call he did not want traced.

Downstairs, the dog began to bark. Sweating from the exertion of his climb to the attic—and the heart-freezing conviction that some Gestapo types would kick in his front door and catch him—Sam went to the attic window and used a yellowed section of newspaper to dust it off. Almost immediately, he spotted a van bearing the logo of a Dallas TV station and a miniature satellite dish on its roof.

Edging away from the window, he listened, teeth gritted, as someone knocked below. But with his truck out of sight in the locked garage, the vultures quickly lost interest, and soon he caught a glimpse of them—a female reporter and a cameraman, climbing back inside the van and disappearing.

He imagined they had only gone so far as next door, to shoot footage of the charred rubble that comprised the crime scene. And almost certainly, they would not be the last to think of asking him to comment. Though Sam had no intention of saying one word to any reporter, they could make it damned tough on him if they decided he was worth harassing. Eager to frame a story, they might easily cast him—with a little help from the authorities—as the potential villain of this modern tragedy. The quiet neighbor who kept to himself when not dismembering those who swiped his morning paper.

The thought broke him out in another layer of cold sweat.

After finessing the insulation back into place, Sam hauled himself painfully to his feet and climbed down the attic ladder to the second story. Walking from the master bedroom to the empty guestroom to the upstairs bath, he made a last check of all the windows, which gave him a clear view of the dimming sky, the cypress-studded lake, and his own front yard, where the deer had again returned to graze. He looked carefully, taking a pair of field glasses with him, and waited for ten minutes until he spotted the green and white Dallas news van leaving.

With any luck, there were no more teams out of sight behind the trees and the investigators would believe his injuries were keeping him at home. With even more luck, he hadn't missed spotting someone specifically left in place to watch him.

By the time he made it back to the ground floor, he

wanted nothing more than a long nap on his oversized sofa, or at least to veg for a while in front of the TV. Instead, he shuffled to the kitchen and downed a pain pill with a glass of water. Thus fortified, he whistled for the dog.

"How about a boat ride?" he asked Java. "But we have to keep it quiet."

Barking with excitement—to Sam's chagrin—the Lab spun around and raced to the old sleeping porch. The door creaked as she pawed it open, and she disappeared inside, only to return seconds later with Sam's life vest clamped firmly in her jaws.

"Good girl," he said. "Let's see if we can sneak onto the water before we both get in big trouble."

Heart thrumming, he took the dog out and started the bass boat's nearly silent electric trolling motor with the cell phone in his pocket, illegal intention in his heart.

The boatman liked to watch the blood pool. He liked it even better than the shock he'd glimpsed on her face, the disbelief that he could be here, that he could do this to her. That her life could be distilled into a spreading, crimson puddle.

When he had the time, he liked to stick around, to watch the gleam dim from sparkling ruby to a flat rust color. Dulling at its edges first, then filming, the brown eating its slow way toward the center like a cancer.

But the watching was pure pleasure, and this, regretfully, was business. He didn't have the time today, and he had neither twenty thousand acres of water nor a hungry alligator handy to conceal what he'd been forced to do.

Fortunately, in this case, he didn't need to hide his victim. In fact, he realized, her discovery could serve his purposes far better, if he planned things carefully.

But then, he always did, for it was that care which

differentiated him from shadows, which set him above the common lot of those who called themselves professionals.

The thought warming him, he went to find a larger knife.

CHAPTER TEN

The best lack all conviction, while the worst
Are full of passionate intensity.

—William Butler Yeats,
from "The Second Coming"

As she sat at her desk perusing the file on Leroy "Coffin" Coffer, Justine Wofford caught herself wishing it had been Deputy Savoy who'd been blown out of his shoes on the front lawn of the Monroe house. Not killed, certainly, but put out of commission for a while, like the rookie Calvin Whitaker.

Because as often as Calvin had annoyed her with his overly crisp *yes-ma'ams,* his obvious infatuation, and his thousand and one questions about his shiny new career path, he was one hell of a lot easier to take—and certainly simpler to direct and divert—than a seasoned investigator like Savoy.

And unlike Roger Savoy, Calvin didn't resent the hell out of her, didn't weigh her every decision against the gold standard of her husband's. Thinking of Lou, Justine cursed aloud, furious all over that he hadn't bothered changing his insurance policy's beneficiary in the two years they'd been married. That as a result, every dime of a half-million-dollar policy was going to his ex-wife while Justine and her son were left with . . .

Guilt struck her like a logging truck, grief pooling in its tracks. The suddenness of the stroke that had left him dead within an hour had given her no chance to say good-bye, much less ask his forgiveness. And certainly no opportunity to check to be certain he had made the arrangements he'd promised that evening, close to three years earlier, when he had blindsided her with his proposal.

"I know it's a surprise," he'd told her after they'd met in the neutral territory of a motel room. Met and had surprisingly energetic sex, despite their twenty-two-year age difference and the two-hour drive between their jurisdictions. "I know you've hardly been thinkin' about dating, much less remarriage, what with workin' nights and keepin' things together on the home front like you do. But a man my age doesn't want to waste time—and I'm sure as hell not comfortable with sneaking around like a damned teenager."

"But my job—" she'd protested, though she was really thinking about Noah. How long it had taken to settle him down after his father had skipped town and vanished, how upset he still became at any change to his routine.

But heaven forgive her, she'd been thinking, too, of how hard she had to struggle to provide for her son's special needs and how ruinously expensive it was proving.

"Hell, you marry me and you can turn in your badge," Lou told her earnestly. "I'll take care of you and Noah. I'd consider it my privilege."

"You awake, Justine—I mean *Sheriff?*"

Starting, she turned her head toward Savoy, who was standing in the doorway holding another mug of coffee.

"If you're thinking of showering me with any more caffeine," she said, "you can get the hell out of my office."

He flinched at her tone. "About that, Sheriff. You know I'd never—"

"Forget about it," she snapped, angry with herself about bringing up the incident. He'd apologized already, and her father, a retired lawman in his own right, had advised her not to be pulled down into such horseshit. "So what can I do for you, Deputy?"

"Just wanted to let you know we got a tip off the AMBER Alert line. A possible sighting of Misty Bailey in the area a few days back. She was in a black car driven by a white male with facial tattoos."

As his boat drifted over lily pads, Sam realized he had no right to expect his ex-partner's forgiveness, and even less to think Luke Maddox would be willing to risk helping him. No right, but Sam hoped anyway, because he knew the kind of man his old friend was.

"Do you have any idea how much damned trouble you caused?" Luke demanded. "Since you've been arrested, I've had to personally visit every client, do nine kinds of groveling, and swear on a stack of Bibles I didn't have a thing to do with your actions. And I still ended up losing more than half of the accounts."

"I'm sorry," Sam told him, repeating what he had said so many times before. Though Luke said nothing, at least he didn't hang up.

Sam took advantage of the lull to explain, "I never thought about it coming back to bite you, never thought of anything but those corporate bastards screwing over their own retirees." It still pissed him off royally, the way the corporation had dissolved and "reallocated" the pensions and health-care costs people like his neighbors had worked for decades to earn. Intent on covering its ass, the company had reformed under a new name, using carefully hidden financial assets.

And then its officers had made the mistake of hiring Sam—whose expertise ran to following money trails—to help them keep their secrets hidden.

"Save it for the jury," Luke said. "Oh, wait. That's right. They didn't buy into your bullshit, either." After a brief pause, the harshness ebbed from his voice. "Listen, I feel for your friends, too. Harry and Mona are good people, and what happened to them is dead wrong. But this was never your fight, Sam. They should've gone to the authorities or found an attorney."

"They tried. Again and again, but all they heard was how it was all loophole-legal. By the time they came to me, they were desperate, frightened—"

"If you'd wanted to do something, you could have quietly steered them toward one of those media crusaders."

Sam didn't say that he had tried that, didn't bother explaining that reporters hadn't been in the least interested until he'd leaked the California-based company's internal e-mails . . . along with the principals' financial records.

"But, no," Luke went on, "instead, you decide it's your damned place to out our client, without ever once discussing it with me."

"You're absolutely right," Sam said. "And I'm really sorry, Luke. I screwed up. And worse yet, I screwed over someone who used to be a damned good friend."

When he heard nothing in response, Sam thought he'd lost the cell phone signal, in spite of all the new towers put in place after the last hurricane.

Finally, Luke answered. "Maybe I'm an idiot, but I still do consider you a friend, Sam. Maybe that's why it hurt that you didn't come to me before you went off half-cocked and dropped us both into a shit storm. You could've asked for help, man. Don't you get that?"

"Well, I'm coming to you now. I'm asking."

Instead of hanging up, as Sam more than half expected, Luke listened while Sam explained his present situation. As they talked, it felt almost like the old days, when the two of them had brainstormed over barbecue in Austin. But when Sam mentioned what he needed, his former partner blew up on him.

"Haven't you learned a thing from all this trouble?" Luke demanded. "What you're asking—no way in hell. If it were only me, I'd think about it because it does sound like you're getting a raw deal. But, Sam, I just can't risk it, especially not with the way things are at home now."

"Is something wrong?" Sam's stomach muscles tightened. "Susan and the baby—they're all right, aren't they?"

"The baby's doing great but not such a baby anymore," Luke said, speaking of his son, Jake. "And Susan's pregnant again, but the doc's got her on bed rest. I have my hands full, I can tell you, keeping her from climbing the walls and taking care of a rambunctious three-year-old."

From Luke's voice, Sam could tell his old friend didn't count such work a burden. His family meant the world to Luke, and Sam respected his refusal to gamble with their future. Especially considering how damning it would look if he were caught helping the same disgraced partner whose prior illegal acts he'd disavowed.

Once their conversation ended—more or less amicably—Sam wrapped the phone in plastic. His vision blurring from the pain pill, he dropped the phone inside an empty wood duck house. Since the ducks almost universally preferred the naturally occurring hollows of cypress trees to the state's well-intended wooden shelters, he wasn't too worried about disturbing a pair should he ever need to come back to retrieve the phone.

Not that there was anyone else he'd trust to call. As Sam pondered how he might possibly pull off what he planned without outside help, the boat drifted ever nearer to the skeletal remains of a dead forest, the moss-covered bones whose thin fingers reached toward blood-tinged wisps of cloud.

She'd been gone with Elysse's car far longer than she should have, Ruby realized as she noticed the reddening of the western sky beyond the treetops to her left. Surely, Elysse must be worried by now, possibly even angry that Ruby hadn't at least called her to say where she was.

Guilt coiled snakelike, squeezing at her stomach until Ruby pulled to the roadside and reached for her cell phone. Yet she couldn't force herself to call, couldn't imagine sharing what she'd overheard Sheriff Wofford saying.

Ruby's throat knotted and tears threatened at the recollection of the way she'd excused herself—after telling the lie that she was all right—and then bolted from the sheriff's office. Frantic, she'd jumped in the car and started driving back toward Cypress Bend Road and the ruins that had once been her lake house.

With a defeated sigh, she dropped the phone back inside her bag and told herself she was nearly there already. She might as well finish what she'd started. Then she'd drive straight back to apologize to Elysse for being gone so long.

A few minutes later, Ruby wandered near her ruined house, her nose clogging with the wet-charred stench. She thought of when she'd first moved here with Aaron, how they'd worked together so hard—doing everything from the painting, to woodwork, to tile repairs themselves for lack of money. They'd been so eager to make his parents' neglected weekend house their first real home. She remembered when she'd walked, heart in throat, onto the back porch, to tell Aaron that their home test kit had read positive. She'd watched him nervously, worried since they had only recently argued about finances, but he had yelped with joy and lifted her right off her feet to kiss her. So many sacred moments lay here in the ashes, so many dreams destroyed. She had to forcibly wrench her thoughts from the past into the present, as ugly as it was.

The authorities had driven stakes into the ground and roped off the area around the rubble, had posted official-looking KEEP OUT signs around the blackened heap. A moat of sorts surrounded it, deep puddles from the volunteer fire department's efforts, which had served to keep the blaze from spreading to the trees. Deep footprints pockmarked ochre mud, from the boot craters of those who'd worked the scene to the smaller, shallower steps that must have come from the dogs they'd used to search for bodies.

She realized now that she'd been out of her mind coming here. She would find only despair in the ruins of her life, not answers. So instead, she walked down to the dock and to the water, went to it for solace, as she had so many times in her life.

As a dragonfly skimmed the tops of the lake weeds in front of her, she stopped short, then stared down at a strip of long brown grass, barely discernible in the deep-hued twilight. Shaped like a canoe, it marked the spot where Aaron's old boat had been chained these past few years, upside down to keep the rain out. Had Misty gotten rid of it for some reason, or could it have been stolen last night?

Shaking her head, Ruby gave up on the question. What did it matter anymore, if Zoe was dead? What had any meaning, if everything she'd worked for, everything she loved now lay beneath the surface of Bone Lake?

"Bullshit," she burst out, pouring all her defiance, all her will to fight into the two syllables. Because it *was* bullshit, contemptible and inexcusable to stand here drowning in self-pity while there was even a sliver of a possibility that her child and her sister still drew breath. So what if Sheriff Wofford was having the damned lake searched? She'd suggested earlier that Misty had simply run off with Ruby's money and her daughter. The lake bottom was only one more theory, one more possibility to be checked out, then discarded. A hurdle—perhaps the last—on the way to a reunion, a reunion Ruby would be damned if she gave up on.

It was time to stop this, time to get her pathetic ass straight back to Elysse's, to call everyone they knew to join the search. Ruby thought of Myrtle Lambert and her prayer circle, Paulie and Anna Hammett and their many friends. She'd ask all of them for their help, make whatever pleas she had to, get down on her knees and beg on the television news. And she would follow up with the sheriff, hound her for more information, not only on this "Coffin," but also concerning Misty's call to Sam.

All her life, Ruby had been the sort of person who felt better with a plan. Galvanized by this one, she ripped the car keys from her pocket and started walking back toward Elysse's Corolla. But she didn't get three steps before she heard the deep-throated rumble of a boat motor closing in behind her.

Head swimming with the pain meds, Sam was nearly home when Java started fanning her tail furiously. Following the dog's nose, he spotted a lone figure standing on the bank near the Monroes' dock.

"Oh, hell," he said, assuming it was some law enforcement type who would demand to know what he'd been doing. But as she turned, he recognized Ruby in spite of the dim light. Squinting, he realized she was waving at him—no, waving him *toward* her.

He turned his bass boat, a sporty red and white model that cost more than the Chevy Yukon he had bought to tow it, and let it drift the final few feet before it bumped up against the old tires nailed to the dock at water level. After tying up, he shut off the engine and heard the subtler chorus of frog romance, insect battle, and bird business.

As he climbed out of the boat and said hello, Ruby was standing at the grass's edge, near the place the dock's end rested. Though she said nothing, he quickly recognized her set, determined body language and the suspicion on her face.

Growing up, he'd seen that expression way too often, had heard the whispers that went with it when he'd walked through local stores—always under observation—or past the teachers in the halls at school. It was the look that said they'd decided to give someone like him a wide berth, or else to go ahead and hit him with a preemptive strike before he had the chance to stir up trouble.

But Ruby Monroe had never looked at him that way before, which meant, Sam realized, that Sheriff Wofford or Special Agent Felker or Acosta had been talking to her.

"I would have thought you'd be in bed today," she said, and in her voice he heard ambivalence: concern mingling with caution.

"Might have been," he said honestly, "if I hadn't kept getting interrupted by Sheriff Wofford and those DEA guys. You talk to those two yet?"

She shook her head but kept her eyes locked with his.

Long-lashed, pretty blue eyes, he realized, though he'd never really noticed them before.

"What did they say?" she asked.

"They weren't so much inclined to give me information as to try and get some. I did hear that the fire marshal's thinking some people cooking up drugs might've accidentally set off the explosion."

"That's more than anyone's told me directly," she said, "but I figured it was something like that. No news from the AMBER Alert yet, but I do know Misty wasn't in that house—the medical examiner's report made it official."

"That's great news," he said, his relief so palpable he felt dizzy. He wobbled and took a step to regain his balance.

"Careful there," Ruby warned, "before you end up going ass-over-teakettle into the drink."

Though "the drink" this close to shore only amounted to a foot or so of slimy, green-brown water, he stepped off into the grass, grateful he hadn't humiliated himself by landing headfirst in the muck. "Guess maybe I wasn't up to boating after all."

"Why on earth would you even try it if you're that weak? Or did they give you something?"

"Pain pills," Sam admitted. "And I realize it was stupid to take off—"

"Every bit as irresponsible as getting behind the wheel drunk," she interrupted, but there was no heat in her words. "You okay now? You look sort of green there."

He felt it, too. "Maybe I ought to sit down for a minute."

When she took him by the hand, he tried not to like the feel of her fingers, smaller and much smoother, against his rougher skin. "Thanks," he said, "but I think I'm doing . . ."

Better, he'd been about to say, before the world careened around him.

"Try the grass here. It's dry," she suggested. "And I don't see any fire ants."

She settled down to sit near him, though out of arm's reach. For a minute or two, they rested in silence.

Finally, Ruby said quietly, "I have something to ask you."

Nodding, he closed his eyes against the dizziness.

"Were you sleeping with my sister?" she asked. "And did you *just happen* to end up with her money?"

Ruby watched as his face darkened. Watched as the hurt in his brown eyes was swiftly walled off behind growing anger. Fear pierced her ambivalence about him, and it struck her that she'd taken an insane risk, pushing him like this when there was no one else around.

Jaw tightening, he growled, "No and no—and so much for goddamned gratitude. If I recall correctly, I scaled the porch roof of your burning house trying to save your sister and your daughter. Next time, I'll mind my own damned business."

"I *am* grateful, and I told Sheriff Wofford if she had heard you last night, if she'd seen what you did, she'd know. She'd know the way I knew—"

"The way you *knew*?" He shook his head, then winced and put a hand up to his temple.

Seeing him in pain upset her, until she reminded herself of her conversation with the sheriff, the questions she had raised. "I didn't buy it when she suggested you might've helped Deputy Balderach's murderer escape last night."

"Someone escaped?"

She nodded. "That's how it looks—because Balderach was shot and your johnboat is missing."

Sam stared at her, the shock clearly written on his face. "He was *shot*?"

"Before the explosion, they think. And your boat was gone, so—"

"I thought it'd been impounded."

"That's not what I heard."

Sam grimaced. "Well, anyone could've taken off in that one. It's got an old pull-start motor. You don't even need a key."

"I was here," she said, "and I can't see how you could've done it. There just wasn't time."

"So why all but accuse me of stealing from your sister? Other than being a McCoy, what the hell have I ever done to make you think I'd—"

"It's not what you did," she said, "but what you didn't. Why didn't you tell me? Why didn't you say anything about Misty calling your house?"

"Calling?" Sam's forehead creased, making him look genuinely confused. "*When?* I haven't heard from Misty. If she'd called, I would have—"

"Five forty-two a.m., March thirtieth, she called you. It was on her cell phone records, the last day anyone heard from her."

"March thirtieth . . . that would be . . ." His gaze slid away from hers. Frowning, he tapped his own fingers as he counted backward. "Last Monday, right?"

She nodded. "Tomorrow, it'll be a week. Surely, you haven't already forgotten."

Sam snapped his fingers and looked back at her, his expression focused. "That would be the day I took out this pain-in-the-ass client. He wanted to go early, be out on the water by the time the fish got up for breakfast. So I was out already by then—I can show you my log-book."

"You keep written records?"

Nodding, Sam explained, "Anna Hammett talked me into writing everything down so in case something ever happens on the water, people would know where to look, who I'm with, that sort of thing. And besides, it helps me with my taxes."

"Taxes?"

"I'm not so much inclined to screw with Uncle Sam since I discovered he has teeth."

"Gotcha." Ruby wrenched the subject back to Misty. "Did she leave you a message?"

"No. No, she didn't. But that was the same day—the last day, come to think of it—I remember seeing her. Both her and Zoe, out on the back porch with those people, like I already told you."

"You're sure? About the message?"

He didn't hesitate an instant before answering, "Absolutely. And I can't imagine why she would've called me, unless the raccoons found their way back in."

"Raccoons got in the *house?*"

Sam nodded. "A couple at least, up in the attic. She knocked at my door one day last . . . I don't know, must've been last fall sometime. She acted kind of embarrassed about asking for my help, 'going all girly-girl' was how she put it, but she said they were keeping her and Zoe up all hours, havin' a hell of a party up there."

Ruby smiled a little at that, hearing her sister's voice with her words. "So you helped her?"

He shrugged. "Just made sure the overstuffed fuzzballs were gone, then nailed a board back over a hole I found. It was no great shakes."

"Well, *I* appreciate it," Ruby said.

Java wandered to her and pushed against her hand, and Ruby automatically rubbed her ear.

Sam's gaze flattened. "So does that mean you're through listening to Wofford's bullshit? Because that's all it is. They're reaching, Ruby, looking for the easy answer. But not necessarily the right one."

Ruby stared at him, weighing her need, her instinct to believe against the knowledge that he'd had plenty of time to construct a credible lie. Plenty of time to practice telling it.

"Aaron and I were close, for a long time," Sam said. "We trusted each other. And his parents—whatever happened later, the Monroes saved my life."

"I was wondering when you'd bring them into this." She scowled, thinking that this appeal could have been rehearsed, the playing of his trump card. "I can tell how important Aaron must've been to you from all your calls and visits. And the way you showed up at the funerals, first his parents' and then his."

Diabetes had killed Shirley Monroe—who'd outlived her husband by only two years—just six months before Aaron's accident. A whole family wiped out in short order . . . a much-loved family, judging from the number of friends and former foster children who had shown up at the services.

But not Sam McCoy, though Ruby recalled he had sent flowers. Whining, the dog looked up at her, eager for some more attention.

"You don't want to believe me, fine." Sam slowly rose, face flushing. "Why don't you just come right out and ask me what you really want to know? Did I take Zoe and Misty somewhere? Did I murder them?"

"You son of a bitch." Her vision blurred with hot tears. "Don't you sit there and use a word like *murder*. Not in connection with my family."

"I'm sorry I upset you. Maybe I was a little harsh. But I get to feeling pretty harsh when I'm unfairly accused. Especially of violence."

"I'm not accusing you," she said, "but I'll be damned if I'll pussyfoot around any questions that need to be answered because you might get hurt feelings. Not with my daughter out there somewhere. Not with Misty missing."

"I got that." He nodded, his jaw tight and his expression guarded.

"So what do you know," she asked, "about a guy named Leroy Coffer? Or maybe you'd know him by his nickname, Coffin."

Sam shook his head. "Never heard of him. Who is he?"

"Someone else my sister called, supposedly quite a few times. Might've been that guy we saw. The one with the tattoos."

"I don't think I ever saw him before last night," Sam said. "I was hoping the son of a bitch was one of those killed in the explosion. Are they thinking maybe he was Balderach's shooter?"

She nodded. "He has a history of drug-dealing. And a history of violence toward women, too."

"Your sister didn't seem the type to put up with that sort of thing," Sam said. "I've seen her deflect trouble-makers over at Hammett's more than once. She has a real talent for insisting on good manners, making sure folks treat her with respect without pissing them off. Even the guys in the Play Room, from what I've heard. And everybody seems to like her for it."

Ruby felt a rush of gratitude to hear this reminder of the sister she believed in, the sister she had trusted with her only child. "Misty has plans for her life," Ruby agreed, "and they don't include hooking up with losers. But even smart women get fooled sometimes, and if this really was the guy . . ."

Fear strangled the thought, fear of what a man like Coffin could have done to Misty—or especially to Zoe, who was too young to defend herself.

"I have to go now," Ruby said. "Elysse is expecting me."

"Are you okay to drive there?" he asked. "You look pretty shaken up."

"I'll be fine, but what about you? You want me to drive your boat over to the dock? You're really not in any condition—"

To her astonishment, he took her hand and squeezed it as he held her gaze. "You just worry about yourself and your family, Ruby. I've been in charge of looking after Sam McCoy a good long while."

As he headed toward the dock, Ruby stood watching, astonished at the chasm of need that had opened with his touch. She'd been four years without a man in her life; would the ache have been so deep with any male contact, no matter how innocent?

Or did something about Sam McCoy leave her vulnerable to the same charms that had already hurt Elysse— and maybe Misty, too?

CHAPTER ELEVEN

A few people laughed, a few people cried, most people were silent. I remembered the line from the Hindu scripture, the Bhagavad-Gita. Vishnu is trying to persuade the Prince that he should do his duty and to impress him takes on his multi-armed form and says, "Now, I am become Death, the destroyer of worlds." I suppose we all thought that one way or another.

—J. Robert Oppenheimer,
speaking of the detonation of his invention,
the first atomic bomb

Of course he'd waited for her, even as night fell all around him.

Once committed to a plan, a project, or a promise, he could wait tirelessly, heedless of the hunger, fatigue, and impatience that would compel any of the hollow men, the shadows, to give up.

It was one of his gifts, and one that caused others to seek him out and offer contracts, for he was the one factor upon which his employer might rely, the single constant in a world inconstant.

As well, it was a point of pride, and so the boatman waited in a spot where the boughs bent near the sunken dock, a place where silvery green moss hung like a crone's hair, its tips grazing the surface of the water. It formed a shroud of sorts, made acrid but more bearable by the familiar reek of burning tobacco. Thus hidden, he sat watching through field glasses for a silhouette, watching for the woman to pass before the outside light.

Watching and waiting for the moment he would rain fresh hell upon her head.

Ruby tried calling several times on her way back, but Elysse's line kept kicking over to voice mail. Ruby hoped like hell that didn't mean her friend was busy calling out the National Guard to hunt her down.

But that didn't make sense, since Elysse hadn't tried her cell phone. More than likely, she was simply caught up recruiting more volunteers for the search effort. Elysse might stink at romantic relationships, but she had always had a talent for organizing people in efforts ranging from their ten-year class reunion to a blood drive put together for a girl badly injured by a hit-and-run driver.

By the time Ruby reached Elysse's neighborhood, she'd long since turned on the headlights against the deepening gloom. With no street illumination, she relied on an occasional outside security light to mark her progress. Some of the houses were lit from the inside, too, but at least half remained dark, more evidence that many of the canal properties were vacation homes or rentals more often occupied during summer vacations.

She was glad to see Elysse's place lit and an outdoor light left burning at the corner of the house. After parking the Corolla underneath it, Ruby climbed out and headed toward the wooden staircase.

On the second step, she paused, hearing a bubbling thrum so familiar it shouldn't trouble her; it did anyway. Boat motor, she decided, but very near. She turned her head toward the canal but saw nothing in the moonless darkness, unless . . . oh God. Was that tiny orange glow a burning cigarette?

The motor suddenly cut off, and a warning skittered cockroach-quick up her back. Though it might be nothing, just a neighbor out for a last smoke and a cold brew, raw instinct sent her pounding up the steps.

Bolting through the screen door—thanking God Elysse had unlocked it for her—Ruby whipped around and flipped the latch behind her. Though she saw no one in the circle of light below, heard no sound to alarm her, she let herself inside the sliding glass and locked that door behind her, too.

So it was that the first blood she saw came as a splash of crimson in her peripheral vision, a sidelong glimpse as she turned. Before her mind could frame what she'd seen with any semblance of meaning, she saw Elysse's black cat huddled in a corner, its fur bristling and its whiskers dangling with fat, red globules weighing down its ends.

Still uncomprehending, Ruby stared at the Persian, who flattened its ears and hissed, its orange eyes huge.

"What's wrong, Bubba? Are you hurt?" Ruby asked.

Turning, she called, "Elysse, there's something wrong with your—"

First, Ruby spotted the telephone, left off its hook atop a counter. Behind the kitchen island, the line of one bare leg caught her eye. A bare leg lying in an impossibly huge puddle, a dark slick bordered by two sets of smeary footprints: the small, red tracks left by the black cat and two larger ones from what appeared to be the sole of a man's boot.

She jumped when the phone tucked inside her purse began to ring.

CHAPTER TWELVE

We are battling fanatics who kidnap and behead civilians and shoot fleeing children in the back. There can be no dialogue with such people. . . .
　　　　　—U.S. Senator Kay Bailey Hutchison, Texas

Ignoring the phone, Ruby thought: *This can't be. It can't be right.*

She peered around the corner of the kitchen island, then sank into a squat, her legs trembling too violently to hold her, her eyes closing against a sight too unspeakable to absorb in one glimpse. She wrapped her arms around her knees and whispered to herself that this had to be some kind of flashback, some remnant of the war lodged in her mind like shrapnel.

Kidnappings weren't a daily fact of life in Texas.

Friends weren't butchered like cattle—no, *executed*— in their kitchens.

Regroup, Ruby. Take a deep breath.

But the heavy stench of blood tainted the air filling her lungs, and when she opened her eyes, the same carnage filled her vision.

Like Carrie Ann, Ruby's mind screamed, though Elysse had not been decapitated. Quite.

Ruby turned aside and gagged, ignoring her cell phone, which had once more begun ringing. And then, abruptly, she remembered the glowing cigarette outside, the muted throb of an idling boat motor.

"You son of a bitch," she shrieked, rage propelling her to her feet, giving her strength to reach the kitchen island. Averting her gaze from her friend and avoiding the puddle, she grabbed the wooden knife block, from which she drew the second largest blade.

The largest slot, she saw, lay empty. *Call the sheriff,* the voice of wisdom—or possibly self-preservation—whispered. *If he's out there, he's waiting for you. He's waiting and he's capable of . . .* Grief tore through her at the thought of Elysse. . . . of anything.

As she reached inside the shoulder bag to find her cell phone, it started ringing for the third time. Blinking away tears, she flipped it open and cried, "Please—please, you have to help me. I need help here fast, at Elysse Steele's house. Call 9-1-1 and tell them it's—it's on—"

While she stammered, trying to pull the street name from her shocked brain, the caller interrupted.

"Now that I have your attention," an unfamiliar male voice said, "let's talk about something I have that you want. And something you have that I'm as eager to procure."

"Wh—*what?*" she asked, unable to believe what she was hearing.

"Don't play stupid with me," he ordered. "We know you have the files, and we want them returned. And if we find they've been opened or copied or tampered with in any manner, I promise you, I *will* take out my disappointment on your loved ones. In the same manner—"

"No!" Her head spun with the realization that she truly *had* drawn home the violence of the war zone, that by foolishly taking the risk of smuggling back the flash drive with a dead woman's insurance against DeserTek—documents detailing the names of "problem" employees, dates of transfers to high-risk assignments, and mysterious payments made after their deaths—she had endangered her daughter, her sister—and had gotten her best friend in the world killed.

And thanks to a petty thief inside the Dallas/Ft. Worth terminal, Ruby didn't even have the item this man had gone to such lengths to reclaim. But no way was she admitting that, no way would she risk provoking him into killing Zoe and Misty.

"Let them go. I'll give you anything. Please." If she could set up some kind of exchange, she would think of something—find some way to get her family clear. If she had to kill the bastard, she would. She would find a way, and she would shoot or slash or blow him all to pieces and then dance on his damned entrails.

"You *will* give me everything. No arguments, no tricks, and don't even think of telling the authorities or anyone from the media about this call. Defy me, and I promise you I'll be the first to know," he hissed. "And the next body you find is going to be your daughter's."

"Let me talk to her," Ruby blurted, thinking that something in his voice, something buried in his malice, was familiar. "Please, she must be so scared, and I—I need to hear her voice. I have to, you know, to—uh, to assure myself that they're both really okay. That you have them and they're still safe."

"But they *aren't* safe. And they won't ever be safe unless you follow my instructions to the letter. Can you do that, Ruby? Can you follow them exactly?"

"I swear I will. Just don't hurt—"

"Then wait for my next call. And remember, whatever you say to the authorities, any authorities, will come back to my ears, so have a care. . . . You don't want to go and lose your head. *Or theirs.*"

"Please." She didn't want to beg, but with Elysse's body offering the evidence that this bastard had no qualms about committing such atrocities, the dam of Ruby's self-control gave way. "Please let me hear her voice. Let me talk to Zoe."

When no response came, she looked down at the phone and realized the caller had already disconnected. From outside, she heard an emergency siren fast approaching. Glancing toward a window, she made out a flashing red light.

Pleading, praying, cursing, she fumbled with her cell phone until she hit the call-back button. She *had* to hear her child's voice, had to make the kidnapper understand that.

On the second ring, a man said, "Preston County Sheriff's Department, how may we assist you?"

Her heart stuttered to a standstill and then jerked wildly back into rhythm. The speaker sounded friendly, down-home—nothing like the maniac she had talked to moments earlier. But that made no sense, unless . . .

Outside, the sirens swelled, and the person on the phone repeated, "Preston County Sheriff's Department. Is someone there? Do you need help?"

Disconnecting, Ruby checked her phone's list of received calls. And found that, to her horror, the threat had come from *inside* the department.

She shuddered uncontrollably, thinking of the sadistic

threats—and the man's assurances that he would be "the first to know" if she reported his call.

Sickened, Ruby snapped her phone shut and clutched the knife as footsteps hammered up the outside stairs.

CHAPTER THIRTEEN

There will be time, there will be time
To prepare a face to meet the faces that you meet;
There will be time to murder and create,
And time for all the works and days of hands
That lift and drop a question on your plate. . . .

—T. S. Eliot,
from "The Love Song of J. Alfred Prufrock"

April 6

When the pounding began around dawn, Sam dreamed they were returning to arrest him. The knocking started Java barking, and he woke, head swirling with the details of the search the night before, from the humiliation he'd felt while standing helplessly, watching a pair of sheriff's deputies paw through his possessions, to the moment an emergency cut short their visit. Sam hadn't heard the call itself, which they had gotten via cell phone, but from what little he'd gleaned, a killing must have taken place near the lake closer to town.

A murder he prayed had no relation to anyone he knew.

Downstairs, the racket continued unabated, Java barking near the front door, the hammering insistent. Cursing, Sam pulled on a pair of jeans and grabbed a T-shirt from a pile of clean but as-yet-unfolded laundry he'd tossed into the wicker chair beside his bed.

By the time he made it to the front door, he'd at least assured himself he wouldn't be dragged out of the house half naked. But instead of the hard looks of law enforcement he expected, Sam opened the door to Ruby Monroe, looking so pale, exhausted, and miserable that he instinctively reached for her.

"Ruby, come inside. Please. Sit before you fall down." Forgetting his lawyer's and his former partner's warnings to stay out of this, Sam wrapped an arm around her shoulders and helped her to the sofa.

She slipped off her tennis shoes and drew up her knees in a near-fetal position. Gray and filmy, morning light streamed through the large window overlooking the lake, but Sam switched on a small lamp to better see her.

"She's dead," Ruby told him, her eyes gleaming with unshed tears. "He—he's killed her."

An image flashed through Sam's mind: Zoe laughing, chasing Java, Misty watching her with a stunning smile, her hair golden in the sunshine. Dread sucker punched him, dropping Sam onto the sofa's opposite end.

"No," he pleaded, his throat tightening as, outside the window, a huge white egret wafted to the water's edge. "Zoe?"

Ruby shook her head. "It's Elysse."

He jerked back, unable to make sense of what she was saying. "Elysse?"

"Last night—last night I found her. Just after dark, at her house. It was terrible."

He remembered Elysse's house on the canal, not far off the main body of the lake. A house that had been the scene of laughter and good times—and later on, some very bad ones as Elysse gradually forgot his warning that he wasn't interested in anything serious.

"Elysse *Steele*? That can't be right," he said. Vital and passionate, Elysse was a force of nature. Needy, sure, in that kind of crazy-girlfriend way that sent men running, and with a vindictive streak once she was hurt, but so vibrant and so funny and so . . . hell. "What happened?"

"He—he cut her. Killed her." Ruby sputtered, tried to say more. Failed.

"*Who* cut her?" Sam demanded.

Ruby pinched the bridge of her nose with trembling fingers. As if she hadn't heard his question, she said, "I had to tell them, Sam. I'm sorry, but I had to. They knew already, and they asked me—"

"Asked you what?"

"If you were the last man Elysse dated."

Sam's stomach tightened. "I was, I guess, until I ended things a couple months back. But that doesn't mean I—"

"Of course it doesn't." Leaning forward, Ruby looked at him directly, conviction burning in her reddened eyes. "Because I know it wasn't you."

Sam opened a drawer in the lamp table and pulled out a pack of tissues. Plucking several from it, he pressed them into Ruby's hand.

"*Why*, Ruby?" he asked quietly. "Why would you trust me now when the authorities clearly don't? They were here last night, searching my place, when a call came in about—it must have been about Elysse. What is it you aren't saying?"

Trembling visibly, Ruby wiped her face, then crumpled the tissue tightly in her fist. "At this point, they don't trust me, either. I was questioned by deputies and Wofford half the night."

"Surely, they can't think you would hurt your own friend. Why would—"

"They don't think I killed her," Ruby told him. "For one thing, it took someone powerful to—to do what was done to Elysse. She's—she was taller and quite a bit heavier than I am. Athletic, too, and besides, I didn't leave those great, big, bloody boot prints in the kitchen."

Sam wanted to ask for more specifics, but Ruby looked so close to breaking down completely that he didn't push it. Besides, he was having enough trouble wrapping his brain around the fact of Elysse's death. He wasn't sure he could yet handle knowing the details, so instead he focused on the way Ruby avoided his eyes.

"If they know you couldn't have killed her, why do you think that they distrust you?" he pressed. "What do they suspect?"

Her shuddering intensified. "I don't know what to do, Sam. This morning, I went to Misty's friend, Crystal, but she was too scared to let me stay there. She has a little boy, and—and she'd already heard about the murder. Then Myrtle Lambert, Zoe's sitter, said I must've gotten caught up in some evil, that God's punishment seldom comes unearned, and I—I must have done something so terrible that I deserved—"

"That's bullshit," Sam insisted, unable to imagine someone saying something so cruel, especially in the name of a merciful Creator. "You couldn't have possibly—"

"He—he cut Elysse's—her throat—her neck was nearly sliced through. She was my best friend, and I loved her, and he took her life because of me."

These last words, coming as they did on a choked whisper, finally shattered Ruby, though she'd managed to stay upright through the shock of learning that her family was missing, of finding a dangerous intruder in her home, of discovering her best friend butchered. Stunned, Sam gathered her into his arms and held her, allowing her to sob against him as he tried to think his way past his own horror.

"Ruby," he said, whispering into the soft hair near her temple. Rubbing light circles along her back, he felt her struggle for control, her effort to weep quietly. He felt, too, his physical awareness of her warmth and closeness, and he hated himself for it. Carefully, he stepped back.

"Please, Ruby, tell me," he said. "Why would you blame yourself? Why would anyone imagine you're somehow to blame?"

She wiped her face again and stared at him, eyes wide and, unless he was mistaken, terrified.

He passed her the entire pack of tissues. "What is it?"

Her gaze slid away from his. "I—I haven't told the sheriff this. I couldn't, but right after I found Elysse, a man called. The man who killed her. He said he had my family, said he wanted . . . something I brought home with me. Something from Iraq."

Sam stared at her, asked harshly, "What kind of shit have you gotten yourself into?" *Not to mention me.*

It was hard to imagine a young mother, the kind of woman a straight-arrow guy like Aaron Monroe would have married, involved in smuggling. Tough to accept the idea that such a person would risk everything on the chance for a big score. But he reminded himself he didn't really know her, and that the lure of easy money had made fools of a hell of a lot of men and women. His work in the computer security field, where he'd tracked down numerous embezzlers, had taught him greed had its way with people every day.

"When I was overseas, I had some trouble," she admitted. "I was driving buses, mostly transporting contractors from secured compounds back and forth to worksites, but Jake Hennessy, my immediate supervisor—what a nightmare. I tried to stay away from him, did my best to keep my distance, but every time I brought the bus in, he'd manage to be right there, brushing past me, rubbing up against me, making disgusting remarks about how my uniform hid too much, how he'd like to get me naked. What he'd like to do and how he'd make me want it. And the more I told him to back off, the tougher I got about setting boundaries, the harder he came at me."

"Sounds like a grade-A asshole." Just hearing about it made Sam feel like a jerk for noticing the soft contours of Ruby's body in those brief moments he had held her.

"I don't like the idea of whining to management, like it better if I can take care of things myself. But this guy was getting dangerous, hanging around near my quarters, turning up in odd places to try to corner me alone. And I knew it was escalating, that the harassment could turn into rape if I didn't do something about it, so I went to the company's command post and asked for an appointment to see someone. But when I explained the reason I was there, this redheaded twenty-something out of Oklahoma, an administrative assistant named Carrie Ann Patterson, starts looking nervous and whispers for me to meet her in the ladies' room. And that's where she tells me I should consider other options."

"Why? I'd think a woman would support another woman."

"She'd seen too much, she said, women reporting harassment, men *and* women reporting health and safety violations. Nothing ever happened to the people who got reported, but the ones reporting ended up transferred to more dangerous areas. And more than you'd expect ended up dead. She'd been keeping track, she told me. Keeping records of what happened. She said she was privately talking to some people back home about it—including someone connected to a congressional committee looking into U.S. contractors in the war zone—but she didn't want me ending up as one of the suspicious deaths on her list. She said she could use my help."

"So what did you tell her?"

Ruby's color deepened. "I said I was just a bus driver looking out for my family. I thanked her for the warning, but said I couldn't get involved. And then I turned around and walked out of there in a cold sweat. Later on, I spoke to a couple of the guys I knew around the compound, some of the male drivers and the truck transport personnel, about my problem with Hennessy. They were helpful," she said wryly. "Had a talk with Hennessy that took care of the trouble. Told him if that didn't work, he'd wake up without the necessary equipment to bother any other women."

"Good for them," he said.

Ruby stroked the dog's broad, brown forehead. "I could really use some coffee, if it wouldn't be too much trouble."

"Sure," he said. "I'll go start a pot. Be back in a minute."

When he returned, he found Java on the sofa with her, her head in Ruby's lap. Both the woman and the dog had closed their eyes. Knowing how exhausted Ruby must be, Sam hated to wake her, so he waited until the coffee finished its drip cycle.

"Ruby," he said. His hands full of two huge mugs, he nudged Java with a bare foot. "Move it, you big lug. Off."

As Ruby snapped awake, the Lab shot Sam an aggrieved look and jumped down. "I didn't mean to—" Ruby started. "How long was I out?"

"Just a few minutes," he said. "You need more. I imagine you're running on nothing but adrenaline and fumes now."

She reached for the coffee, cupping the earthenware in both hands. "And caffeine. Can't forget that."

"Black all right?" he asked her. "I have milk, and some sugar, too, I think."

"This is fine, thanks." She shook her head as if to clear it and swept the hair from her face. "What was I telling you?"

"How your problem with your slimeball boss was solved," he said.

She nodded. "I thought that was the end of it until the day I passed by Carrie Ann. She had a bag over her shoulder, and she looked scared as hell. Said she was supposed to go home the next week, but DeserTek was reassigning her down to their operation near one of the most dangerous cities—the fighting was so heavy there, they sure as hell weren't running buses. But a supply convoy was going, and they told her she had to go with the truck driver or they'd fire her and strand her in-country."

"They can do that?" Sam asked. "To an American citizen?"

She nodded. "These big contractors are pretty much a law unto themselves. The normal legal protections don't apply outside of the states."

Heaving a sigh, she let her head hang forward over the steaming mug. "But I should have found some way to stop them from taking Carrie Ann. Should have hidden her in my quarters and bribed my snitch of a roommate into shutting up about it. I was—I'm ashamed to admit it, but I was too scared to get involved, especially with Carrie Ann panicking the way she was. They came and hustled her off, so damned fast there was hardly time to think. And that was the last I saw of her. The last anybody did except the insurgents who waylaid her transport. She and the driver were both missing for two days. Before they were found beheaded, with their bodies burned."

"Like Elysse," Sam said, a chill exploding inside him at the thought of the way her throat had been cut. She'd been brutally murdered for no other purpose than to intimidate Ruby.

"Before she left, she gave you something, didn't she?" Sam guessed. "She passed you some kind of evidence against them."

Ruby nodded. "She pushed a flash drive into my hand. I didn't want it, but there was no time to argue. And afterward—I thought I could just drop it in a mailbox somewhere after I got home. Anonymously. But now, if I don't turn it over, he's going to butcher my daughter and my sister."

"You haven't told anyone?" he asked.

"God, no. The call—that call I got last night came from the sheriff's office."

"You're kidding."

"When he hung up on me, I hit the call-back button. I was desperate to convince him I had to talk to Zoe. But a deputy answered and said *Preston County Sheriff's Office.* And the guy who'd called had warned if I told anyone, anyone in law enforcement, he'd know right away and kill my family."

"Did you check the call log?"

"I did—you can look if you want to. That call definitely came from the sheriff's office."

Sam rubbed his thumb along a jaw gone prickly with stubble. "Can't discount the possibility it was a spoofed call, Ruby. There are services online that let you enter someone else's phone number on a form, along with the number you want to call. Then the service patches you through, and the fake number shows up on the other party's caller ID."

"That's legal?"

He nodded. "As far as I know, it is. Supposedly for

playing *jokes* on your friends, but a lot of bill collectors
and stalkers know about it. And the way it works, if you
hit REDIAL, your call would go back to the fake number
and not to the real caller. So it's perfectly plausible this
guy's not law enforcement, just someone interested in
keeping you from going to the authorities—which, in my
opinion, is exactly what you ought to do. You can't handle
this yourself, no way."

"You don't understand. By the time he broke off the
connection, Deputy Savoy was already in the neighborhood. He told me the sheriff herself had sent him, said
someone had called her personal phone number with an
anonymous report of a disturbance."

"The sheriff?" Sam remembered his father carrying
on about the department's harsh treatment of "undesir-
ables," from midnight beatings to planted evidence and
nudge-and-a-wink public defense in trials where the
suspect's guilt was a foregone conclusion. But as suspicious as Sam was of law enforcement and as much as he'd
hated Justine Wofford's needling, it was hard to imagine
her involved in a conspiracy involving murder and abduction. It was especially tough to imagine she'd choose
to work with Roger Savoy, a man whose ugly election
tactics had provoked many to sympathize with the former sheriff's widow.

"You have no idea how much money is at stake," said
Ruby. "DeserTek's the leading competitor for a huge,
new government contract—hundreds of millions hanging in the balance. I'm not saying Wofford's necessarily
the one, but you could buy any number of Podunk
county sheriffs for a fraction of that price."

Sam thought about the diamonds sparkling on Wofford's ears and finger, her sleek, expensive look, and her
embarrassment about the condition of her run-down de-

partment vehicle. He recalled, too, the regret that filtered through her words as she'd spoken of the child victim of a hit-and-run driver. Could Wofford really be involved with anything that put a little girl at risk?

"Or you could buy off deputies or feds or I don't know who all else," Ruby said. "And since all the agencies investigating are coordinating their efforts through that office, I can't take any chances. I won't."

"So you plan to hand over the flash drive?" She'd get herself killed, Sam thought, and he was just supposed to sit by and let it happen? Protect his own ass while this bastard carved up innocents?

Ruby blew her nose. "I'd give it to him a hundred times over, but I . . ."

She choked up, but he waited her out, fighting the desire to haul her into his arms once more, to make her problems his.

When she looked at him again, her eyes looked bluer than ever against the reddened corneas. "I don't have that drive, Sam. And there's not a damned thing I can do to get it back."

She told him about a snatch-and-grab that had happened at the airport, told him of a theft that sounded random, yet Sam couldn't help wondering if it had been . . . or whether someone other than DeserTek had been willing to resort to desperate means to get those files.

CHAPTER FOURTEEN

We took risks, we knew we took them; things have come out against us, and therefore we have no cause for complaint, but bow to the will of providence, determined still to do our best to the last.

—Explorer Robert Falcon Scott,
from a letter written shortly before his death
during a South Pole expedition

Tasting blood, Ruby realized she was biting into her own lip. Chewing away while wondering if she'd just made the worst mistake of her life. Bad time to make such a huge decision; shock and exhaustion were playing hell with her thought processes, grief and guilt crashing down her judgment like a wrecking ball.

"They wouldn't let you live." Sam looked into her face, into *her*. "Even if you had the drive and gave it to them, they'd have to kill you to keep you quiet. That's the whole idea, right? They mean to isolate you long enough to shut you up forever."

Ruby set down her coffee mug and reached into the purse she'd left beside her on the floor. Pulling a handgun from its depths, she ground out, "Not if I get him first." Just holding the weapon brought a welcome surge of energy, an antidote to the sense of powerlessness that had swamped her. She'd been so scared for so long, so afraid to act, but what good had being passive done her?

"Whoa, whoa," Sam burst out, holding up his palm. "Point that somewhere else, why don't you?"

Ruby redirected the snub-nosed revolver toward the floor, her face burning. Her father, an avid sportsman who had taught her about gun safety, was probably spinning in his grave. "I'm sorry."

Sam leaned forward to better see it. "Looks like something Humphrey Bogart would've carried in an old black-and-white movie. What'd you do?" he asked. "Knock over a museum?"

From some unknown reserve, she mustered up a smile. "Don't worry. It can still shoot holes in someone."

"That's what's got me worried," Sam grumbled.

Ignoring him, Ruby argued, "Mrs. Lambert said her husband took excellent care of it." No need to add that the man had died some fifteen years back, around the time of her own father's final coronary . . . and the beginning of her mother's downhill slide into the bottle.

Sam looked skeptical. "Mrs. Lambert? This is the same woman who thought God must be pissed off at you?"

"Guess she was hedging her bets on that one, in case the Lord was siding with me after all. Either that, or she was glad enough to help as long as I wouldn't be drawing trouble to her house." Ruby grimaced. "I can't really blame her on that count, or Crystal, either. I'm not exactly the safest of companions."

"Trying to scare me off?"

She held his gaze for a moment that expanded like the morning taking shape outside the window. "You don't look like you scare all that easy."

"Oh, I scare, Ruby," he told her. "Right now I'm scared for you and for your family. I'm scared you'll all end up dead if you think for half a second you're going to walk straight into an ambush and get the jump on a professional, or a whole pack of 'em, for all we know, with that relic you're holding. And I'm afraid I'll be the one who ends up taking the fall when it's all over."

Ruby held her breath, wondering if she'd guessed wrong about him, if he would simply tell her to get the hell out of his life. But before he said another word, the dog lifted her ears and growled in the direction of the street, where a car or truck door closed.

"Oh, shit," Sam told her. "If that's someone from the sheriff's office, they'll have a lot more questions when they see us together."

But Ruby had already started toward the front door. Peeking around the curtain covering the sidelight, she said, "Unless they're hiding deputies in yellow DHL vans these days, I'd say you have a delivery."

When she glanced back at him, he still looked worried, but at least he hadn't thrown her out like Crystal or Mrs. Lambert. Yet.

"Think I'll grab another cup of coffee while you get that," Ruby suggested, to give him the space he needed. "Need a refill?"

When he shook his head, she picked up her mug and purse and made herself scarce, pushing open the swinging door and ducking inside a dated, but clean kitchen.

Sam was right, she knew, that investigators would likely take a dim view of her visit here. Especially the sheriff, who not only seemed to suspect Sam of some involvement but had lashed out at Ruby herself last night while questioning her.

"You're not telling me everything." Glaring like a thunderstorm, Wofford had towered above her. "And until you decide to do that, the chances are we won't find your family—or at least not in time to do them any good. Besides that, Deputy Balderach and your friend Elysse won't end up with justice, either. You want all that on your conscience, Mrs. Monroe? Can you live with it?"

Ruby had nearly spilled it all then, but something—maybe it was the hardness she saw in the sheriff's nearly black eyes—warned that she might be testing Ruby, that she might be poised to call the man holding her family. So instead, Ruby had sworn that she'd shared everything she knew. Sworn it and saw either exultation or frustration flash over Justine Wofford's expression as she turned away, supposedly to attempt to track down Elysse's stepbrother.

Ruby poured herself a second cup of coffee from the half-full pot on the burner, but this time she spooned in some sugar from a bowl she found beneath one of the painted white cabinets. As she stirred, she heard the front door closing.

A few moments later, Sam came through the door and told her, "Coast is clear, if you want . . . to come back out." Distracted by the shoe-box-sized package he was holding, he stared down at its shipping label.

"Forget what you ordered?" she asked.

"Haven't ordered anything I remember, and I don't recognize this address." He shook his head and set the mailer on the counter. "Probably one of those sample fishing gizmos these companies send me now and then. I'll look at it later. Right now I'm making us some breakfast."

"Breakfast?" Ruby shook her head, confused. "I thought—I thought you were worried about someone seeing me here."

He glanced up at her. "Right now I'm more worried you're going to keel over on me, Ruby. So sit down before you fall down."

"But I'm not—I couldn't possibly—"

He slapped the top of one of a pair of stools beside a speckled countertop. "Come on over here. We can talk while I cook. What we can't do is make a decent plan on empty stomachs."

She'd been so braced for failure, so prepared for him to look out for his own interests, that she didn't know how to handle the simple kindness she heard in his voice.

When he went to the refrigerator, she dropped mutely onto one of the bar stools, where she watched him pull out a carton of eggs as if this were any other morning. As if Elysse weren't dead and Ruby's family held hostage.

He pulled a striped bowl from one cupboard and began cracking the white eggs, one after another, their slimy yellow innards sloshing down.

"I—I'm feeling really queasy." She panted out the words, blackness fizzing at the edges of her vision.

"Just turn away from me," he said. "Look out the window and start talking. Tell me again about what happened last night. Tell me everything you remember."

She swiveled on the bar stool until she could see out the window above the sink. Her view was of the lawn and thick trees that had stood between their homes for decades. Touched by the sun's first rays, the damp grass sparkled as plump blackbirds pecked industriously among its roots. Filling her lungs, she willed the dewy green to saturate her awareness, willed it to fill those hollows left by the desiccated tans and beiges of the desert.

Yet inside, she remained arid and empty of emotion as she retold her story, beginning with the idling boat motor and the cigarette's glow in the darkness and ending with Deputy Savoy's arrival. As Sam cooked—she was vaguely aware of the scents and sounds that marked his progress—she went on speaking, feeling her soul peel back from the horror like a sunburn, exposing the raw flesh beneath.

Outside, the grass and trees swam in her vision, and eventually, she grew conscious of the warmth and weight of his hand resting at the juncture of her neck and shoulder. When she stared at him, he jerked away—his expression of surprise turning into dismay.

Clearly, he hadn't *meant* to touch her. He was feeding her in the same way a man might toss scraps to a starving stray, but when it came to a personal connection . . . she'd seen the struggle written in his golden brown eyes. And she couldn't blame him one bit.

Turning from her, he dropped slices of bread into the toaster. "You said he wouldn't let you speak to either of them?"

"No," she said, "and I've been thinking about that. Maybe he didn't have my family with him when he called. If he was really in that boat nearby, he must have left them somewhere. Tied up, maybe, or locked someplace, or . . ." *Or dead.*

Sam pulled a pair of plates from a cabinet. "What if he doesn't have them? What if he never did?"

She opened her mouth to argue, but the sense in his suggestion stopped her. Rubbing tired eyes, she allowed the thought to permeate her brain. "I guess . . . I suppose that's possible. Since I found Elysse and he called, I can't think of anything but what he'll do to my baby and my sister if he finds out I lost the flash drive."

"What if—and this is one hell of a big leap, so bear with me—what if the phone call *wasn't* spoofed, and your caller really is tied up with law enforcement somehow? And what if, knowing the details of your family's disappearance, he decided to take advantage of the situation—to pretend he has your family to get you to give up the evidence?"

"So why did he kill Elysse like that? To convince me it was all tied up with DeserTek?"

As he buttered the toast, Sam nodded. "That and to leave you too terrified to do anything but blindly obey his instructions. To get you so off balance, you wouldn't wonder about other possibilities. Such as why drug dealers would set up shop in your house."

Ruby sighed and set down her mug. "I can't imagine what DeserTek could possibly have to do with that. Or why my sister would empty out our bank accounts."

As she explained what Wofford had said about it, Sam used his spatula to lift the fried eggs onto two plates. "Want to eat here at the counter or the table?"

"Sam. I told you I can't—"

"Come on, Ruby. You're asking me to violate the terms of my probation. I'm only asking you to eat."

She shook her head. "*What?* I'm not asking you to—"

The heavy white plate clunked down onto the counter, and Sam put his own beside hers, then pulled forks and paper napkins from a drawer. "Maybe not in so many words, but you came here looking for help, didn't you? To a guy who does computers, not guns. I'm the wrong McCoy for that. Or maybe it's my criminal expertise you were after."

In his voice, she heard a sneering cynicism that instantly raised her hackles, a complete about-face from the compassion she'd heard and seen and felt only moments earlier. Was this his way of pulling back, of distancing himself from uncomfortable emotions? Or was it the jerk in him coming out of hiding?

"What a load of crap," she shot back. "I came over here to tell you about Elysse and warn you Wofford's gunning for you, that's all." She glared at him even as it dawned on her that maybe, on some level, he was right. She had been praying for a miracle—and maybe, at least subconsciously, she'd grasped at the straw of his knowledge of technology in the hope that he'd be able to unearth some kind of clue.

Rather than admit it, she used the side of her fork to cut into an egg, then took a tiny bite. Sam, too, started eating.

"Don't worry," he assured her between mouthfuls. "I still mean to help you. But it's only because I have a vested interest in finding your family. Because I have no intention of getting this pinned on me."

"Fine, Sam." She choked down another bite, not because he'd told her to, but because she needed to remain strong. Strong enough to trust a man she shouldn't trust. "I'll take whatever help you want to dish out for whatever reason you sling my way. And if the help comes with a side of attitude, so be it. Because I have more than a 'vested interest' in this. I have absolutely, positively *nothing* left to lose."

THINGS FALL APART

Crying again. *Zoe.* Louder this time, slicing through the blurred dreams. Numb dreams where Misty still remembered how to smile. Where she hadn't screwed up everything so badly that . . .

The child's voice was bird-shrill, probably complaining about watching the same DVD of Jasmine and Aladdin, celluloid companions who'd long since outstayed their welcome. She was probably sick, too, of living on cereal and water and the stark horror of forced isolation.

Misty woke shuddering, guilt giving her the strength to fight free of the drug's grip. Blinking in the filmy light, she looked around the living room. Checked to see if anyone was sitting in the kitchen or passed out on the couch.

She spotted no one but knew better than to assume *he* wasn't here. He might be sleeping in the second bedroom, although he'd left the radio playing in there as usual, emitting the muted murmur of male voices that formed the background noise of her dreams.

Her breath hitched at the thought of what had happened the last time he was wakened, when he'd exploded out of that room. . . .

"Please, Aunt Misty. *Please* talk to me." Zoe's voice edged toward hysteria.

Fear cut the last threads of inertia. "It's okay, sweetie," Misty rasped, her throat so raw each word was agony. "I'm here. I'm awake now."

"Can I come out now? Can I? I have to go potty and the can's all smelly and—"

"Keep your voice down, Zoe." Misty glanced back toward the other bedroom. "If he hears—"

"The pink phone isn't working." Zoe sounded mad now. "I pushed the numbers like you taught me, but no one came to help me."

Misty blinked, heart pounding, and tried to recall tossing her cell phone into the depths of Zoe's backpack. But those last minutes at the house had been so scrambled, so frightening, she had no clear memory of doing so—or whether she had gotten around to paying the overdue phone bill, much less charged the cell.

But one thing was for sure. *He* would go crazy if he heard that Zoe had it. And like every four-year-old on the planet, she had no concept of how to keep her voice low.

Misty managed a hoarse whisper. "You have to hide it. Hide it quick, or he'll be very mad."

"I don't care! I want to get out of here and I want my mommy and my kittens and . . ." The defiant little voice slid into tears.

Just as Misty heard heavy footsteps from the front porch. Footsteps moving swiftly toward the door.

CHAPTER FIFTEEN

It is the same thing: killing, dying, it is the same thing:
one is just as alone in each.

Jean-Paul Sartre,
Dirty Hands, act 5, sc. 2

Sam watched with mixed emotions as Ruby drove away in the white Corolla, which Wofford had granted her leave to continue driving until Elysse's stepbrother could be reached in one of DeserTek's Iraqi compounds. Thinking of the exhaustion written in Ruby's every motion, he thought, *I should've made her stay and rest, never should've let her take off in that condition.*

But part of him had been glad to hear her argue that there was no time to waste. For one thing, she was right; for another, he needed to plan his actions carefully, and his logic short-circuited whenever he glimpsed the heartbreak in her eyes.

It hurt almost as badly thinking about her daughter—Aaron's daughter—scared or injured or bound or even dead along with Misty, almost as badly as it hurt to think about Elysse's death. He hated, too, hearing himself lie by telling Ruby he would only help her for his own sake. Standing by the window, he told himself he was a grown man, long past the days when he'd been just another freaking foster kid with his nose pressed to the glass. Forever looking in, but never quite belonging, always longing for the love, the goddamned *trust*, that Aaron Monroe had claimed as his birthright.

Son of a bitch. Could it be true? Had his recent legal troubles sent him sliding backward, regressing to a place where he coveted the woman and the child simply because they had belonged to the "brother" who'd betrayed him?

"Bullshit." Sam's outburst spooked the dog, who tucked her tail between her legs and slunk toward the kitchen.

"Oh, come on, you big baby. C'mere, Java. It's okay, girl." He followed her into the room, where he caught the adolescent Lab consoling her bruised feelings with her front paws on the counter.

"Down from there. No, Java." He grabbed her collar and pulled her head away from a leftover piece of toast. Before he could drag her from the treat, her tongue shot out, quick as any bullfrog's, and she snagged and swallowed the bread down without chewing. But Sam considered it progress that at least it had been actual food this time. Only two weeks earlier, she'd eviscerated one of his down pillows and—for reasons he could not begin to fathom—gulped his watch whole.

Mission accomplished, Java dropped down onto her haunches, then cocked her head as she eyed the package Sam had left on the counter nearby. Figuring she might still be hungry, Sam stepped between her and the item and then turned to stare at it as well.

The box was ringing, its sound muffled but steadily rising in volume. A cell phone, unless he missed his guess. But who on earth would be sending him such a thing, and who mailed an activated cell phone anyway?

He grabbed a knife and slit open the package but paused, wondering if this could be some kind of setup. What if someone, maybe the DEA guys who had been here, *wanted* him to violate the terms of his probation? What if they, or maybe Wofford and her deputies, were poised to "happen by" with another warrant after intentionally putting a forbidden item in his hands?

Stupid to worry about such a possibility, he decided, when he'd already given Ruby cash to buy a laptop. Besides, if the authorities wanted to set him up, there were a thousand ways that they might do it, from planted drugs to a fabricated "journal."

By the time he pulled the cell phone, an inexpensive disposable model, from the shredded cardboard used to cushion it, it had stopped ringing. He checked out the phone itself. There were two "Missed Calls," both listed as "Unavailable."

He pulled out the packing material in the hope of finding a note of explanation or an invoice. Instead, he heard the light tap of something plastic against the countertop. Tail wagging, Java tried to horn in, but he pushed her head away and scooped up the thin black case. Only a few inches long, with a tiny flashing green light and a small exterior antenna, it had to be a GPS tracking device, one inserted in the package to allow someone to remotely keep tabs on when this package arrived.

Once more, the cell phone started ringing. This time, Sam answered, his curiosity outstripping his caution.

"McCoy here," he said.

"About damn time," a husky female voice responded.

"Sybil?" Sam broke into a wide grin and thanked God for his former partner, who had clearly decided to risk calling on his sometime "associate" for help. Sam had never actually met the hacker who helped out when "extralegal" methods were the only means of protecting their clients' interests. More than likely, Luke, who claimed to have known her for years, had never met her personally either, for "Sybil" was as notoriously shy of direct contact as she was bold in terms of riskier endeavors.

Electronic contact, however, was another story, as long as a potential client came recommended and was willing to abide by her precautions to the letter. And as long as her fee was deposited in an untraceable offshore account.

"So what can I do for you?" she asked, sounding impatient as ever, probably annoyed that Luke had called in a personal favor and distracted her from whatever moneymaking mayhem she was currently into.

Her attitude changed once Sam explained his situation, including those portions he'd prefer to leave to someone with her expertise—as well as her complete lack of regard for the finer legal points.

"So let me get this straight," she rasped. "You've got a badass big-time contractor who'll stop at nothing to get back its property, no property to give back, drug dealers, DEA, ATF, and locals all involved . . ."

"Could be some FBI, too, considering the missing child."

"The FBI . . ." she echoed.

With a jolt, Sam remembered Sybil's history with the bureau, her starring role, courtesy of one grainy photo and a whole lot of conjecture, on an episode of *America's Most Wanted*. Since then, he'd heard she'd become lower profile and more paranoid than ever. Had he screwed up entirely, scaring her off by reminding her of the danger?

Instead, she laughed, a sound that sparkled like glassy shards in sunlight. "I am loving this already."

He hoped that meant that she was glad to get the chance to once again run circles around her federal adversaries. And not that she had figured out a way to sell him and Ruby out to either the authorities or—worse yet—to a company with pockets as deep as its collective morality was shallow.

Because whatever the debt the mysterious Sybil owed Luke Maddox, Sam had always suspected that her first and foremost loyalty was to padding her offshore account.

After a certain point, not even caffeine is enough. Ruby nudged past that point some thirty miles north of Dogwood, when the car drifted onto the road's gravel shoulder and jostled her awake.

Crying out, she fought to keep the Corolla from running off into a drainage ditch bordering the tree-lined road. For an instant, she had no inkling of where she was, no idea who had put a thick, green forest in the middle of an Iraqi desert.

Heart ricocheting around her insides, she slowed, then stopped the car along the grass just off the shoulder. From the two-lane highway, the driver of a van honked as if to scold her, but continued on its way while other passersby ignored her.

Ruby unwound her clenched hands from the wheel and slapped at her cheeks to rouse herself—as if the surge of adrenaline hadn't been enough to do the trick. About a quarter mile ahead, she caught sight of a long-closed lumber company, a familiar landmark that told her she was less than halfway to her destination, a city of about fifty thousand. Though she was afraid the kidnapper might call her back at any moment, she and Sam had agreed the cash purchase would attract less attention in a larger community than Dogwood.

She would also attract less attention if she didn't get herself killed on the way. To help wake herself, Ruby walked around the parked car while she sipped from the can of Coke Sam had offered before she'd left.

"Come on, Ruby, you can do this. Not for Sam or for yourself. For *them*." As close to the edge as she felt, she couldn't bear to say the names of her missing loved ones.

What she could and did do, however, was to climb back inside the car and crank up one of Elysse's retro-rock CDs. Though she tried to focus on the beat rather than the blaring lyrics, Pat Benatar's "Love Is a Battlefield" pounded its message through her defenses, leaving her in tears before she reached her destination.

"If anyone asks, you have no idea where I've gone," Sam said as Paulie Hammett, standing just outside the restaurant's delivery door, held out a set of keys he'd asked to borrow. "Maybe on an overnight fishing trip with an old client. All right?"

Rather than dropping the key ring into Sam's outstretched hand, Hammett instead pulled off his gimmee cap to scratch a salt-and-pepper brush cut. "I gotta tell you, Sam, I don't want to end up with any trouble over this. Anna won't stand for it."

"You loaned me the cabin keys a while back," Sam improvised, knowing that it was Paulie's resistance and not his wife's that must be overcome. "I must have copied them without permission. That's what you'll say if you're ever asked about it."

Still, Paulie hesitated, shaking his head. "I've worked too damned hard to build this business. If people start thinking I'm somehow involved in this situation—"

"Why would anybody think that?"

Hammett rubbed his whiskers. "Well, Misty and I had a real blowup, in front of staff and customers and God and everybody, the day she walked out. That and the fact that I'm a fat old man with money and people've been speculating that Misty might have gotten herself in a family way."

"Pregnant? You're saying Misty's pregnant?" Sam had a feeling Ruby knew nothing about this.

Paulie massaged the back of his neck. "Hell if I know,

and even if it's true, I couldn't begin to guess who did the deed. All I know is gossip—nothing stops it. Not money, not influence, not the fact I've been faithful to my wife since I went all moon-eyed over that girl back in high school. And now I gotta worry over some waitress getting in a snit, maybe even takin' off like this to spite me."

Sam shook his head. "Come on, Paulie. That was nothing. Everybody knows she was being touchy with everybody—and nobody'd ever believe that you and Misty—"

"Thanks, dick-weed. That makes me feel a hell of a lot better."

"Because you're a man of honor, that's all I meant. And if Anna found out you were screwing with the help"—Sam made a snipping motion with his fingers— "let's just say that meatballs would be the daily special."

"Yeah, sure, that's what you meant." Paulie glowered at him. "Why are you a suspect anyway? Why don't you tell me that?"

Sam grimaced. "What have you been hearing?"

"Some people have been in asking questions. People with shiny federal badges, not to mention the usual county mounties and, God help us all, reporters, wanting to shoot my damned sign in the background of their stories. Even that asshole Roger Savoy has been out." Paulie had never gotten over the deputy arresting Dylan for possession years before. "Surprised you haven't had them swarming all over your house yet."

"What makes you think I haven't?" Sam asked. The vans had disappeared, but he suspected they'd swarm back in greater numbers once someone got the bright idea to dig into his background.

"Anna asked me point-blank if I thought you were involved." Paulie broke eye contact. "If you might have it in you to hurt a sweet young lady and a little girl."

Sam turned away, looked out toward the clouds reflected by the water. A movement caught the tail of his vision, and he turned in time to see an old black woman with a cane pole lift that night's dinner, a fat catfish, into a beat-up, wooden boat. Even from this distance, Sam could hear its muscular body thumping against the hull as the fish flopped. Could almost feel it struggling for life.

"What did you tell your wife?" he asked quietly, sickened that two people he had known for decades, the same two people he had lived with, laughed with, would be asking themselves if the bad blood in him had won the day. After the foster system had cut him loose, the Hammetts had put Sam up for a while—despite the Monroes' warnings to watch him like a hawk. Sam had been a source of cheap labor, Paulie had insisted gruffly, but there had been no mistaking his pride when Sam cobbled together enough scholarships and part-time work to go away to school. Sure, he'd squandered the opportunity, marrying ridiculously young and dropping out when the relationship unraveled a few turbulent months later. But when he'd finally gotten his shit together and made good in the high-tech world, Paulie and Anna had been thrilled to bursting, had even come to visit him a few times at the luxury condo he'd bought on Austin's Travis Lake.

Yet in the end, when push came to shove, he was still nothing but a McCoy to them. A freaking liability.

"I told her you damned near got your ass blown to pieces trying to help a neighbor." Paulie tossed him the keys. "And as far as I'm concerned, that's all there is to your involvement."

Sam forced himself to look up into the older man's eyes. "Thanks, Paulie. For everything." Though that didn't cover it by half, Sam couldn't manage more. Clenching the key ring, he dropped it into his pocket. "I promise, I won't give you any reason to regret it."

"Don't you put it that way." His voice rumbling like a bear's growl, Hammett's expression hardened. "Don't you dare say those words."

Taken aback by the abrupt change, Sam stared at him. "What's the problem?"

This time, it was Paulie's turn to look out toward the water, but not before Sam saw the suspicious gleam in his eyes. "Sorry, kid. It's just that Dylan used to say that when he took my truck keys. Used to say it every time the little son of a bitch was about to go out on a bender. I always wanted to believe him, always argued with his mother. And half the time I ended up cleanin' up another of his fucking messes."

"You two have another blowup?" Though Hammett's son was more than ten years younger than he, Sam had always gotten on fine with Dylan. But father and son clashed as violently as storm fronts, though it was clear Paulie loved Dylan, in his fierce way.

When Paulie wouldn't answer, Sam reminded him, "Listen, your kid's been straight and sober a long time now. Settled down with Holly, doing great work around town, from everything I hear—and you've gotta admit, he ripped a page straight from your playbook in terms of bringing in the business."

After buying his retiring boss's remodeling business— almost undoubtedly with his parents' money—Dylan had immediately changed its name to Tex-Appeal Exteriors and sprung for a huge sign featuring a winking, beefcake handyman holding one heck of a long tool. The sign had incited (or *ex*-cited, Sam suspected) some church ladies, whose angry buzzing drew reporters, resulting in a controversy that had attracted enough business to keep Dylan in the black for years.

"My idea in the first place, that sign." Worry tempered Paulie's half smile.

"People change," Sam went on, "they reinvent themselves and make good. One mistake, or even a series of 'em, doesn't have to mean the end."

Paulie's gaze snapped back and locked on to his. "Is that what you're doing now, Sam? Are you 'reinventing' yourself the way my boy has? Or are you sliding back into the same territory that got your ass arrested?"

Sam gave him a hard stare. Wondering what he could say to Hammett's question when he didn't know the answer himself.

CHAPTER SIXTEEN

"Certainly there is no hunting like the hunting of man and those who have hunted armed men long enough and liked it, never really care for anything else thereafter."
                                   —Ernest Hemingway,
                        "On the Blue Water," *Esquire*, April 1936

On her way back to Dogwood with the laptop and other items Sam had asked for, Ruby's cell phone rang. She fumbled for it, pulse rate soaring, as she pulled over near the bridge that crossed Cane Creek north of town.

The phone's screen said *Private Number,* which meant it could be him. The kidnapper, wanting an exchange she and Sam hadn't yet had time to set up and a flash drive she didn't have. Despite her shaking hands, she managed to shut off the car's stereo and croak out a greeting.

"This is Ruby Monroe."

"Are you being a good girl, Ruby Monroe?" came the man's voice. In the background, she heard a child crying, not the frantic shrieks of immediate pain or terror, but the fretful whimpers of one who had been fussing for so long she had lost hope.

"Is that my daughter? Is that Zoe?" When no answer came, her fear and stress changed to fury. "Let me talk to her, you murdering bastard. Let me talk to both of them or I swear I'll—"

"You must be very cautious, very sensible about the way you finish that sentence, Mrs. Monroe." His voice was positively glacial, a stark reminder of the brutality of Elysse's murder. "Because I've never responded well to threats. Particularly not when my patience has been worn thin with all this insufferable noise."

Frozen to the marrow, Ruby stopped herself. Was Zoe sick or injured or simply scared and weary of confinement? "Let me speak to her. *Please.* I'll make her stop crying for you. I promise, I'll make things easier for you if you'll only—"

"You. Will. Have to wait. Do you understand me? Do you?"

An image appeared in Ruby's mind: the corpse she'd found in Elysse's kitchen shrunk to childlike proportions. Ruby's teeth chattered so hard that it was barely possible to speak. This man, this *monster* held her beating heart in his hands. "I do. So wh-when do you want to make the exchange?"

"I'll call again tonight. After I've arranged the details. In the meantime, keep avoiding the reporters as you have been," he said with what sounded strangely like approval, "and keep your mouth shut about our talks or *I will know.*"

"But I—" she began before realizing the line had gone dead.

For several minutes, she sat rocking back and forth and rubbing her cold arms. Then Sam's words came back to her, something he'd said about the kidnapper wanting her rattled and off-balance, too terrified to think.

Maybe she hadn't heard her daughter's cries at all, but those of some other child. Or, if this man had been savvy enough to spoof a caller ID last night, could he have thought to record the weeping and replay it in the background to convince her Zoe was alive?

Popping the heel of her hand against the car's dash, Ruby gave an anguished cry, then fought to lock her fear down tight. Because as long as she allowed this *terrorist* to paralyze her, she wouldn't be doing a damned thing to save the people she loved.

Some thirty minutes later, as she followed the map Sam had drawn out for her, the wind flipped up the silvery green skirts of the hardwoods and showered the road with rust-colored pine needles. With every mile she drove, the clouds above contorted, twisting themselves into rumbling gray towers that presaged a thunderstorm.

She hoped like hell the rain would blow past, since she'd hate to get caught on this pothole-scarred back road in anything heavier than a sprinkle. Low in places, with portions of its asphalt washed away from past floods, it made her wish she were out here in a four-wheel-drive vehicle.

The sky's growl deepened and she spotted a white flash to her right. Great.

Frowning, Ruby drove right past the crossroad and had to back up to turn off in the same direction as the lightning. Ahead of her, overarching trees hugged a dirt track. Overhead, their branches writhed as if in pain. Though what looked like fresh tire tracks assured her that someone—Sam, she hoped—had passed this way not long before, she still worried she'd find herself in a mud hole, stuck and unable to comply with the nameless kidnapper's demands.

Farther in, the tree-cave cast her into such deep shade that the car's automatic headlights came on to light her passage. A dark length dropped in front of her, and she stopped short, narrowly avoiding a bough as thick as her leg.

Looking upward nervously, she blew out a shaky sigh and rolled slowly over the limb. Peering into the gloom, she kept her eyes peeled for the "Hamm's Hideaway" sign that Sam had mentioned.

According to what he'd told her, the place was a bayou fishing cabin, one of those weather-beaten shacks often passed down through the generations. Too dilapidated and isolated to make a worthwhile rental, Paulie had held on to it only out of sentiment—and as a place to smoke cigars and stare out at nothing without Anna getting after him. Probably a heck of a dump, Ruby suspected, if he wouldn't let his wife set foot inside it.

About the time the first, fat raindrops popped against the car's exterior, Ruby glimpsed something red—Sam's Yukon, behind the screen of trees. She never did spot the sign, but the SUV's bright color led her like a beacon to a cabin perched tentatively along the curve of a meandering, wide stream, its muddy, green-brown water rippling with the wind.

Like Elysse's place, Hammett's getaway was elevated. But that was where the resemblance ended. The cabin consisted of warped, unpainted boards weathered gray by the elements, except where it was stained green by algae. Spanish moss had webbed not only the overhanging live oaks, but the shack's roof and porch as well.

She parked, then popped the trunk and hurried to grab her purchases before the sky opened up completely. She'd expected to hear thunder, or the stillness that often preceded a big storm. Instead, a mechanical hum met her ears, the sound of a gas generator that explained the welcome, yellow glow she spotted through a grimy window.

Sam emerged from inside and rushed down the steps. As he jogged toward her, he flashed a truant's smile, his face still handsome despite the small Band-Aids he'd placed over his stitched cuts. "Hey, there. Let me get that for you before it really starts to come down."

No sooner had he spoken than the rain came in a torrent, pelting them with stinging drops as it rattled like a million pennies striking the cabin's tin roof, the car, and both of them. Scooping up plastic bags and boxes and slamming the trunk shut, they raced for shelter, hurtling up the steps and running inside. They stopped, panting and dripping, on a patch of peeling linoleum in the center of a kitchen that, for all its dust and grime and musty smells, made Ruby think of her clean-freak grandmother.

Once they'd put down their packages on the floor and on top of a square, wooden table, the two of them stared, each taking in the other's drowned-rat appearance. To Ruby's astonishment, they both burst out laughing.

Laughing, like two kids on an adventure.

Laughing, as if the exhilaration of a dash through the rain had washed their memories clean. Except hysteria edged this mirth, an explosion only a hairbreadth from helpless tears.

Mortified, Ruby abruptly fell silent, and Sam sobered just as quickly, his gaze locked on to hers.

Outside, the rain rattled off the roof and a window showing a slice of gray sky dark as dusk. Combined with their isolation and the weak illumination from an old tin-hooded lantern, the effect was to make the small room feel tiny, the moment intimate.

"I'm sorry, Ruby." Soaked to the skin, with his short hair flattened and his T-shirt clinging to the contours of his muscles, he looked genuinely contrite—and uncomfortably appealing. "I don't want you to think I'm making light of any of this, but—hell, sometimes you have to laugh or completely break down. You understand?"

Nodding, she said, "Yeah," and struggled to stop thinking about the way she'd lit up inside at her first sight of his smile. Emotionally at sea, she couldn't risk losing her focus for a moment.

"Have a towel." He pulled several from a cardboard box perched on the counter of an antique Hoosier kitchen cabinet.

She gratefully accepted, and he took one for himself and used it. As she dried, she took in the white enamel cookstove and shelves stacked with various supplies, from canned foods and batteries to cleaning items. In one corner, someone had set a large red and white cooler.

"Did you bring all this stuff?" she asked as Java danced an enthusiastic welcome near her feet.

"Most of it," he said. "I don't want to waste time driving to town for supplies or risk being followed back here, so I tried to think of everything we might need for as long as a few days."

She rubbed the Lab's soft brown ears with one hand, a reflexive act that did nothing to ease her worry. "I don't think we have a few days. He called me, in the car."

She told Sam about her conversation with the man who claimed to have her family. Though she struggled to get out the words, she added her suspicions that he might have used another child's cries or a recording to make her believe that he had Zoe.

"Go lie down," Sam said to Java, who had gotten too insistent in her quest for attention. When the dog obeyed, he praised her, sounding pleasantly surprised.

Looking back at Ruby, he asked, "Did you hear Misty, too? Did he mention her?"

Ruby rubbed her arms. "No, I didn't hear her, and he's refusing to give details. All he does is make threats, and I don't doubt for a second that he's capable of anything. Anything at all. If you only heard that voice . . ."

She shivered, and Sam pulled a larger, newer-looking towel from his box, which he wrapped around her gently. Using the absorbent tail of the white cloth, he blotted cooling moisture from her cheek, then cupped her jaw, caressed it lightly with his fingers.

"We're going to do this, Ruby. We're going to do everything we can to track your family, get phone records, your sister's financials, see if we can prove they're somewhere else."

She looked at him intently, clinging to the gentle strength in his words, the assurance in his eyes. "How, Sam? Even with the laptop and the air card for the Internet, I don't see how that's possible."

"It's possible," he told her. "Especially with the help I've come up with. The best kind of help."

"*What* kind?" she asked.

He shook his head. "Don't sweat it. Just know that somebody's on our side. Someone who doesn't have to bother with technicalities or bosses or running to get every move approved by some judge."

She realized he was speaking of a criminal, yet she was still relieved. They could use any kind of ally they could get at this point. Particularly one whose actions wouldn't make their way back to a bought-and-paid-for deputy or sheriff.

"Meanwhile, we'll use the laptop and that flash drive you bought to make a mock-up. You find a pretty close match to the one that's missing?"

"They're both red, and I think they're close in shape,"

she said dubiously. That was as much as she recalled about the drive she'd sewn into the lining of her backpack. In her desperate rush to get it out of sight before she was caught with it, she'd paid no attention to the brand or any markings.

Sam nodded an acknowledgment. "It won't be perfect, won't be identical to the one the thief took—especially in terms of the contents—but we have to both believe it's going to fool him long enough."

Outside the window, lightning flashed and a boom followed, causing her to jump. Trembling even harder, she shook her head. "This is never going to work. He said they'll know if the files have been copied or examined. If they can tell all that, they'll figure out a fake in no time."

"He can't know about the contents at a glance. That's bullshit. So what we have to do is figure out a way to overpower him while he's distracted. Or plant a GPS tracker on him somehow—I've got one we can use to follow him back to wherever he's stashed your family, if he has them."

"How can we possibly—"

"Shh." Sam stepped closer to her, near enough that she felt the heat of him, felt the tidal pull of man to woman. And she wanted so badly to believe him, to buy into his skill and competence, that she didn't step away from him, didn't move a single muscle, even when she realized he was bending to seal her mouth with a kiss.

Her heart bumped at first contact, and her head tilted backward to allow it. There was no hurry in his kiss, no expectation or even possibility. No fireworks went off— not even another stroke of lightning. Yet the warmth and comfort and simple human connection sent fatigue cascading off her, smashed through the glass shell of her grief and isolation.

She could have stood there for a long time, drinking in the sweetness. Instead, when it felt like enough to sustain her soul awhile longer, she spread her hand against the wall of his chest, applied the gentlest of pressure, and felt disappointment mingling with relief when he stepped back to look her in the eye.

"You want me to lie to you, to tell you I'm sorry?" he asked her, the gentlest of smiles warming his eyes. "I'm not much of a liar, Ruby. Couldn't beat a six-year-old at poker."

She shook her head to answer, unable to speak for fear of what she might say. She knew she was a wreck now, knew she was in danger of mistaking gratitude for more.

The safest thing, she decided, might be a change of subject. "There isn't much time."

Nodding, he said, "Of course," before putting his back to her and beginning to unpack the electronics she had purchased.

But he didn't turn quite fast enough to keep her from seeing the regret in his expression. Regret and sharp desire crumbling beneath the force of will.

CHAPTER SEVENTEEN

"When you have a child, the world has a hostage."
—Ernest Hemingway

With Ruby in the next room slipping on a clean, dry shirt he had offered, Sam set up the computer at the table and cursed himself for a fool. After realizing he was no better at relationships than any other McCoy, he'd learned to content himself with good-time girls, all of them too short-term to give a damn about his background. All of them too shallow or too selfish to break his heart when they left.

Though it was hard to think about her now, he knew Elysse had been his first real slipup. She was neither self-centered nor superficial, a woman whose biggest flaw had been a tendency toward self-delusion. She'd longed for a life partner and a family, but she'd been too quick to settle for a man who wanted nothing of the kind.

As bad a mistake as it had been to get involved with her, it didn't hold a candle to the sin of playing with the emotions of his foster brother's widow. Turning his head, he listened for Ruby but heard nothing except the diminished rattle of the rain.

"You finding everything okay?" he called, the thought running through his mind that he should tell her what Paulie had said regarding the rumor about Misty's pregnancy. That he had no right to keep such information, no matter how dubious, from Ruby.

When she didn't answer, he went to the open doorway and peered into the living room. He smiled, surprised to see her curled up on a red slip-covered sofa, her head tilted against her outstretched arm, her features slack with sleep. Exhausted, he thought, to conk out like that so quickly, but it was probably the best thing for her.

Before she'd succumbed, Ruby had pulled off her jeans and T-shirt and dressed in a long-sleeved guide shirt that was miles too large for her. Sam rummaged in a dented metal chest and shook out an old but reasonably clean throw he discovered. He hesitated for a moment, admiring her bare legs before guilt cracked its tiny whip.

As stupid as this attraction was, it wasn't about Aaron, Sam realized as he covered her and grabbed a fresh shirt for himself. It didn't have a damned thing to do with jealousy or with paying him back for what had happened with the Monroes when they were both just kids.

But it wasn't about Ruby either, *couldn't* be, in such a short time. So it had to be the situation, the vortex of the shit storm forcing the two of them to work together. After changing shirts, he went to the kitchen and rebooted the computer—yet another forbidden desire—to activate the newly installed air card.

He had to keep his mind on his task and off the woman. Anything less would be unfair to Ruby, even cruel, considering her situation. Only a first-class asshole would move in to take advantage, would go back into the other room, slip his hands beneath the blanket, and caress that creamy skin.

Scowling at the computer's progress, he forced his mind back on track. A few minutes later, he used cell phone technology and Ruby's log-in information to connect to what he'd come to think of as Nirvana: the untamed Internet.

"That's right," he said aloud, his blood pumping and fingers tingling as thoughts of Ruby's body—along with Pacheco's warnings—faded.

Sam's first stop was a free Web-based e-mail account Sybil had promised to set up for short-term contact. Finding no messages, he opened a second window and busied himself seeking out and reading all he could find regarding DeserTek.

There wasn't as much as he might have expected. Though the company was mentioned in a few news feeds listing overseas contractors, critics appeared focused on the largest and most infamous of the "wartime profiteers," several of which were being forced to publicly account for themselves in congressional hearings beginning next week. DeserTek's public face, its Web site, was decidedly low profile, and it took Sam quite a bit of digging—and a couple of exercises that proved he hadn't lost his knack for circumventing firewalls—to find the names of the company's CEO and board of directors.

From there, he followed strands as faint and fragile as the most delicate spiderwebs, but it was a simple Google search leading to the archived "Celebrations" section of the *Houston Chronicle* that caught the first fat fly. A wedding announcement showed DeserTek director Alexander Jason Merrill with his new bride, Hollis Marie Leighton. Hollis Leighton, who'd been given into holy matrimony by her father, U.S. Senator Richard Leighton. The lucky groom, Sam decided, looked too damned baby-faced to sit on the board of such a company, a suspicion he confirmed by finding Merrill's name listed in an alumni association's rah-rah announcement congratulating a prestigious private college's recent honors graduates. Very recent, as in last spring. . . .

Which led Sam to dig deeper on the other members of DeserTek's board, to see if he could find out into whose bulging pockets each of the puppet's strings led.

When Ruby opened her eyes, the air above her shimmered, laced with moving filaments of light, threads of sun that filtered down past floating plants, through algae, past the strands that undulated all around her. Golden strands of hair, her hair, though her hair was neither so long nor so light in color . . . Was it? And how was it she was looking up through water, through a silvery school of minnows sparkling just beneath the surface, looking toward the silhouette of lily pads above them?

Panic slashed through her like a razor, and she sucked in a breath to scream. Except she couldn't do it—wasn't breathing, because she'd awakened too late. Because she had already been dead, dead and anchored to the bottom far too long.

Anchored not far from the body of the tiny blonde, beloved child who had been her charge.

CHAPTER EIGHTEEN

*Yes, the Dead speak to us. This town belongs to the
Dead, to the Dead and to the Wilderness.*

—Carl Sandburg,
from "Yes, the Dead Speak to Us,"
Smoke and Steel

With the first scream, Sam lurched to his feet. By the
second, he was kneeling beside the old sofa in the living
room, shaking Ruby as he called out her name.

"Nightmare." His heart thudded as he tried to explain
it. "You were having a nightmare. It's all right now."

Ruby stared upward, reached upward, her fathomless
blue eyes focused on something he could not see.

"Can't—can't get to the surface. Can't breathe," she
whispered. "Something's holding me down."

"Wake up, Ruby. It's a bad dream." He took his hand
off her shoulder. "I'm not holding you down. You can
breathe now."

She blinked, and her white-rimmed eyes turned to
take in the sight of him. With a noisy gasp, she pushed
herself into a sitting position, her body shuddering.
"Misty. Misty's down there. At the bottom of the lake.
And Zoe . . ."

"You can't know that," he said quietly and a hell of a lot
more calmly than he felt. "It's a nightmare, that's all, fears
working themselves through your head while you sleep."

Ruby jerked, remembering. "They're dredging the
south end of the lake for bodies. I heard the sheriff say so.
She thinks Zoe might be . . ."

Sam hugged her trembling body, as much to calm

himself as to offer comfort. After making a shushing sound against her temple, he whispered, "You can't give up now."

"I—I was Misty, in the dream. And there was something heavy weighing me down." Rocking herself, she added, "And I—I think she was upset about Zoe. . . . What if Zoe's down there with her? What if they're both really—"

"We can't afford to think that," Sam said. "We just have to keep working on the assumption that we'll get them out alive. I've already found something. Something that could help us."

"You have?" Ruby shifted, and Sam helped her to her feet.

As they moved back toward the kitchen, he explained about the senator's son-in-law, along with a second connection he'd uncovered linking another DeserTek board member, a woman whose leadership experience appeared to be limited to an elementary PTA, with a high-ranking State Department official who happened to be her brother. "If I can come up with anything that financially connects them, we'll be in business."

Ruby rubbed the sleep from her eyes. "I don't get it. What do you mean?"

"I mean, I might not be able to load that flash drive you bought with the same files that were stolen, but I'll come up with enough incriminating information that we could crush the company's chances to secure that fat new contract if it were made public. Maybe I'll even get enough to take them down completely. All we need here is a bargaining chip."

He didn't bother to explain what he'd been building as he went along, the components he'd uploaded to a safe location. Time enough to fill her in on that later.

"Something to trade for Misty and Zoe's freedom,"

Ruby added, nodding, as she stared down at the computer. "I should have been here helping you. Why did you let me sleep?"

"You were only out for a few—"

"It's been *hours*." She pointed out the time on the corner of the laptop's screen. "It's already past four."

Embarrassed at having lost track of the time, he glanced at the now-sunlit window and said, "You really needed the sleep. No one can run on fumes forever. Besides that, I work faster on my own."

A chiming sound from the computer alerted him to the presence of an e-mail in his in-box, one bearing the hall-of-fame spam header DEFILE HER EXPECTATIONS WITH UR NU LONG SCHLONG!

He grinned, recognizing Sybil's sense of humor in both the header and the sender's name, Blessing R. Cummings. But the smile died on his lips when he read the contents of her e-mail.

"What is it?" Ruby asked him.

"Nothing I wasn't expecting. Not really. My— uh—my associate couldn't get a bead on the signal for your sister's cell phone. Which means the battery's out of juice—"

"Or underwater." Ruby's eyes looked haunted.

"Or damaged somehow or maybe even turned off," he added, "so we'll start working on plan B now."

Sybil, using the information he'd e-mailed her, would start working to track the DeserTek players' financials. If no more profitable opportunities turned up in the meantime.

"It's a bad sign, isn't it?" Ruby asked him. "That and the fact that Misty hasn't used her credit cards."

"She could be spending cash." Tactfully, he didn't mention Ruby's looted accounts. "Would make sense if she doesn't want to leave a trail."

The silence made even more sense if Misty was a captive. Or a corpse. But Sam saw no need to state the obvious. Ruby understood the reality as well as he did.

"How about a sandwich?" Rising, he reached for a loaf of bread and took stock of the other items he'd brought. It was a pretty limited assortment, but at least he'd thrown in the jalapeño potato chips that he found so addictive. Given those and a supply of iced-down Dr Pepper, he could function until his arteries begged for mercy.

"I suppose," she said as he pulled open the bag. "But let me feed you this time. You keep working."

"Are you sure?"

She nodded her head. "I need—I have to do something. Think I'll start by putting my pants back on."

He wanted to tell her they would still be damp but figured she'd know self-interest when she heard it. So instead he went on explaining, speaking loudly so she'd hear him, his suspicions regarding DeserTek's real leaders.

"I knew they were well connected," she called back, "but I had no idea that the board was nothing but a front. And heck, what did I care, as long as they paid me a great salary to drive their buses?"

He heard the irony in her voice, the bitterness and self-recrimination.

"We can keep a copy," he said. "Send it to somebody with that congressional committee. Or put the press on their scent with an e-mail."

Reemerging, she shook her head. "If I can pull Zoe and my sister out of this alive, I'm willing to let the rest go. As long as they'll leave us in peace, I have to, no matter what this has cost me."

"How about what it cost that woman who was killed after she warned you about complaining, and all those other workers? How about what it cost Elysse Steele?"

Ruby winced, flushing deeply. "I'll never forgive

myself for my part in this—don't you understand, my
heart is broken. Elysse—I've known Elysse for half my
life, Sam. But if I'm allowed a miracle, if I ever see Misty
and Zoe again, how can I risk their lives? Especially if it
turns out it was really my involvement in this whole
scheme that put them in danger in the first place. These
people, these powerful big shots pulling down hundreds
of millions—they aren't about to let some little cog in
their machine destroy them."

"That's what they want all us 'little cogs' to think.
And if you can't stand against systematic murder, then
what can you stand against?"

"I stand for my child, Sam, and the sister I practically
raised. If I'd remembered them and only them, they
wouldn't be in danger, so you can stow the lecture. I feel
plenty bad enough already."

"All right, Ruby," he said carefully. Of course, she'd put
her family before the need for vengeance. Maybe justice
was a luxury, a nebulous concern only applicable to those
who could afford it. Or those, like him, with no family to
put first, and only a hollow shell of a real life to return to.

A chiming interrupted. "Better check out this new
message."

"Sure. Go for it." Ruby's voice was crisp, her agitation
obvious as she turned toward their food supplies.

Not knowing what to say, Sam turned back to the
message. This time, the sender's name was a random
string of digits, and the header contained only the words
I'M OUT.

"What the hell?" he said. Clicking to open it, he
quickly read the contents.

  *DT's contracted Hobson Best to troubleshoot a *personnel
  issue.* I've seen Best's work, seen the way he *solves**

(!!!) people's problems, and I won't cross him, won't chance hitting this bastard's radar screen. You got good sense, you'll get clear of this mess in any way you can. Make a run for it if you have to. Ditch the woman and go off-grid. Now, before it's too late.

Just disappear and I'll contact you later—could use a sharp mind & skill set like yours. Could make it worth your while.

"DT," Sam growled through clenched teeth, hating DeserTek more with each passing minute. How arrogant, how dangerously amok this corporation had run, to hire a pro killer to obliterate the evidence against them.

"Hobson Best," said Ruby, who'd come to lean over his shoulder. "My God, it sounds so . . . I don't know, like a small-town preacher, or the local bakery on Main Street. And here it turns out it's one of the devil's other names."

Sam looked up to see the stark horror in her eyes, even more troubling than the chill in her voice. "Best won't be his real name, and he isn't supernatural. He's just a hired gun."

"Your friend or whatever he is doesn't think so. Seems pretty spooked to me."

Sam didn't correct Ruby's assumption as to Sybil's gender. It was a moot point anyhow, since the hacker had made it clear that she had no intention involving herself in anything to do with Hobson Best. Shrugging, he said, "Good help's hard to find. Guess this is gonna have to be a do-it-yourself project."

Ruby studied his face. "You mean you're not taking his advice about running?"

He shook his head and ground out, "Not on your damned life."

The tension in her shoulders eased, and she sighed. "I hope you don't come to regret it."

He could have said more. How he'd felt more alive in the past two days than he had the last two years. How quickly the idea of exacting righteous vengeance for Elysse's death and Ruby's suffering had taken root. How, despite the horrific circumstances, he felt content here, doing the kind of work he should be doing, after wasting his talents, even his life, for far too long. How turning tail and selling out to a slippery mercenary like Sybil tempted him not for a moment.

But he held his peace, partly out of an instinct for self-preservation and partly because he realized he still hadn't talked to Ruby about Misty. As succinctly as he could, he went ahead and shared what Paulie had told him, though he was careful not to mention Hammett's preoccupation with his own reputation.

Worry lines creased Ruby's forehead. "Crystal mentioned the same thing, said she even asked Misty about it point-blank. Misty denied it, got pretty upset. Too upset, if you ask me. It really makes me wonder—"

Ruby's phone rang, and she all but dove to reach it on the Hoosier's pull-out countertop. Picking up, she said, "Crystal? Is it really you?"

Ruby relaxed, her body language revealing that she'd half expected it would be the man claiming to have her family. Which would make sense, if Hobson Best knew technology as well as he did terror.

But new tension coiled in her voice as she asked, "What did you hear about my sister? Tell me." While listening, she paced, moving from the kitchen back into the tiny living room.

"Who?" asked Ruby. "Tell her I need to know now." After a long pause, she added, "Come on, Crystal. I don't have the patience to play these kinds of games. *Fine,* I'll meet you there in about forty minutes. Please don't go anywhere until I—good, and thank you. Thanks for calling me."

Lowering the phone, she frowned. "Crystal's been digging around some, talked with a running buddy of hers who ran into an old friend who . . . I really don't know how they're all connected, except this woman, this friend of a friend, is in her thirties but still parties heavy-duty, sleeps with the kind of men who leave marks. . . ." Ruby turned away from Sam to look out through a window streaked with dirt and rivulets of water. "And she says she was out one night not long ago with Misty. Says my sister was hanging on some wasted dude's arm, if you can believe that."

"When?"

"Maybe a week ago."

"Do you buy it?"

Ruby blew out a breath and shook her head. "I'm not sure anymore. I want to believe she and Zoe aren't with Best, but considering what was going on at my house in my absence . . . I need to check this out. Crystal says the friend dropped off this chick at Paulie's, and she's pretty messed up. She won't talk to law enforcement, swears she'll take off if Crystal tries to force the issue. But she wants to talk to me."

"To you? Do you know her?"

"Crystal was all freaked out 'cause Paulie's giving her a hard time. I couldn't get a name out of her to save my life. Right now Crystal's plying this person with coffee to try to get her sober. But she can't keep her in Paulie's office long, so I'd better get there fast."

"You all right to drive?" he asked. "You still look pretty beat."

"I'm doing better; I'll be fine. I'll go and talk to her. At least I'll be doing something more productive than sitting around watching you work on the computer. Just call me if there's anything I can help you with."

"Before you leave, do me one favor." He thought of the soft warmth of her lips, the way she'd felt to the touch. The way it would feel if the two of them were other people and the circumstances different.

Her throat moved as she swallowed, looking at him so intently that he had to glance away, over to the Hoosier cabinet, where she had left the bread out. Lying beneath the spot, Java tried to look innocently disinterested in her proximity to human food, but the drool gave her away.

"What is it?" Ruby asked him.

"I want you to have a sandwich. Before my dog helps herself to it."

Ruby's nose wrinkled as she pulled a set of car keys from the pocket of her still-damp jeans. "She can have it. I'm sure as heck not hungry."

"Java's got her own food, but you need to eat something," he insisted. "I know damned well you haven't had anything since this morning."

She looked annoyed. "So now you're, what? My mother?"

"Like it or not, I'm your partner in this," he said, going for the peanut butter and a knife. "And I'm not sticking my neck out for some woman who doesn't have the sense to take care of herself. So humor me, Ruby."

"Fine," she said, and grabbed the jelly, then helped him slap several sandwiches together. Once they'd finished, she wrapped one in a napkin and said, "I can eat and drive at the same time. And, just for the record, I thought you were only sticking your neck out for your own sake."

He grimaced, hating having his own words thrown back into his face. But Ruby's smile snipped the thread of his annoyance.

"Whatever your reasons," she said quietly as she looked at him, "I want you to know that I'm grateful—truly thankful—to have you on my side. And if you help me get my family back, I swear to you, I mean to spend a lifetime paying off that debt."

He wanted to tell her that seeing her family safe and whole would be plenty of reward for him, that seeing himself exonerated was all he wanted personally.

Yet he hesitated for some reason, remembering a time when he had dared to ask for more from life. Remembering those first, fantastic days with Elysse, before everything had gone wrong.

And in that moment, Ruby said good-bye and slipped outside, without even allowing him a chance to tell her to be careful. Without even allowing him a chance to consider the fact that he should be the one throwing himself at her feet to thank her.

CHAPTER NINETEEN

For your hands are defiled with blood, and your fingers with iniquity; your lips have spoken lies, your tongue hath muttered perverseness.
> —The Holy Bible (King James Version),
> Isaiah 59:3

Less than a mile down the road, Ruby's cell phone rang again. One glance at the caller ID had her pulling over.

DeserTek, the screen read, a name that sucked the air out of her lungs. She could scarcely believe they would have the balls to phone her directly. Unless their bribes and connections made them feel immune to prosecution.

Fighting to keep the quaver from her voice, she braced

herself for another conversation with the devil. "This is Ruby Monroe."

"This is Graham Michael Worth calling from the Dallas office." The voice was officious, even pompous, but not at all alarming. "You may remember meeting me when Jeremy Bray brought you for your initial interview—"

"I remember." Ruby pictured the man whose lumpish, graying looks had stood out in such contrast to Elysse's stepbrother's meticulously toned torso and dark buzz cut. Had the midlevel personnel recruiter been left out of the loop about her family's abduction? Surely, Worth wasn't about to repeat the ridiculous offer she'd already turned down in Iraq. As she resumed driving, she asked, "What can I do for you?"

"This is a bit awkward," he began. "But I've been asked to remind you, in the strongest terms, of the confidentiality agreement you signed as a condition of your employment. I need to emphasize that our attorneys are prepared to litigate any breaches to the fullest extent of—"

"You're threatening me with *lawyers*?" Why bother when they already had her family? With Zoe's and Misty's lives on the line, some nebulous threat of a lawsuit couldn't mean less to her. She guessed he really had been left out of the loop about her family's abduction. But then, it wasn't the sort of thing the guilty put out on an inner-office memorandum.

"It's come to our attention that you have taken DeserTek property in an attempt to sell trade secrets to our competitors, who would happily use the information to cut us out of the running for—"

"You've got this all wrong," she said, more confused than ever. He thought she was after money, taking those files from the country?

"Fortunately," the corporate mouthpiece went on, "the stolen files have been recovered."

Ruby's heart lurched. "*Recovered*? You mean that was your guy at the airport? He was the one who . . ."

She let the question trail off, wondering why DeserTek would take her family if they'd already stolen the backpack and found the flash drive in it. Then why on earth was Best, a hired gun, demanding the drive's return? Unable to make sense of Worth's words, she was terrified to say more. Better first to figure out what he was after rather than to risk saying the wrong thing.

Just keep it together, Ruby. For your family's sake.

"As I was saying, the files have been recovered. Because DeserTek would prefer to avoid any unpleasant associations in the public eye, we are prepared to forgive this clear-cut case of corporate espionage—"

"You're kidding," Ruby protested. "I drove buses for you, Mr. Worth. Bus drivers don't do 'corporate espionage.'"

"Considering that the files were found among your personal possessions, that would be a difficult point of view for you to defend. As well as an incredibly expensive one, should we be compelled to move forward on the civil suit we're preparing."

Ruby's head was spinning. This made no sense whatsoever. If DeserTek really had the files, who else would be willing to use kidnapping to control them? Or was the company's internal communication to blame, with one department completely unaware of what another one was doing? A third possibility began to gel in her mind, the idea that they were after something other than the flash drive, something that she hadn't considered.

Though she wanted desperately to demand that he tell what he knew about her family, she forced herself to couch her question carefully. "What is it you want? Whatever it is, I'm listening."

"We expect you to abide by the terms of your contract. Meaning that no copied DeserTek trade secrets will turn up elsewhere and you will speak to no one attempting to extract privileged information for the purpose of damaging the company's position."

"Trade secrets," she decided, must be code for Carrie Ann's list of dead employees. What Worth wanted, Ruby surmised, was a guarantee that she had no intention of appearing before the congressional committee or the media, no inclination to tell tales of a photogenic young redhead out of Oklahoma who'd been all too conveniently decapitated by "insurgents." God forbid a few dead peons should interfere with DeserTek sinking its teeth into the juicy new contract it was drooling after.

She could almost hear Sam asking her, *"If you can't stand against systematic murder, then what can you stand against?"* Could almost see the disappointment dawning in his eyes.

"And if I give you my word?" Ruby asked, willing to promise anything, surrender any ideal, for the chance Worth would assure her that her family would be released unharmed.

"In exchange for your word," Worth said, his voice hardening with each word, "we're prepared to halt plans to file a six-point-three-million-dollar lawsuit that will bury you in debt and possibly go on for decades. Considering that you're a single parent—I believe I read that in your file—I'm certain you wouldn't wish to put your family through such an ordeal."

Ruby frowned, wondering whether this, too, was corporate-speak from a man who knew better than to mention a kidnapping over the telephone. Or whether he truly didn't have a clue about the abduction. With the strain splintering her patience, she burst out, "Listen, you son of a bitch, I have spoken to no one—not a soul—about this and I never had the desire, the time, or the equipment to copy or e-mail anything. You have it all in your hands. Every damned thing you want. All I'm after is my family's *safety,* their *security.* Right this fucking minute, do you hear me? Or so help me—"

She blew out a breath, thinking, *Way to keep it together, Ruby.*

There was a long pause before the manager said carefully, "I agree, family security *is* important. Which is why, in recognition of your exemplary service to DeserTek, we are prepared, in exchange for your signature on another nondisclosure agreement, to offer you a one-time bonus of fifty thousand dollars."

The idea of the offer—the insult of another bribe after everything she'd gone through—sent yet another hot wash of fury cascading through her system. It was one thing to be blackmailed, quite another to allow this son of a bitch to imagine for a second she'd embroiled herself in this fiasco over money.

"Fifty grand," she snapped. "Do you honestly think for a second that makes up for any of this? My family— the people who mean most to me in this world—and my freaking house, which just *happened* to blow up the night I came back into town and—"

"Y-your house?" Worth stammered, sounding genuinely shocked. "Something happened—and what about your family, Mrs. Monroe? What's going on out there?"

"Bad luck, right? Or maybe you like to think I've earned bad karma, what with interfering with your—"

"Mrs. Monroe, surely you are not implying—a company the size of DeserTek would never stoop to—believe me," he said dryly, "all the teeth we need are in the mouths of our attorneys."

A long pause followed as Ruby wondered what chance a widowed nursing student from East Texas stood against the DeserTeks of this world, with their rabid packs of lawyers and their total disregard for any rule but profit. Well connected as they were, they could murder, steal, abduct, engage in bribery and the cruelest torture, and then assign some well-paid functionary to lie about it all. And no one dared to stop them, not even the U.S. Congress. What had she been thinking to let Carrie Ann give her that flash drive in the first place, much less to attempt to smuggle it out of the country?

"Overnight the form to me at the Dogwood post office, general delivery," she said as she pulled into the parking lot of Hammett's. "Or bring it here yourself. I'll sign anything you want. I just need this to be over, with my family safe at my side."

Ruby hung up, wishing she could believe her nightmare would soon end but unable to bring herself to trust anything that Worth had told her. Until she had her family back, she had to check out every possibility, track down each bit of information—and prepare as best she could to deal with Hobson Best.

As she strode down the hall that led to Paulie's office, Ruby heard Hammett's booming bass voice and saw his back turned to her just outside the door.

"I've got a business to run, Crystal, and the last thing I need is you holding some damned junkie prisoner back here. Let her leave if that's what she wants, and get your ass back out to work."

"But Ruby needs to—"

"Ruby needs to stand out of the way and let Wofford and her people handle this. I'm tired of having my business disrupted, tired of having all these outsiders poking around. Do you know the kind of trouble they could cause me?"

"Hey, Paulie." As he turned toward her voice, Ruby glowered at the huge man and said flatly, "I'm really sorry that my family's disappearance is proving such a *fucking inconvenience* for you."

He jerked back as if she'd struck a blow, his round face blanching. "I'm sorry, Ruby. Really sorry. I didn't mean for you to hear that."

"Probably not," she snapped, "since if it got around, that kind of insensitivity might be bad for business."

"Don't be like that," he pleaded, looking nothing like the intimidating tyrant he could be at times. "You know Anna and I both—we adore Misty and your daughter. We've been on our knees praying the authorities will find them."

Ruby reminded herself that for all his bluster, he'd allowed Sam the use of his personal cabin. That he had been a good, if flawed, boss to her sister for a lot of years and that everyone, including her, needed forgiveness now and then. "I'm sorry I chewed your head off," she said, her voice softening. "Just let me borrow your office for a little bit. Please, Paulie."

As he nodded, Crystal darted a nervous glance toward the door behind her, where they heard something fall.

"Listen, Ruby," she said, "Jackie's getting cold feet. She's climbing the walls in there."

"Who is? Do I know this person?"

Crystal shrugged. "She said something about remembering you from school, but I can't imagine that's right. For one thing, Jackie looks too old."

"Jackie . . ." Ruby rifled through her memory, trying to place the name. "You aren't talking about Jackie *Hogan?*"

"I'm pretty sure that's right."

Ruby probably wouldn't have recalled the name if it hadn't been for the rumor that Jackie, then a senior, had hooked up with a twenty-four-year-old drug dealer who sometimes beat her up. Strange that Jackie would remember Ruby, who'd been two years younger and too busy tending to her mother and her younger sister to have a social life.

"Trash, that's all she's ever been," Paulie grumbled. "Worked here when she was sixteen till I fired her ass for stealing from the register."

Ruby shook her head, confused. "Let me talk to her."

"Only person ought to question her is Wofford," Paulie said. "For all we know, she's heard about Misty and decided she could scam some money out of you for drugs."

"I didn't want the sheriff because I was afraid that Jackie would take off," Crystal said uncertainly, "but maybe Paulie's right."

"Now that I'm here, it can't hurt to talk to her," said Ruby, fingering the side of her purse for reassurance.

From inside the office came the sound of glass shattering.

"Damn it." Paulie threw open the door, where a scrawny woman with dirty mouse-brown hair held up a chair beside a broken window.

Her pale face glistening with sweat, she wheeled around and pointed the four chair legs toward the doorway as if to ward off lions. The spaghetti strap of a filthy top had fallen off a blade-thin shoulder, and her legs jutted beneath a skirt that fit her like a grocery sack. "I fuckin' told you," she said to Crystal in a smoker's voice coarse as a squawking crow's. "I can't wait around here. I told you, I can't do it."

"Put down that chair and sit," Ruby said, stunned to see the wreckage of a trashy but head-turning high school beauty. "You said you'd see me, and here I am. So

I'd really appreciate it if you'd tell me what you know about my sister."

"I gotta go," Jackie repeated.

"Answer and you're free to leave, I promise," Ruby told her. "Otherwise, Paulie's pressing charges for this damage."

"Damned right I am," he bellowed, causing the woman to shrink back. "All I have to do is pick up that telephone, and I'll have deputies before you finish cussing me about it."

The woman looked at each of them in turn, then glanced toward the shattered window as if to gauge her chances of scrambling out before they grabbed her.

"Please tell her about Misty," Crystal said. "This could turn out to be important. This could save a little girl."

"Screw a little girl," growled Jackie, at which point, Ruby pulled the handgun from her purse.

"You don't want to answer for my family's sake, then answer because you don't want me to blow your head off that scrawny little neck."

"Ruby." Crystal shrank back, her eyes huge.

At the same moment, Paulie warned, "Not in my place, Ruby. I won't have this here, you understand me?"

But Jackie stared at the gun before slowly lowering the chair. Perching on the seat's edge, she stared up sullenly, her bruised arms crossed over her narrow chest.

"Fine. I'll talk to you." Her pale blue eyes fastened on to Ruby's before she nodded in Paulie's direction. "Not the pig, not the fluff, just you, Ruby Monroe. And then I walk out with no trouble."

"Deal," said Ruby, then glanced toward Crystal and Paulie. "I need a half hour."

"Ruby, you can't do this," Crystal pleaded, tears

streaming down her face as she looked at her boss. "I didn't know there would be a *gun*."

"This is a family restaurant," Paulie warned. "I've got goddamned little kids out there eating chicken nuggets. I'll give you fifteen minutes to get that woman out of my place. Make it ten, and then I call the sheriff."

"Okay," she agreed. "I'll make it quick, and then we'll be gone."

"Let's go, Crystal." Paulie laid a huge hand on the waitress's shoulder and spoke gently. "We have customers to see to."

Once they left the room, Jackie leaned forward to ask Ruby, "Got any cigarettes?"

When Ruby shook her head, Jackie asked, "How 'bout some cash, then? You know, for smokes and stuff."

Ruby began to suspect Paulie had been right about the woman, that she was simply trying to exploit a tragedy that had caught her ear.

"I don't have any money," Ruby said carefully. "I'm told my sister took off with it. Thought you might be able to offer a little insight on that."

The skinny shoulders shrugged, reminding Ruby of an animated scarecrow.

Jackie's eyes narrowed as she leaned forward. "Here I thought you were gonna turn out to be so fuckin' pure and perfect and smart. All I can say is if you trusted your sister with your money, you're just plain stupid. Nobody can trust nobody these days. Too many damn temptations in this world. Your man sure as hell knew that."

Ruby nearly choked on her own fury. "You didn't know Aaron and you don't know me, so quit with the bullshit before I have Paulie call the sheriff."

If the woman had been worth the effort, Ruby would have added that there *were* good people, people who fought off the kinds of temptations that ruled the creeps in Jackie Hogan's circle. From her neighbor Sam McCoy to so many of those she'd met in the war zone, Ruby had seen people risking everything to help others. People like Carrie Ann, who had risked her life—and maybe lost it—to warn a stranger not to file a grievance against her supervisor.

Guilt stung Ruby's eyes, whispered that she might have saved Carrie Ann if she'd only dared to act. Saved her or lost her own head for a near stranger.

Lips pressed together tightly, Jackie clutched the edges of her seat and glanced toward the door.

"Come on," Ruby urged. "Just tell me. What tempted my sister? You told Crystal you saw Misty. Unless you were lying about that, too."

"I saw her, all right." Jackie wouldn't meet her gaze.

Ruby sat on the edge of a second chair and whispered, "Was my daughter with her? Was my little girl there?"

Jackie nodded, looking up, her gaze hard with disapproval. "She shouldna had her at that party. Shouldna come there with no kid."

Though Ruby tried to control her reaction, the gun shook visibly in her hand. "Was she—was Zoe all right?"

"The kid? She was kinda scared of Coffin's dogs. Those big fuckers are nasty, and his friends aren't hardly any better."

"Is this Coffin the same guy with the 666 on his cheek?"

Nodding, Jackie laughed until she coughed. "That's really somethin', ain't it?"

Heat rushed to Ruby's face, and her knees wobbled with the confirmation. "My—my daughter was with . . ."

"She was there, yeah," said Jackie, "but she calmed down after a while. Dylan got her some toys n' shit to play with. And Misty, she'd rip the eyeballs out of anybody who looked at that kid crosswise. Still, it wasn't right—"

"Dylan? You're talking about Dylan *Hammett?*" Ruby broke in.

Jackie once more glanced at the door, then nodded. "Yeah, Dylan. Misty showed up to get him."

"Showed up where?"

Another shrug. "At Coffin's mama's place, back in her pool house. But don't tell Dylan's old man he was hanging with us. Dylan can't handle any more of his shit right now."

"You're saying Misty's involved with Dylan Hammett?" Ruby asked, still unable to believe it. Sure, the two of them had been close at one time, but their platonic friendship had ended when he'd refused to take responsibility for Crystal's pregnancy. Besides, Dylan was married, and married men were something Misty didn't do. Ruby felt sick, wondering how she could accept the word of some skanky, drug-riddled "witness" over her knowledge of her own flesh and blood.

But she could no longer ignore the signs that something had gone very wrong with Misty, something she had clearly taken pains to hide. As she might hide a pregnancy resulting from an affair with a married man, especially one who'd fathered her own best friend's child. . . .

Jackie nodded. "Hell, yeah, she was into Dylan. She was hangin' all over him. Leanin' on his shoulder, pullin' on his arm. But when he wouldn't leave with her, she stuck around and chilled awhile. So we talked about some people we both used to know. And she told me you was the one my Aaron Monroe finally hooked up with."

A warning prickled at the base of Ruby's neck, but she

reminded herself that now was no time to worry over Jackie's intimations about Aaron. Wrenching her mind back to Zoe and Misty, Ruby asked, "Who else was there? Anybody named Best? Hobson Best?"

Jackie shook her head. "Never heard of him."

Ruby wasn't sure whether to believe her. But then, it seemed ludicrous to think that a professional assassin sent in by DeserTek would hang out with the local stoners. "Was my sister using at the party? Did you see her take any—"

Jackie's gaze snapped back. "Did one visit to Coffin's turn her into some kind of crack whore, you mean? What's the matter, you worried I'm contagious?"

"No. I don't—" But Ruby didn't know what she meant. "Please, my daughter. I just have to know about my daughter."

Jackie's expression softened, so her pale eyes looked inhabited instead of empty. "Listen, put away the damned gun. I'm here because I heard Aaron's kid was missing and because"—she tapped a chest diminished from its glory days—"because, hell, I still got a heart in here, you know?"

Ruby slipped the handgun back inside her purse. "I'm sorry about that. It's been a hell of a last couple days, and I'm feeling pretty desperate. The sheriff thinks—she's got an idea Coffin might have them. Or might've hurt them, depending on how things went."

"Coffin? That son of a bitch would sell his mother's kidneys if could find a payin' market. He liked the look of Misty, kept going on about what a 'prime piece' she was, which frankly pissed me off. But Dylan made it clear that she was his, you know? Told Coffin that no matter how much he owed, she and the kid were both off-limits."

If they could be found safe, if all this really turned out

to be related to some drug deal, Ruby thought she might kiss Dylan's cheating lips instead of wringing his neck.

"Do you think Dylan and Misty might still be together?" Ruby asked. "Do you think he could've run out on his wife and taken my sister and my daughter somewhere?" *Somewhere safe* . . .

The blade-thin shoulders hunched another shrug. "I don't know. Could be, I guess. What I told you's all I know about it, really."

"What about my house? Have you and your friends ever been to my house?" Two of those friends, Ruby suspected, had never made it out.

Jackie darted a look toward the window. "Do you think Hammett's already called the deputies? That fat shit's always hated me, accused me of stealing when I didn't."

"We still have a few minutes," Ruby assured her, though she hadn't bothered to keep track of the time. "So answer me, please, Jackie. Were you ever—"

"You're stalling, aren't you, Ruby? Trying to get me thrown in jail."

"Were you ever in my house?" Ruby demanded.

Jackie's anger shifted to a look of slyness, making Ruby instantly regret her question.

"Guess your husband never mentioned me, huh?" asked Jackie. "Never talked about our way-back-when? Yeah, I've been to your place. Sneaked in through a back window."

"Why are you lying to me?"

Jackie laughed, clearly amused by her distress. "Fucked my brains out in his bedroom, with his mama and his daddy fast asleep down the hall. That foster kid, too— we laughed our asses off to hear Sam snoring in the next room, never guessing, while we went at it like—"

"I don't need to hear this." Even if it were true, Ruby

told herself it didn't matter. Aaron had never pretended to be a virgin.

Yet the other woman's sneer, her unspeakable claims, made Ruby want to pull the gun out of her purse and pistol-whip her.

"Don't worry," Jackie said. "It was over in no time flat, once the stick turned blue."

"You lying bitch." Furious, Ruby was reaching for the bag when, with a startled gasp, Jackie jumped up from her seat. But she wasn't worried about Ruby. Instead, her gaze was on the parking lot, where Deputy Savoy was climbing out of a marked SUV.

"Oh, shit," Jackie announced as she shoved past Ruby on her way to the door. "That rat-bastard Hammett."

Ruby didn't try to stop her as she bolted down the hallway. But Jackie didn't get far. Chaos erupted in the dining room, in full view of Paulie's customers, several of whom panicked when Jackie snatched a knife off a table as she raced past.

Assessing the situation quickly, Deputy Savoy yelled, "Freeze. Sheriff's Department," and rushed after her with his gun drawn.

Emerging from the kitchen with an apron tied around her thick middle, Anna Hammett shrieked at the sight of the knife-wielding woman rushing toward her. Customers screamed, and children's heads were pushed down beneath tables. One man started swearing at the deputy, and a quick-thinking waitress—the same young black woman who had retrieved Crystal for Ruby a day earlier—shoved a chair out into Jackie's path.

With her frantic gaze flicking from the deputy to Anna, Jackie never saw it coming. Catching one leg on the chair, she flew over it, then landed with a sharp cry.

"She's on the knife," screamed the waitress. "Oh God, she came down on the—"

"No! Goddammit." Struggling to get up, Jackie streamed profanity and pressed a hand to her thigh, which was spouting blood. The blade clattered to the floor, and quick as thought, the waitress kicked it spinning out of reach.

"Calm down, Jackie. Please calm down." Grave and dignified in spite of his hard breathing, Deputy Savoy approached the injured woman, whom Ruby suspected he'd arrested in the past.

She edged backward, thinking that she'd seen enough.

A hand clapped down on Ruby's shoulder. "Where're you off to?"

She looked up at Paulie Hammett. "I'm going to stop by for a visit with your son. Jackie says she saw him with my sister. At a party. And he was messed up, Paulie. Messed up the way he used to—"

"That's horseshit. Dylan's been over all that for a long time." Paulie loomed above her. "You can't seriously believe her. Ever since the first time I set eyes on that Jackie, she's been trouble."

Paulie glanced back toward the dining room, where parents were gathering their children, others were shouting for their checks while Anna fluttered among them and appealed for calm and reason. "I have to get back out there, try to convince folks Hammett's is a safe place. Meanwhile, you leave Dylan out of all this."

"Listen, Paulie, if he's seen my family, if he's wrapped up with drug dealers—"

Paulie's face went crimson and he scowled at her, more threatening than ever. "Dylan's put that all behind him. Only twenty-seven, and he's already running his own remodeling business. Married a sweet girl, and they're thinking of starting a family, giving us a real grandchild, any time now. You want to spoil that for him, Ruby? Want to screw up the life he's worked so goddamned hard to build? Undo all of Anna's and my work—your sister's, too—and let's not forget the tens of thousands we spent on rehab and helping him buy the business. You want to wreck everything on the word of some damned junkie?"

"Of course not. That's why I have to go talk to him. Where's he living these days?"

Paulie glanced back toward the diners, then said, "All right, Ruby. I'll give you the address on one condition."

"What's that?"

"Leave that gun you're toting locked inside my desk drawer where it can't hurt anyone."

CHAPTER TWENTY

"Blondes make the best victims. They're like virgin snow that shows up the bloody footprints."
—Alfred Hitchcock

He'd thought he had her figured. Terrified, weak, and probably none too smart, his little bus driver should have gone to ground like a scared rabbit and stayed there, waiting for him to call her next move. Delay, he'd learned from long experience, drew panic tight as a noose. Uncertainty made things worse, and he'd done all in his power to keep her bewildered. Because his employer valued the quality of the target's fear, her sense of helplessness, nearly as much as the item sought.

Because when the time was right, they needed the word of it to spread like oil on the water, a toxic nightmare that would be spoken of for years.

And yet he spotted Ruby Monroe, roaring down the road in her dead friend's car. Racing along as if she meant to skip town . . . or was in the midst of carrying out some plan.

Braking the vehicle he'd "appropriated," he made a three-point turn to follow. Because whatever she was up to, it was his business to find out. And to make her understand that he was in control here, that she was completely helpless.

He needed her to know that nothing she did would make a single bit of difference. That like the predators of this realm, he would deal out death as he saw fit.

That once this was all over, once he had the item she had hidden, he would leave her broken, bleeding, just another bloody corpse to feed the stinging ants and worms and serve as warning. Another chance to prove that he was always—no exceptions—as good as his word.

For most of his professional life, Sam had played the part of hacker, testing security systems for governments, businesses, and, most often, financial institutions. He worked for hours, sometimes days straight, probing weaknesses, slicing his way inside, and then suturing shut the same loopholes he'd exploited.

But today, he wasn't looking to correct an Achilles' heel. All he cared about was working his way through the labyrinth of defenses of one particular bank. With no time to reinvent the wheel, he risked logging in to and harvesting some code he'd stored in an online vault before his arrest, code he modified to build an SQL injection attack.

Without Sybil's assistance, the attack could be traced back to him if the breach were discovered and the right investigator dug into it. Sam figured it could cost him at least twenty years in custody, since the feds had zero sense of humor when it came to bank intrusions. . . .

And all for a woman, the woman and the child of the foster brother who had gotten him thrown out of the only stable home he'd ever known. Sam could almost hear his lawyer screaming, calling him a dumb-ass gringo. Could almost see himself nodding his head in agreement.

Because he went ahead and did it, thinking that the preservation of his half-assed life scarcely tipped the balance when weighed against the safety of two women and a child.

Java whined and shuffled her paws, then shot him the long-suffering look of a Lab with a full bladder. Though he hated the interruption, Sam pushed his chair back from the table and scratched her ears, then took his best friend outside.

Only then did Sam notice that the sky, though clear, was dimming. Shouldn't he have heard from Ruby by now?

Back inside, he used the phone Sybil had sent to call Ruby's number. To his relief, she answered on the second ring.

"Hello?"

"It's Sam," he said, hearing the anxiety in her voice. "Just wondering if you'd found out anything. Did you meet with Crystal's friend?"

"Yeah, and what a trip that was. But she gave me some information." Ruby detailed the conversation, including the woman's claims that Misty had been with Dylan Hammett, who had supposedly fallen off the wagon with a thud.

"Paulie's going to go ballistic." Sam figured that he and Anna had dug deep in their own pockets to allow their son to buy Tex-Appeal Exteriors. And Paulie Hammett, for all his money, had never been the type to part with his funds lightly.

"He already has, but if there's any truth to Jackie's story, I'm about to find out," Ruby told him. "I'm in Dylan's subdivision now."

"You're going to his house? Did you call first and check if he's home?"

"I was afraid he'd take off if I gave him any warning," she admitted, "especially if his wife's around."

"Holly thinks he hung the moon," Sam warned, thinking of how happy, how vivacious the bubbly brunette had been at the wedding, imagining her joy extinguished like a burning match dropped into water. "So you might try to get him off by himself, or he'll never talk."

He probably wouldn't anyway, Sam realized. People lied when they were caught relapsing into addiction. He thought about his father, breaking promise after promise. Thought of how his failures—including his physical abuse—had dimmed the light behind Sam's mother's eyes.

"I'll make Dylan understand," said Ruby. "I'll convince him somehow. If he's still around, that is. If he hasn't run off with my family."

"I'll try tracking him from this end."

"One more thing," Ruby added. "I had a really strange call from a personnel guy named Graham Michael Worth at DeserTek. He's claiming they have the flash drive."

"What?" Sam's brain scrambled for purchase. If DeserTek really had the flash drive, why would they risk something as drastic as kidnapping? "You're sure this Worth's with DeserTek?"

"Positive, and I didn't understand it, either. First, he threatened legal action if I didn't keep my mouth shut, and then he offered me a fifty-thousand-dollar 'bonus' if I'd sign another confidentiality agreement. The way he was talking, I couldn't figure out if he was offering my family's safety or he didn't have a clue about what's really going on."

"What did you tell him?"

"I was afraid to give away too much, so I said I'd sign anything he wanted. All I'm after is my family's safety."

"This is really strange," Sam said. "Makes me wonder who—hell, I don't know what to think about it, either. Could it be a case of the left hand not knowing what the right is doing?"

"Makes sense that only a few key players would know. God knows what'll happen when Elysse's stepbrother finds out his own company was involved in her death. Did you know Jeremy works for DeserTek? He's helped a few people from the area get hooked up with them."

"Bray?" Sam remembered that asshole from high school. Not fondly, either.

"He's a safety engineer now. Still kind of a jerk—loves lording it over anybody he's helped—but he did pull some strings to get me started."

"That was quite the favor," Sam said dryly.

There was a long pause before Ruby said, "Listen, I'm almost at Dylan's now. So let's try to figure all this stuff out later."

"Call me as soon as you talk to him. And I want you to be careful. Because at this point, Dylan Hammett's got a lot to lose."

"And I've got a lot to get back." Ruby sounded fierce, determined. "So maybe he's the one who'd better watch his step."

CHAPTER TWENTY-ONE

Murder, though it have no tongue, will speak
With most miraculous organ.

—William Shakespeare,
Hamlet, act II, scene ii, ln. 630

The shadows had grown long by the time Ruby found the right street, but there was still light enough to see that Dylan's neighborhood was new, with many of the houses still under construction. The entrance of the up-scale subdivision boasted a large stone sign bathed by a fountain, which endlessly anointed the words LAKEVIEW VILLAGE ESTATES. Ruby noticed, too, that most of the old trees—including some sprawling grandfather live oaks, had been spared in the building process instead of being bulldozed as they often were at less expensive building sites.

Either the new wife had big money, or Dylan's contracting business was bringing in a lot more than Ruby would have guessed.

The Hammetts' handsome brick one-story house, with its two-car garage, was situated atop one of Preston County's highest points. Dylan and his bride had chosen well, orienting the back of their home to overlook a broad and sparkling arm of the vast lake several hundred feet below. Better yet, the view behind the house was almost pristine, thanks to the wooded state preserve lands on the opposite shore.

But Ruby knew if she had a pair of field glasses she'd be able to pick out the side-by-side lots where Sam's house kept watch over the ruins of her own. In a fast boat, a person—say, a cheating husband—could reach those ruins from the subdivision's boat docks in less than twenty minutes, though it would take more than twice that long for a car to make the trip.

She wondered if Dylan had a boat, then decided she'd be hard-pressed to find a man who'd grown up on this lake who didn't own one. Especially a man who'd been brought up doing every job there was at Hammett's, including boat maintenance and guiding.

Looking at the house, with its well-tended lawn and blooming spring flowers in the beds, made Ruby doubt the story of its owner's relapse. Addicts didn't rake or pull weeds; they didn't mow or edge lawns. But as she walked toward the front door, she noticed subtler signs of neglect. Yellowed newspapers in their wrappers bordered the white driveway. Every shade was drawn, with the dried husks of dead flies lying on the sills behind them, and the delicate filaments of spiderwebs strung across the doorway.

Did that mean something was amiss, something that could not be cleaned or covered up by a yard service? Or were the newlyweds just more fascinated by each other than housecleaning?

Sex definitely ranked way ahead of housework in Ruby's book. Not that she'd had any of the former since Aaron—she hadn't even dated, not once, since he . . .

A flush singed her cheeks at the realization that, for the first time ever, it was not her husband she pictured when she thought of making love. It was Sam McCoy, who was risking his freedom in an attempt to help her family; Sam, who cared whether she slept or ate and whose kiss had lit a long-untended fuse at the least likely time imaginable. Though his kiss had alighted on her as gently as a dragonfly, she felt the trembling of its wings still: diaphanous, unceasing, and warming her in spots left far too long untended.

"McCoys steal—everybody knows that." Elysse's voice whispered through her memory like a breeze stirring the tips of the tall grasses that grew near the lake's edge. *"Expect anything different, and you've got nobody but yourself to blame."*

Fresh grief sucked the air from Ruby's lungs, hazed her vision with unshed tears. Pushing it aside, she forced herself to ring the bell.

When neither Dylan nor his wife came to the door, Ruby wondered if it was possible the two had left for a vacation. Or maybe both of them were working late.

Sighing, Ruby pulled her phone from her purse and called Hammett's, where she asked for Paulie.

"Do you have Dylan's work number?" she asked as soon as he came on the line.

"He's not home yet?" Paulie asked her.

"No one's answering. He hasn't said anything to you about going away, has he?"

"No, but to tell you the truth, I haven't seen him the last couple weeks. He's been busy, we've been busy—doesn't mean the boy's in trouble," Paulie hastened to assure her. "Doesn't mean a damned thing, except he and Holly prefer a little privacy."

Ruby was in no mood for Hammett's bluster. "I'm not saying it means anything, but how about that number? Or do I have to call directory assistance?"

"No need to snap at me. I'll give you his cell phone. That's what he uses for his business."

He rattled off the number, which Ruby scribbled on the back of her hand with a pen.

"And don't jump all over his ass when you call him," Paulie warned. "I don't give a cockeyed damn what that sleaze Jackie told you. My boy's got nothing to do with your sister and Zoe going missing. Not a thing. You hear that?"

"Sure thing, Paulie," Ruby told him. Hell, as loudly as he was shouting, half of Dogwood probably heard him. "And speaking of Jackie, is she okay?"

"They took her to the hospital, but she'll be in the county jail before long. Take more than a sliced thigh to kill that one." Hammett sounded almost disappointed.

After hastily thanking him for the information, she ended the call and punched in Dylan's number before turning toward the sound of a car's passing. As an older-model Ford Mustang with tinted windows slipped around the corner, she turned her attention back to her phone.

Dylan's line rang four times before going to voice mail. Unsure of whether to risk spooking him by leaving a message, Ruby hesitated. Before she made up her mind, an automated voice told her the customer's mailbox was full.

Frowning, Ruby wished she'd asked for Dylan's new wife's number. But Ruby couldn't imagine asking a total stranger, *"Is your new husband screwing my sister? Have you found crystal meth or condoms in Dylan's sock drawer lately? Or maybe not the condoms. I'm thinking he might not've been using them with Misty."*

Stupid, she was being stupid, allowing squeamishness to throw a barricade in her path. Or maybe it wasn't that, but Ruby's vivid recollection of a time when she had been a young bride, with complete trust in her husband. A time before financial worries and the deaths of Aaron's parents had intruded on their bliss. . . . Like a fool, she had assumed that time remained for them to rebuild, had never guessed more tragedy was waiting in the wings.

With no time to finesse, Sam downloaded all the data files he could get to before someone discovered an intrusion and shut down the system. As a result, he had access to financial records not only from Misty Bailey's and Ruby Monroe's accounts, but from those of a number of locals who did business with Dogwood's largest bank.

Splitting his display screen, Sam pulled up two sets of records and carefully compared them, then flipped through several more . . .

Until one pair had him swearing, his hand darting for the cell phone to call Ruby. To call Ruby and to warn her that danger could be coming from an unexpected quarter.

Not wanting anyone to see her damp face, Ruby didn't turn toward the sound of another vehicle on the street behind her. Instead, she waited for it to pass by before peering up and down the block.

Since the only sign of life she spotted was a pair of squirrels, she walked the house's perimeter. Along its side, she stopped and stood on tiptoe to look inside through tiny gaps between a shade and window casing. The rooms inside appeared dark, and not even cupping her hands around her eyes to block out the fading light helped.

She had nearly reached the backyard when she heard a noise—a click, she thought—though she couldn't say from which direction. Her first impulse was to freeze, heart thumping, but soon she looked around, taking in the light breeze chasing through the tree branches and carrying the sound of children's voices, perhaps from the next street. Could the noise that had startled her have been a bat cracking a baseball? A bicycle's tire rolling over pebbles?

Neither possibility concerned her, so she continued moving around a bed containing white azaleas and into the backyard. There, a patio had been built behind a set of huge back windows, left uncovered so the newlyweds could take in their expensive view of the lake below the hillside.

Though a spectacular sunset was taking shape in that direction, Ruby had no interest in looking out over the water. Instead, she hurried toward the windows—only to be stopped dead by the sight of the back door, left ajar.

Her heart pounded a staccato warning. Was someone hiding inside, someone who had chosen to ignore the ringing doorbell? Could that same someone have been watching her progress as she walked around the house?

But that hardly made sense, for if anyone had seen her, wouldn't he or she have closed and locked this back door? And when Ruby looked through the large windows, she saw no lights left on inside.

But she could make out what looked like one hell of a disaster. Despite her caution, curiosity had her edging closer, moving close enough to press her face against the glass.

Inside, the kitchen cabinets were all open, their contents spilled out onto countertops or smashed on tile floors. Drawers had been pulled out and dumped in the family room, and someone had slashed the cushions of an expensive-looking sectional sofa and overturned some potted plants. The unexpected violence of the destruction had Ruby sucking in a sharp breath and instinctively taking a step backward, which gave her a watercolor view of the reflected sunset . . .

And the murkier reflection of a large man rushing at her from behind.

Screaming, she wheeled around to face him and ducked reflexively at the sight of something—maybe a length of two-by-four—swinging like a baseball bat toward her head. The movement saved her skull, but before she could get out of range, her attacker leapt at her, knocking Ruby off her feet.

She caught the barest glimpse of tattoos as the horizon tilted and the back of her head cracked against the window glass. She collapsed as if he'd ripped the spine out of her. And as she lay on the concrete, blinded by the starbursts of bright pain in her vision, she felt rough hands knot in her clothing, heard the harsh scrape of foul breath and the tearing of her shirt.

When his hands fumbled at the fly of her jeans, a cry of pure rage erupted from her lungs. Adrenaline ripping through her, she clawed and kicked and rammed her stiffened fingers into one of his eyes.

"Fucking bitch," he bellowed, grabbing the torn neckline to shake her like a terrier dispatching vermin.

She fought to pull her knees up and landed a mule kick to his rib cage, but her attacker backhanded her hard enough that fireworks exploded before her eyes in reds and whites and livid purples.

The last thing Ruby sensed, before the colors faded, was a crack that exploded loud as lightning close beside her. A crack that was accompanied by a sharp, burnt-bitter stink that shouted, *Bullets!*

CHAPTER TWENTY-TWO

I am not resigned to the shutting away of loving hearts in
  the hard ground.
So it is, and so it will be, for so it has been, time out of
  mind:
Into the darkness they go, the wise and the lovely.
  Crowned
With lilies and with laurel they go; but I am not re-
  signed.

—Edna St. Vincent Milay,
from "Dirge Without Music"

As Sam mashed down the Yukon's gas pedal, Pacheco's voice held court in his head, where it ripped into him in a profane pastiche of border slang and English. "You tryin' to send me to Tahiti for my next vacation, *ese?* 'Cause you're digging yourself the deepest fucking hole I ever seen. *Estúpido! Cabrón!* Turn your ass around and get back to your own place."

"No turning back now," he grumbled as he slung the SUV around a sharp turn, one he took so fast, he sent a spray of pebbles peppering the side of a black Mustang that slid past the range of his headlights on its way out of the subdivision.

He had no choice but to act on what he'd learned, information that he suspected would quickly make its way back to Sheriff Wofford—whose bank accounts had swollen like a flood-stage river lately.

But he couldn't imagine turning his back on Ruby, a woman who had trusted him with not only her life, but those who meant the most to her. Maybe it was that very trust that had brought down his defenses. Or maybe he'd simply decided that his isolated existence was unworthy of the cost of keeping the walls standing.

Whatever the reason, he hadn't hesitated for a minute when she didn't answer her phone. Instead, he'd grabbed the laptop and the flash drive, unwilling to risk leaving either, called Java, who would most likely eat something that would kill her if she was left alone, and hopped into his Yukon. Already on the fly, he called Paulie to get Dylan's phone number and new address.

Because Justine Wofford's bank accounts were not the only ones that had shown unusual activity. In the younger Hammett's case, that activity had correlated closely with withdrawals from the accounts Misty Bailey had controlled. Over the past few weeks, various amounts, from a check for fifteen grand to a number of smaller cash deposits, had slowed Dylan Hammett's dizzying, downward spiral, which included numerous cash withdrawals and overdraft charges from the bank in the past months.

Undoubtedly, the stupid bastard would be less than happy when Ruby showed up in the flesh with questions. Though he'd never seemed the violent type, if Dylan felt backed into a corner, God only knew what he might do to break free. Especially if he'd killed Misty—maybe even accidentally—to keep her quiet after bleeding her dry.

Sam slowed to check the numbers on the houses, but as he rounded a curve, he caught sight of Elysse's white car, parked beneath a streetlamp. Gut tightening, Sam glanced toward the dark house but saw no sign of Ruby or anyone at all.

He pulled up behind the car and parked before once more trying Ruby's number and then Dylan's. When both phones rolled to voice mail, Sam said, "Java, stay," and climbed out of the Yukon.

He didn't get two steps before turning back to grab a flashlight. But when he opened the rear door, the young Lab saw her chance and leapt out barking. Though Sam cursed the noise, he decided not to waste time trying to corral her. For one thing, a man chasing his loose dog was far less threatening than a stranger rushing around a dark house with a flashlight.

To beef up the impression, he whistled for Java—who leapt and barked about him playfully, enjoying this new game after a long day spent cooped up in the cabin.

When he reached the door, he pounded and then tried the doorbell. Hearing no response, he called loudly, "Dylan? Dylan, it's Sam McCoy. I've got a flat, man. Can you give me a hand?"

Shutting up, he listened intently, but the only sounds that came to his ears were the buzz of evening insects, the sound of an automatic garage door rising somewhere down the block. Unable to see anything inside, he decided to go around back. Java raced ahead of him, tongue lolling and tail wagging.

Sam spotted something in the grass ahead, something that turned out to be a cell phone. Picking it up, he recognized the phone's spring green outer case as Ruby's—and then he saw a set of keys, including one bearing a Toyota emblem, only steps away.

"Shit, shit, shit." His mouth chalk-dry, he scooped the keys up—then heard, from around the corner, what might have been a human moan.

Java froze, growling softly as the hackles on her neck rose. She rushed forward for a few steps, then chickened out and doubled back to fall behind her owner as Sam crept forward, crouching and cutting off his flashlight. Terrified as he was for Ruby, he still was hesitant to race blindly into a situation he didn't understand and might somehow make worse.

But a soft cry, clearly feminine, made him forget his caution. "Ruby?" he called, racing around the corner and switching on the beam, which he swung wildly as he searched.

Until the light jerked to a stop at the partially nude and bloody human figure lying next to the back window. A figure that was struggling disjointedly to raise itself onto hands and knees.

He stared in horror, unable to make sense of what he was seeing, confused by the woman's bent neck and dripping hair.

Until finally, her face turned his way, and his horror took a sharp turn.

"Misty?" He dropped to his knees. "Misty? Is that you?"

Have to reach the surface. Break it. Kick off the chains and swim up, toward air and light. Toward life.

But the pain settled thick around her. Thick and heavy as the slimy muck of rotting vegetation, yet sticky somehow, like the tarry mud that sucked her feet down through the bottom of Bone Lake.

She felt her legs sink deeper, felt her body slipping through layer after layer of dark ooze. Panicking, she fought and struggled but only settled deeper—until she dropped into a blackness broken only by the leering face of the full moon.

CHAPTER TWENTY-THREE

"There is something haunting in the light of the moon; it has all the dispassionateness of a disembodied soul, and something of its inconceivable mystery."

—Joseph Conrad,
from *Lord Jim*

Instinctively, Sam reached to help the shivering, shirtless woman. Flinching at his touch, she dropped to a seated position, her head drooping as she groaned in pain.

"Easy there. It's me, Sam." He brushed back the stiff hair covering her face. "Misty, are you—is Zoe still with—"

The moment her eyes opened, he sucked in a startled breath, understanding that through some trick of the light and terror and the sisters' shared genetics, he had been mistaken. This was *Ruby,* not her sister.

With both relief and horror pounding through him, he laid his hand on her bare back, avoiding the worst of the blood for fear of hurting her. He pushed back the whining Java and said, "I'm calling for help, Ruby, and whoever did this—he's gone. So be still, lie still if you can and breathe."

"So deep," she moaned. "Under the water. I couldn't breathe. I couldn't—"

"You're nowhere near the lake." Using the light, he scanned her body for a deep cut, a gunshot, any wound serious enough to explain the quantity of blood staining her and puddling on the concrete. If he could find it, he could apply direct pressure, make a bandage, keep her from bleeding out while he called 9-1-1.

Keep her from dying right here and right now.

Yet as closely as he looked, he couldn't find the source. "Where are you hurt, Ruby? What did Dylan do to you?" Sam wanted to choke the bastard, pound his face to pulp—and when he noticed Ruby's open and unzipped jeans, nausea joined the mix of fury and raw fear pounding through his system.

She reached to the back of her head, wincing when she touched it. "Not Dylan. It was that man from the house, that horrible man with all the sixes on his face. I saw his reflection coming at me. Tried to get away, but he jumped me . . . banged my head against the window, there."

Sam turned his beam to follow her hand gesture and saw the faintest smudge of blood with a few hairs sticking to it. Two feet to the left and slightly lower, a softball-sized hole had been blown through the glass. Though he had a vague impression of a hellacious mess inside, he quickly returned the light to Ruby.

To his shock, she was sitting up, shuddering as she hugged her knees.

"There was a gunshot," she said, sounding astonishingly alert. "I heard it. But I don't know—I must've blacked out. We were—fighting. I was fighting because I wouldn't—I couldn't let him rip my clothes off. I tried—I tried to stop him, but he . . . I should've made him stop, Sam. I should have."

Sam's heart broke at the look in her eyes, at the suspicion of the violence done her. Taking off his own shirt, he draped it over her. "God, Ruby. It's not your fault. You couldn't have possibly . . . Hang on a minute while I make that call."

As he punched in the digits, her bloody hand clutched at his forearm. "Please don't," she pleaded. "I don't want anyone to—"

He shushed her as the dispatcher started speaking. Since he had used his satellite phone instead of Ruby's, he had to be transferred to the Preston County dispatch center.

"I'm *not* hurt, Sam, not really," Ruby insisted as he waited to be connected. Gingerly, she poked her arm inside a shirtsleeve. "No cuts, no bleeding, just this bump on my head. Don't you see? This isn't my blood. If I'd lost this much, I'd be dead, or damned close to it."

"They'll need to do some X-rays," he said while on hold. "And you'll need an examination. . . . There'll have to be a rape kit."

She shook her head, then grimaced and rubbed her neck. "I don't think that bastard raped me. I don't think he had time before someone blew him away."

Sam's attention jerked back to the hole through the window, which could very well have been caused by a bullet. So where was the tattooed man? And what about whoever supposedly had shot him?

"Nine-one-one dispatch," the operator said in his ear. "What is your emergency?"

"I need an ambulance. A woman's hurt at—"

"No," Ruby insisted, ripping the phone from him before he could give the address. As she disconnected, she said, "I can't afford to waste time at the ER or in a freaking interview room answering more questions. *He's* supposed to call tonight. About the exchange for my family."

Instead of arguing, Sam asked, "So you really think someone *shot* the guy attacking you?"

"I heard a bang while I was blacking out. And when I look at all this blood—somebody's hurting a heck of a lot worse than I am. I wonder where he went, though. I can't imagine he was in any sort of shape to run off."

"Unless he dragged himself off to die elsewhere, or

maybe the shooter took him along for some reason." Sam cut himself short as she struggled to stand. "Stay down, Ruby. We still have no idea where the shooter is or how badly you're hurt."

"Probably mildly concussed," she said, grimacing as she rubbed her head. "I know the signs. I've studied nursing."

He gave up and took her hand to help her. "Then you ought to know concussions can be bad news."

"Let's worry about that later, once we're out of here. Somebody else could've heard that shot and called the sheriff." She patted her hips, looked down at where her pockets hung inside out. "What happened to my keys?"

"I found them, with your phone, along the side of the house."

"Guess he got my credit card, then. Maybe that was what he really wanted in the first place, not rape."

Or maybe he'd been looking for the flash drive, Sam suspected.

"Hand me those keys, please," said Ruby.

"If you think I'm letting you drive—"

"I'm not abandoning Elysse's car." Bruised and bloody as she was, Ruby was stubbornness incarnate.

But she didn't have the market cornered on that commodity.

"Elysse is gone now, Ruby, and no way am I giving you the keys. Now let me help you to my truck, and let's get out of here before someone shows up."

Ruby pulled away from his grip, but after a few wobbly steps, she bent forward, groaning. He grabbed her arm to save her from going to her knees.

"All right." She shot him a sheepish look. "We'll try this your way, in your truck."

As they walked back along the side of the house, he

looked for any sign of Ruby's credit card, in case it had been dropped with the other items.

Gripping his hand, she whispered, "Listen, Sam. You hear that?"

Sam first heard some kind of mechanical noise—one that reminded him of a dentist drilling—and then made out an engine idling. Mostly hidden by the bulk of his SUV, the dark bumper of some lower-profile vehicle was all he could make out.

"Sheriff's department?" he asked, thinking Ruby might have gotten a better look.

"No flashing lights," she said.

"Let's move over this way, see if we can get a better angle—*hey!*" Sam heard the splash of liquid and belatedly, he understood the drilling sound. Letting go of Ruby, he ran toward his Yukon with Java at his heels.

He made it around the SUV in time to hear a car door closing and tires squealing as an older Mustang—one he recalled from only minutes earlier—took off in a hurry.

"Son of a bitch," Sam yelled, smelling the gasoline gushing from a round hole in the bottom of his tank.

When he saw Ruby weaving toward him, guilt gave him a swift kick. Hurrying back to her side, he said, "We're not going anywhere. Bastard punched a hole right through."

"What are you doing running out here in the open?" she asked. "That guy could've shot you."

He opened the Yukon, the thought jolting through him that the driver of the black car could have made off with their bargaining chips. Relief flooded him when he found the items safe and sound in the under-seat storage drawer where he'd left them. "Thank God, our stuff's still inside. If we'd lost the laptop and the flash drive . . ."

Ruby nodded, her expression grim. "Better forget about the truck for now. We'll take Elysse's car, if he didn't hit it, too."

Sam got down on his knees next to the Corolla but spotted no damage—or any suspicious-looking wires or boxes that might explain why the shooter wanted to force them to use it. Standing, he opened the passenger door for her.

Ruby hesitated, blinking down at the seat. "I hate getting her car all bloody."

"It'll be all right," he said. "We'll clean up her car later. Careful getting in there."

As Ruby sat, she groaned, once more raising her hand to cup the back of her head. When strength and coordination failed her, Sam lifted her right leg inside the car, then pulled her seat belt across her trembling shoulder. The dome light highlighted tear trails cutting through the blood smears, revealing the moon-pale face behind.

Despite the mess, he leaned in to kiss her temple. "Let's get you out of here."

He shut Java into the backseat and then drove out of the subdivision. "No emergency lights yet. Maybe no one heard anything—or understood what they were hearing."

"Another lucky break." Ruby smiled tiredly, the mask of blood smears crinkling. "I'm feeling so blessed."

Sam smiled back, relieved to hear a note of sarcasm. It meant she still had some fight left in her, more than he ever would have imagined. But what was it Elysse had once told him? Some quote about women and tea bags, how you could never guess the strength of either until they were dropped into hot water.

Certainly, that was when his mother's weakness became apparent. When the going got tough, when his father's drinking and disappearances and the constant money problems and sporadic bursts of violence turned too difficult, Brenda McCoy had left him and J.B. playing behind their room at the local motor court while she'd slipped into something more comfortable. Which had turned out to be a Greyhound bus.

Sam shook off the memory of coming inside after J.B.—a bullying ass-wipe even at the age of twelve—had opened a big gash on Sam's shin with the steel blade of a rusted shovel they'd found. The injury had bled like hell, but it was nothing to the pain, and the searing shame, of realizing she'd left them only seven crumpled dollar bills and a six-word parting message, a scribbled note that told them *Sorry, boys. Your mama's had enough.*

As he and Ruby rolled along the dark road, Sam thought about that refuge, the one place where his lame-ass family had remained welcome even in their bleakest hours. For years, he had avoided the place, had avoided the only soul, other than his brother, who knew the entire, sordid story of what it meant to be a McCoy.

"You'll always be safe here," she'd told him, that last terrible day. *"Till the day I die, I swear it."*

He'd sworn he would never take her up on it, would never put himself in a position where he'd be forced to sink so low. But tonight, his pride was going to have to take a backseat, he decided as he cut another look back Ruby's way. She might be a mess now, physically and emotionally, but somehow, she still sat upright with her blue eyes narrowed—looking mad enough to gnaw and claw her way through hell itself for her kid.

"Tell me everything you remember," he said, with the old nightmare of the motor court still rumbling like thunder in his head. "Everything from the moment you got over here. Maybe then, between the two of us, we can figure out what's really going on."

She shuddered, hugging herself inside his shirt. For a

moment, the facade of her strength trembled; then she started speaking. She recounted the facts slowly, taking her time to get details straight. Each time emotion seemed poised to overwhelm her, she took a deep breath, steeling herself to continue.

"Dylan was clean, for what?" he asked. "Four or five years, right? Not a single hiccup . . ."

"Not that anybody knew of. Seemed like he'd found himself, found his calling, when he got into the building trade."

"But when he stumbles for whatever reason, he tanks big time, gets into financial trouble with some very bad sorts. And somehow or other, he drags an old friend— your sister—into it."

"I just don't get it," Ruby said. "Misty and Dylan— they were kids together, working around Hammett's, always cutting up. More like a brother-sister thing than any kind of romance."

Sam, nine years older, had been long gone from the area during those years, but he'd heard as much. Yet the financial records hinted at a different truth. "She gave him money, Ruby. Probably thirty grand all told, according to what I found in her bank records."

"You broke into our *bank accounts*? How could—"

He shrugged. "I made a good part of my living testing bank security. Let's just say, First Bank of Dogwood got a really bad grade. And I hate to tell you this, but most of the money Misty gave him was yours."

"How generous of her," Ruby said darkly. "But it would have to be my money. Misty's been spending every cent she can scrape together on school and that high-dollar equipment she needed for her court reporter training. I imagine that's all up in smoke, too. But I don't give a damn about the money, or the house, either, for that matter, as long as I find Zoe and learn that Misty's all right. And *then* I'm going to strangle her for dragging me through hell."

"So what do you think happened back at Dylan's?" Sam asked. "You think Tattoo Man came looking for him, maybe over money?"

"I'm guessing the tattooed creep—I'm pretty sure he's Coffin—has been tearing apart that house for valuables because he knows Dylan's long gone. Which begs the question, where is *Mrs.* Dylan? Surely, Dylan didn't run off with both his wife *and* my sister."

"Doesn't seem too likely."

Ruby looked away, and several moments later, her voice drifted like that of a swimmer carried on the current. "I keep thinking about that crying, that child crying in the background of the phone call. Best's last call, if that's really who it is. What if he's not bluffing? What if Zoe's really with him, scared or hurting or— What if the DeserTek people tell him they have the flash drive? It's just killing me not knowing which way to turn, which place to look."

As Sam took a corner, Ruby looked from side to side. "Wait a minute. You aren't going—this isn't the way back to Paulie's cabin. Like I said, I can't risk going to the hospital or getting stuck at the sheriff's office, either. I can't take a chance on having Best call and—"

"Don't worry. There's no way I'm letting you within a mile of Wofford." He explained the recent wire transfers, tens of thousands at a time, that he'd found in her personal bank records.

"Wofford? I can't believe it. She seems so . . ."

"Honest? People fake that. Some of them, quite well."

"*Sharp.* I was going to say 'sharp,'" Ruby corrected. "Don't the banks have to report large deposits to the IRS?"

Sam glanced over at her, impressed that Ruby knew this. "Cash deposits, yeah, but she might've slipped under the radar with transfers from offshore if there weren't enough of them to trigger antiterrorism bank-reporting software."

"Where'd the money come from? Could you tell?"

"Some sham front company—Sunrise Happy Doodle International—doing business through a bank out of the British Virgin Islands. All untraceable, of course."

"Sunrise Happy Doodle, my ass," Ruby grumbled. "This has DeserTek written all over it. Still seems weird to think Wofford wouldn't know about those transfers attracting government attention."

"Wofford's local law enforcement, and not especially experienced. Besides, I've spent a lot of time doing computer forensics investigations to catch embezzling employees, and if it's taught me one thing, it's that greed makes people stupid. All kinds of people from all walks of life. They start showing up at work in fancy cars and flashy outfits. Wearing Rolexes instead of their usual cheap digitals, buying vacation condos for their honeys. You wouldn't believe the idiotic shit that people—"

"Where are we going, Sam? You still haven't told me."

"To the Hook-It-Cook-It." Ignoring the tightening in his gut, Sam thought of the horseshoe-shaped, fifties-era motor court he remembered so vividly, a collection of native-stone-walled relics. These days, he knew the rooms were rented almost exclusively to fifties-era fisherman and the occasional lost trucker, but it was the one place he could think of that might do.

"I thought that place was closed down."

"Not as long as Opal Carmichael is still breathing."

"She is? That woman must be—Lord, she was ancient when my family moved to Dogwood."

It didn't surprise Sam that Ruby knew Opal or knew of her. The woman might be pushing ninety, but she was also a Dogwood legend, famously opinionated and just as famously eccentric in her efforts to promote her business.

Now that Sam thought about it, she could have been the prototype for Paulie Hammett. "She's in amazing shape for her age, and better yet, she won't bat an eye when I walk in shirtless and pay cash for a room. Takes a heck of a lot to ruffle Opal's feathers." At least, she'd never seemed troubled whenever Sam's screwed-up family had bounced its unruly way back after an eviction. "She won't tell anyone our business."

"But it's so close to town," Ruby protested. "Someone will see the car or spot us going inside. Paulie's cabin—"

"Paulie's shack doesn't have hot water or a working shower. It doesn't even have a bed, just a nasty-looking mattress lying in a corner. No way am I taking you back there tonight, not in the shape you're in. The Hook-It's old, and it might smell like disinfectant, but Opal keeps it clean, and like I said—"

"When the authorities realize you aren't home, they're going to assume you've run, Sam. They'll hunt you down and catch you with that laptop and the cell phone."

He shook his head. "Doesn't matter, Ruby. What I did today, it's traceable if the right people start looking. And I can guarantee you, they will."

Ruby gave him a look that sliced straight through him. "When this is over, Sam—"

"When this is over, I'll be gone. I'm going to have to skip town soon as I can."

"Oh, Sam, I never meant for you to— Are you *sure*? If I explain why—"

"Last time, I had good reasons, too. I was trying to help an older couple I know, trying to help get back the retirement money that was stolen from them. But the rationale didn't matter then, and it'll matter even less now." He reached over and skimmed her jawline with his fingertips. "Listen, Ruby, don't worry about me. This is about your little girl, that's all."

"You're doing it for Aaron, too, aren't you, Sam? Because you really did care about him."

"Truth is, I hated the son of a bitch," Sam stated flatly.

"You—you hated Aaron, Sam? Why?" She sounded surprisingly troubled by the revelation.

"Doesn't matter, not at this point." Stress might be pulling at the edges of his old scars, threatening to rip them open, but now was hardly the time to dredge up ancient history. "What's important is, I *don't* hate you or Zoe. And Aaron's parents—no matter whose story they ended up believing—I owe both of them big time. This is just a fraction of the payment on that debt."

"Another time," Ruby said, "I intend to make you explain that."

Sam passed a low-slung, mom-and-pop grocery, boarded and abandoned since the construction of a new megamart across town. Most of the businesses along this road had gone the same route, save for a Dairy Queen and the motor court, whose black-lettered yellow sign was missing not only bulbs but letters. "Why don't you wait here while I go in and see Opal. And if anyone comes by, duck. If anybody sees you, they'll call an ambulance for sure."

Her eyes closed, she nodded an acknowledgment.

"Are you going to be all right out here?" he asked, wondering if he should call that ambulance himself.

"Go ahead. I'll be fine."

He hesitated another moment before he hurried inside, leaving the car idling.

A CLOSED signed hung behind the fly-specked window, but Sam saw someone moving inside and the door opened when he tried it. A compactly built woman with a thick brown ponytail stood with her back to him, pulling items from the desk and loading them into cardboard boxes.

"You come for a room, we're closed now," she called over her shoulder, speaking around the lit cigarette that dangled from her lips. "You come to rob us, there's no money . . . but you're welcome to as many of these butt-ugly decorations as you can carry off."

"Is Opal here?" Sam asked, eyeballing the web of tattoo art on the bare arm he could see. With its macabre mix of skulls, hearts, and daggers, it was weirdly beautiful, in a vintage biker art way. "I need to see her."

When the woman turned to look at him, he saw the flinch as she took in his shirtlessness and blood smears. Almost instantly, she recovered, her surprisingly young features hardening like concrete. "Get on out of here. Whoever you are, my grandmother's not well—and she sure as hell doesn't need your kind of trouble."

"I have to see her," Sam insisted. "Old friend. One of the McCoys, you tell her."

She lifted a handgun from the box, a little automatic that she held as if she knew what she was doing. As she pointed it in Sam's direction, her silver nose stud caught the light. "Maybe you didn't hear me?"

"Which one of the McCoys?" an elderly woman's voice called from a back room separated by a beaded curtain.

In spite of the circumstances, Sam smiled to hear it. "Miss Opal, it's me, Sam. Sam McCoy. I need your help."

The beads rattled as she popped her head through. Her hair had thinned and gone entirely white, and the arms poking from the sleeves of her housedress looked more like twigs than human limbs, but Sam would recognize her smile anywhere. "Right answer. If you'd said you were your brother, I might've told my Trisha to shoot you."

"You promised me you'd go rest, Gramma." The younger woman—Trisha, apparently—flicked a hard look in Sam's direction. "And your eyesight must be worse than we thought if you can't tell this is trouble."

Opal waved off her protest and felt her way toward the counter. "Come here, Sam. Come right up close and let me see you."

Trisha rolled her eyes, but her aim didn't budge. "He's bloody. He has no shirt. He could've killed somebody."

Her grandmother's face puckered as she knotted a fist on one thin hip. "How many times have you told me you hate it when people judge you by your tattoo or all those holes you insist on punching through the pretty face your mother and the good Lord gave you?"

Trisha rolled her eyes. "We're talking *blood,* not self-expression."

"A woman's been hurt," Sam said, then spat out the first story that sprang to mind. "Her husband hit her. And he'll kill us if he finds us. This was the only place I knew to go. The only place that felt safe."

"What did I tell you?" Trisha asked her grandmother. "This is *trouble.* I'm calling 9-1-1."

Before she could reach the telephone, the old woman moved quickly to grab it and warned her off with a look. "I'm not yours yet, Trisha, or those hospice people's or the mortuary's, either. I'm still my own, and that means I make my own decisions. For one more night, at least, and *this* night, I intend to honor an old promise to a scared boy. So you put that gun away now, or I'll disinherit you."

"Did you forget? You've disinherited me three times today already," Trisha said with a wry grin.

"Please." Opal's voice cracked on that one word, exposing grief and stubbornness and one last measure of pride.

Heaving a sigh, Trisha lowered the weapon and nodded. "All right, Gramma. All right. Room Twelve's cleaned and ready. I took care of it when we thought Nick could get off work to help us move you."

Grinding out her cigarette in an ashtray, she flicked a glance toward Sam. "My brother. Never met a family obligation he couldn't wriggle out of."

Sam nodded, though he could only think of Ruby, out in the car hurting. "I was wondering, would either of you have any painkillers? And we could both use clean clothes."

"Oh, for Christ's sake," Trisha said. "Anything else, Your Majesty? A getaway car maybe, or an alibi?"

But Opal was already digging in the cardboard box. "I think—let me see. Here's something. Some of those samples they mail out with the coupons. Could be a little out of date, but . . ."

After glancing through the door to where the car sat idling, Sam accepted the two trial-sized ibuprofen packets and thanked her.

"And I'm sure we can find you some old clothing," Opal offered. "Our guests used to forget things sometimes. I've washed and boxed the last of them for the Goodwill people, but it'll take me a few minutes. Trisha, honey, do you know where we left those?"

Scowling, Trisha pulled a room key off the line of hooks on a wall behind the counter. "Go ahead and take care of your girlfriend. I'll pick out a few things and leave 'em in a bag or box outside your door."

"Thank you, both of you," Sam said. "And if anyone comes looking . . ."

"We won't say a—" Opal started.

Her eyes narrowed, her granddaughter interrupted. "You sure you aren't the one who hurt this woman?"

"Hell, no, I didn't hurt her. I would never—"

"I find out otherwise, all bets are off." Trisha glanced down toward the handgun, where she had left it on the desk. "All bets and the safety. Got that?"

Sam nodded. "Loud and clear."

Taking the key and pills, he stepped outside . . . only to find that the Corolla and the woman in it had both vanished as if they had been swallowed by the night.

CHAPTER TWENTY-FOUR

Parting is all we know of heaven
And all we need of hell.

—Emily Dickinson,
from "My Life Closed Twice Before Its Close"

"Where *are* you?" Sheriff Wofford's voice hissed over the phone line. Or maybe the phone's signal was only breaking up.

Either way, Ruby shuddered and scooted lower behind the wheel, though the spot where she had moved the car, out of sight of two men she'd seen walking, lay hidden deep in shadow, between the back of the motor court and the overgrown wooded patch behind it.

"You didn't answer my last call." The sheriff sounded exasperated as she went on. "And when I tried Mrs. Lambert, where you *told* me you were staying, she said you'd made some other arrangement."

"Sorry to put you to any trouble." The words clotted in Ruby's throat, sickening her as much as the blood drying in her hair. All she could think of were Justine Wofford's diamonds, her expensive-looking suits. The fat bank accounts that indicated she'd sold out her integrity— and maybe even Ruby's family. "I'm staying with another friend. What's going on?"

"What other friend?" Suspicion chilled the sheriff's words. "I'll need a name, Mrs. Monroe."

"Why did you call me?" Ruby pushed back. "Have you heard any more news? Gotten any leads? Or has your focus shifted to interrogating me?"

There was a stunned silence on the other end, but Wofford didn't take long to recover. "You're with Sam McCoy now, aren't you? After everything I've told you."

"Sam?" Ruby did her best to sound astonished. "Why would I be—no, I haven't seen him. No."

She winced, hearing the deception in her own voice. She had never gotten away with lying to her parents, either.

"You could be in danger, Ruby. I'm sure you imagine you know this man, but McCoy's history—"

"Sam's been nothing but helpful."

"Just listen, for your own good," the sheriff urged her. "Not only has McCoy's brother been charged with big-time drug-running, but Sam had a long-running grudge against your husband. Sam tried to blame Aaron, but McCoy was charged with stealing three hundred fifty dollars from the Monroes when both of them were high school seniors."

Sam tried to blame Aaron. Ruby frowned at that, unable to imagine her husband taking money, especially from the kind of parents he could turn to for anything he needed. Unless . . .

Jackie Hogan's smoke-roughened voice haunted her, the cruel glee in the addict's eyes as she'd spoken of her past relationship with Aaron. *"Don't worry. It was over in no time flat, once the stick turned blue."*

Had three hundred fifty dollars been the price of an abortion? Ruby thought about the crosses and Last Supper print that had hung in the lake house before the renovations, thought of how her husband had never missed a week at church until his parents' deaths. Knowing they would never understand his failing, had Aaron allowed Sam to take the blame for his sins?

Ruby's throat tightened. So had it been guilt that had prompted Aaron to stick up for Sam whenever his "theft" was brought up? Guilt over Aaron's own misdeeds?

Sam's words pounded inside her head: *"Truth is, I hated the son of a bitch."*

If it was all true, no wonder. Still, she shook her head, thinking it was ridiculous to imagine Sam visiting vengeance upon a four-year-old child and the sister-in-law of her late husband. "That's really the best theory you can come up with?" she asked Wofford.

"It happened in the Monroes' lake house. The one you own now."

"Owned, you mean," Ruby corrected, flames leaping in her memory. "And whatever went on between them happened a long time ago. It has nothing to do with—"

"Don't be stupid, Ruby. Listen to me and I'll be sure you're kept safe."

Ruby's mind flashed to the image of a silvery stream of bubbles rising from the bottom of Bone Lake. Had her dreams been her intuition's warning, not that Misty and Zoe lay beneath the water, but that her own life was in danger from an unexpected threat?

"I can't be *kept safe."* Ruby heard the sharp lash of her own hostility, but couldn't contain it. "Can't sit somewhere on my hands while you're tossing off stupid theories and keeping *secrets* from me."

"All right, Ruby. If this is how you want to play it, I'm just going to go ahead and let you know what we've found." The sheriff's voice gentled. "I'd rather not have done it this way, but—"

"You—you've *found* them?" Ruby felt a tearing start deep in her stomach and rip straight through her heart. "You have, haven't you? You found my family, and they're—they're dead, aren't they?"

When Wofford explained the situation, Ruby couldn't draw air enough to scream, couldn't even react to the sudden pounding at the driver's window just beside her.

"Ruby?" Sam's voice, though not his worry, was muffled by the glass. But right now everything seemed muffled.

Silenced.

Ruined.

Lost.

CHAPTER TWENTY-FIVE

I shut my eyes and all the world drops dead;
I lift my eyes and all is born again.
(I think I made you up inside my head.)

—Sylvia Plath,
from "Mad Girl's Love Song"

Though Sam finally coaxed Ruby into unlocking the car door, she lowered the phone from her ear without saying a word or making eye contact. Sitting upright in the driver's seat, she stared straight ahead, her gaze unfocused and her body still as death.

"Did Best call again?" he asked, knowing how much each conversation with the man had cost her. When she didn't answer, he gave her shoulder a light shake. "Ruby? Ruby, I need you to talk to me or nod or something."

She did nod, a movement so subtle it was nearly imperceptible.

"Good, now let's get you up. There'll be a shower and a clean bed. Heavy curtains on the windows and a good lock on the door." When she failed to respond, he let the dog out of the backseat. Returning to Ruby, he plucked her from the car and used his knee to bump the door shut. With a push of the key fob, the alarm chirruped reassurance.

As Sam carried her to the door of the end unit, Ruby curled against his chest, her hand still clutching her pale green phone. Inside, he flipped a switch, igniting a pair of low-wattage lamps with paper shades. The rest of the room was much as Sam remembered from his childhood. Same rough, pine-planked walls, same yellowing acoustical tiles checkerboarding the drop ceiling, same thin, muddy-colored carpet, with darker, worn paths pointing the way between the tiny kitchenette and the cramped bathroom.

A shadow, the ghost of his much-younger self ducked behind the queen-sized bed. Sam sucked in a sharp breath, a mistake, since the room's odors triggered yet another avalanche of memory, every damned bit of it bad. Grimacing, he stepped inside and lowered Ruby into one of two off-kilter, wooden chairs.

With Java wagging her tail beside him, Sam knelt down in front of Ruby and gently pulled the phone from her hand. She didn't seem to notice when he laid it on a low, round table whose once-white top bore so many dark rings from coffee mugs and soda cans, they formed a subtle pattern on the surface.

Ruby didn't react, either, when he took both her ice-cold hands in his and looked her in the eye. The blankness he saw there frightened him.

"Talk to me," Sam pleaded. "Let me know I didn't screw up bringing you here instead of the ER."

Her head shook slightly. "It's fine." The voice was listless, a soft murmur. "The room'll do fine."

Impulsively, he hugged her, as much to reassure himself that she was real and solid as to offer comfort. "Opal's granddaughter's going to leave some things outside our door. So if you hear a knock in ten or fifteen minutes, don't be startled."

"What things?"

"She said she'll send some clothes for us. Might be a little short on style, but they'll be clean. And I've brought something for your head, too." He pulled a two-pill packet from his pocket. "How about some water?"

Ruby made an affirmative sound, her gaze still unfocused. In the kitchenette, Sam found a glass and brought her water, then fed her the tablets, one at a time, though he suspected the dose wouldn't be enough to do more than blunt the edges of her pain.

"I have to go back to the car now," Sam explained, "go get the computer. I want you to stay right here. Stay here and do not move."

When he came back, he found she hadn't. Not a millimeter. But he heard her sigh slide out, heard a slight hitch in her breathing.

"Who was it you talked to, out there?" he asked.

She looked up, her eyes shining. "Sheriff Wofford. She says they've found my sister's car. It's underneath the water. Underneath the water and . . ."

Keeping his distance was impossible. He pulled her to him and rocked her gently, saying, "Tell me it was just the car." His words were hoarse with emotion.

"They brought up Misty's wallet with her license and some torn clothes. And the divers are recovering some chunks of . . . something that looks human, not far from the Bone Yard back off Coot Channel Road, that little pass near Hammett's."

"I know the place." Sam pictured what locals called the Bone Yard, the flooded hollow filled with the bleached skeletons of dead trees. Passing through the center of this navigational hazard, Coot Channel had been named for the ducklike, black water birds so common to the area, but Sam knew the spot for its lunker bass and ancient catfish.

Along with big-ass alligators, such as the enormous specimen he'd heard bellowing not two weeks before. One evening, out in the johnboat, he'd seen the dark gray monster—maybe fourteen feet in length—take one of the stunted island deer that had ventured to the water's edge for a final, fatal drink. Sam couldn't forget the image of the huge creature exploding from the shallows like a steel-jawed trap. The client in Sam's boat, an experienced outdoorsman in his fifties, had given a teenaged girl's scream, and Sam's gut turned to ice water at this vision of death at its most primordial.

He shoved it out of his mind, telling himself that Misty and Zoe, if they were gone, hadn't died by any act of God or nature. But the hand of man could be even more cruel.

"I told Wofford I need to be there," Ruby said. "I need to see . . . But she told me they've blocked off the road, that they aren't letting any civilians back there until they clear the scene."

"There's nothing you could do there. And besides, you're in no shape to—"

"Do you think . . ." Ruby's gaze flicked to meet his.

"Am I deluding myself to keep hoping they're alive? Am I just another of those pathetic family members you see on TV, the ones who always think the body found is going to magically turn out to be somebody else's? That they're going to be the ones to get the miracle?"

"There's nothing pathetic about hope, Ruby. And nothing in the least pathetic about you."

Fingering the blood-stiffened strands of her hair, he waited perhaps a minute before adding, "Except maybe that death-metal neopunk look you've got going."

He lobbed the jest with utmost care: a life preserver to a fallen swimmer. To his relief, she made a grab for it, responding with a brief and rueful smile.

"I should clean up," she said. "This feels—it smells—I have to get it off me. Have to get ready for whatever comes next."

Struggling off the chair, she climbed to her feet before he could assist her. Once there, however, she swayed, her eyes closing and her forehead wrinkling.

"One step at a time," Sam said. "Only focus on that."

As she moved, he ached to see her pain, his own healing injuries giving a sympathetic throb. "You're going to have to let me help you. Otherwise I'll be peeling you off the bottom of the tub."

"Oh, hell." She sounded resigned to the necessity, though none too happy. "What's a little dignity between friends?"

Sam helped her into the bathroom and lifted her like a child to a perch on the counter. "So we're friends now, are we?" Important to keep her talking, he reminded himself. Keep her mind off both her physical pain and the torment of imagining what the recovery divers might be finding at this moment.

As he untied and pulled off each of her shoes, she said,

"Of course we're friends, Sam. What you've done—what you're risking . . . in spite of what happened between you and Aaron."

He hesitated, frowning.

"Wofford tried to tell me—she said you have a grudge against him."

"I did, for a long time."

"Did he pin the blame on you, Sam? Or did his parents just assume and he said nothing? Maybe because he was a scared kid, or just weak in that moment?"

Sam shook his head, wondering what Ruby had guessed and resisting the temptation to say that he'd been scared, too, going to that group home after six years with the Monroes. But seeing her empathy, her willingness to listen even in these circumstances, made him more determined than ever not to tell her what the man she'd loved had done. "We're not having this conversation, hear me? We're taking care of you now."

He began unbuttoning the shirt she wore, his shirt, now smeared with blood. And in spite of everything, in spite of the filth and their varied wounds and the dread he knew both felt about what would come during the next hours, the reprobate McCoy in him noticed the female form beneath the cloth.

"I don't understand," she whispered. "I don't know why you're doing all this. Why you're helping me if you and Aar—"

"I was only out to save my own skin," he reminded her, his lie serving as penance for the lustful thought.

Pain spasmed across her features as he helped her slip the shirt off. He focused on that pain, that face as he stood her up to unfasten her jeans.

"Maybe that's the way it started," she said.

Her fingers bumped his, at her zipper, and their hands

shot apart, as if each had felt the shock. As if each recalled the kiss they'd shared the last time they'd been in such close quarters.

"Here, let me start the water." Sam quickly turned from her, from the low rumble of sexual awareness between them. "Maybe a bath and not a shower, so you won't have to stand up?"

"A shower, I think. I want this blood, this day, to run right off me."

Sam moved the ivory shower curtain to start the water running, and the ancient plumbing groaned in the same pained tones that he remembered. And he thought that in this place of all places, he wanted to deserve grace. He wanted to believe in the man Ruby saw instead of the man who'd thrown away every good thing that had ever come his way.

He wanted to be stronger than his history of screwups and suspicion, stronger even than his DNA, to give her the tenderness and care she needed. From a *friend*.

But when he turned back to Ruby, she was completely naked, her limbs trembling, but her head held high. He swallowed hard and said, "Let me—let me check this water."

When he stuck a hand in, it remained cold.

Ruby, still behind him, clutched his shoulder, her short nails digging in. "Sorry. Accidentally checked the mirror. Got a little dizzy when I saw the blood."

"That makes two of us." After unwrapping the soap, Sam fumbled a small bottle of shampoo onto the tub's edge, beside a folded washcloth. "You going to be all right?"

"If you can give me a hand in."

As the water warmed, he pulled the curtain back and all but lifted her inside. Instead of standing, however, she sank down to her knees as her legs gave way. Sam bent with her, struggling to support her—and getting thoroughly soaked in the process.

"Shit," he said, on all counts. Then, after a hesitation, "How about some help there, Ruby?"

She groaned in reply, turning to sit on the tub's bottom, the warm water sluicing over her back. Her hair darkened, some of it falling into her eyes, and ruddy streams trickled from her body to swirl down the drain.

Sam's resolve threatened to do the same, but he stepped in, jeans and all. "Scoot forward. Can you do that?"

When she did, he knelt behind her, trying to distance himself from the purely physical reaction of his body. He fixed his attention on the movements of his hands as he unscrewed the shampoo's top, on the cool slick of the liquid pooling in his palm. On Ruby's needs and not his own.

"Tip back just a little," he said roughly.

"Thank you," she said quietly.

He rubbed in the shampoo, his fingers slipping through strands whose stiffness melted into silken warmth. A lightly evergreen scent sprang up, clean and woodsy, vanquishing the pungent, iron reek of blood.

Ruby sighed. "This—this is good. I can't remember the last time someone did this for—" Air hissed through her clenched teeth.

"Sorry." Moving his hand from the sore spot, he gently untangled her hair with his fingers as the water washed it clean. "You all right?"

"If I can stay right here," she answered, craning her neck to regard him. "Right here, inside this second. If I don't think about the past or future. If I don't think of anything except . . ."

The look she gave him sent a jolt of pure desire through him. Stifling a groan, he reached for soap and washcloth.

"Let's finish cleaning you up." Lust roughened as his words were, he refocused on the necessity of cleaning her skin. Of washing every speck of blood and dirt and violence from her body.

But it was torturous, watching that tautly curved flesh come clean, steadying her with one hand while running his other—behind the thin square of white cloth—over creamy skin, or gliding over small but beautifully formed breasts whose rosy nipples peaked with his touch. Just once more, he lathered her breasts, his overheated brain supplying the excuse that he needed to be extra certain she was clean there.

Teeth gritting and wet jeans growing even tighter, he screwed shut his eyes, thinking it might be easier if he couldn't see her. But still, he felt her sleek limbs as he washed them, memorized the curve of her back, the sweet flare of her hips.

When he reached the juncture of her legs, he told her, "I'm sorry, but you're going to have to—"

"You're doing fine," she whispered, and guided his hand with her own.

The cloth fell from his hand as it lingered.

"Ruby . . ." Control breaking, he arched above her to mouth her neck, to press his nose against the clean, sweet fragrance of her hair.

And she twisted round, taking the soap from him. One finger trailed down toward his fly. "Please, Sam."

Relief flooding through him, he undressed as she washed him. Except that when the cloth again fell, she didn't bother picking it up.

She kissed his mouth fiercely, sleeked her slippery hands along his chest, and crawled onto him, her slim thigh nudging his rock-hard erection. He felt no languor in her movements, not the slightest hint of caution—only a desperation to lose herself completely, to give away her consciousness, if only for a while.

As the hot rain pelted his skin, as his mouth found her breasts and his fingers found their way inside her, every reality but instinct disintegrated and washed away completely. Until the only thing left was the rhythm, the power of their bodies joining, a relentless, rocking maelstrom that neither of them could control, a storm that broke when Ruby cried his name, when all too soon, he spilled his lust inside her, unable to hold back.

Ruby curled against Sam as he lifted her from the tub, her body swaddled in white towels that felt scratchy against her pink flesh. Stripping off the bed's comforter, he laid her on the soft sheets. Her body felt limp and loose and utterly relaxed. Though her head ached vaguely, her mind drifted, blankly restful, content to allow Sam to do what he wished.

Pleased that what he wished seemed to involve a slower, gentler round of touching, beginning with undemanding kisses that lingered at her mouth, she gave in to sensation. All conscious thought submerged into an oasis of taste and scent, of every sensation she could take in as the two of them made love with a languid ease that slowly built to a devastating climax.

Devastating, because as the world around her shattered, so did the cell-thin barricade between shock and pain, crushing blow and comprehension. In the wake of physical release, the reality of her situation struck her like an axe blow.

She cried out, her pleasure turning inside out, her tears rolling to soak into the pillow. When Sam wrapped his arms around her, she pushed him away.

"I haven't been with—this was my first time since—" She couldn't even finish, couldn't force Aaron's name past the grief knotting in her throat. "And to do it now, with my daughter out there somewhere—to drag you deeper into this instead of handling it on my own—"

Lying on his side to face her, Sam carefully pulled up the sheet to cover her nude body, then placed his hand atop the back of hers. "Stop. Right there. You're human, Ruby, and human beings reach out for comfort, for contact when they're hurting. Because nobody's equipped to get through something like this on her own."

She stared at him as her emotions turned kaleidoscopic, a shifting pattern of guilt and need that gradually gave way to gratitude. For in Sam's eyes, his touch, his voice, she read nothing but acceptance and a depth of comprehension she'd never before known.

"And you *aren't* alone," he added, "no matter how tough this gets. Because I swear to you, I mean to see you through as far as I can."

"Thank you." She wanted to say more, but the sincerity of his vow overwhelmed her.

"Absolutely, you should thank me." He feathered a touch beneath her chin, a wicked grin slanting across his handsome features. "Sacrificing my virtue like this, it's one hell of a job."

A smile slipped up on her, took her by surprise. And for the first time in a long while, she felt the possibility of joy beyond a distant horizon, the faint glow of the unseen edge of dawn.

Justine Wofford hated like hell to leave the search scene, especially to Savoy, who would end up using it against her in one way or another. But Harriet Wickenfield had called, screeching like a barn owl about Justine's son, Noah. No matter how hard she tried to calm the older woman, Mrs. Wickenfield kept going on about the boy's having broken something. As she flipped on the siren and raced toward home, Justine prayed it wouldn't prove to be his neck.

Already, Justine had been shaken by the grim scene along Coot's Channel and her phone call to Ruby Monroe. Worse yet, Justine was horrified by the suspicion that her own failings, her own weakness could have played some part in the case's sad conclusion. She was sickened, haunted by the thought that everything she did, everything she'd touched since the election was tainted. Including the only pure relationship she'd known in all her life.

She turned onto a road far from the water, a potholed, single-lane that wound past well-spaced, older homes surrounded by fenced pastures. In spite of her anxiety, her spirits lifted just a little at the sight of horses of all sizes, from the brown and white minis to the black and sorrel Morgans, grazing in the lush spring growth. When a pair of huge white dogs—Lou's dogs—loped out to meet her, she convinced herself that everything was all right, that the only thing her son had broken was another drinking glass, left carelessly within reach.

But as she pulled up beside the white two-story, Harriet Wickenfield boiled out of the back door with her flabby white arms waving.

"What's going on?" Justine asked as she bailed out of the same ragged-out Expedition Lou had bitched about for one hundred and six thousand miles.

"Noah won't come out. He's locked himself inside—"

"Is he hurt?" Justine was already trotting toward the back door, the rush of adrenaline cutting through her fatigue.

The caregiver panted in her wake.

"No—no, ma'am," huffed Mrs. Wickenfield. "What I meant to say is he's busted out a window in his bedroom. You can see it from here."

Justine looked up, heart falling as she caught sight of the missing pane. Too small for the nine-year-old to climb out, but that didn't guarantee her son was not in danger.

"Where is he now?" Justine demanded. "You didn't leave him with the broken glass?"

"He's blocked the door somehow. He—"

Without waiting to hear more, the sheriff sprinted for the house, her long strides rapidly outpacing the older woman's. As Justine reached the door, she flung it open, wishing for the thousandth time she'd found someone better trained than a retired grocery store clerk, someone more prepared to handle Noah's special needs after school hours. Justine would see to it, she swore. Screw the trouble, screw the legal problems keeping her from accessing her and Lou's joint accounts and forcing her to sell her mother's jewelry bit by bit to pay the bills. Risky or not, Justine *had* to use the money, the money she'd vowed to return or at least report, to get good help before her son . . .

"Noah," she shouted, reflexively looking toward the kitchen floor, where he spent hour after hour banging pots and their lids, delighting in the harsh metallic jangle. The noise had driven off at least two previous caregivers and at times drove Justine wild, yet at the moment, she'd give anything to hear it, anything at all to see the child who wouldn't let her touch him and couldn't seem to show he loved her back.

Making for the stairs, she called his name again and listened. Not for a vocal response—she'd learned it was useless to expect that—but for the reassuring jingle of a ring of keys or the rattle of one of the cans of pebbles, bolts, and spare change that Lou had welded shut for safety.

Struggling not to choke up at the memory, she reached

the door and tried it. Though the knob turned, something blocked the door itself, as if something heavy, like his dresser, had been shoved against it.

Justine couldn't imagine that Noah, always small for his age, had found the strength to move a heavy piece of furniture, and the smaller items had been bolted to the floor. Which meant that instead of using weight, he had made a wedge. No matter how delayed he was in other areas, her son could be very clever about such things.

She pounded on the door and shouted, "Noah, open up for Mama. It's time for your favorite grilled cheese."

Of course, that wouldn't work, she realized. Noah—who timed his schedule to the nanosecond—would know it wasn't grilled cheese night, would figure out she hoped to trick him. Which meant he'd never open the door, even supposing that he noticed all the shouting and the banging.

She shouted downstairs for Mrs. Wickenfield to bring a screwdriver from the kitchen junk drawer, but in her panic, the woman couldn't find one—or do anything but burst into useless sobs and wail that this job was too much for her nerves.

Justine found a pair of scissors in her child-proofed bathroom cabinet. Sliding the blade beneath the door, she eventually managed to poke loose the toy that had been jammed there. Flinging open Noah's door, she took one look inside and cried out at the sight of all the blood.

CHAPTER TWENTY-SIX

How does one kill fear, I wonder? How do you shoot a spectre through the heart, slash off its spectral head, take it by its spectral throat?

—Joseph Conrad,
From *Lord Jim*

Ruby sat up in bed as her phone began ringing, her chest constricting with dread that it would be someone from the sheriff's office with even worse news.

After a reflexive glance toward Sam, she hit the speaker button so he could hear as well. "Hello?"

"Mama, come and get me. I'm scared. I want to go home—"

"*Zoe?* Zoe, baby . . ." Ruby choked out on a sob.

Beside her, Sam clicked on the light and leaned close to the phone, but Ruby scarcely noticed as she asked, "Where are you, honey? Tell me and I'll—"

"Mama, don't let—"

"I've been concerned about you, Ruby Monroe," the glacial voice of the kidnapper interrupted. "Concerned your daughter wouldn't have a mother to come home to."

"*Wait!* Give her back the phone, please," cried Ruby. "I have to talk to Zoe. I have to—"

"You'll talk to her tomorrow if you do as I tell you. First of all, I want you keeping out of sight and out of volatile situations. Because the next time, I assure you, there'll be no last-second miracle to save you."

"You were there. At Dylan Hammett's, weren't you?"

In her mind's eye, Ruby saw the tattooed man rushing at her, felt Coffin's rough hands tearing at her clothing. Not to rape her, as she had feared, but searching her clothes and pockets for an item he had not found in her luggage.

"You meant to *steal* the flash drive," she accused, though she couldn't make herself believe she was speaking to the same man who'd attacked her. More likely, she was speaking to the shooter.

Clearly, he had no clue that his employer already had the files. If she told him, would he simply kill Zoe, as he had probably already murdered Misty? Ruby's instincts, and the cruelty in his voice, warned her that volunteering information could prove deadly.

"It's true you wouldn't be alive to carry on this conversation if you'd been foolish enough to have the item on you," he said, "but that's not important now, since you will bring it to me. Tomorrow afternoon, at precisely twelve thirty-five p.m. You will come alone and place the item in a bright orange duffel bag I've left at these coordinates."

"Why tomorrow? Why not now?" She flashed on a vision of herself retrieving the gun from Paulie's and putting Best down the way she had the charging mastiff. Long shot or not, she saw nothing to be gained by delaying. "I have the drive. I need my daughter."

"I suggest you write down these coordinates," he said, ignoring her suggestion. "I will not repeat myself."

Sam whipped open the nightstand drawer and pulled out a pen and a yellowing motel postcard. Ruby snatched them from his hands as Best slowly, clearly read off the long string of digits composing both latitude and longitude.

Despite her shaking hands, Ruby managed to record them, even had the presence of mind to read them back to the kidnapper as if she were confirming something as mundane as a credit card number for a catalog order.

"You listen beautifully." Best's praise flicked like a serpent's tongue in her ear. "Keep listening, and your family will survive this."

Shivering, Ruby asked, "You'll be waiting there with Zoe? You'll let me take her home, right? And my sister—will my sister be—"

"Follow my instructions, and you will all be re-united."

Ruby recalled the vivid images she'd dreamed of the lake's depths. But Zoe's voice had been real; Ruby had no doubt.

Sam laid a hand on her knee, gave her a look that helped to ground her.

"When?" she pressed Best. "I have to know when I'll have them back."

"When I've assured myself you haven't tampered with or duplicated the material. When I've assured myself you've spoken to no one."

"Of course I didn't talk to anybody," she exploded. "I never even wanted that flash drive in the first place. Never bothered looking at the thing," she claimed, "and I still have no idea what's on it."

"Don't play stupid, Ruby Monroe. Don't pretend that anything's so simple."

Taken aback, Ruby tried to fathom what he knew and how he knew it. Sam's hands made a rolling motion, urging her to keep the killer talking.

"It *is* simple," she insisted. "You come meet me tonight, right now. Have my family with you. I'll give you the flash drive; you let them walk away." She pictured a new scenario: Sam hiding near the exchange site, armed and ready—shooting the kidnapper as soon as he assured himself her family was safe. *If* Sam could be persuaded to take yet another risk. Hadn't he told her—quite emphatically—that he didn't do guns?

"Tomorrow afternoon," Best told her, "twelve thirty-five, exactly as I've instructed."

"How do I know you won't ambush me? How do I know you won't kill them?"

"You want *assurances?*" The flat menace of his words electrified the band of nerves around her stomach. "How about an *assurance* of how you'll find your family if you deviate in the least from my instructions?"

"No, I—" Ruby couldn't breathe, remembering how he'd used her friend to prove a point the last time. Seeing the shining pool of blood and Elysse's neck sliced in a grisly smile. What if he carved up Misty—if she weren't dead already? Or would Ruby find pieces of her only child? "I didn't mean it. Please, please don't tell me—"

"You might check the trunk of your car," he said, just before the line—and all the fight in her—went dead.

"Ruby? Ruby, are you with me?" Sam took her hand and squeezed it, then pulled the blanket to her shoulders to warm her. But it was her face that worried him most, from its pallor to its slack look of defeat.

"I don't want to see it." She shook her head emphatically, looking more like a lost child than the sensual woman he'd made love to, the strong woman who'd stood up to terror with such courage. "I—I can't look this time."

Sam pulled on his wet pants, then checked outside their room's door, where, as good as her word, Opal had left the bag of clothing she had promised. Bringing it inside, he picked through the assortment until he came across a faded, navy T-shirt that would fit him. Most of the items were too large for Ruby, but he found one pair of cropped jeans and a striped top that looked as if they could have belonged to that rarest of Hook-It patrons, a fashion-conscious twenty-something. No undergarments, but Ruby didn't protest as he helped her to dress.

"You don't have to come out," he said. "Let me take the keys and check the trunk."

"If—if it's my sister this time . . . If it's anyone I know . . ."

Sam touched her cheek and softly kissed her temple. "I'll be right back."

Ruby hugged herself and rolled away to face the wall as he slipped out into the night.

Except for the filmy veil of starlight, the darkness was complete now, particularly in the spot where the small sedan crouched beneath low pine limbs like an animal in hiding. Seeing no one else, Sam approached, dread burning through his veins like acid, drying the moisture from his mouth.

His flashlight's beam landed on a slow drip coming from beneath the rear bumper. A drip that splashed down into a dark spot on the gravel.

Sam understood the damage to his truck now. The reason that the kidnapper had wanted to be certain they drove away in Elysse's car. Squatting down behind it, he used the light to confirm what he knew already. The streaks showed up brilliant red against the white.

Call 9-1-1, estúpido, Pacheco's voice screamed at him. *Don't touch that trunk lock. Don't touch anything. Just make an anonymous phone call and vamoose.*

"Too damned late," Sam growled, thinking of his prints all over the car and his vehicle's presence at the home of Dylan Hammett, a house where any idiot could tell someone had met with violent death. If Wofford had reason to deflect the blame onto him—or even if she merely connected dots and looked no further—he was likely to need a whole different brand of lawyer. One who specialized in defending clients charged with murder.

With little to lose, he decided to learn the identity of the victim of his alleged crime.

"Don't let it be Misty. For Ruby's sake, please don't," Sam prayed as he popped the trunk and looked inside.

CHAPTER TWENTY-SEVEN

This is the Hour of Lead—
Remembered, if outlived,
As Freezing persons, recollect the Snow—
First—Chill—then Stupor—then the letting go—
                    —Emily Dickinson,
                    from "After Great Pain"

The body was in bad shape, the fatal wounds horrific. But it was the injuries inflicted after death—or at least Sam *hoped* it had been after—that had him turning aside and retching violently.

With its throat slashed and its tongue gouged from its bloody maw, this corpse—its chest blown open by a bullet—had been left as a message, a message no less clear than the one embodied by Elysse Steele.

But as terrible as the sight was, neither he nor Ruby need mourn this victim, the tattooed man who had taken over Ruby's home and assaulted her just prior to his death. Spitting to clear his mouth of the foul taste, Sam wondered that Ruby's tormentor had chosen to save her life.

At least until he got the flash drive from her—or found out she didn't have the right one.

The sound of fast-approaching footsteps attracted his attention, prompting Sam to slam the trunk reflexively, his runaway heartbeat drumming in his ears. His next move was to kill the flashlight, but apparently he didn't get it switched off fast enough.

"Sam McCoy?" The voice was young and female, the speaker's breathing ragged. "Sam, it's Trisha. My gramma asked—asked me to come tell y'all—"

She had to stop and catch her breath.

"Easy," he coaxed, wanting to calm her quickly and get her out of here before she caught a whiff of blood and vomit, before she realized she was within a few yards of a corpse.

"I freaking knew you would be trouble. But Gramma wants me to let you know there's some kind of cops asking about you—DEA guys, I think. She's talking to them up front, putting on her senile act, but . . ."

From around the corner, Sam made out the approaching glow of headlights. In a split second he reacted, bolting not toward the room, which would have forced him into the agents' path and led them straight to Ruby, but for the shelter of the trees behind the motor court.

Within seconds, his own shadow stretched and swung before him as what must be the agents' vehicle came around back. He imagined himself running, silhouetted, pictured an SUV's window rolling downward and a marksman taking aim. So clear was the premonition that Sam zigzagged in what he prayed would be the right direction, his instincts throbbing out a warning that a bullet was ripping its way toward him, about to leave him every bit as dead as the tattooed corpse in the trunk.

Dread pounded at his temples, hammered at his chest. Panic sharpened by regret that he had no time to warn Ruby, no time to help prepare her for the—

When it came, the crack was sharp and sudden, a crack that sent him pitching forward, hurtling toward a darkness slick and glassy as his recent downhill slide.

Ruby waited, with every passing moment tightening fear's grip. Frozen with anxiety, she couldn't move a muscle, couldn't even glance at the clock to note how long it had been since Sam had left her.

What if he'd found Misty? What if Best had done to her what he had done to Elysse? Had Zoe watched her aunt's murder? And what about the body parts recovered along with Misty's Honda? Horror bubbled up inside Ruby, her mind fixated on an image of a body breaking loose and floating up to Bone Lake's surface, of reptilian eyes watching from a distance. Eyes gleaming coldly in the twilight as they glided ever closer.

Ruby gasped, sucking in a breath that exploded the vision and finally shattered her inertia. Rising, she shoved her feet into her untied shoes and hurried toward the door, unable to wait another second to learn what Sam had found inside the car's trunk.

But with her sudden change in elevation, her sight dimmed and the muted notes of pain inside her skull roared to a crescendo. Gritting her teeth, she reached for the wall and braced herself as waves of dizziness broke over her.

She waited for the room to right itself, for the crashing surf in her head to subside. Waited and wondered if Sam had decided to cut his losses, to use her keys to get as far from this mess as he could. Wickedly sharp, the suspicion sliced through her, but she told herself that despite the brief respite she had found in his arms, she had no right to expect more from him, no right to begrudge him his own survival.

She told herself all this but still could not accept it,

could not begin to fathom that he might be as lost to her as Elysse.

Ruby's eyes widened as she imagined something altogether different from abandonment. An idea far more horrifying. What if Sam himself had been attacked, if the killer had been lying in wait as he made the phone call?

As she looked around the room for anything she might use as a weapon, Ruby's gaze struck on the nearer of two tired-looking, wooden chairs beside the coffee-ring-stained table. Lurching toward it, she picked it up and, with a surge of pure adrenaline, smashed it down as hard as she could against the floor. A leg cracked and she struck again, then twisted the wood until a sharp-ended length snapped off in her hand. Not much against a gun, a knife, or a madman, but she had to find out what had happened to Sam. What chance did she have of saving her family without his help?

Unwilling to leave the flash drive behind, she plucked it from the laptop's USB port, then tucked it into her pocket as she hurried for the door. As she left the room with Java close on her heels, she tried to tell herself that her family was the only reason she was going out there, that her heart wasn't pushing her to risk getting herself killed—and dooming Zoe—for a far more foolish reason . . .

An attachment she had no damned business forming to a man who'd already warned her he was skipping town the moment he could.

Exhausted from his tantrum—and probably to some extent from blood loss, Noah slept where he lay on the ER waiting room's floor. Sitting cross-legged beside him, Justine ignored the black looks of those waiting, though she felt like flipping every one of them the bird.

Intellectually, she got it, knew they were all wondering what sort of mother allowed her child—who was so perfectly, heartbreakingly normal in appearance—to carve designs on his own forearms, then couldn't even blot the crusting blood without inciting a near riot. They had no way of understanding that the same boy who apparently hadn't felt pain as he'd scored his own flesh with a shard of glass screamed in agony at the pressure of a warm, damp washcloth or—God forbid—a hug.

Besides, if it got around that Justine Wofford, Preston County sheriff, had been tossing off obscene gestures in the ER, she could kiss her chance for reelection goodbye. And after what she'd done to win even the brief privilege of filling the remainder of Lou's term . . . Justine swallowed to clear the taste of bile at the thought of the shortcuts she had taken, the innocence she'd sold along the way.

She had no choice except to call her father, despite the understanding that he would pelt her with I-told-you-so's. If he figured out what she'd done, the retired Morton County sheriff would be the first to report her actions, or maybe even lock her up. She still cringed at the memory of his idea of support when she'd told him of her plans to claim Lou's office.

"Even if you have the stomach, even if you win it, those deputies'll never accept a woman as their sheriff, especially one who didn't pay her dues by comin' up through their ranks. And if you ask me," he'd warned, not caring for a minute that she hadn't, "you'd be better off movin' back home and findin' yourself something more suitable. I've still got plenty of pull back in Morton County. You want, I'll see about getting you something more fit for a single mother. I hear the evidence tech's retirin'. That's indoors, safe . . ."

And boring as hell, Justine thought as she stroked Noah's

soft brown hair, on the long side because cutting it was such an ordeal. Asleep as he was, she could touch him, as long as she was careful. Her heart ached with the need to pull him into her arms, to ask her son whether she'd been right to want more than her father offered: the challenge of the career she'd watched her husband handle so well; the fulfillment she had left behind when leaving her position as a Morton County deputy to take a second chance on marriage. And the money, too, for a sheriff's salary would allow her to keep her independence.

Swallowing her pride, she made the phone call. When her father answered, she said, "I need your help, Dad, and I need it right away."

"I've still got that spare room, sugar. And you know Noah's always welcome."

"I do know, and I appreciate that," she said, thinking that his acceptance of her autistic son might be the only reason she and her dad still spoke. Unfortunately, he'd never been nearly as accepting of the other facets of her life, from her choice of jobs to what he saw as her piss-poor taste in husbands. "But right now I need you to come here instead. Please, it's only forty minutes if you hurry."

Though she'd often wished he'd stayed in Morton County, tonight she thanked God he had chosen to retire to a rural ranch so close by.

"What's wrong?"

"We're in the emergency room, waiting for some stitches. Noah's cut himself."

"How'd he manage that?" Her father was familiar with the lengths to which Justine went to keep the boy from hurting himself.

"Best I can figure, he banged his head straight through the window, then used a jagged piece of glass to cut his arms."

"How bad is it?"

"His head is just fine, and most of the cuts look pretty superficial. But there are a couple of deep spots—I figure no more than eight or ten stitches this time. Thing is, Noah's caretaker's walked out on me, and I'm smack in the middle of this huge case—"

"The AMBER Alert? I saw that on the TV. Saw you, too, at the press briefing." Her father waited a beat before adding the rim shot. "You looked a little overwhelmed."

"Just tired." *Of your assuming that you—or any male sheriff—could handle it all better.* "This case is tough enough without having both the media and outside agencies all over my ass. Besides, I've lost a good man."

Oscar Balderach had tried hard to talk her out of running for her husband's seat, had had the nerve to tell her Lou would never have approved. Still, he had been her husband's good friend, and more importantly, his safety—the well-being of all those who served in her department—fell firmly on her shoulders.

"It happens, Justine. Happens to the best of us." Her dad's tone left no doubt that he didn't count her a member of that club. "So you're in over your head—that's what you're finally admitting."

Justine felt the corner of her mouth tic downward. "Okay, so you were right, I'm fucking drowning out here. The question is, Dad, are you gonna toss me a life jacket or a boulder?"

"I'll be there. When haven't I, when you've been inclined to ask?"

As she was ending the conversation, another call came through. Switching over, she said, "Wofford here."

"Sheriff, this is Ichabod."

Justine felt her brows rise in surprise that Larry Crane would use the hated nickname. "What can I do for you, Deputy?"

"Those body parts brought in from the lake—thought you might want to know we've got an ID."

"You're sure about that?" The last Justine had heard, they'd only found small pieces.

"Brought up a head later, in halfway decent shape, too. Stashed down in some cypress roots. Gators like to do that, like to age their meals before—"

"Whose head?" Justine interrupted. "Could anyone tell whose head the divers brought up?"

Someone in the waiting room coughed, prompted her to look up, to notice a half dozen or more patients and their family members staring. A couple looked on in slack-jawed horror, while the rest bore the same expression of morbid fascination she'd seen in rubberneckers driving past a fatal wreck. Though she preferred it to the you-have-to-be-the-worst-mother-on-the-planet looks she'd scored after her son's tantrum, she frowned and turned away from them, cupping a hand around the receiver as Noah shifted, sighed, and laid his head against her thigh.

When Crane named the victim, Justine screwed shut her eyes. "You're sure?"

When he replied in the affirmative, she breathed a curse. She'd thought herself ready, braced for any eventuality. But this? This was going to be more difficult than anything she had imagined.

"Roger's all set to notify the next of kin," he said, referring to Deputy Savoy, "but considerin' their history—"

"You tell Roger, I'll break the news myself as soon as possible, so keep it zipped until then. Any media out there yet?"

"No. We had a lucky break in the department. Most of 'em lit out to cover that church bus wreck on I-10."

Though Justine, too, was glad that the reporters had left

the county, she couldn't help wondering how many lives
their "lucky break" had cost. "Well, let's make sure they
don't hear about it for the next few hours, and if you find
anything—anything at all—I want you to call me first."

"But Savoy's handling the—"

"I'm interested in his version, too. Mostly interested in
how far it differs from the facts. So are you willing to
help me on this, Larry, or do you really want to be the
guy they call Ichabod, the guy the others stick with every shit detail, until the day you die?"

She left the question hanging, left the deputy to think
his slow way through the implications . . . and choose his
loyalty.

CHAPTER TWENTY-EIGHT

The blood jet is poetry,
There is no stopping it . . .

—Sylvia Plath,
from "Kindness"

Sam gasped with pain, biting back a curse as sweat poured
off his body. His left ankle was swelling quickly, a souve-
nir of the thick branch that had snapped beneath his
weight and sent him crashing into the underbrush. For a
few moments, he'd kept still, praying that the agents
hadn't spotted him. But his hopes crumbled as what he
assumed to be the DEA's dark SUV barreled his way,
jouncing over tufts of grass and flattening the mounds of
fire ants.

Seeing their approach, he'd turned and limped deeper
into the brush. Back in the day, a bayou had flowed be-

hind the Hook-It. Decades before, its waters had mysteriously changed course, drying up the motel's fortune and leaving the nearly impenetrable low area now filled with trees and undergrowth—and plenty of bugs and snakes as well. But Sam was willing to risk them if he could just lose his pursuers.

Running, however, was proving a hell of a lot more difficult than he'd imagined. With every step, fresh agony shafted up his leg—making him want to scream curses at the top of his lungs.

Still, he staggered forward, moving deeper into a damp tangle populated by thick swarms of mosquitoes as scores of sticks did their utmost to scrape, trip, and impale him. When one snagged his shirt, he paused to disentangle it and sucked in huge draughts of humid air. Peering back over his shoulder, he spotted no lights coming his way, but alarm jolted through him at the crunch and crash of something moving toward him through the underbrush. Moving fast enough to make him wonder if the agents had night-vision goggles or thermal imaging to pick up the heat of his body. Would they have special scopes, too, for their weapons, giving them the means to drop him the instant one of them got a clear shot?

For Christ's sake, don't give them a stationary target.

Adrenaline spiking through his system, he forgot the ankle, forgot the possibility that he might put out an eye on a low-hanging branch or break his neck stepping in a hole. Forgot everything but the imperative to keep moving, to put distance between himself and the men who, for all their tools, were unfamiliar with the area. Who, for all their training, lacked the sense of direction he'd honed from years of motoring around the area's tangled network of waterways.

Using the motel behind him to orient himself, he moved deeper into the grove and prayed the snarl might slow his pursuers. The trouble was, it would also make it harder for him to get out—and give them time to call for enough backup to draw a noose tight around the area, around all of Dogwood if that was what it took.

So he had to get clear of it while he could.

Because he was in deep shit now, serious shit, with his SUV abandoned near what he now knew to be a murder scene and a body in the trunk of the car he had just driven. If he ended up arrested, how could he be of any use to Ruby? He'd never promised her—nor had she expected him—to do hard time on her account.

Sam's injured foot caught on a fallen tree trunk, bringing him down hard as his knee gave way. He landed in a tangle, his breath pumping through his shredded lungs, a stitch in his side adding to his pain. But the physical agony was nothing compared to the thought of letting Ruby down. Of leaving her to face Best and maybe Wofford on her own. Or would she be caught in the hotel room, now that the Corolla had been spotted? Would she be taken into custody, along with both the laptop and the flash drive? If Best learned that she couldn't make the rendezvous, would he kill Zoe and Misty in retaliation?

Lying prone and frozen, Sam saw a beam of light, its movement splintered by the myriad branches. Instead of rising to run, he lay still and listened, praying that the fallen tree and silence would be enough to hide him.

He nearly jumped out of his skin when something close by chittered, a night bird or some huge insect. In the distance, he heard the sound of traffic—traffic, but no sirens—from the road. A minute more and he heard tramping, the sound of heavy footsteps and then a radio.

"You got a bead on him?" a canned voice asked, an accented voice that had Sam flashing on the face of Special Agent Acosta.

Sam felt a pinching at the back of his neck—and resisted the urge to slap at the offending insect. Or *insects,* from the feel of it. Nasty little bastards.

"Negative." Only a few feet distant, the speaker stopped, standing with his back to Sam. "I lost him."

Sam cringed, startled by the agent's proximity, and tried to recall the name of Acosta's partner of the peach-fuzz hair and expensive wraparound shades. The one who'd been moving through the brush with the stealth factor of an elephant on stilts.

"I don't see him, either," said Acosta on the radio. "Let's pull back to the motel, call for K-9 backup. Let the dogs flush him out of this shit."

"Or let the fucking alligators eat him," Peach Fuzz grumbled.

"Works for me."

As the agent signed off, Sam's hand curled around a stout stick, and he pictured himself rising up and using it to take out this pursuer, then using the man's weapon to get Ruby and himself, not to mention his personal canine, out of this mess.

Sam felt the capacity for violence stir inside him, sharp and vicious as anything J.B. had ever dealt out. All his life, Sam had understood it lay there, dormant. Had known it waited, coiled like a viper.

And all his life, he'd feared it, shunned it, for unlike his brother, or even the slimeball of a father who had spawned them, Sam understood the consequences of raising his fists or picking up a weapon, understood how quickly things could spiral out of control.

Understood how, even if he managed to avoid getting

his untrained ass killed, he couldn't swing a stick at a man's skull, couldn't pick up a gun and charge toward another armed man without the very real possibility of committing murder.

I'm not my brother. Not him. Not for any price.

All this blazed through his brain like lightning before the chance evaporated as the agent walked away.

Leaving Sam to wonder how the hell he was going to get out of this mess. Leaving him to listen for the howling of the sirens and the barking of the dogs.

Moving quietly, Ruby made her way behind the motel, the chair leg clutched like a baseball bat in her hands. Java sniffed around industriously, looking more concerned with finding the perfect place to squat than with her master's absence.

Ruby spotted the Corolla, parked where she had left it in the shadows. So Sam hadn't used the keys to take off, but then where had he gone?

She peered into the star-softened darkness. Though she saw nothing, heard nothing anywhere near the car, her gaze was drawn to the taillights of an idling vehicle—an SUV, she thought—near the trees some forty or fifty yards back.

Its presence unnerved her, though it could easily belong to a pair of trysting lovers or some teenagers out drinking. But she could stand here spinning out possibilities all evening. None of them would explain Sam's absence, or why he'd taken off without a word.

"Sam?" she called softly, moving closer to the Corolla's trunk. Could whatever was inside have frightened off a man brave enough to risk a fiery death? A man who'd done things for her that might send him back to prison?

Ruby swallowed hard, clutching her makeshift weapon

more tightly. "God, please help me," she whispered. "Don't let him be dead, too."

Her stomach went cold as terror prickled at the base of her neck. Had her prayer come too late for Sam?

Unable to accept that possibility, she shook her head, a movement she instantly regretted as firecracker bursts of pain popped in her ears. Groaning, she felt Java's tongue, warm and wet on the back of her hand.

"He wouldn't have left *you*," Ruby said, her gaze latching on to the SUV at the wood's edge, her body trembling at the thought of risking not only her life but her daughter's on the astronomically small chance that she might be able to rescue her "partner" with a chair leg. If Sam was even out there, still alive.

The fine hairs behind her neck rose, warning her to stay put—or better yet to run back inside the room and lock the door. Warning her that Zoe had to be her focus, Zoe's welfare her real responsibility.

Java raised her head and growled, and from the direction of the woods, Ruby heard a staccato burst of gunfire.

Her choice made, she spun on her heel and bolted, intent on getting back to safety . . .

And totally surprised when she ran headlong into its polar opposite.

CHAPTER TWENTY-NINE

I never hear the word "escape"
Without a quicker blood,
A sudden expectation,
A flying attitude.

—Emily Dickinson,
from "I Never Hear the Word Escape"

Bleeding and exhausted, Sam waded, swam, and fought his way along the slimy loop of bayou. Disgusting as it was, he'd been damned lucky to fall, then slide his way down into it while running for his life.

The shooting had stopped as quickly as it started. Thinking the agents had already left the wooded area, Sam had nearly gotten himself killed by moving too quickly. Now he just hoped the shooter had mistaken Sam's sudden disappearance for a kill—a natural mistake since the drop-off couldn't be seen from his angle.

Sam figured he didn't have long before the agents figured out where he'd gone. But they wouldn't know he hadn't been shot, just scraped and cut up from his tumble. And they wouldn't know, as he did, that this stinking mud hole connected at one end with the navigable waterway—if he could make it without becoming mired in the muck or succumbing to fatigue . . . or running into something huge and hungry.

At some point, Sam had read about the rarity of alligator attacks in Texas, about the total lack of verified fatalities. Still, he was powerless to keep the primordial terror at bay, the marrow-deep fear of being eaten, of being snapped and broken and torn to bite-sized bits.

An image of the doomed deer jolted through his awareness, compelling him to fight even harder to make progress.

Cheer up, he thought as he struggled to pull a leg from the deep muck. *You'll probably drown a hell of a long time before you're eaten.*

Pathetic as it was, the thought struck him as funny, and a muffled snort of laughter gave him the burst of energy needed to reach deeper water. As he began to swim, he forced himself to slow his breathing, to focus on his strokes rather than the panic roaring through his brain. Worrying about alligators, DEA bullets, and what was happening to Ruby wouldn't save him—no more than it would help her. Even so, it took a long time for the cool water to slow his racing thoughts.

And even longer to quiet the suicidal temptation to turn back.

Though Best had precisely measured the amount of veterinary tranquilizer in the hypo and jabbed the full measure in her upper arm, Ruby was still struggling, reminding him that even the snared rabbit is capable of drawing blood.

He should have fucking known, should have realized after watching her tear into Coffin. It had been Best's pleasure, killing the foul bastard who had long since served his purpose. But as Ruby fought on, Best feared he'd have to kill her to keep her from ripping out his eyes or biting through the hand he used to muffle her screams. Desperate to subdue her, he pinned her with his greater weight, pinned her until her kicks wound down to mere twitches. Until she finally went limp beneath him.

By that time, he heard sirens. Kicking a large dog to send it yelping out of his way, he tossed the woman in the trunk of the Mustang, then ran around the corner to find a room with its door ajar. Within moments, he emerged with a laptop computer and sped off, intent on finding out exactly what he'd captured.

CHAPTER THIRTY

The idea of death, the fear of it, haunts the human animal like nothing else; it is a mainspring of human activity—designed largely to avoid the fatality of death, to overcome it by denying in some way that it is the final destiny of man.

—Ernest Becker,
from *The Denial of Death*

April 7

This time, she lay submerged just inches beneath the water's surface, only her eyes and nostrils protruding as she watched the paddle dig and twist, a trail of bubbles rising with each blade-stroke.

Tucking her short legs against her body, she used her tail to propel herself in the intruder's wake, not because she recognized the metal beast as prey but because its size and shape nudged another instinct, one that compelled her to defend her territory against others of her kind.

Her interest waned as thumps and vocalizations reached her ears, sounds she associated not with saurians but humans. She went still among the lily pads but didn't withdraw, mostly because she had sometimes known the boatmen to clean their catches on the water and toss the heads and entrails—an easy meal—over the side.

Even a decade earlier, she might have been frightened off by

the increasingly loud noise: the scraping, banging, and the hu-
man's strange grunts. But large as she'd grown, she feared little,
so it was not until something heavy flopped awkwardly into the
water that she flipped her powerful tail and disappeared into the
depths . . .

Until she was drawn back a few hours later by the scent of
blood seeping from the plastic. Suspecting a trap, such as the one
that had shorn off half her rear leg many seasons earlier, she
swam away and returned to it several times, until the sweetly
enticing scent of decomposing flesh finally lured her back for
good.

At long, long last, Sam was living up—or down, he realized—to the McCoy name. Though he'd fought the
stigma of the family reputation all his life, he felt only
exultation as he untied the boat from its dock and mo-
tored off, grateful to the owner, who'd hidden a spare
ignition key so carelessly.

He'd write a thank-you note from the penitentiary,
or—if he got extremely lucky—from whatever foreign
clime he chose for his retirement. Somewhere tropical,
he thought as he shivered in his sodden clothing. But it
was no more than a fantasy, a derelict's dream of finding
a winning lottery ticket in the gutter. Realistically, Sam
figured that his days—hell, his *hours*—as a free man were
numbered.

For one thing, the DEA agents who'd come after him
weren't stupid, nor were any of the other law enforcers
who'd be called in to assist in the manhunt. If they'd
decided he was involved in meth production and was
possibly a murderer, they'd spare no effort to hunt him
down.

Ruby, who was almost certainly in custody, might
protest, but they weren't likely to buy whatever story she
concocted. Even with the laptop and the flash drive in

hand, it would take days or weeks for law enforcement to unravel all the questions. Days or weeks when Zoe Monroe might have no more than hours.

So what are you going to do about it? What can you, at this point?

As a breeze ghosted along the starlit bayou, Sam's teeth began to chatter. Though a temperature in the low sixties wouldn't ordinarily pose a problem, his wet clothing, his prior injuries, and the aftermath of his exertion made for an uncomfortable—potentially lethal—combination.

Which meant that before he considered what, if anything, he *could* do, he was going to need to find his way to shelter and dry clothing—to help, if he could come up with anyone he might trust. And he was going to have to find it on the water, in the darkness, with a large group of professionals out to bring him in . . .

Or maybe they were looking to bring him *down* instead.

"Ruby. Ruby, wake up. Please—it's been *hours*. Wake up before he comes back."

Like newsprint in the rain, the edges of the words blurred. Eventually, emotion bled through. Concern, regret, raw terror. Odors, too, musty, muddy, woodsy. Something like the scent of Paulie's cabin, except—could that be blood?

The last of these pulled Ruby closer to the dream-lake's surface, close enough to finally recognize the voice. With a start, she sucked in a breath—or tried to, then choked on panic before she understood her mouth was taped. Bucking, she jerked forward, pulling taut against whatever held her upright and immobile.

"Don't try and fight it," warned the speaker. "Please don't fight it. You can breathe through your nose if you calm down. But you can't let yourself get upset; you'll clog up and you'll suffocate."

Misty, Ruby realized. It was her sister talking to her, helping her breathe underwater. Ruby allowed herself to drift along with this new current, allowed the air to ebb and flow from her lungs.

Yet this time, she remained anchored to her body. To the sick throb at her temples and the wrenching ache in her joints. She tried to shift, to curl into a less painful position, yet the bonds pulled at her flesh, uncomfortable, unyielding, and altogether real.

"He taped you to the chair. Don't struggle." Misty slurred her words, sounding tired or drugged or maybe sick. From somewhere more distant, perhaps inside a nearby room, a radio played what sounded like a car dealership commercial.

Desperate to see her, to assure herself that Misty truly was alive, Ruby tried to open her eyes. But it was dark— pitch-black in this place, or maybe she'd been somehow blinded?

Or she could be dead. Dead along with Misty: a pair of rotting bodies at the bottom of the lake.

"Your—your mouth and eyes are both taped. But if . . . if you tilt your head toward the sound of my voice, if you lean toward me just a little," Misty whispered, "I may be able to reach the edges of the pieces on your face."

Ruby tried as hard as she could, frantic to see, to breathe freely and speak. And needing—yet terrified— to ask about her daughter. She heard Misty straining, heard her whimper, too, as if whatever she was doing was costing her pain.

"I can't—I'm just a couple of inches short, but I'll never reach it this way." Misty sounded near tears, yet somehow unfocused. "I'm so sorry . . . you can't ever know how sorry. This is my fault, all of it. I don't understand, but oh God, Ruby. I really screwed up."

Unwilling to give in, Ruby tested her bonds' weaknesses and her own strengths. She found little to give her hope. Her fingers moved but her wrists and elbows were taped firmly to the seat back. Her ankles gave a little, more so as she flexed them. With nothing else to do, she continued working them while Misty whispered to her.

"I gave Dylan a big deposit for materials. He was supposed to come out with a crew and take care of the roof and that other stuff you and I talked about. But he kept making all these excuses, and then he quit returning my calls."

Ruby was surprised, but mostly aggravated. She didn't want that story now, while she was frantic to know about her daughter. Why couldn't her sister understand that? And why did she sound so *off*? Had she taken something, or had Best forcibly injected her with whatever he'd used to nail Ruby in the upper arm?

"I should've gone to Paulie or talked to you about it, but instead I tracked down Dylan and cornered him at home. He was screwed up, Rube, way strung out—I haven't seen him like that ever, not even in his bad old days right after high school.

"It took me a while, but finally, he broke down and told me he was the driver who hit the little Bradley girl last year." Misty wept audibly as she continued. "He knew he hurt her real bad, but he panicked and took off in his truck. Afterward, he sat home crying, waiting and waiting for someone to show up and arrest him. But nobody ever came, and that messed with his head even worse."

Ruby heard her sister's compassion, but she didn't share it. Why hadn't Misty mentioned Zoe yet? Was she purposely avoiding the subject or too overwhelmed by her own emotions to comprehend that Ruby cared for nothing else now?

"As the months went by, the guilt got worse," said Misty. "He couldn't eat or sleep. That's when Dylan started with the cocaine, started blowing tons of money on it, neglecting customers. Finally, Holly couldn't take it anymore. She moved back to her parents' place in Longview a couple of weeks ago.

"All I did was try to help him. I swear, that's all I really wanted. I thought together, we could beat it like I helped him beat it last time. Then he could fix up your house and everything could get back to normal. And you wouldn't have to know I'd nearly lost your money."

Ruby didn't understand. If this was about Dylan—and her sister's naive tendency to believe the best of people— how did DeserTek fit in? DeserTek and the flash drive Ruby had so foolishly smuggled out of Iraq.

"But he was in a lot deeper trouble this time," Misty said. "These drug people he was wrapped up with found out about the accident somehow, and they were black-mailing him to keep it quiet, especially from his dad. They drained Dylan dry and refused to believe him when he told them he was out of money. And they were going to hurt him—maybe even go after Holly—if he didn't come up with it. But it was never enough, Ruby. No matter what I gave him, they always wanted more."

Finally able to reach the floor with her feet, Ruby used them to scoot herself closer to her sister. Pain flared with even that small movement, but she gritted her teeth and fought past it.

"Yes, that's it," whispered Misty. "That's it, just a little—careful. Don't tip over. If you fall, he'll hear us— and if he does, it's over. As horrible—as awful as it was with Coffin, this guy's so much—when you look into his eyes, there's nothing in them, nothing human."

Ruby's flesh crawled with a fevered chill, for she knew without a doubt that Misty had to mean Best. Recalling the horror of their phone calls, the nightmare of what he'd done to Elysse, she wanted to scream at her sister, *Where is he?*

Was he in the room with the radio, where Ruby heard the muffled sounds of what sounded like a baseball game? Was he in there with Zoe, doing something to her? At the thought, Ruby's eyes burned behind the tape, and her nose grew stuffy. As breathing grew more difficult, she used her feet to scoot a little closer.

"There. Right there." Misty's words were followed by more straining sounds and breathy sobs of pain.

Ruby's heart bumped went she felt the first touch, when she felt a pulling near her mouth. The pressure hurt; the damned tape must be wound around the back of her head, but at last, Misty must have found an end, an end she started working to peel away.

Don't cry, Ruby ordered herself, since already, she felt suffocated. *No matter how much it hurts, you can't afford to cry.*

The tape proved stubborn, coming away in tiny increments. But at last, just as bright warnings flashed across the black field of her vision, the corner of her mouth was freed, allowing her to suck in the most welcome breath she'd ever taken.

"Zoe," she attempted to say, but for all her urgency, the name came out indistinct and muffled.

But judging from Misty's sharp inhalation, she must have understood Ruby's meaning nonetheless.

"Zoe's right here," she said, "locked in the next room. I saw her a little while ago. He brought her to me with a basin of water and a cloth to let us wash a little. You'll be proud, Ruby. Proud of how she's holding up."

Ruby silently thanked God that her daughter lived

and was nearby. Still, it seemed intolerably cruel to be so close to her yet absolutely helpless to go to her, to hold her, or get her to a place of safety. Once more, she struggled against her bonds, as if her will alone could break them.

"Shh, be still," Misty warned her. "I'm getting there, a little at a time. If he comes out, though, if he sees what I've done . . ." Anxiety tightened her voice.

As more tape came away from her mouth, Ruby managed, "He hurt Zoe?"

"Her arm's sore. That bastard Coffin twisted it, trying to make me—but physically, she's not in bad shape. Scared, mostly."

Locked up and terrified, and crying for a mother who couldn't come to get her. What would that do to a child's psyche? Ruby worked her stiff jaw, a thousand questions squirming in her brain.

"I almost have it," Misty whispered, "but you have to promise to be very quiet. He's only in the second bedroom. He took something from your pocket and shut himself in there with a computer."

He had the flash drive, Ruby realized, heart jumping inside her chest. She didn't know which scared her more, the thought of what he'd do if he believed somehow he had the right one, or how he would retaliate once he learned he didn't.

The last of the tape pulled away from her mouth, so suddenly that some of her hair came with it. Ruby bit her tongue to keep from shrieking.

"Sorry," Misty said, lightly stroking Ruby's cheek with her fingertips. "But if you can stand it, I'll work on your eyes, too. It'd go a lot faster, if I had both hands."

"You're taped, too?"

"Chained to this bed frame, wrist and ankle. Or what's left of 'em anyway."

"What do you mean, Misty? Did they hurt you?" Ruby asked, worried by what she heard in her sister's voice.

"Doesn't matter right now. Except—the skin, where it was broken . . . there's a pretty bad infection, from where I tried to work myself free."

Ruby felt the movement of her sister's fingers, the careful search for the end of the tape covering her eyes. Thinking of Best, so nearby with the flash drive, she struggled to imagine some scenario where this would come out all right. Maybe he'd decide he'd gotten what he'd been paid to get, then leave them. Soon after, perhaps the DEA or some deputies or she didn't care who would burst onto the scene to save them. Or maybe they'd come early, arrest or, better yet, shoot Best full of more holes than a bombing range.

But when Ruby came to a fantasy where Sam smashed down the door, her breath hitched painfully. For instinct told her that he hadn't risked so much, given up his future, only to get cold feet and bail out—that when he'd climbed onto the porch roof of a burning house, when he'd come after her at Dylan's, when he'd eased the horror of the situation by making love to her, he'd shown her the real man behind the reputation, the man who'd already screwed up his life once to help someone in need.

The man she'd miss forever, because this time, she was sure he'd died helping. Had been murdered by Hobson Best to keep him from interfering in the man's plans to abduct her. Trapped behind the mask of tape, she shook, her hot tears burning, and she prayed, prayed with everything left in her, that his ending had at least come swiftly, that Best had been too distracted to make Sam suffer, too hurried to carve him up as he had Elysse.

Loosened by the moisture, the tape pulled more easily

from her eyes. She blinked, trying to clear them, and struggled to focus on the face of the sister she'd thought dead.

At first, she saw nothing but a silhouette, a dim shape backlit by the cheap fluorescent lighting from what appeared to be a nearby kitchen. She had a vague impression of old paneling and an ugly mustard-and-brown-striped sofa shoved back in a corner, but her attention remained fixed on Misty, sitting on a wrought-iron bed of some sort. Misty, whose image slowly cleared.

Ruby gaped to see her looking nothing like the sleek, blonde beauty she had left a year before. Though she struggled not to react emotionally, there was no stopping the flow of tears at the sight of her younger sister's bruised face, tangled hair, and thin frame, swimming within the remnants of torn clothing. Misty's gaze slid away, and Ruby was hammered with the brutal suspicion that powerless to stop it, her sister might have been raped.

"Oh, Misty."

"Let me tell you, sister," she said around a pained smile, "you don't exactly look like Miss America yourself right now."

Flippancy. A good sign. "Yeah, well, as soon as we get out of here, I'll be sure to schedule us a day spa package," Ruby promised. "Ultramega makeovers all the way."

Misty looked away again, then whispered, "They made me get your money, Ruby. Coffin and his girlfriend, Jackie, and their scuzzy friends took Zoe from me, wouldn't let me see her until I brought the—"

"I don't give a damn about the money, Misty. I don't care about a thing you did to stay alive and keep my daughter safe," Ruby said, though anger roared inside her at the news that Jackie had been more involved than she'd admitted. She hoped the bitch had stuck herself deep when she'd fallen on that knife at Paulie's.

Using her feet, Ruby concentrated on scooting closer to her sister.

"But I—" Misty started before she recognized what Ruby was doing. Straining toward Ruby's bound wrist, she whispered, "It hurts for me to reach down, but just . . . a little . . . bit more . . ."

Both sisters' heads jerked toward a sound and the rattling of the doorknob of the nearest closed door. Before Ruby could react, a muffled voice called, "Aunt Misty, who ya talking to? Has my mom come to get us yet?"

Eyes flaring, Ruby sucked in a breath to call out to her daughter, but Misty clapped a hand over her sister's mouth and darted a nervous glance toward a closed door on the opposite end of the room. Light seeped from around its edges, a sign the man inside was very much awake.

"If you'll go to sleep like a good girl," Misty told the child as tears leaked from Ruby's eyes, "I think your mom might come tomorrow."

"But I want to go home *now*," Zoe whined. "I want my own bed and my own—"

"Quiet, Zoe, or he'll hear you." After a warning glance at Ruby, Misty dropped her hand and resumed speaking to the child. "Just go to sleep and you can have some good dreams. I'm counting on you to tell me about them in the morning. Tell me all about the kittens."

"I'm dreaming about hamburgers tonight," Zoe said. "And macaroni and chicken and peas and mashed potatoes. Every kind of good food."

"Mmm," said Misty. "You're making me too hungry. Off to bed now, sweetie. Hugs and kisses."

"Hugs and kisses," came the small and sleepy-sounding voice.

Ruby's focus hung on her daughter's words, on the fact that she was miserable and hungry, trapped, and, worst of all, only a few feet away yet so far out of reach. And a rage boiled up inside Ruby, a murderous fury that made her want to punish everyone responsible. Including herself for sitting here, completely helpless.

As emotion threatened to consume her, she pictured herself locking her heart inside a chest, then pushing it into the lake's depths. Later, when things were settled, she could dive down and retrieve it. She would weep for hours then, over Sam, Elysse, and the terrifying ordeal her child and her sister had gone through. But for now, Ruby understood her strength was needed, her determination. And a courage that she did not feel but must somehow scrape together.

"I'm sorry," Misty whispered, lowering her voice further. "But if she hears you, there'll be no controlling her—and no saving her, either."

She resumed working on the tape at Ruby's wrist, her gaze straying to the limned door and the muttering of voices on the radio.

Nodding, Ruby whispered, "The thing Best wanted, the thing he took off of me. It's not what he expected. Not what he's been demanding. So I have to—*we* have to get out of here before he figures out—"

"That's what I don't understand. What is it? Why did he come looking for you? I was already in too deep, letting Dylan stay with us at the house—your house—to try and get his act together. But the stupid shit invited Coffin and those other creeps to hang out, said they were his *friends*. But everybody was Dylan's friend when he was using.

"It didn't take me long to lose control completely," Misty added, shaking her head. "And when those bastards started cooking drugs, they wouldn't let me take Zoe and leave."

"I had something," Ruby told her, "something I brought

back with me that could damage the company I worked for. Someone was murdered for it, but she passed it off to me first. That's what they're after, Misty. Sorry I got you wound up in this. If I'd had any idea they knew, I never would have—"

"The man in the other room—he showed up at the house and talked to Coffin last week. I got the idea they knew each other from prison. Still, I tried to talk this new guy into helping me and Zoe. Instead, he offered a pile of money," Misty explained, "to *buy* us and hire Coffin to do him a couple of favors. I had no idea what he wanted. I thought it was some sleazy sex thing, so I panicked and grabbed Zoe to make a run for it. When Coffin tried to stop me, Dylan went for his throat."

"Because you were carrying his child," Ruby guessed.

Misty looked up at her sharply. "I might've been stressed out, even moody lately, but no matter what you've heard, I'm not—Dylan and I never—he was my *friend*. *My*—" Choking up, she moved on. "Screwed up or not, he would've killed Coffin except the moneyman—I guess it's the guy you call Best—shot him. Shot him right through the throat."

"He killed Dylan?"

Misty nodded, moisture glimmering on her face. "God, it was so horrible—the gurgling, the kicking. But then Best shot him again, chest this time, and he and Coffin wrapped the body and put it in the canoe. I think Best took it out somewhere and dumped it in the lake."

Ruby thought about the chunks of human flesh recovered, thought about her grief when she'd believed the corpse was Misty's. "Your car was dumped not far off. Your driver's license, too. When they found it, I thought . . . everyone thinks you're dead."

"I am—we all are—if we can't get away from him.

Because he'll kill every one of us with less thought than you'd give to swatting flies."

Ruby heard, as well as felt, the tape rip loose from her wrist. At the same moment she heard heavy footsteps before a radio switched off behind the door.

Footsteps next, a big man striding toward them.

For one heart-freezing moment, Ruby's gaze met Misty's. With nothing to be done to disguise the torn tape, both of them feigned unconsciousness, prayed for invisibility, exactly as newborn fawns will when confronted by the wolf.

THE CEREMONY OF INNOCENCE

Zoe tried to sleep, but all she could think of was her mom coming to get her. Her mom was very brave—Misty and Mrs. Lambert always said so—so maybe she would stop the bad men and then take her and Aunt Misty far away. Or maybe her mom would bring a whole lot of police and they would put the men in jail. On the way home, she would buy everybody pizza.

Zoe rolled over, feeling gritty and sticky and too hot in her blanket. And then she started thinking of the Bad Man making her get off his phone almost as soon as she had started talking. It made her stomach hurt because she'd had a whole lot of things to tell her mother, things she couldn't wait to say until tomorrow.

So as quietly as she could, Zoe crept from her nest to the closet and pulled it open. Slipped inside the blacker darkness and hoped the spiders were asleep in their beds.

Once there, she found Aunt Misty's telephone and

started pushing at the keypad, pretending she was dialing her mother's number.

Except this time, something happened. She didn't know what different thing she'd done, but the phone lit up and made a funny whooshing noise that it had never made before, not even after her aunt whispered instructions on how to turn it on. Maybe she'd done it wrong before because Aunt Misty had said the battery must be dead and though Zoe couldn't see her, she had heard her crying for a long time after that talk.

But now that it worked—really worked—Zoe pushed three buttons, the three buttons from the song her aunt sang with her. The three buttons she had promised would always bring help.

CHAPTER THIRTY-ONE

"The consequences of our crimes long survive their commission, and, like the ghosts of the murdered, forever haunt the steps of the malefactor."

—Sir Walter Scott,
From "The Heart of Midlothian,"
The Waverly Dramas

When karma came back to bite a person's ass in Preston County, Justine Wofford decided it did so with a vengeance. While holding her howling, shrieking wildcat of a son through the ordeal of stitches, she missed a slew of phone calls. She'd neglected to put her cell on vibrate, and the repeated intrusion—an annoyingly insistent jingle she'd let Noah choose—only added to the exam room mayhem.

"No touch, no touch," he cried, a phrase that had

become his favorite since he'd finally started speaking three years earlier, at the age of six.

"Listen, listen, Noah," Justine said in the calmest voice she could manage. "Listen to the sound you picked. Listen to the pretty ring tone."

He quieted—making her wish she'd tried that particular distraction ten minutes earlier—and tilted his head toward the sound. The doctor's shoulders heaved and his lips moved through what looked like a prayer of gratitude as he worked. Meanwhile, a graying nurse sporting multiple chins stood nearby, rubbing at the elbow Noah had kicked and treating Justine to an especially hateful variant of the hairy eyeball.

Exhausted, stressed, and with her ears ringing from the noise, Justine forced herself to grind out, "I'm sorry you were kicked, Ms. Del Monte. Autistic kids don't intentionally set out to hurt others. Noah's just reacting to his own fear and discomfort."

"Reacting to being spoiled, if you ask me," the woman grumbled.

During the years she'd spent in law enforcement, Justine had been shoved by addicts, hit by a belligerent wife beater, and on one especially memorable occasion, pissed on by a drunk. Yet somehow, she had never wanted to shoot anyone more than she now did—Justine glared over at the name tag affixed above a drooping bosom—Marguerite Del Monte, LVN.

Before she could say anything regrettable, Noah did it for her, echoing the nurse's words, down to their snotty intonation: "Spoiled, if you ask me."

Caught off guard by Noah's pitch-perfect imitation, Justine laughed at the shocking outrage blooming in the woman's eyes. Which, quite predictably, infuriated her even more.

"Why, of all the disrespectful—"

"That's enough, Marguerite," said the doctor, a Nordic giant who looked better suited to the college gridiron than a small-town ER. "Why don't you take a break now? Go and put some ice on that elbow."

"Gladly." She huffed out of the room.

Noah, completely unmoved, watched fascinated as the doctor knotted the last stitch. "Flash-flash," he sang.

Justine smiled, pleased to comprehend. "He means the needle," she translated. "He's into the way it gleams when you move it. Careful he doesn't find a way to pocket it when you're not looking."

The doctor, who had earlier introduced himself as Ross Bollinger, glanced up at her. "I'm sorry for what she said to you. I could have her written up or, worse yet, counseled on dealing with our special needs patients."

Justine smiled. "Would it do any good?"

"For that one?" Humor glinted in a pair of gray eyes that crinkled at the corners. "Want the truth, or what the hospital'd expect me to tell you?"

Before she could answer, or decide whether he was flirting, her phone interrupted.

"Sorry about that," she said, with a glance at the caller ID window. "Work's a bitch some days."

"Bitch some days," Noah echoed, leaving her to hope it wouldn't be one of those phrases he would take a shine to and repeat for months on end. Including at the latest Sunday school, where he was already close to wearing out his welcome.

"Go ahead and take it," Dr. Bollinger invited. "Noah and I are doing just fine."

"You're sure?"

"Absolutely, if you're not too long."

The knot in Justine's stomach loosened slightly. Nodding, she reassured him—and herself—by saying, "I'll be right outside."

The ringing stopped, and she took advantage of the lull to check her voice mail, frowning through the news of the disaster found at Dylan Hammett's house—including the presence of a pickup registered to Sam Mc-Coy, who couldn't be located. When she heard about the fresh blood on Hammett's back patio and the hole drilled through the bottom of the truck's fuel tank, she wondered whether McCoy was a murder victim or the perpetrator.

In a subsequent message, she heard the concern in her deputy's voice at the news that Holly Hammett, Dylan's wife, could not be found. The deputy—a competent eight-year veteran named Caruthers—reported that he was going to see Hammett's parents in an attempt to find out what they knew about the situation. . . .

"Oh, shit," she breathed. Caruthers *couldn't* get to Hammett's on the Lake before she did, couldn't be the one to break the news to Paulie that his son's body—or parts of it—had been pulled from the lake. Glancing down at her watch, she checked it against the time the voice mail had been sent.

Too late, she realized. *I'm too damned late already.* As if that weren't disaster enough, the next voice mail brought her a report that a witness had seen Ruby Monroe abducted, thrown into the trunk of a dark Mustang. Parked nearby, another car—the white Corolla she'd been driving—had held a tattooed body, one matching the description of Balderach's suspected killer.

But with the body count increasing by the hour now, Justine couldn't glean a moment's satisfaction that her deputy had gotten justice. She was too busy wondering what other disasters karmic payback would heap atop her tainted term of office . . . a term whose final price she could not yet begin to guess.

One part of Ruby warned she shouldn't look at his face, that if she did, this man would have to kill her.

The other knew that in the end, it wouldn't matter, that her fate and the fates of her family had far less to do with her actions than with this murderer's whims . . . or more likely with the orders some higher-up at DeserTek—maybe even a U.S. official or a senator—had given.

So she looked up at the bastard who had bought her sister and her daughter from a drug dealer as leverage. The bastard who had slaughtered Elysse Steele simply to send Ruby herself a message—her stomach spasmed with the thought—and killed Sam McCoy to keep him from helping her.

Defiantly, she glared, taking in the murderer's short hair and dark eyes, the hard muscles of a weight lifter's physique. With her loathing and her fury and her terror for her family all crowding to the forefront, it took her a full minute to register the dangerous wrath in the man's expression.

It took her even longer—seeing him in this shocking context—to understand who this man was, to realize she knew Hobson Best's real identity.

Which, she understood with sickening horror, dropped her odds of survival even further.

"You—you killed—he was your—" she started.

"You thought I was so careless"—her captor stalked toward her, his gaze as cold as any hunter's—"so fucking *incompetent* that I wouldn't even check the flash drive?"

Eyes wide, she cried out when he caught her by the throat.

"You thought I was nothing but a *shadow,* a man who'd accept a contract with no thought"—he raised his free hand, revealing the coiled, orange extension cord he carried, its metal pronged end drooping toward her, threatening as a serpent's head—"absolutely no intention of keeping my word."

He released her neck and grabbed the cord, about three feet down from its plug. Without asking her a question, or even allowing her more than a split second to fill her lungs, he lashed her, raining his fury in the form of blows that split flesh at her chest, her elbow, thigh, and face. Screaming, sobbing, she lost track of the places that the cord struck, lost track of everything except the terror that she would die here, without a prayer of saving her child.

Misty, too, shrieked, begging him to stop. Yelling that Ruby couldn't answer questions, couldn't be of any use if she died. His red-faced frenzy didn't slow a moment until Misty cried, "How will you keep your word now? How will you keep from turning into a shadow if you can't stop?"

The killer froze, his fist raised, the snakelike cord dangling limp beneath it, dripping with Ruby's blood.

It was only then that the pain hit her, pain that obliterated all other awareness, from the sounds of her own daughter's frightened wails behind the closed door to her desperate need to think of something—any lie or promise—that would save them.

CHAPTER THIRTY-TWO

Between the idea
And the reality
Between the motion
And the act
Falls the Shadow

—T. S. Eliot,
from "The Hollow Men"

Sam's fingers shook so badly he could barely punch the buttons of the cell phone he'd recovered from the nest box. Dangerous as it had been to venture so far on the lake, he'd risked replacing the phone he'd ruined during his swim. Risked being caught by armed agents on the water.

In Paulie's shack now, he shuddered beneath layers of towels and blankets he'd wrapped around himself and wished for Ruby's warmth. Or Java's, or even his truck's heater. All of which lay far beyond his grasp.

"McCoy? That you?" Paulie slurred, sounding strange, as if he had been drinking heavily. "Do you know already? Do you *fucking* know—"

"I—I know they're looking for me." Sam had trouble speaking with his teeth chattering so hard. "Know I have to get a car before it's too late."

"That bitch Wofford sent someone to tell me Dylan— they're saying my son's dead, Sam." Paulie sounded as if someone were sawing through his arm with a dull blade.

"Dylan's dead?" The news hammered flat Sam's lingering hope that Dylan might be keeping Misty safe, that the two of them had gone somewhere together. Sam squatted down on his heels and pulled the towels around him tighter, needing warmth to make sense of what his friend was saying.

"They found his—found someone in the lake, but it can't really be him, can it? How could he have been out there—supposedly for days? I would have fucking known it. And Anna, she's his mother. Wouldn't she have felt it? How can parents not know that their only child's gone?"

Sam flashed onto a memory of Paulie clapping Dylan's shoulder at his wedding and trash-talking about stealing away his son's bride, both father and son grinning from ear to ear. "I don't know what to say. I'm sorry, Paulie, sorry for your family."

Had Dylan's body—or parts of it—been the one recovered close to Misty's car? Or had both of them been murdered—two obstacles in the path of the kidnappers' ideal hostage, Zoe?

"What the fuck do you know about sorry?" Paulie demanded. "What do you know about my boy? They sent—sheriff sent a goddamned deputy to tell me—her freaking lackey, after everything I did for that bitch."

Sam wondered at the edge of fury in the man's voice, and at the *"after everything I did for that bitch."* He'd known Paulie was dead set against his old enemy Roger Savoy winning the sheriff's office, suspected that Savoy might shine too bright a light on Paulie's Play Room—a place Sam scrupulously avoided—if he were elected. But Sam had had no idea Paulie had played a major role in helping Justine Wofford defeat the man.

"They're telling me they found your goddamned truck at Dylan's," Paulie told him. "And there were windows smashed and blood in back. They're telling me you might have—"

"You have to believe me," Sam said. "I had nothing to do with what happened to Dylan. This evening, I went over to find Ruby—"

"She was going to see him—" Paulie stammered. "Goin' because that crack whore Jackie said she saw Dylan with Misty. Ruby swallowed those lies, even though I told her my son had nothing to do with all that. He's a happily married man with a—with a business—and I—I love him, Sam. I love my boy. . . ."

Hammett broke down completely, causing Sam to close his eyes against the force of the man's grief. To think that everything Paulie and Anna had been through with Dylan, all the love and all the struggle, had boiled down to this loss. The sadness and waste of it tore the breath from Sam's lungs.

And reminded him of Ruby, in the midst of her own fight to save her child.

"Could Ruby have hurt my son?" Paulie asked Sam. "Could she—people do things when they're desperate. They get crazy."

"You said yourself the deputy told you Dylan had been in the lake for days. Besides, somebody jumped Ruby this evening at your son's house. Probably the same person who hurt Dylan."

"Who, Sam? Fucking *who*? Because when I find out, I'm going to kill the bastard."

"Too late," Sam told him, thinking of the tattooed body he'd found in the trunk. "I'm pretty sure it's already taken care of."

"What do you mean by that? What do you have to do with this, Sam?"

Realizing he'd get no help from Paulie, that his grief was quickly turning to suspicion, Sam said, "Nothing. But please tell Anna I'm sorry. I'll keep both of you in my thoughts."

"Keeping both of us in your thoughts? You think those kinds of fucking platitudes are—"

A beeping interrupted, and to Sam's astonishment, he realized he had an incoming call on a number he had given no one. On a number he had used but once.

"—are worth shit," Paulie finished. "I want answers, that's all I want, and I fucking know you have 'em. So where the hell're you now? You back at the cabin?"

"I'm heading out of town. I've gotta run now, Paulie." Though he felt horrible about it, Sam cut off his old friend to accept the second call.

"I'm here," Sam said, not sure whether to expect Luke or maybe Sybil, if his former partner had given her the number.

Or for all he knew, it could be the feds calling to let him know they were just outside the cabin and a sniper had his ass in his sights.

"Sybil warned me to stay out of this, but I talked her into forwarding the information," Luke told him. "Once I saw what you were tangled up with, there was no way I could let you—listen, Misty Bailey's cell phone was turned on tonight, and I've got a bead on the GPS coordinates. It isn't far from your house—not far at all, it looks like."

Sam scrambled clumsily for a pad and pen among the supplies he had cached earlier. As he forced his stiff fingers to do his bidding, Sam was humbled by the chance his friend had taken, especially with his current family situation. Whether Luke had hacked into a cell phone system or the sheriff's office computers, he'd taken the kind of risks he normally farmed out to Sybil.

"Thanks, Luke, and let me copy down that information."

"You know, the emergency responders could have gotten the location, too," Luke assured him. "They'll be hot to save this kid, or at least to get the guy who murdered one of their own. Every cop on the planet *lives* for chances like this."

"Unless their boss has been paid off to suppress the information." Sam briefly explained what he had found in Sheriff Wofford's banking records. "Or worse yet, she could warn the kidnapper somebody's using Misty's cell phone."

"You can't go charging into this," Luke said. "If you need to bypass the sheriff's department, make an anonymous call to one of the other agencies involved."

The risks swarmed in Sam's head like hornets, from concerns that the information would leak back to the locals to the knowledge that he'd be giving away his own location with the phone call. He weighed them against the lunacy of the only plan he could come up with.

But time tipped the scales of his decision. His gut told him the killer would learn of the call made from Misty's phone at any moment. Once he found out, would he destroy it and change locations? Or would he be enraged enough to slaughter the person who had dialed?

"I need those coordinates," Sam insisted. "And if you can, go to your computer and plug them into Google Earth. Get me an address or some landmark."

Without a GPS device on hand, he'd have to rely on the global mapping software, with its street address layer, to help him find the place. And he'd have to pray that it was close enough to the water's edge for him to reach by boat.

"Shit, Sam, you think I'm calling to get you *killed?* You can't go charging over there, especially on your own. Sybil spoke to me personally, told me some of the things she'd heard about Best. This psycho will take you apart. Literally. And what's more, he'll enjoy the hell out of it. I wouldn't walk into that with anything less than an army."

"Just give me the information, and I'll call in the cavalry," Sam promised, eager to get Luke off his back.

"Who? Who are you going to call on this one? Tell me now, or this conversation's finished."

"The Texas Rangers." Sam recalled reading somewhere that the legendary law enforcers sometimes investigated sheriff's department officials accused of corruption. So hopefully, his story would ring true to Luke.

"You'd better. Because Susan says she misses your visits to the ranch here. Told me to quit my damned pacing around and do what I had to do to help you."

Sam smiled, relieved to know both Maddoxes had elected to forgive him. "Thanks, man, and give that gorgeous wife of yours a big hug for me," he said.

The two men exchanged information, Luke giving Sam landmarks as well as the phone number of the nearest company of Rangers. Sam, for his part, shared with Luke the password to allow access to his online storage vault, along with instructions on launching the same automated e-mail program he'd used to expose the California-based company that had screwed thousands of its own retirees.

"Isn't this the kind of thing that nearly landed your ass in jail the last time?" Luke reminded him. "Come on, McCoy. You ought to know better than anyone that the feds have gotten really good at tracking this kind of—"

"It's not going to launch. It's just a fail-safe, meant for leverage." He explained his plan to his old partner, with one notable omission.

"If this comes back on me," Luke said, "if it ends up hurting my family—"

"It won't," Sam promised, knowing that the signs, the

m.o., would all point back to him. And if the program launched, it would mean he'd been killed, after which he wouldn't give a damn what was said about him.

It wasn't as if he had a good name to worry over, or any real familial connections.

Regretfully, he thought of Aaron's daughter, his not-quite niece, and his bond with Luke's family, threads so tenuous and fragile the slightest breeze would break them. And he thought of Ruby Monroe, a connection he had even less right to consider, but one his heart claimed nonetheless.

"What. Did you do. With the flash drive your *friend* gave you?" Trembling with rage, Best stood over Ruby Monroe, the extension cord still dangling from his hand.

With one eye swollen shut, the other fluttered closed as her head drooped to one side. Already injured and still drugged, she'd been in no shape to take a beating. Perhaps in no shape to survive it.

What on earth had he done, to toss aside his obligations—and all logic—to indulge a fit of temper? Maybe it was coming back here, festering in the same swamp that had spawned him, that had shorn him of his hard-won, carefully crafted composure. But how could he live with himself, fail to deliver on the promise he had given his employer? How could he bear the rest of his life stranded in the realm of shadow?

"Please." Tears streamed down Misty Bailey's dirty face. "Unchain me so I can take care of my sister. If she dies now, what use has this all been? How will you ever find what it is you're looking for?"

He stared at her, suspicious but desperate to recover control of the situation . . . and himself.

"I can help you," she said. "I can get her to say what

she's done with—what did you say it was? A flash drive? She'll tell me if I ask her . . . as soon as she can speak."

Misty yelped, flinching at his sudden movement as he dropped the extension cord and tore off the bedsheet covering her lower body. The horror in her eyes told him she feared he'd rip off her filthy shorts and rape her, that she believed he was no better than the revolting animal he had pulled off her more than once.

Rather than touching her, Best looked down at her chained ankle, found it red and oozing, badly swollen. If she ran, she wouldn't get far on it, and besides, he had long since shattered the thin veneer of her courage. Had long since destroyed her capacity for resistance.

"If I unchain you, and you try to run"—he stared into the depths of her blue eyes—"I will find you and I'll make you watch me kill them. I know how to make it last a long time. Do you believe me?"

She nodded, and he saw a woman broken. Broken to his will.

"Do you?" he roared, coming within inches of her face.

"Yes, I do believe you, and I promise—"

"I promise *you*," he whispered, warming to the sense of power, of total domination. And feeling the start of an erection that had nothing to do with the lithe body on display before him and everything to do with the weakness he exploited. "I promise you, you'll be the one to cut the child's throat, that by the time I offer you that chance, you'll thank me for giving you the means to silence her screams."

"Whatever you want, you will have it," Misty promised. "Just let me help my sister. And let me help you. Please."

Confident of his control, Best went to his bedroom to

retrieve a basin of water, a sharp knife, and the keys to the two locks he'd used to secure her.

Bringing them back out, he told Misty, "You have an hour to extract the information. Exactly one hour before I begin my work."

CHAPTER THIRTY-THREE

The belief in a supernatural source of evil is not necessary; men alone are quite capable of every wickedness.
—Joseph Conrad

When Justine's father arrived and gave her the chance to finally listen to all of her voice mail, Paulie's Hammett's grief-soaked fury made her blood run cold. Wincing at the stream of profanity, she disconnected, jumped into her SUV, and started driving toward the South Lake area, heedless of her son's blood, which had stained her white silk blouse.

In his present state, Hammett might do anything, *say* anything to anyone. He was the proverbial loose cannon, his fuse lit by a pain too unspeakable to bear.

On some level, he must understand that she had nothing to do with Dylan's death. But in all the years of the younger Hammett's screwups, there had always been a Wofford there to protect him from the consequences of his actions. Her husband certainly had, allowing Paulie to spirit his son away to rehab rather than forcing him to face charges, and later, after Dylan had redeemed himself, overlooking several complaints about the way he did business.

So Paulie had felt comfortable, he'd told Justine a few weeks after Lou's death, keeping a Wofford in office rather than seeing "that hard-ass Savoy" claim the sheriff's badge. When Paulie had first approached her with an offer of support, she'd thought he and his friends, a handful of the county's most influential business leaders, only meant to help with the fund-raising. A crawfish boil at Hammett's on the Lake, perhaps, or at most, a sit-down dinner at the local country club.

What she hadn't understood was the meaning of an "offer of support" in a Preston County race, and the shocking ease with which an outsider could be sucked into the area's influence machine. To complicate matters, Hammett and the others felt certain she must know, since they had "worked closely," as they put it, with her husband over the course of his six terms.

By the time Justine understood that her new allies intended to steal the election for her, there had been no way to extricate herself. Not without destroying her own career—possibly even earning jail time—and not without bringing Lou's own crimes into the public eye.

So she'd allowed herself to be talked into accepting the unthinkable. Told herself it was for the good of the citizens of Preston County, who would be better off without a sanctimonious prick like Roger Savoy in charge of law enforcement. Once in office, she could change things, let the county's movers and shakers know her influence was not for sale.

It had been a hopelessly naive thought, a damned case study of how a public servant fell into corruption.

"You think you can just accept our help, and then play the Virgin Mary?" Hammett had asked her. "You buck us, it'll come out, and we both know whose damned name will be splashed all over the headlines. And what'll happen to that boy of *yours* when you're serving your sentence?"

Justine had consoled herself with the thought that it wasn't as if these men, Dogwood's most influential business leaders, expected a whole lot for their money. A "lost" traffic ticket, stepped-up patrols around their properties, personal attention when they or their families were in need.

But this evening, that unspoken contract had been broken. Hammett thought she'd deliberately blown him off, sending a deputy to break the news to him that his only child had been found dead. And worse yet, she had been the Wofford on duty when the consequences of Dylan's actions had finally, fatally caught up with him.

But only minutes away from Hammett's, a call came over her radio. A report of a 9-1-1 hang-up made from the phone registered to Misty Bailey.

Lacking the army Luke had suggested, or even access to any weapon other than a utility knife on his belt, Sam had risked placing an anonymous call to the Texas Rangers before returning to the stolen boat. With only moonlight and a more powerful flashlight he'd picked up to guide him, he raced in the direction of a bayou he knew well, a trip that would have taken only twenty minutes in daylight.

Before setting out, he hesitated, then made another call, this time to information, which he asked to connect him to the main office of the Hook-It-Cook-It Motor Court.

Opal answered on the sixth ring, her creaky voice tightening when she realized it was he. "That woman— the woman who was with you—Trisha saw him take her. Saw him toss her into his trunk and drive away."

Sam's heart slammed against his sternum. *Ruby.* "Who did? *Who?* Did you call and report it?"

"The car was a dark Mustang—that's all she knows. And some deputies are here already. They found—they say they've found a body in the back of that white car you were driving. Did you kill that man, Sam McCoy? Did I shelter a killer?"

"No, ma'am. I swear you didn't," Sam said. "I'll explain it all to you as soon as Ruby's safe."

"Trisha found your room's door kicked in. If you left any valuables, they're gone now. Except . . . she found a dog whining near the door."

"Hurt?" Sam asked, heart sinking.

"She's fine. We have her at the office. At least until we have to leave tomorrow evening."

After thanking her, Sam disconnected and started the boat's motor. Because if Best had Ruby—and undoubtedly both the laptop and the flash drive—Sam couldn't afford to wait for the Texas Rangers—or to risk finding they'd doubted his anonymous information and called Wofford. He couldn't sit around or run to save his own hide while the woman he cared for—maybe even loved— was slaughtered with her family.

He set off at an insane speed, counting on his memory and knowledge of the waterways and praying he wouldn't smash the boat's hull against a cypress knee and kill himself before he reached his destination.

Water wakened Ruby, the lake's waves rolling over her face as she lay on her back.

Except this time, the nightmare had a sound track, its dark imagery overlaid with Misty's voice.

"You have to wake up, Ruby. You have to talk to me now."

More moisture. But Ruby recognized the coolness of a damp cloth touching her face. It touched off a cascade of a pain so overwhelming that her vision dimmed once more.

Misty grabbed her shoulder, shook her. "No, Ruby, you can't pass out. There's no time for that."

"Don't touch—don't touch me," Ruby begged. "It hurts. Hurts so much. Let me go back to—"

"*No.* Don't you get it? He'll kill Zoe. If you don't tell him about the flash drive, he's going to cut her into pieces!"

Ruby's eyes shot open. Or at least one of them did. She wasn't even certain she still *had* a left eye.

But adrenaline jolted with one last burst of energy, giving her the strength to sit upright on the bed. Only now Misty sat in the chair, festooned with scraps of duct tape. As far as Ruby could see, she was free, and the kidnapper was gone.

"Tell me," Misty pleaded. "Tell me before he comes back. What did you do with it, Ruby? We only have a few minutes left before he—"

"We have to grab Zoe and get out now."

"Are you *crazy?*" Misty demanded. "I can barely walk, and you're half dead."

With a superhuman effort, Ruby struggled to her feet. A wave of nausea rose to meet her, but she forced herself to fight it off, to stagger toward the door that would lead her to her daughter. The room whirled around her head, stars exploding in her vision.

"Just give him what he wants," Misty whispered furiously. "For once in your life, why can't you listen to me?"

Using the doorknob to hold herself upright, Ruby lowered her voice. "Don't you think I would've given him the damned thing if I had it?"

Though the knob turned, the door merely rattled when she tried to push it open. From the other side, her daughter called, "Mama, did you come to get us? Did you come to get me like you promised?"

"I'm here, Zoe. I'm here, baby." With her vision nearly useless, Ruby felt along the door's seam. Until she found the latch and combination lock that secured it.

From behind her, Ruby heard a metallic clicking, the unmistakable sound of a gun cocking.

"Perhaps I can help you with that," came the even more alarming voice. "Let me get that door and bring out your daughter for you."

CHAPTER THIRTY-FOUR

"What we fear comes to pass more speedily than what we hope."

—Publilius Syrus,
from *Moral Sayings*

Emotion overwhelmed Ruby, dropping her to her knees. Relief to see her child, after twelve months and a journey through hell. Fury at the sight of Zoe's tangled hair and thinness, the terror in her eyes. Love and fear and overwhelming pain, far surpassing the physical agony Ruby had endured.

She wrapped her bleeding arms around her daughter and kissed the child's temple. For her part, Zoe cried and shouted at their captor with every scrap of outrage a four-year-old can muster, "You hurt my mom! You're a very bad man."

"Shut up, if you don't want me hurting her a lot more." He grabbed Zoe's arm and pulled her toward him.

Refusing to let go, Ruby rose to wedge herself between the two, turning her body to force him to let go. He quickly jammed hard metal against her temple. The muzzle of the handgun she'd heard cocked.

"Do you really want her to watch you die like this?" whispered the man who called himself Best, the man who could only be J. B. McCoy. "Do you want her showered with your brains and bone and blood before I cut her to pieces?"

Rage welled up, bubbling past all else. Letting go of Zoe, she turned to glare at him, only inches from a familiar face warped by a sadistic psyche. A face that looked less like his brother Sam's, she thought with a stab of raw grief, with each passing moment.

"You really get off on the sick threats, don't you?" Since he clearly meant to kill them—would *have* to kill them, even if she'd had the damned flash drive to give him, her only hope was to knock him off-balance for an instant, an instant she prayed would give her even the smallest chance of changing the outcome for her family. "You're a real freak, aren't you, *J.B. McCoy?* Not half the man your brother was."

As if in slow motion, she saw his face contort and his hand move, trigger finger tightening as the barrel swung toward Zoe's chest. Too late, she realized he meant to punish her by killing Zoe. Too slowly, Ruby dropped her shoulder with the intent of driving it hard into his sternum.

But she was too close for a solid hit, too slow and weak to make a difference.

Instead, it was her sister, Misty, who attacked, smashing the water basin behind his head. Misty who sent him staggering, his hand flailing as the gun fired, sending a bullet ricocheting off something and shattering a window near what appeared to be the front door.

J.B. fell hard, with Ruby coming down on top of him, screaming at Misty, "Get Zoe out. Now!"

One of Ruby's knees slammed down on J.B.'s gun arm. He was so much larger, so much stronger, there was no way she could grab or keep the weapon pinned down.

No way she could do anything but knot her fists and do her damnedest to distract him for as long as possible.

From the instant Sam had heard the gunshot, every last vestige of restraint shattered. Shoving his way through undergrowth, he leapt onto the front porch, where he looked through the jagged edges of a broken window.

He heard Ruby's frantic *"Get Zoe out. Now!"* Saw Misty looking back, too dazed to drag the shrieking child to the window. He looked farther in to see the desperate struggle on the floor. And understood at once that Ruby had gambled everything, had sacrificed any chance of her own survival in a desperate bid to allow her family to escape.

Yet Misty and Zoe stood frozen, too horrified to react.

Using the flashlight in his hand, Sam smashed out the remainder of the glass and leaned through to grab Misty. *"Get out. Move,"* he shouted at her.

She turned to look at him, eyes huge, before he pulled first her and then Zoe outside.

"Ruby," Misty cried.

"Take her. Run," Sam shouted as a second shot exploded from inside the house.

CHAPTER THIRTY-FIVE

"Let man fear woman when she loves: then she makes any sacrifice, and everything else she considers worthless."

—Friedrich Nietzsche,
from *Thus Spake Zarathustra:
A Book for All and None*,
translated by Thomas Wayne

The sound of shattering glass mingled with Zoe's cry of terror. Then Ruby heard a second male voice—*Sam's?* Sam, alive and here to help her family?

Next came a crack, like the crack of the world splitting asunder. The acrid smell of smoke. The shocking impact of the hardest punch she'd ever taken.

Stunned, she rolled over, her hand moving reflexively to an explosive pain in her side, a pain that dwarfed all others. Right palm slicking with the hot spurt of her blood. Brain reeling with the knowledge that it hadn't been a hard punch, that she'd been shot. The crash of comprehension grayed her vision, hit her even harder than the bullet, and she went still, not even daring to draw breath against the mindless shriek of each nerve.

J.B. must know she was finished, for he rolled to his feet in one swift motion. He launched himself toward the window, toward Misty and toward Zoe, his gun hand rising in an arc toward Sam's face. Toward Sam, who tackled him as more gunfire erupted.

Only this time, she realized, the shooting was coming from the darkness outside, where she'd just sent her family. Outside, where she could do nothing to save them.

Where she wouldn't even have the chance to say good-bye.

Sam plowed into the man, bringing them both down before it registered that J.B.—his cruel asshole of a *brother*—was here somehow. That the drunken disaster of ten years earlier hadn't been arrested in New Mexico as the peach fuzz drug enforcement agent had claimed but must be working for the assassin, Hobson Best, helping him to find his way around the area.

But Sam didn't give a damn about the particulars, not with the sound of shooting outside, shooting that made him fear that Best was out there somewhere, that he was firing on Misty and Zoe.

Sam grabbed J.B.'s wrist, grappling for control of the gun while his brother tried to bring up a knee to kick him in the groin.

"You always were"—Sam twisted to avoid the cheap shot and rolled on top of J.B.—"a fucking dirty fighter."

As Sam slammed his brother's forearm to the hard floor, he heard the crack of bone and caught a glimpse of Ruby.

Ruby lying still, blood leaking through the fingers she'd pressed over her side. Blood all over her. In an instant, he took it all in, right down to the realization that her hand was limp, that *she* was limp and staring.

That she could be dead.

With a shout of pure rage, Sam embraced the violence he had shunned all his life. When several hard blows failed to make his brother drop the gun, Sam used his free hand to pull the utility blade from its pouch on his belt and brought its point around.

"You're only shadow. Less than nothing," J.B. roared just as his left fist struck the side of Sam's skull.

The impact sent Sam reeling, sent the blade spinning

from his grasp. He felt the world turn over, realized too late that his brother had regained the advantage and flipped him onto his back.

That his brother, sweating and panting with exertion, had shoved the muzzle of the gun beneath his jaw. For the first time, Sam focused on a changed man, a man who had traded the sloppy viciousness of a mean drunk for something far more alarming. Something that made Sam wonder what hellish metamorphosis he'd undergone in prison, what could account for the murderous new light in J.B.'s stone-sober eyes. Was he—could a two-bit criminal have possibly grown into the assassin known as Hobson Best?

"You always—always thought," J.B. said, sneering, "that *you* were the only one with substance. The only fucking one who deserved a decent family, a fucking college education. The only McCoy who could become a real professional or figure out his goddamned way around computers."

"If you want to think spoofing a few phone calls makes you a—"

"And now look at you, loser," J.B. went on as if he hadn't heard. "Going to die like a fucking dog as soon as you tell me where the files are. Tell me what you did with them because now I know you're in on this. I know you were the one who took them from her."

He jerked a nod toward Ruby, on the floor behind him. Ruby, who was moving her hand and rolling onto her side.

So she's alive, for now at least.

But Sam had no idea how to keep her breathing.

Justine stayed low, shallow breaths gusting past the edge of panic—a panic it took all her resources to push past.

She still had no idea who'd shot at her, only that her

flashlight's beam had caught two people moving, both dressed all in black, down to the night-vision goggles they were wearing. She'd shouted a command to freeze, identified herself, and watched the pair split, wheeling and firing as they'd rocketed off into the brush.

Professionals for certain and not the common run of East Texas meth-heads she'd been half expecting. Switching off and holstering her flashlight, she picked up the gun she'd dropped, her hand shaking so hard she'd be lucky if she could hit a stationary target.

She was in huge trouble here, could be picked off at any moment. And it was her own damned fault for breaking department policy. Rather than waiting for backup as she should have—both her own men and the DEA agents with whom they'd liaised were on the way—she'd taken off running when she'd heard a shot.

Taken off running toward the possibility of a redemption that couldn't be bought, a stupid risk that could damned well leave her child orphaned. All the shooters had to do was circle back to take her out, or intercept her as she made her way back to the SUV she'd left parked down the road, its lights off. She thought she might have hit—maybe even killed—one during the exchange of fire, but their night vision and their obvious training gave them a formidable advantage.

She rose to a crouch and took a step in the direction of the road, only to whirl toward the sound of someone crashing through the brush behind her.

Before she could fire, a woman called, "Help—you have to help us. My sister—Ruby's back there and he'll kill her."

"Misty? Misty Bailey?" Astonishment goosed Justine's already racing heartbeat. "Do you have Zoe with—"

"Sheriff Wofford?" Misty stumbled through a patch of moonlight, a child in her arms.

In that split second, Justine glimpsed the chance she'd been praying for these past months. The chance to give her career—and the devil's bargain she had made to claim it—meaning.

"This way," she ordered, more confident, more *competent* than she had felt in years. "I'm taking you somewhere safe."

"But my sister—" Misty protested over the sounds of Zoe's weeping.

"Help will be here soon." Justine prioritized her mission in her mind. The child's safety had to come first, then Misty's and her own. Outnumbered and outgunned, Wofford knew she'd done the best she could.

And from what she'd seen of Ruby Monroe, the woman would likely count her family's safety as enough.

CHAPTER THIRTY-SIX

"Where there is mystery, it is generally suspected there must also be evil."

—Lord George Byron

"Now that she's dead," Sam said coldly, "I'll sell you what you're looking for. Sell it to you for half a million."

Ruby's vision swam, pain forming eddies that threatened to drag her under like a riptide, pain that overwhelmed her relief that Sam still lived. Did he really think her dead now? And could he really be so callous that he'd seek to turn her tragedy to profit? Or was he simply scrambling for some way to save his own life?

So what? Isn't that what you did when you let Carrie Ann

go on the supply truck? Didn't you tell yourself that her problems weren't yours?

As J.B. pushed himself off his brother, Sam's gaze flicked to hers for a split second. In that moment, Ruby understood his gambit, understood that he was looking for some chance to save her.

Don't, Sam. Get yourself out. This was never your fight in the first place.

Now sitting, J.B. kept his gun on Sam and his back to Ruby, a sign that he, at least, had dismissed her as a threat. As well he might, with the agony of each breath tearing through her, with her life's blood pooling on the floor around her.

Just like Elysse's . . . Ruby thought of her friend, dying alone and terrified, dying with so many of her dreams unfulfilled. Fury sparked in Ruby's heart, a tiny flame that made her grit her teeth and cling fiercely to consciousness.

And she remembered something, something she'd heard slide across the floor while the brothers were fighting. Praying it would be a phone, she swept her hand across the floor in an attempt to find it. Though she couldn't risk speaking, maybe she could dial 9-1-1. Maybe it was too late for her, but Ruby prayed Sam and her family, at least, might be saved. And that J. B. McCoy would pay for what he'd done.

"If I kill you, I get it anyway, along with the computer you used to create the fake." Best—or J.B.—sounded amused as all hell. "Besides, what my employer really wanted here was an illustration. An example of how far DeserTek's willing to go to protect its—"

"You can't think I'd come here with the real drive on me," Sam said. "Besides that, if you kill me, you'll have no way of preventing the automated e-mail blast that's going to expose DeserTek's secrets to every major media outlet in the country. It's already in motion—and can't be stopped unless the money is deposited in an account set up to—"

J.B. laughed at him. "What makes you think I'm in DeserTek's employ? And what makes you think exposing them isn't what we've wanted all along?"

Ruby's fingertips bumped something. Something just out of her reach. Ignoring J.B.'s ridiculous denial, she gritted her teeth and used her feet to push herself toward the object.

Fresh pain blanked out her vision, yet she reached through it until her fingers curved around something hard and plastic but the wrong shape and size for a phone.

Disappointment burned through her, sent hot moisture rolling along her face. Grief that so much suffering— from Carrie Ann's to her family's to her own—would make no difference, that Sam's sacrifice, the possibilities she'd once sensed for them were doomed to shatter beneath the wheels of corporate greed.

Sam was talking, arguing loudly with J.B. now, but the present was beginning to sink beneath memory. Submerging her beneath Bone Lake, where the lapping wavelets echoed an earlier conversation.

"If you can't stand against systematic murder, then what can you stand against . . . against . . . against?"

As her awareness faded, Ruby's fingers skimmed cool metal, and her own words glittered above her, a host of silvery minnows whose meaning sparkled in the sunlight.

"I stand for my child, Sam, and the sister I practically raised. . . .

"I stand . . .

"I stand . . ."

With a tremendous effort, she *stood*, breaking through

the surface, surging to her feet. Flowing only briefly before ebbing.

Yet her fall gave her momentum, strength enough to plunge the blade in J.B.'s neck as he swung toward her and fired off a wild shot.

Sam kicked away the falling gun as J.B. dropped it, his hands flying toward the knife jutting from the side of his neck. As Ruby collapsed, Sam tried to stop his brother, tried to keep him from pulling the three-inch blade free.

But with a howl of pain, J.B. jerked it out, showering Sam with an arterial spray of blood. Sam dove for the gun, but still on his knees, J.B. ignored him, turning instead toward Ruby and raising the knife as if to strike.

But he fell instead, spasming on the floor with a hand clasped to the spouting neck wound.

Ignoring him, Sam stuck the gun beneath his belt and went to Ruby, his eyes burning as he took in her injuries.

Lifting her hand, he said, "You did it. You saved Misty and Zoe. And you saved us."

He wasn't certain she had saved her family, much less her own life. Wasn't sure of anything except her courage and the way his heart contracted when her blue eye met his.

And the pain he felt when that eye drifted closed. Until she whispered, "*We* did. Because of you, Sam."

With a splintering crash, the front door of the house flew open. Two men dressed in commando-black burst in, what looked like assault rifles at the ready. Federal agents, Sam thought, until the first in, a man larger and more muscular than the most imposing bouncer, shouted at Sam, "DeserTek security. Back away, hands up, unless you want to die now."

But Sam couldn't move from his spot in front of Ruby. "She's seriously wounded. I'm not letting you take her. I won't."

To his surprise, instead of shooting him, they went to J.B. While one man covered Sam, the second jerked J.B.'s hand from the spurting wound and pinned his wrist down with a booted foot.

"Are you working for Colo-field, Incorporated, or Global Missions?" the buzz-cut private soldier demanded.

J.B.'s eyes rolled back into his skull, his body bucking and convulsing.

"Which one hired you?" screamed the soldier, but J.B. was well past answering, his breath rattling from his body, a sudden, shocking stillness taking hold.

Dead, Sam realized. The tormenter of his childhood, this resurrected nightmare. But he doubted he'd live long enough to feel relief.

Confirming his fear, the man guarding him yelled, "On your knees—now."

He glanced back at Ruby, who lay so still, save for her breathing, that he thought she must be unconscious. He decided there was no place he would rather die than by her side.

Kneeling, he followed the order to lace his fingers behind his neck. Closed his eyes while one soldier began searching the cabin while the other stepped behind him. Inside his head, he ticked off his last moments, his mind filling with the taste and feel of Ruby, the sacred moment when they had eased their pain with the joining of their bodies, the way he'd thrown off his isolation and immersed himself completely in one shared task, the quest to free her family.

And as he did, he regretted not the briefness of his life, but all the years he'd wasted with his nose pressed to life's window. The years he'd spent as a foster child and a criminal's son instead of really living life as Sam Mc-Coy.

"All right, we're done here," called the soldier who'd been searching.

And to Sam's astonishment, the two men ran out the front door, leaving him alive and—he soon discovered—leaving Ruby bandaged to keep her from bleeding out.

CHAPTER THIRTY-SEVEN

"It is by going down into the abyss that we recover the treasures of life. Where you stumble, there lies your treasure."

—Joseph Campbell,
from *The Joseph Campbell Companion*

Four months later

"I'll leave you two to discuss it." A Dallas attorney in a killer suit glided to the door of an office rich with distressed leather, walnut, and a hand-knotted Persian rug. With her hand on the knob, Delia Scott turned back toward her client, her expression sympathetic. "When you've decided, Mrs. Monroe, you can ask the secretary to call me back—I'll be working in the conference room. Or if you need more time, just call me."

She closed the door behind her softly, leaving Ruby and Misty alone, the shock of the unexpected offer still reverberating through them. Ruby had never thought this day would come, had been warned that DeserTek would try to wear her down with delay upon delay followed by as many appeals as it took.

"I don't get it." Though Misty sounded perplexed, she looked far healthier, and less haunted, than she had in months. In honor of their trip into the city—and her sister's first day trip after her long convalescence—she'd taken care with her appearance, pulling up her long hair and wearing an aqua sundress that highlighted her sleek, blonde beauty.

The free community counseling, Ruby decided, had been worth far more than its price implied. For all of them, including Zoe, who was thrilled to be back with her friends at Mrs. Lambert's day care.

"The media's been all over DeserTek's case," Misty continued, "and your testimony led to—what was it—a half dozen officials' arrests. They have to hate your guts now. So why offer to settle?"

"For the same reason they saved my life." Unconsciously, Ruby touched the healing scar at her side. Though she was well on her way to a complete recovery, the wounds to her soul lingered, and the memories—so many memories—marked her like brands. "They're hoping to salvage what's left of the company—and recast themselves, at least in part, as good guys who've been wronged in all this."

Misty rolled her eyes. "Quite a trick for a company accused of killing off five workers overseas."

Ruby nodded absently, wondering if it was true that the majority of DeserTek's management staff knew nothing of the murders—including Elysse's stepbrother and Graham Michael Worth from personnel, who had sent in a pair of DeserTek's private security contractors after her comments had raised his suspicions.

"They wouldn't have a prayer of skating through this," Ruby said, "if Global Missions hadn't gone after them through me—through you and Zoe—here on U.S. soil."

During her hospitalization, Ruby had been astonished

to learn the Florida-based corporation—a competitor for the six-hundred-million-dollar contract hanging in the balance—had orchestrated her family's ordeal. All for the purpose of hijacking DeserTek secrets and destroying the better established, and notoriously cutthroat, company with negative publicity. Instead, it had been the upstart Global that went under, while DeserTek struggled to salvage the millions the government had locked down by freezing its assets.

"If we settle, DeserTek stands a chance," Ruby explained. "If we keep fighting, the media will stay on them, and any jury's likely to award us way more than three-point-eight."

Three-point-eight million was the current offer, once Ruby's attorney claimed her percentage. After that, she would split the settlement into thirds, one for herself, another for her sister, and a final third to ensure her daughter's future. Though the government, too, would take its toll, in the form of taxes, the amount still staggered Ruby, the financial weight assigned to so much wrong.

"So what do you want to do?" Misty asked carefully, hardly daring eye contact.

Ruby understood. DeserTek was offering to swiftly end the daily dredging up of memories, offering a way out if she could only let go of the fight . . . and justice.

Gazing toward the window, which overlooked the city's sun-soaked downtown, she thought of other fallout: allegations that Justine Wofford, along with her late husband, had accepted bribes funneled through an offshore company, allegedly to protect several local, less-than-legal gambling operations; Paulie and Anna's crushing grief over the murder of their son; and Sam—God, it still sliced her to the bone to think of Sam's plight, locked inside a federal prison for violating his probation.

Locked away because he had refused to leave her side to run, even in those moments when he thought it would cost him his life.

Swallowing back tears, Ruby looked at her sister. "I know you're ready to finish up your classes and get out of that crappy house we're renting."

"It *is* a little crowded," Misty remarked.

"You say that so casually, as if you weren't the one to bring home two full-grown animals from the shelter instead of 'one tiny kitten.'" Ruby softened the statement with a smile, still touched by Zoe and Misty's conspiracy to rescue both Elysse's cat—which Ruby had renamed Beelze-Bubba—and Sam's young retriever, Java.

"*You* say that so casually," Misty countered, "as if *you* weren't the one who cried your eyes out when you came home from the hospital and saw them."

Ruby's throat thickened with the reminder that both animals had been just days away from euthanasia, of becoming the two last victims of this debacle.

Would she allow those others who'd been harmed to suffer, simply so she could make her family secure? Would she turn her back on Carrie Ann Patterson one last time and give up on the man who'd risked everything to help her?

Decision made, Ruby stood abruptly. "I'm sorry, Misty. I know you want this to be over, but it won't ever be—it can't be. Not until DeserTek takes care of the families of the people they got killed in Iraq. And not until the big shots running the company pull whatever strings necessary to spring Sam McCoy. Otherwise, *Today Show,* here I come."

Two weeks later, Ruby and her sister drove back to Dallas, where they once more met with the attorney. As

Ruby read over the agreement, she sensed her sister watching carefully, probably wondering whether Ruby could bring herself to sign it.

Hesitating, Ruby looked up at Delia Scott across the table and said, "I'm still not satisfied."

Her disappointment ran far deeper than DeserTek's claims they could do nothing to influence a federal judge. Her eyes burned at the thought of Sam, who had refused her request for visitation at the penitentiary. Though he insisted, through his lawyer, that he didn't want her seeing him in custody, she couldn't help imagining, night after sleepless night, that the real reason for his refusal was anger. That he blamed her for sending him to prison and regretted those hellish days they'd spent together.

Hellish, but for his generosity, his offer of comfort. Hellish, but for the love and gratitude that had welled up in Ruby's heart during these past few months. Hopeless love, it seemed.

"You've done a great thing for those families," Delia said gently. "Without you, they'd be tied up in court with this for years. You're a hero, Ruby."

"*Sam's* the hero." Tears sliding down her face, Ruby made up her mind, put the pen to paper. "And just look where that's gotten him."

Smiling as Ruby handed back the pen, Misty suggested going out for lunch. "Come on, Ruby," she coasted. "Maybe it is only a partial victory, but we both know life's too short not to grab every chance we can to celebrate."

Misty looked so concerned, so hopeful, that Ruby spontaneously hugged her. After everything her sister had suffered, she deserved her moment of closure, a small celebration to end this painful chapter of her life.

"You're absolutely right," Ruby said, forcing cheer for

Misty's benefit. "Let's get out of here. Your big sister's going to buy you lunch at the snootiest, most overpriced restaurant Big D has to offer."

As Misty asked a friendly paralegal for a restaurant recommendation, Ruby thought she saw the woman wink. But before she could wonder what that was about, Misty hustled her out, distracting her with chatter about her plans to resume her court reporter training in the fall semester. Twenty minutes later, the two of them pulled into the restaurant in the smoke-belching wreck of a car they'd been sharing. Misty covered her mouth to keep from laughing at the horrified expression of the uniformed valet when she tossed him the keys.

"Careful not to get any scratches on it." As they walked toward the ornate double doors, Misty grinned at Ruby. "Think they'll throw us out?"

"If they do," Ruby said, forcing a smile, "let's just blow this Popsicle stand and find ourselves some cold beer and hot barbecue and a couple of even hotter cowboys."

Misty's head swiveled to stare at her, probably because it had been so long since Ruby had even attempted a joke. Yet in spite of this one, sorrow sheened Misty's eyes, a depth of empathy that sobered both of them.

Once they were seated, Ruby said, "Did you pass that maitre d' a note?"

Misty gave a who-me shrug and shook her head. "I just handed him a tip, that's all. Isn't that what you're supposed to do in fancy places like this?"

Studying Misty's blush, Ruby was momentarily suspicious. But according to their counselor, part of the healing process involved learning to trust her sister again, so Ruby forced herself to put it out of her mind.

As if Misty had sensed her doubt, she grew quiet until after they'd been served their fussy little salads. "I know you're just faking it for my sake," she said softly. "I know you're disappointed with the deal, and I know why."

Ruby looked up, a bite of crab trembling at the end of her fork. "Why?" she asked, as if she could forget even for a moment.

"Come on, Ruby. You don't have to pretend for my sake. It's Sam, isn't it?"

"*Stop.*" Ruby moved crisply, laying down her fork and dabbing at her mouth with her cloth napkin. "Stop right now. Don't—let's not spoil this."

But before the words were out, her shoulders slumped in defeat.

More quietly, she added, "Sam's right not to let me see him. The situation's impossible. We could never—not for years and years. There's no parole in federal—"

"You love him, don't you?" Misty sounded awed by the idea. "You're in love *with* him."

Unable to bring herself to admit the words aloud, Ruby said, "I'm grateful to him, Misty, and it breaks my heart that he's locked up on my account. But as far as 'love' goes, we were only together for a few—"

"People can learn a whole lot in a few days under fire," Misty assured her. "More than some people figure out in a whole lifetime. And besides, Ruby, I have to tell you that Sam might be—"

"Let it drop, please. I have a daughter to raise." Ruby stared a plea into her sister's eyes. "A life I'm going to have to do my best to get on with. And if I'm going to do that, I have to learn to be thankful for what I got back, not miserable about what I can't have. I'm getting past him." Ruby swallowed audibly and forced herself to add, "I'm going to be just fine. Fine without . . . *Sam?*"

Both sisters stared as a tall man barged past the puffed-up little maitre d', who huffed after him protesting the invader's worn Levis and missing tie. Completely ignoring the penguin in his wake, Sam McCoy looked around until he spotted Misty standing and waving her arms to capture his attention.

"I'm really sorry, Ruby." Flushing furiously, Misty hurried to explain, "The FBI's been trying to hire Sam as some kind of consultant—financial cybersecurity, I think. But nobody was sure when, or even *if*, the release could be arranged, so we decided—I couldn't stand to see you crushed if it didn't happen, and . . ."

Whatever else she said, Ruby missed it as she shook off her shock and threaded her way toward Sam. In that last moment before they reached each other, she saw the answer to her doubts and fears, saw the reflection of all the pain and love and longing she'd known in his absence.

But it was in his kiss, as Ruby melted into his arms, that she found so much more. While the restaurant's patrons gasped and whispered and the maitre d' protested the "unsuitability of such personal displays," Sam wiggled a folded bill between his fingers to bribe the little man to back off.

And consumed by passion, Ruby at last let go of her misgivings . . . and let her heart give in to hope . . .

To joy . . .

And to a dawning faith in their shared future.

ICE

SOMEONE IS WAITING

Most people find beauty in Alaska's austere mountains. To Kaylie Fletcher, there is only death—her whole family gone after a disastrous climbing expedition. Then again, maybe not. A raspy call in the middle of the night leads Kaylie to believe her mother might still be alive. For now...

SOMEONE IS WATCHING

A strange message in a bar. A bloody knife. A fiery explosion. There's a killer inching closer, but Kaylie has nowhere to run. Except straight into the arms of Cort McClaine. The rugged bush pilot is too much of an adrenaline junkie to be considered safe, but Kaylie can't resist the heat of his touch amid the bitter cold.

SOMEONE WILL DIE

Caught in a high-stakes race against a murderous madman, Kaylie and Cort know that with one wrong step they'll be...iced.

STEPHANIE ROWE

ISBN 13: 978-0-505-52775-2

To order a book or to request a catalog call:
1-800-481-9191
Our books are also available at your local bookstore, or you can check out our Web site **www.dorchesterpub.com** where you can look up your favorite authors, read excerpts, glance at our discussion forum, and check out our digital content. Many of our books are now available as e-books!

ELISABETH NAUGHTON

Antiquities dealer Peter Kauffman walked a fine line between clean and corrupt for years. And then he met the woman who changed his life—Egyptologist Katherine Meyer. Their love affair burned white-hot in Egypt, until the day Pete's lies and half-truths caught up with him. After that, their relationship imploded, Kat walked out, and before Pete could find her to make things right, he heard she'd died in a car bomb.

Six years later, the woman Pete thought he'd lost for good is suddenly back. The lies this time aren't just his, though. The only way he and Kat will find the truth and evade a killer out for revenge is to work together—as long as they don't find themselves burned by the heat each thought was stolen long ago . . .

STOLEN HEAT

ISBN 13: 978-0-505-52794-3

To order a book or to request a catalog call:
1-800-481-9191
This book is also available at your local bookstore, or you can check out our Web site **www.dorchesterpub.com** where you can look up your favorite authors, read excerpts, or glance at our discussion forum to see what people have to say about your favorite books.

TRIPLE EXPOSURE

"[Thompson] more than holds her own in territory blazed by Tami Hoag and Tess Gerritsen."
—*Publishers Weekly*

COLLEEN THOMPSON

Better than anyone, photographer Rachel Carson knows the camera can lie. That's how lurid altered photos of her appeared on the Internet, starting a downward spiral that ended with her shooting a nineteen-year-old stalker in self-defense. Fleeing the press and the threats of an un-identified female caller, she retreats to her remote home-town in the Texas desert. In Marfa, where mysterious lights hover in the night sky, folks are used to the unexplainable, and a person's secrets are off-limits. But recluse Zeke Pike takes that philosophy even further than Rachel herself. In her viewfinder Zeke's male sensuality is highlighted, his unexpressed longing for human contact revealed. Through a soft-focus lens, she sees a future for them beyond their red-hot affair, never guessing their relationship will expose the lovers to more danger than either can imagine.

ISBN 13: 978-0-8439-6143-0

To order a book or to request a catalog call:
1-800-481-9191
This book is also available at your local bookstore, or you can check out our Web site **www.dorchesterpub.com** where you can look up your favorite authors, read excerpts, or glance at our discussion forum to see what people have to say about your favorite books.

CHRISTIE CRAIG

Macy Tucker was five years old when her beloved grandfather dropped dead in his spaghetti. At twelve, her father left his family in the dust. At twenty-five, her husband gave his secretary a pre-Christmas bonus in bed, and Macy gave him the boot. To put things lightly, men have been undependable.

That's why dating's off the menu. Macy is focused on putting herself though law school—which means being the delivery girl for Papa's Pizza. But cheesier than her job is her pie-eyed brother, who just recently escaped from prison to protect his new girlfriend. And hotter than Texas toast is the investigating detective. Proud, sexy…inflexible, he's a man who would kiss her just to shut her up. But Jake Baldwin's a protector as much as a dish. And when he gets his man—or his woman—Macy knows it's for life.

Gotcha!

ISBN 13: 978-0-505-52797-4

To order a book or to request a catalog call:
1-800-481-9191
Our books are also available at your local bookstore, or you can check out our Web site **www.dorchesterpub.com** where you can look up your favorite authors, read excerpts, glance at our discussion forum, and check out our digital content. Many of our books are now available as e-books!

✂

☐ **YES!**

Sign me up for the Love Spell Book Club and send my
FREE BOOKS! If I choose to stay in the club, I will pay
only $8.50* each month, a savings of $6.48!

NAME: _____

ADDRESS: _____

TELEPHONE: _____

EMAIL: _____

☐ I want to pay by credit card.

☐ **VISA**   ☐ **MasterCard**   ☐ **DISCOVER**

ACCOUNT #: _____

EXPIRATION DATE: _____

SIGNATURE: _____

Mail this page along with $2.00 shipping and handling to:
Love Spell Book Club
PO Box 6640
Wayne, PA 19087
Or fax (must include credit card information) to:
610-995-9274
You can also sign up online at **www.dorchesterpub.com**.
*Plus $2.00 for shipping. Offer open to residents of the U.S. and Canada only.
Canadian residents please call 1-800-481-9191 for pricing information.
If under 18, a parent or guardian must sign. Terms, prices and conditions subject to
change. Subscription subject to acceptance. Dorchester Publishing reserves the right
to reject any order or cancel any subscription.

GET FREE BOOKS!

You can have the best romance delivered to your door for less than what you'd pay in a bookstore or online. Sign up for one of our book clubs today, and we'll send you *FREE* BOOKS* just for trying it out... **with no obligation to buy, ever!**

Bring a little magic into your life with the romances of Love Spell—fun contemporaries, paranormals, time-travels, futuristics, and more. Your shipments will include authors such as **MARJORIE LIU, JADE LEE, NINA BANGS, GEMMA HALLIDAY,** and many more.

As a book club member you also receive the following special benefits:
- **30% off all orders!**
- **Exclusive access to special discounts!**
- **Convenient home delivery and 10 days to return any books you don't want to keep.**

Visit www.dorchesterpub.com
or call 1-800-481-9191

There is no minimum number of books to buy, and you may cancel membership at any time. *Please include $2.00 for shipping and handling.